Paranoid

Paranoid

Steven Axelrod

FOR NICK AND CAITY

ONE:
INNOCENTS

2733-AXEL

1

For Tom Jaglom, it began on the November afternoon when the Mafia killed Alfredo Blasi. He didn't know it, of course—we often don't know when things begin until after they've ended. The moment when forces that are going to change the world assemble and begin moving together is a question for hindsight and historians and college kids playing the if game in late-night dormitories—if the Arch Duke Ferdinand hadn't been assassinated in Sarajevo, if Hitler had attacked the British Army before they fled at Dunkirk . . . or, in this case, if a reporter named Jim Gramble hadn't been on the steps of the Criminal Courts Building that day, standing in the raw wind, asking questions—what might have happened?

The question would have bored Tom Jaglom. He was a practical person. He had no interest in speculation; besides, on the day in question he had something much more important on his mind.

He was falling in love.

He was walking in Central Park with Amy Elwell, holding her hand inside his coat pocket, watching the wind scatter her long red hair, feeling truly happy for the first time in years. He felt too large for his skin. It was almost painful. The park was deserted in the bitter cold and it felt like their private estate.

They had been together all morning. Tom was supposed to have picked her up at ten, but he'd arrived at her apartment two hours early. He had been up since five. By seven he was on the street, buttoning his coat against the cold. The wind running between the grimy buildings felt as clear as stream water. He gulped it as he walked. MacDougal Street was peaceful in the sharp morning light, the shops and cafes closed, litter blowing across the pavement. He saw no one but bums and joggers, a kid on a skateboard, a little man walking five big dogs. The city was at rest, unclenched. It absorbed his energy.

He had started walking without conscious direction; nevertheless, within an hour he was at the front door of Amy's apartment house. She lived on the fourteenth floor. The elevator was slow, the hallway was silent. He stood in front of her door for a moment, bracing himself. Then he knocked. He heard footsteps, then the cover of the peephole sliding. Locks clicked and then the door was open and she was standing in front of him in a bathrobe, her hair wrapped in a towel. She smelled of soap and steam.

"Come in." she said, smiling, startled but happy to see him. "I just got out of the shower. I didn't expect you for hours."

"Sorry—I couldn't wait."

He stepped inside and she hugged him. He could feel the firm length of her naked body loose under the terry cloth. She pulled away an inch or two, kissed him lightly. "Let me just get dressed," she said. "There's coffee in the kitchen."

Tom walked into the cramped, sunny room, and poured two cups of coffee. He sat down at the little table Amy had jammed into a corner by the window. He pulled off his coat and sweater; like most New York apartments, Amy's was brutally overheated all through the winter.

He sipped his coffee. Intruding on this ordinary part of her day gave him a sudden vision of what life might be like if he lived with her, if he were really at home in this little kitchen, as if he had awakened beside her in the pale sunshine, made coffee while she showered.

These were not fantasies he could have imagined himself inventing even two months ago. But everything was different now. He saw beautiful women and he didn't care. He saw children and he wanted his own. He hadn't said all this to Amy yet. He wasn't sure how to do it. He didn't want to scare her; and he was a little scared himself.

She came in wearing jeans and a t-shirt. Toweling her hair. They chatted while she ironed a shirt. They went downstairs after awhile. The city was waking up. They had a quick breakfast at a Bagel Nosh and then walked—uptown through the garment district and then across town at forty-second Street, past Grand Central and then north on Lexington, looking in shop windows, talking about mid-terms and parents, politics, poetry and pizza, long easy threads of conversation unspooling block after block as the city unpacked itself around them.

Eventually they wound up in Central Park. Walking in lazy circles towards the West Side and lunch. Amy's hand was warm inside his pocket, her fingers laced tight with his as she talked.

"I'm just not sure why I even bother at this point," she was saying. "They like the idea of me being home for Christmas, but it always turns into a nightmare."

"Why? I mean—what happens?"

"I don't know . . . everything I do is just a little bit wrong. It's like there's some abstract version of me in their heads and I don't measure up."

Tom smiled. "What's she like?"

"Well—for one thing, she accepted that Juilliard scholarship. Music is the whole world to her. She's not recklessly throwing away her God-given talents."

"Oh boy."

"All she wants to do is practice. It's great—she makes them so proud. She's going to be the first woman Concert Master of the New York Philharmonic some day."

"She sounds like a bore."

Amy laughed, and at that precise moment, Tom realized they were being followed. Under normal conditions he would have figured it out much more quickly. But he was distracted. Amy kept talking, but he was counting pairs of footsteps now, estimating weight from foot falls—three, four, five altogether. Jumbos. And they were speeding up. Amy finally sensed that something was wrong and started moving faster herself. This was the worst possible response. Tom tugged on her arm, pulled her back into a casual stroll.

"Don't hurry," he whispered. "Don't turn around. Just keep talking." There was still a chance that this whole absurd circus could be avoided. But Tom had been trained well, by his father and others, and he knew it wasn't likely. The group was dividing behind them. At the moment he knew the gang was going to attack, all he felt was embarrassment——this kind of situation made him feel like a freak.

Two gang members trotted ahead of them, blocking the path while the others caught up.

This was it. Tom sighed.

"What's your hurry, pal?" the leader asked conversationally. Tom had made a point of not hurrying, but he decided against pointing this out. The gang ranged in age from about fifteen to twenty, big heavy white guys wearing bulky coats and packing guns under them.

"He don't wanta get robbed," one of the others suggested.

"Yeah," a third one agreed. "You gotta be careful around here. This is a high crime area."

"Let's kill 'em both!" the youngest one burst out suddenly, unable to control his enthusiasm.

"No," said the leader. "That would be a waste. We'll kill him—the girl we take with us. We can have some fun with her. He pulled out a switch knife and let the eight-inch blade snap out dramatically.

Tom cleared his throat.

"Hold on a second,' he said. "You're making a big mistake here. No—really. Look, this may seem a little bit hard to believe, but . . . .I'm the son of the President of the United States. It's true. And wherever I go, these Secret Service guys follow me. Big guys. With guns. They shoot first and ask questions later."

The leader thought this was hilarious. He barked out a short laugh. "Oh yeah?" he said.

Tom shrugged. "Well—no, actually. They don't really ask questions later. Except for stuff like, 'Where are the body bags?' and 'Who's going to get the brains off this wallpaper?'"

"Cut the crap, buddy—"

He never finished the sentence; Ira Heller's Secret Service crew finally made their appearance. Three men in gray trench coats carrying AK-47 attack rifles. The gang burrowed into its jackets, and in a moment they were armed the same way. Heller, a jowly, graying man in his fifties who looked like the ex-cop he was, spoke in a tired voice with a faint Brooklyn accent.

"Okay," he said. "Put the guns down."

The leader was clearly intimidated but determined to hold his ground. Tom realized he was probably more dangerous now than he had been before—fear would make him unpredictable.

"No way, man. Don't mess with me."

"Don't prolong this." Heller was fighting a yawn. "Drop the guns—now."

Tom inched closer to Amy. No one noticed. He decided it was safe to whisper. "Do what I say," he breathed in her ear. That was all. It had to be enough. She nodded—the smallest inclination of her head.

"You drop your guns!" the leader was shouting, and the others were cheering him on with "Yeah! Do it! Up yours!"

Tom took a step forward.

"Wait a second. Let's not start World War III here. Can't we just talk about this? I'm sure if we all calm down and take a couple of deep breaths we can—"

Everyone was beginning to be lulled by the sing-song diplomacy in Tom's voice. He struck in the middle of a sentence, with no warning. While he was speaking he had been choreographing the whole event in his mind, just as Jake Gritzky had taught him to do, calibrating his moves against the relative positions of the gang members and the Secret Service guys. It worked in his head but you could never be sure until it happened.

Tom spun on the leader, breaking his wrist, disarming him and throwing his knife. The metal butt cracked one gang member just above the nose as Tom launched into a spinning back kick that connected with another one's jaw like an ash-wood bat on a slow pitch—it actually lifted him off his feet and propelled him backwards against a tree. As the kid's gun clattered to the asphalt, Tom yelled, "Amy! Down!" and was pleased to see in a flicker of perception as he blocked another clumsy attack that she dropped to the pavement instantly. Tom took out a furiously swinging kid with one clean elbow strike to the throat. Behind him, a Secret Service guy knocked a gun barrel up before it could be fired and then decked the hood with a rifle butt to the face. Tom dove for the fallen AK-47, grabbed it and twisted over to aim it at the last gang member. But he was a

little late—three other rifles were also aimed at the kid. He
looked very young.

His finger was on the trigger.

Heller shook his head. "Don't even fantasize about it."

Another agent stepped forward gingerly and took the
gun from the boy's hands.

It was over.

Tom helped Amy up. She looked shaken and angry
and scared and confused, all her emotions stoked by
adrenaline. Heller was calm to the point of boredom. He
snorted irritably, "You're gonna get yourself killed one of
these days, kid. You gotta be more careful."

Tom gave Amy a hug, ignoring Heller.

"Are you okay?"

"Sure—I think so . . . I just—"

Heller closed in on them. "Hey—I mean it, Tom. You
get killed, that's it for me. I'm selling encyclopedias somewhere."

Tom laughed and patted Heller's shoulder. "Now don't
you get sentimental on me, Ira. It's bad for your image."

Tom took Amy's arm gently and started walking her away.

"You're shaking, "he said.

"That man, that agent . . . he was right. We could have
been killed. Those guys—"

"Nobody fired a shot."

"I know, but . . . anything could have happened. I thought
one of them was going to shoot me, I felt it in my stomach, I
can still feel it, it's like a cramp—and that little boy he was
just—"

"I know. But you did the right thing. 1 was impressed.
You hit the ground like a real soldier."

They walked on, closer to Central Park West now. Tom
noticed that Heller and one of the others were following
them.

"How did you move so fast?" Amy asked after a while.

"I've never seen anything like before. You were much faster than those Secret Service men."

"That's not really fair—they're trained to defuse situations and negotiate. I was trained to attack."

"Trained?"

"I've studied martial arts since I was eight years old and I've been working with small arms since high school."

"But why?"

"So I can kill people," he said.

"You . . . want to—kill people?"

"No. But I have to know that I can, if it's ever necessary. That's what it's all about. You study for years so you'll be prepared at certain moments. So that you're ready when it's life or death."

"But what if those moments never come? You'll have wasted your life."

"They come, Amy. A 15-year-old kid just stuck an assault rifle in your face."

"But this is Central Park. This is New York City. Couldn't you move to Iowa or someplace—Nantucket? Your family has a house on Nantucket. Why not live there? You don't have to live in the capital city of violent crime."

"Iowa isn't safe. Neither is Nantucket. No place is safe. You're just kidding yourself if you think that."

They walked along in silence. It had started to cloud over, dark metallic clouds that promised the first snow of the season.

"I just wish it were a better world," Amy said at last.

Tom shrugged. "This is the world. If you want civilization you get violence. That's the deal. You can pretend it won't happen to you, or you can prepare for it. You can learn how to control it. That's what the study of martial art is really about—controlling violent situations."

Amy shook herself. She was chilled. She slipped her arm around his waist and held him tight.

"Well, you certainly controlled that situation," she said. "Do you really need those guys following you all the time?"

"I don't have any choice. But I love ditching them. Want to try?"

"But, Tom . . . they just saved your life. I mean—"

"That was the first time they've ever actually helped me. And it'll probably be the last."

"But they'll get in trouble if they lose you."

"Exactly."

"I don't understand."

Tom squeezed her shoulder. They walked along in silence for a while as he collected his thoughts.

"Heller isn't just trying to protect me, Amy. He has some kind of grudge against me. Or he wants something and he thinks he can get it by spying on me. I don't know. But he's way out of line. He's using directional mikes to eavesdrop on my conversations. He's bugging my phone. He's opening my mail. And that's just the stuff I've noticed. I asked him point blank if he thought I was a security threat of some kind and he was just like no, no, don't be ridiculous. Like I was crazy or something. I complained about it. But he just denies everything and nobody takes me seriously, and he's still on my case twenty-four seven. So what am I supposed to do?"

"I don't know."

"I didn't either. For a long time I just let it happen. I told myself it didn't matter anyway. I mean, I have nothing to hide. I'm not a spy or a terrorist. But it was driving me nuts. You can't imagine what it's like, never having any privacy, knowing people are watching you all the time. So I decided to fight back the only way I could. If Heller wants me under constant surveillance—fine. But I make it as hard as I can for him. That's the game we play now. Once in a while I win and I get a few moments to myself. Mostly I lose. But it's always fun and even Heller would have to admit that it keeps him on his toes. So—shall we?"

His grin was infectious. Amy felt herself being caught up in the game.

"O.K.," she said. "What do we do?"

"I think of something ingenious. You follow orders— just like you did back there."

"Yes, sir," she gave him a mock salute, then leaned over and kissed his cheek.

There was an idea Tom had been meaning to try for weeks. It required a two-way street, so Central Park West was perfect. There was usually at least one Dodge sedan with a full radio set-up involved in his surveillance, and as soon as they came out of the park he saw it parked at the curb, glaringly obvious in its futile efforts to appear unobtrusive. Heller and the other agent trotted over to the car as Tom and Amy ambled toward the curb. Tom was checking the traffic: light to moderate, just what he needed. The Secret Service guys were in the car now, and the engine was running. Amy stepped off the curb to hail a cab. Tom took her wrist and brought it down gently.

"Not yet," he said. The cab went by. So did several others.

Heller would start getting suspicious any second. He had a good eye. Then Tom saw what he wanted—two cabs with their vacancy lights on approaching each other on opposites sides of the avenue. The one headed downtown was a block further away.

It was now or never.

Tom hailed the uptown cab and they climbed in. He was already pulling out his wallet. "Pull into the traffic slowly and stop when I tell you. I'll give you twenty bucks. Come on—let's go!"

"Awright, awright, keep ya shirt on."

As they started up' Tom saw the Dodge two cars behind them, easing into a routine tail. The other cab would come parallel in five or six seconds, but someone had stepped into the street hailing it. They were out of time.

"Stop—now!"

The driver jammed on the brakes, heaving Tom and Amy forward. Horns brayed behind them. Tom caught Amy, threw a twenty at the driver and slammed out of the cab just in time to get the other driver's attention with an ear-splitting, two-fingers-in-the-mouth whistle. He caught the driver's eye, opened the door and piled in, with Amy right behind him. The cab never even stopped.

"Downtown—and step on it!"

Tom and Amy crowded the back window to see what Heller's Dodge would do. Inside the car, he was shouting, "Turn it around. Turn it around."

"Okay," said the driver. "I got them in sight. No problem." He had been through a six-week course in tactical driving, and Tom's cab was only a block away in light traffic.

It should have been no problem. The switching-taxis ploy was just juvenile grandstanding and effective pursuit would make it look as silly and ineffectual as it really was. Heller sat back and made a conscious effort to relax his bunched shoulders. He felt a headache coming on.

The Dodge swung into a U-turn—and then there was a van in front of them. Some old guy was doing a slow right off Seventy-Fourth Street onto Central Park West. Heller's driver laid on the horn.

"What the hell! Move it! What the hell are ya—? Goddamn it! Jesus!"

At the sound of the horn, the old guy in the van came to a complete stop and ceremoniously gave them the finger. Then his van stalled. The engine wheezed and stuttered as he tried to get it going again. Traffic was lining up behind them.

Heller crushed his eyes shut. There was no way to explain this. The kid had a horse-shoe up his ass. That was all. By the time the van was finally out of the way, Tom's cab was long gone. Now he'd have to waste a half-dozen men staking out the usual locations.

"I'm gonna kill that kid myself," he growled, chewing down on three aspirin, swallowing them dry. "I'll sell encyclopedias, that's beginning to look pretty goddamn good."

"They'd put you in jail if you killed the kid, boss," the driver pointed out.

Heller sighed. "So I'll go to jail. I don't care. I'll sell encyclopedias in Sing Sing. I'll go cell to cell. It'll be worth it."

Amy shouted, "We did it! We did it! That was great!"

She hugged Tom and his nose was full of the smell of her hair, the heat of her neck. He held her awkwardly, sideways on the seat.

Giving the slip to the Secret Service had long ago become a stale game, a joyless rebellion against the constant invasion of his privacy. But today it was an adventure.

They had tricked the bad guys, gotten lucky and escaped. It was fun.

Amy's lips found his and kissed him. Desire rumbled through him. It parched his throat, pulled his face tight. When she drew back her face was wild. She was staring at him, and he was held by that fierce probing look. He longed to say something. But he didn't dare move or speak. He had no idea what he would actually do or say—Tear her clothes off? Propose marriage? Anything was possible.

But she spoke first.

"Let's have lunch," she said. "I'm buying."

Eighty blocks downtown, Alfredo Blasi was thoroughly enjoying the last two hours of his life. He walked down the wide main concourse of the Criminal Courts Building flanked by policemen with his lawyer beating off questions from more than a hundred and fifty reporters. Cameras were rolling, flashbulbs were popping. The place was going crazy and it was all because of him.

Blasi was a Mafia hit man and a renowned cop killer who, according to his own testimony, killed cops for fun. "Hey, it's a great hangover cure," he had gloated just over a month ago when he was finally arrested. And now he was going to rat out the entire Nosiglia crime family, so all was forgiven. Blasi was smarter than the usual gangster. He had been to college and a year of business school. He had a good sense of humor, and the irony of this situation amused him. After all these years, the cops were on his side, protecting him like he was one of their own.

You had to laugh.

"What deal did you cut?" reporters shouted at him past the wall of uniformed cops as the crowd moved slowly towards the front doors. There were more of the press on the steps, with camera crews and sound vans spilling out onto Centre Street.

"Is Blasi getting immunity? Is there a book deal? Is there a movie deal? What's he going to say? Are you afraid of Mafia retaliation? How much does he know?"

Blasi's lawyer raised a hand to silence them. Joe Chiaromaro was a burly giant with a dense beard, granny glasses and a bass voice that hypnotized juries. He cut a moment of silence out of the hubbub.

"It's very simple," he said. "Mr. Blasi knows everything. And he's going to tell it all."

Jim Gramble followed the crowd at a slight distance. He didn't shout any questions. He didn't take any notes. He just watched and listened. He was often quiet when other people were shouting. That was one reason he had won two Pulitzer Prizes in the last 10 years for a struggling little newspaper called the *Journal Examiner*. He was a heavy-set black man and was occasionally mistaken for various retired football players, none of whose names he ever recognized.

He strolled behind the swarm of reporters as they emerged onto the broad steps of the Criminal Courts Building. A thin snow was starting out of the iron sky. Jim was watching the cops. They bothered him and he wasn't sure why. Something didn't add up, and that was just the way Jim liked it. He had made his career on other people's false moves, on the alibis that didn't quite account for all the facts and the politicians who dodged the hard questions. He was a gentle cynic and he knew that in a world where no one had anything to hide, he'd be out of a job. Deceit was like a colleague; so were avarice and envy, sloth, anger, vanity, lust and even gluttony from time to time. He was on close personal terms with the seven deadly sins—as well as the 70 or so mildly incapacitating ones. Every good reporter was.

Casual, that was the word he was looking for. The cops were too casual. Of course they hated Blasi, but their jobs were on the line if anything happened to him. Besides, the Mafia had been known to be sloppy in its single-mindedness—if his soldiers happened to take out a few policemen along with Blasi, Dominic Nosiglia was not going to be upset. So the cops had every reason to be alert—furiously, intensely alert, with the attention to every detail of every moment you'd expect from a 15-year-old boy playing Russian Roulette.

But they weren't.

They were just going through the motions, as if they knew nothing was going to happen to Blasi or didn't care. Jim watched the throng approaching the three unmarked police cars that would take Blasi to the FBI safehouse, feeling worse and worse about the whole set-up. He should go inside now, he knew, and phone in a quick report to Sam Crawley at the city desk. But he wasn't sure what he could say.

This story was incomplete.

He stood on the high steps, watching the press and the police, the cold wind snapping at his clothes.

He didn't have much time to decide, but there weren't many options, anyway. He chose the riskiest one, risky not least of all because he was parked two blocks away. If he had trouble starting his car or snagged a few red lights, he could miss everything. All the more reason to get moving.

He took the steps two at a time.

His car, an old green Volvo station wagon, started on the first try. It usually did——not bad after 120,000 miles. He made all the lights and soon he was following the police motorcade over to the West Side, uptown to 39th Street and through the Lincoln Tunnel to New Jersey. He didn't crowd the cops; he stayed just close enough to keep them in sight. Once they were headed northwest on 495, it was easy. They cruised toward Passaic, and he had time to think about what he hoped to accomplish. Even if he made it to the safe house, no one was going to grant him an interview. He wouldn't be able to get within fifty yards of Blasi and the cops wouldn't be in the mood to chat. They' might arrest him—that was about as good as it was going to get.

Still, he felt this was the right thing to do. He couldn't explain why to anyone else—he had tried to justify his hunches before. After the first Pulitzer six years ago, he had been invited to lots of journalism schools. He had attempted to explain to the appallingly young students (most of whom were planning careers in television anyway) the absolute necessity of following your hunches and trusting your senses. If something sounded a little odd to you, it probably was. If you felt the need to do something peculiar—like following a mob informant to an FBI safe house—then you had to do it. Even if you weren't sure why. Figuring out the reasons took too long, it wasted valuable time.

All Jim could have said now was that he wanted to keep Blasi in sight a little longer.

There was more to see.

The safe house turned out to be a fenced-off group of three houses in the cul-de-sac of a Passaic housing development. Few of the other houses seemed to be occupied and the subdivision looked particularly stark because there were no trees or shrubs or hedges. Just brown grass and asphalt. Jim parked as a plainclothes cop opened the gate in the chain-link fence to allow the motorcade inside. There were other cops roaming the grounds. Jim counted 30 of them. He approached the fence and two big guards converged on him.

"This is a restricted area, sir,' one of them said.

"No unauthorized personnel permitted," the other one added.

They must like talking that way, Jim thought. He pulled out his press card.

"Hi,' he said. "I'm Jim Gramble, with the *Journal Examiner*? I was wondering if—"

"Turn around. Walk back to your car. Get in and drive away. Otherwise I'm gonna have to put you under arrest."

In the compound, Blasi was climbing out of the lead car. Jim could hear him faintly as he said in a nasal whine, "I gotta take a crap—does one of you want to come with me for that, too?"

"Go right ahead, Mr. Blasi," one of the cops answered. "You're entitled to your privacy."

Blasi laughed. "Polite cops make me nervous."

He walked toward the middle of the three houses.

"I'm not telling you again, buddy," the guard said to Jim. "Get the hell out of here, now.'

Blasi disappeared inside the house.

There was an eerie pocket of silence before the explosion, as if everybody had stopped breathing at once. The guard grunted and threw himself at Jim, bringing them both down hard onto the street. As they were falling, the house detonated, erupting into a fireball with a deafening thunder and a flat smack of white heat. Jim lay pressed to the street, his pants ripped at the knee and his cheek bleeding. Glass and dirt and chunks of timber rained down all around him.

He pulled himself to his feet, noticing that part of a refrigerator had landed less than a foot away from where he had been lying. There was frying junk everywhere. The house was a ruin, flooded with fire that breathed and crackled while an immense tower of black smoke twisted up from the blaze. The stench of burning plastic and paint and carpet was overpowering.

Jim had to get back to his car, and fast—but he paused to take another head count before he fled. Those old speeches to the journalism students came back at him— trust your senses, believe what you see.

One of the cops started shouting after him as he sprinted to the Volvo, but the voice was squashed by the growing wail of sirens. Jim jumped into his car, gunned the motor and skidded away from the curb. A fire truck tore past him, and then another. He glanced in the rearview mirror. No one was following him.

The explosion was still reverberating inside his body. It felt like his bones were trembling. Alarms were going off in his ears and his head throbbed. He didn't even want to look at his knee. His cheek was still bleeding. But none of it made the slightest difference. He was ecstatic—his instincts had paid off like the dollar slots in a Las Vegas casino. He was suddenly rich in the only way that had ever mattered to him. He was the only civilian eye-witness to a gangland execution, but that was just the beginning. He had seen much more than that.

He was onto the story of his life—if he could stay alive long enough to tell it.

2

At that moment, Tom Jaglom and Amy Elwell were standing at the crowded counter of the Papaya King stand on 86th Street and 3rd Avenue, eating their second hot dogs (Big signs that had been on the walls since Tom's earliest childhood proclaimed them to be "Better Than Filet Mignon!") and drinking fresh-squeezed orange juice from paper cups.

"Well—you're a cheap date, anyway," Amy said between mouthfuls.

"It used to be a lot cheaper. But what the hell–after all, these hot dogs are better than filet mignon."

Amy raised one eyebrow dubiously.

"Okay, okay . . . maybe they're not quite as good as filet mignon."

They took their last bites, drained the last of their juice and walked out into the windy snow. They were walking downtown on 3rd Avenue when Tom stopped suddenly and took both her hands in his. He had found a way to tell her part of what he needed to say.

"I just had a great idea. You should spend Christmas with my family."

"That's sweet, Tom, but—"

"Nantucket's gorgeous at Christmas. It's almost too gorgeous. The first time you see all those Christmas trees lit up on Main Street with the cobblestones and the old elm trees in the snow, you're gonna think 'This has to be fake. It's too picturesque.' But it's real."

"Tom, your parents—"

"They'd love to have you."

"They don't even know me."

"They don't even need to know you. I know you."

"My family might be—"

"You're going to spend the holidays with the President of the United States. They'll be thrilled."

"They're republicans."

"They're Americans. Look—I met George Bush—George Bush, senior. I spent the whole day before this big charity dinner rehearsing all the nasty things I was going to say to him. I ended up asking for his autograph. It was a thrill. Sorry, but it was."

"Tom—"

"Look, the way I see it is . . . at a certain point you have to sort of . . . choose your family. Choose the people you love and make them your family, you know?"

Amy smiled. People pushed past them on the sidewalk.

"That's a nice thought, Tom."

"Then choose me. At least for Christmas."

There was a pause. Then she said "Okay" so softly, he had to read her lips.

The *New York Journal Examiner* was the only newspaper in town that still used copy boys. They used the same typesetting machinery that the paper had started with in 1949—and quite a few of the same Linotype operators. Those old men set the type by hand every day. It was an extinct skill, and they were like an exhibit at the Smithsonian. When they started dying off it would be the end of an era and the paper would

have to move into the modern world. It would be sad. Jim
liked the *Journal Examiner* just the way it was, creaky and ar-
chaic, stubborn and grouchy like the city desk guys Crawley
and McDonough, who would have looked perfectly comfortable wearing green eye shades. There were no computers on
the premises, except in the accounting department. Reporters were lucky to get working electric typewriters.

Despite all that, the paper stayed competitive. Its main
assets were lounging around the city room this afternoon,
Jim thought as he walked through it, nodding to old
friends. Some of the best journalists in America worked in
this shabby, office, and at least fifteen of them were banging out stories now, though the evening edition deadline
was still hours away.

Then there was the managing editor, Roy Fisk. He had
been with the paper since the fifties, starting as a copy boy
and working his way up with a total dedication which some
cynics suggested was the result of his nonexistent private
life. He had never married and he had no friends outside
the office. The *Examiner* traditionally offered either Christmas or New Year's Day off—Roy had never taken either
one. It was easy to pity him, but pity missed the point. Fisk
was a happy man. And he was the perfect managing editor, at least as far as Jim was concerned. Fisk could take five
words out of a seasoned reporter's story and double its
impact, focus a young kid's thinking or tell him which coun-
cilmanic aides were willing to talk off the record about
city council business.

The first rule never changed, and he had hammered
it into an endless procession of college boys and old hacks—
"This is a local paper! How does it affect New York?" No matter what the story was, whether you were writing about Albany,
Manhattan or Moscow, the rule never changed.

Fisk was a frighteningly obese man with a skimpy beard

that he clipped carefully himself to give the illusion of a jaw-line. It was his one vanity.

Jim walked into his office without knocking.

"I'm getting a lock for that door," Fisk said irritably. "What if I had a girl in here?"

"You wouldn't."

"You never know—I might decide to have a mid-life crisis or something. Man needs some privacy."

Jim sat down. The room stank of Fisk's cherry blend pipe tobacco, as usual. The *Journal Examiner* was not a smoke-free workplace. Fisk wouldn't stand for it.

"I want the Blasi story," Jim said.

With Fisk you were best off getting right to the point. The editor wasn't much good at small talk. He didn't follow sports and he never noticed the weather. He put a lighter to his Kaywoodie pipe and sucked down flame. His head was lost in smoke for a second or two.

"What are you going to investigate? The mob takes out some two-bit squealer—so what? Happens all the rime."

"Not like this. Blasi had been a wise guy for almost twenty years. He could have taken the whole Nosiglia family down. That's why the witness protection arrangements were so tight. Nobody even knew what state he was in . . . supposedly. But they nailed him anyway. And that's not even what bothers me."

Fisk took the pipe from between his teeth and examined the inside of the bowl approvingly. "Okay," he said. "What bothers you, my friend?"

"First of all—I was able to follow that motorcade. I'm good but I'm not great, Roy. They would have tagged me in the first 10 miles if they'd been paying attention."

"Go on."

"The cop who protected me from the blast. He took me down *before* the house exploded. I remember the sequence exactly, Roy. He tackled me and the house blew as we fell."

"Jim—"

"There were 30 cops in that compound."

"So?"

"So none of them were hurt. Nobody even needed a Band-Aid."

"What are you saying. They were in on it?"

"I don't know."

"The TPF units, the D.A.'s office, the FBI? They were all in on it?"

"I don't know."

"I hate it when you say that."

Jim grinned—he had the story.

Fisk shook his head. "Just be careful, willya?"

"Thanks, Roy."

"Mention it."

He gave Fisk's damp massive paw a quick shake and then left the office before the big man could change his mind.

Stan Polidakis was scared.

He was about to betray everything he had ever loved. He was about to become a pariah and a target. And a hero, he told himself. But he couldn't quite make himself believe it. Doing what was right should have felt better than this. It should have been cleansing. But it wasn't—he felt dirtier than ever. Still, this was his duty, as far as he could still understand the word. And as a cop he had always done his duty, regardless of how he felt. He didn't let fear or shame affect his actions any more than he would let a head cold keep him from work. The image was no accident— just yesterday the doctor had told him he had something called "walking pneumonia." The walking part was all that mattered to him. He coughed, shivering in the icy wind, and drank some more water from his hip flask. The doctor had prescribed tetracycline and told him to drink at least three quarts of water a day. That was a hardship. He never drank water if there was anything else available to drink. Now he had to piss constantly and he felt like he was floating. But at least he was on his feet.

He was standing on the observation deck of the Empire State Building, waiting for Jim Gramble. *The Journal Examiner* was the only paper in town he still trusted, the only one that was still owned and operated by people who cared about the city. He took another swallow of water and reached for his pills. It was almost four hours.

Then he saw Jim, coming around the corner of the deck, taking his time, easing himself past the knots of tourists, side-stepping to avoid some running kids. As he passed, Stan turned from the rail and the intricate gridwork of the glittering city below, and started walking beside him.

"What have you got?" Jim asked. Stan let two couples walk past before he spoke.

"It's this corruption thing, Jimmy. You're pissing a lot of people off. They're gettin' nervous, and you don't want to make these people nervous. You don't even want these people to know your name.

Jim spoke just loudly enough to be heard over the steady rush of the wind. "Which people?"

"Oh man—you never let up, do you?"

"How high does it go, Stan?"

Stan glanced at his watch and then pulled out his tetracycline capsules. He was glad to stop the conversation for a few seconds, glad to have something to do with his hands. "Hold it," he said. "Just gimme a minute here." He fumbled out two pills and swallowed them with the rest of the water in his flask. It tasted like metal piping.

"How high, Stan?" Jim asked again.

"Higher than you could possibly imagine. It's——" A shaft of pain cut into his stomach like a scalpel. His face went white and he doubled over, clutching at his mid-section. "Oh, God, I—uhhnnggghh—" He staggered backward. Jim grabbed for him and missed.

"Stan! What is it?"

Before Stan could answer there was a hideous muffled explosion, a sound out of Jim's childhood, the resonant thud of a cherry bomb flushed down a toilet and going off under water, as Stan Polidakis' stomach detonated outward, shredding his clothes, lashing Jim with blood, bile and chunks of flesh. A bone fragment, part of a rib, tore his forehead open like shrapnel. Jim staggered backward, pawing at his soaked coat and his bloody temple. He was steaming in the cold, and so was the pulpy crater in Stan's corpse. All around him people were screaming. People were running away, knocking into each other, jamming the gift shop doors. The smell was thick and ripe and sour; a little boy got a sniff and started vomiting. His mother ran to him, and saw him and fainted.

Jim was on his knees in a congealing puddle, cradling Stan's head in his arms, hoping that by some miracle . . . but the world had no miracles to offer this afternoon. No heroic recovery, no last gasp revelations; nothing. Just a dead man, pulverized from the inside as if he had eaten a hand grenade.

Jim found his voice. It seemed like he had been mute for hours, though less than a minute had passed since the explosion.

"Call an ambulance, call the cops! Somebody do something!"

Somebody did. Half an hour later, three plainclothes guys, a couple of detectives, the crime scene unit and the medical examiner were on the windy deck ,going through the usual motions. Jim hovered near the policemen waiting the be interviewed. He had taken off his coat—it was garbage now—and stood shaking, teeth chattering, pressed against a wall out of the wind. His hands were trembling. He held them away from his chest and watched their palsied twitching. Nothing like this had ever happened to him before. He'd been in fights and car accidents; a week ago he'd watched a house explode and burn with a man inside. But he hadn't seen Blasi die, he didn't know Blasi. He hadn't held Blasi's head in his arms while flesh thickened in the surly resistance of death.

Like most people, Jim had a sort of callous over his psyche, and most day-to-day events failed to penetrate it. But now that callous had been torn off, exposing all the soft membranes below. He was stripped, peeled to the raw nerves.

His hands continued to jump on the stalks of their wrists. He jammed them in his pockets. He was going to have to talk to somebody before they let him go home. He realized suddenly that he was exhausted. What he really needed to do was sleep.

One of the detectives, a 10-year veteran of the 31st Precinct Homicide Squad, finally approached him. The man's name was Armand Taliafero. He was tall and bony with a neat pencil mustache that made him look prim and fussy. In fact, he was just the opposite—loud and vulgar, famous for his dirty jokes and racial epithets. Jim braced himself for some trivial obscene remark, but the afternoon's events seemed to have had an effect of Taliafero as well. No nigger jokes today.

He asked for and made notes on Jim's official statement—a solid, eyewitness description of the event. Jim was surprised to find that his voice was normal. The flash of hysteria had faded. Taliafero closed his notebook.

"Any idea what Stan wanted to talk about?"

Jim looked up. He took a deep breath and let it out slowly. "It was personal," he said.

Taliafero gave him a cold smile, tugging up the corners of the his mouth slightly, without including his eyes, which remained cold and wary and attentive. "That was old Stan," he said slowly. "Stan took everything real personal. He took his job home with him. When you're a cop you can go a little crazy doing that. You start to get a little overeager, a little sloppy . . . next thing you know, you're street pizza. Know what I mean?"

Jim stared back at the cop. "No. I don't know what you mean. Why don't you explain it to me?"

Taliafero shot him another one of those non-smiles. "I don't want you to end up like Stan did, that's all. Do like I do—keep it strictly business. Don't get involved, Mr. Gramble. That's my professional advice." The smile widened for a moment into a sly grin. "Nothing personal."

Taliafero strolled away. Jim's hands were clenched tight in his pants pockets. He wanted to jump on the smug, sleazy cop and start hitting him and keep on hitting him until his knuckles were all broken and he couldn't lift his arm anymore. He did nothing, of course. He would find a way to hit Taliafero, but not here, and not with his fists.

Wally Kellerman, the medical examiner, was scribbling some notes, frowning with his usual intensity. At age twenty-eight, he was the youngest ME in the city's history. He had given up a rich practice and a comfortable life for this. Jim had asked him about it once. He had answered with a rueful smile, "I just like crime. It's so interesting."

Jim stood beside him. "What have you got?"

Wally blinked. "Right now? I've got a splitting headache and a bag full of Stan Polidakis."

"Sorry—dumb question."

"After all this, you're entitled. Come down to the lab tomorrow. I may have something by then. I'm not quite as backed up as usual."

Jim nodded and moved off. No one else had anything to say to him. He stepped gratefully into the chalky warmth of the gift shop and pushed his way through the crowd of reporters, nodding hello but not answering any questions. He knew he had to file a story on this. Fisk would fire him if he didn't. But first he had to get home, take a shower and pour himself a drink. He had to get away from here—he felt paralyzed inside and he was afraid it would spread outward, through his nerves and muscles, stilling his body like a statue of grief and horror, halfway through the lobby of the Empire State Building.

It was strange, but the thing that troubled him most wasn't the explosion itself, or being hosed with Stan's insides, or even the way Stan's body looked afterward. No, the worst part was the look on his face just before it happened, when he knew absolutely that he was going to die. There had been no time for fear in those few seconds, but the expression of wounded surprise and bewilderment that filled the man's face was enough to populate a lifetime's worth of bad dreams.

And why? Why had Stan Polidakis been killed? Why did it happen that Jim Gramble had been an eyewitness to a pair of murders in a single week? Cops and reporters hate coincidences. But even if he had been able to believe that there was no connection between the two deaths, Taliafero's little warning would have clarified matters. He didn't doubt the warning. He knew he was in danger now. But halfway home, sitting in a dirty checker cab, the outrage finally kicked in.

He was surprised that it had taken so long; for the most of his life it had been his primary response to the world. A continuous, appalled anger had driven his life and shaped his career. He had worked in the Civil Rights movement because of it. At 19 he had been a Freedom Rider, registering black voters in Mississippi, getting chased and beaten (and almost killed on one occasion) for his efforts. But he had registered more than a thousand voters. He was 25 when Martin Luther King was assassinated, and to him that was the central event in the politics of post World War II America. Everything had changed after that. Hope no longer redeemed his anger. All the other outrages followed—Watergate, Abscam, Iran-Contra, the 'right-to-lifers' who let poor children starve to death in the streets, the homophobic congressmen who refused to fund AIDS research . . . it was an endless list, and it was growing all the time while his own city, his home town, teetered on the edge of bankruptcy, strangled by police corruption, union corruption and bureaucratic dry rot. Donald Trump outraged him, the IRS outraged him, so did the Amidou Diallo slaying and clear cutting in the National Forests and the impossibility of finding a decent egg cream in Manhattan. Everything outraged him—that was what got him up in the morning.

And now, two people had been killed right in front of his eyes and a policeman had threatened him with the same fate, and for what? To protect someone's dirty little secret. Someone had sold out to the mob, someone was on the take and it was all the same. It all cheapened life, turned people into problems that had to be disposed of and then turned them into garbage. Killing for convenience wasn't some new horror, it was the next logical step. Give one of these guys a political agenda and you had the next Hitler. The details were different, the scope was smaller, but it all smelled the same. And then you had Detective Sergeant Armand Taliafero of the 31st Precinct Homicide squad, the perfect emblem for everything Jim hated, a preening mascot for the other side, with its sneering use of fear to control people. Taliafero lived in a bully's world, where the most vicious people got what they wanted and everyone else got a gun in the ribs and ate the leftovers.

This was essential: The world did not belong to Armand Taliafero. It did not belong to the brown shirts and the white sheets and the CIA gray flannel goons who were making the world safe for McDonald's and Chrysler and Coke. But they would take it if you let them—taking was what they knew how to do best.

Jim had a shower when he got home, but he never poured himself that drink. He needed to be alert.

He had work to do.

The Office of the Medical Examiner for the Borough of Manhattan occupied the first floor and the basement of a grimy, nondescript building on First Avenue and 30th Street. In an average week the staff of more than 50 men and women saw an average of 15 murders, nine manslaughter cases, 20 accidental deaths and four suicides. There were drug overdoses, of course, and in any case most of the other fatalities were in some way drug related.

As Chief Medical Examiner, Wally Kellerman had dealt with shotgun wounds, machine gun slayings, fatal punctures from knives, ice-picks, shard glass, teeth (animal and human), pencils, pens, awls and screw-drivers. He had seen bludgeoning with bats and tire irons, bottles and two-by-fours and (in one recent case) a hardened paint brush. He had seen every kind of sexual abuse and torture. He had seen body parts pressed to electric stove burners and corpses whose mouths had been forced against holes in high pressure steam-heating pipes until their insides par-boiled. He had seen bodies without nails and teeth, people blinded by Clorox and force-fed everything from broken glass and cat litter to their own hair. He had written up amputations, beheadings and dismemberments of all kinds, deaths by drowning (in Borscht and egg-nog as well as water), murder by electrocution and vivisection. He had examined bodies whose vocal cords had been abraded into granular jelly just by screaming. He had pieced bodies together from parts found in all five boroughs, traced a car from the tire tracks across a child's body, found every known poison in the bodies of the deceased.

He was a hard man to impress.

Still, he had never seen anything quite like the cratered remains of Stan Polidakis. It took him more than a week to find out what had caused the detonation. There were no residues of ordinary explosives in the body, and no sign of any other instigator until the blood-work came back—a full five days after he asked for it. There were traces of metallic sodium in the lining off the stomach, and a couple of simple chemistry experiments made everything clear.

That afternoon he was standing in the narrow cement court yard behind the building with Jim Gramble. He had been putting off his friend for more than a week, but now he finally had some hard information to present. They had a bucket of water borrowed from the janitorial staff. The grimy little square of paving was a wind break and a sound baffle. The air was still and the traffic on First Avenue seemed very far away. Although they could be seen from at least five dozen windows, there was a sense of privacy about the little court yard, and it made sense: This was New York. Nobody cared; no one was going to look.

Wally had a small packet of tissue, taped at the edges.

"If the Boy Scouts were into murder you could pick up a Merit Badge for something like this," he said. "Someone took the tetracycline out of Polidakis' capsules and replaced it with metallic sodium. It was all the water he was drinking that really did it. When you add metallic sodium to water it liberates the hydrogen in the water and the heat of reaction is so intense it forces the hydrogen to recombine with oxygen and . . . well, see for yourself."

He tossed the little square of Kleenex to Jim.

"There's roughly two capsules worth of the stuff in there. Throw it in the bucket and stand back. It'll take a few seconds for the water to saturate the tissue."

Jim dropped the tiny parcel into the water and retreated. Before he had taken three steps there was a sharp crack like a rifle shot. Water was spurting upward over his head and the ruptured plastic bucket was bouncing across the cement. It hit a wall and rebounded, rocking on its bottom rim for a moment before coming to rest right side up. Echoes snapped between the walls of windows, and still nobody looked.

Jim was staring at the bucket. His left side had been caught in the spray. After a while he said, "Wow."

"The man has a way with words."

"Let's think about this for a second. Whoever did this had to be around Stan enough to know what he was taking."

Wally nodded. "And intimate enough to make the switch."

"Family?"

"An uncle in Dubuque. That's it. The Department was his family."

"Cops," Jim said.

Wally nodded. "Cops."

They cleaned up the mess and then ended up eating lunch together at a little joint on Second Avenue. Like most such places in Manhattan, it was run by Greeks and served aggressively American food. This one even called itself The American Restaurant in case you had any suspicions going in.

"I'm telling you," Wally was saying, "the city is falling apart. I can't even do my job anymore. And Sally was saying—you know Sally?"

"We've met."

Kellerman's wife was a small, energetic blond who wore cardigans and calf-length skirts with ankle socks and white bucks. Jim had seen her last year at some Democratic function. They were seated at the same table and Jim had ended up eating most of her food.

"I guess you know she teaches in the public schools—whatever that means. Crowd control, mostly. Her one big fear was that the kids would attack her, but they don't even notice her. They're too busy fighting with each other. Every day she has a new horror story. As for me . . . well, I was just approached about going back into family practice in Greenwich, and I'll tell you, Jim, I'm giving it some serious thought. I have no budget, I can't keep good people, I can't buy any new equipment. The reports I do submit get lost or misfiled or stuck in some 'oversight committee' until after the trial date . . . it's like—how would you feel if you wrote a great story and the paper didn't even print it?"

"I'd go crazy. I'd quit."

"Yeah? Well, that's what I feel like doing. At first I thought—hell, this is New York. Things are supposed to be screwed up. But this . . . I don't know. Sally and I were really Pollyanna types when we started out. Sure, things were bad, but we could make a difference. There were setbacks, but so what? We had energy, we were optimistic. We figured that was enough. Well . . . Pollyanna should try working for the City of New York. She'd wind up muttering 'People are shit' and taking pot-shots at them from a roof-top somewhere. I mean it."

Jim swallowed a bite of turkey sandwich. "Do you think," he said slowly, "that all of this delay and obstruction could be connected?"

"How so?"

"Could it be intentional? Some sort of conspiracy?"

"To cover up a murder or go easy on a crime family or something? No. I don't buy it. It isn't one killing or one group of people. It's the whole system. It's everything. This city doesn't need a conspiracy to make it fall apart, believe me. If there was one, it wouldn't work. Why should it? Nothing else does."

"I guess."

"I'd love to give you a hot story, but I can't. Unless you think you can sell papers with rust. Because that's what it's all about. The water pipes are rusting, the bridges are rusting, the bureaucracy is rusting. The people are rusting, Jim. Nobody cares. At least in a conspiracy somebody cares. Somebody is trying to do something. That would be a refreshing change around here. Don't get paranoid on me, Jim. You start writing about conspiracies and all you're gonna do is alienate the cops. It ain't worth it."

"Maybe you're right."

"So are you gonna forget about this cockamamie conspiracy stuff?"

Jim smiled. "Nope."

Wally shrugged. "Whatever. Just don't expect to call a cop if you get in trouble."

"That's okay, Wally. I never did."

Jim left $25 on the table and parted from Wally in the street, promising to keep in touch. He walked north towards Grammercy Park, thinking about Kellerman's malaise. Cynics, it seemed to him, had a much easier time. He himself expected situations to be frustrating and assumed that most people were dishonest and stupid. He was rarely disappointed and once in a while he was pleasantly surprised. It was a healthier way to live.

Still, Wally's theory was unsettling. Maybe he was in fact seeing nothing but random social disintegration—a society in the final stages of some terminal disease. Attributing the collapse to conspiracy, looking for some particular intention in the mess, was like trying to see God in the shape of a sea shell. Jim was agnostic; he felt that this was an accidental world which seemed inevitable only because it happened to have turned out this way. Why should New York City be any different?

Well, maybe it wasn't, but he still had a job to do and that job usually involved assuming that things made sense, that if you found enough pieces, they would all fit together somehow, even if the picture was too ugly to look at.

He shrugged, turned right and started walking uptown towards the Fourteenth Precinct station house. A few more questions wouldn't hurt.

The Fourteenth Precinct had been Stan Polidakis' real home for almost twenty years and it seemed like a good place to start poking around. It was a solid old building, bulky and pre-war, all grimy brick and heavy stone orna-

mentation. The tropical air inside smelled like dirty laundry
and cigarette butts and burned coffee. At two in the afternoon it was relatively quiet. Jim heard someone shouting but
the yell was cut off suddenly, as if by a closing door. Typewriters clattered, phones rang. Someone had the ball game on
the radio.

Jim asked at the desk for Carlos Ruiz, Stan's partner,
and was sent up to vice on the second floor. Ruiz was alone
in the squad room, typing a report with two fingers. After
decades of typing reports, he no longer had to hunt and
peck—he just pecked, like a rooster savaging a barnyard
enemy. He paused for a few seconds, glaring at the page
in front of him.

"Hello," Jim began, "my name's Jim Gramble and—

"I know who you are."

"Good—that saves a little time. I'm trying to find out
as much I can about Stan Polidakis—"

But Ruiz was typing again, even more furiously than
before. When he finished a page, Jim pounced on the sudden silence. "I'm trying to figure out why he was killed.
For instance, did anyone at the station house know he was
coming to see me? Have there been threats against him?
What sort of work had he been doing? And what was his
state of mind, I mean, did he—

Ruiz stood suddenly, and stared at Jim. He spoke quietly, with a deadly little space between each of the words.
"Get. Out. Of. Here. Now."

Then he sat down, rolled another page into the typewriter
and started jabbing the keys again. Jim stood looking down at
him for a couple of stupid moments, and then turned away.

Outside in the street he saw two cops headed for their
cruiser. He jogged up to them, but they ignored his questions with absurd stony faces until they were safely in their
car. Then they backed up so fast they almost ran him over,
and burned rubber as they headed for the street.

Jim stepped back, watching them go. Wally was right—
the police did hate him. But hatred of this intensity became another aspect of his story, another clue: these cops
hadn't been taught the techniques of deception. Their
clumsy anger was endearing to Jim. He felt bad for them.
They should have been smooth and cordial, pleasantly
referring him to some dough-faced spokesman from media relations on the tenth floor of One Police Plaza. But
they couldn't even pretend to be calm—these veteran street
cops were actually frightened.

But of what?

One thing was certain—they weren't scared of ordinary social anarchy. Society had been crumbling around
them for years. They might not like it but they were used
to it by now. No, Wally was wrong: This was something different. There was a major story here. But Jim still had no
idea how to find it.

Two weeks later, on a sleeting Wednesday night after
the late news, he began transferring his notes into his computer at home.

He had bought the Macintosh at his wife's insistence
with some of his Pulitzer Prize money, and he was quickly
won over. Soon he had his entire writing life—from the
novel he was working on to the big book he was doing on
the Lindsay administration—scanned into the machine
with back-up copies sitting on his bookshelf. He was using
it for his taxes, his journal, his correspondence . . . everything. And he was careful: he bought a surge suppresser and
an uninterruptible power source. He never traded software.
No viruses, no accidents—and best of all, no more drudgery.
He still had his old Olympia portable in his closet, but only
because he was a nostalgic pack-rat. It was just a relic to him
now, like a bulky black-and-white television with a tiny screen
and a 'rabbit ears' antenna sitting on top of it.

Eleanor had tried to take the computer in the divorce,

and his friends had chided him for not letting her have it—
he would have had the perfect excuse to buy a more sophisticated, fancier machine. But he was perfectly happy with the
machine he had. In the end, he had let Eleanor have everything but the computer and the rent-controlled apartment,
which, after all, had been his before they met. The lease had
his name on it and had five more years to go.

It felt good. His life was clean and uncluttered. All evidence of his wife and their life together had been
scrubbed away from the big sunny rooms. He bought himself
a bed and some comfortable chairs, a simple dining room set,
Teflon pans, plastic-handled stainless steel flatware and a GE
boom box. He hadn't replaced his television yet.

He was sitting at the new table now, updating the Blasi
file. It was disheartening work. There wasn't a whole lot to
add. No one would talk to him. Street cops, department
brass, secretaries at One Police Plaza, FBI people, witness
protection people, even his pal in the State Attorney
General's office. Nothing. He tried the mayor's office, the
organized crime task force, congressional staffers in Albany, city councilmen and their aides. Nothing, not a word.

For the first time in his career, Jim Gramble didn't
know what to do next. He had followed every lead and
gotten nowhere. When he went to bed that night—it was
almost two in the morning—he had decided to give up on
the Blasi story. Fisk would be amused; this didn't happen
very often. Well—let him laugh. Jim was actually relieved.
The people who were trying to scare him had succeeded.
He got to sleep without aspirin or a shot of whiskey for the
first time in weeks.

He was halfway across the City Room the next morning
when he heard his phone ring. He was going into a meeting
with Fisk. He was planning to request a new assignment—
the sewer construction kickbacks, maybe, or the union mess
in Brooklyn.

"Mr. Gramble! It's for you! It's important!"

Jim turned to the copy boy who was holding his telephone.

"It's Chief Quinn! He wants to talk to you."

Ex-Chief of Police Desmond Quinn's deathbed phone call wasn't personal, he made that clear right away. It was business. Jim had questions. He had answers.

"So get down here fast. I could die any minute."

Jim took a cab to Mt. Sinai Hospital and was met at the door by two plainclothes cops who frisked him and rode up with him to the sixth floor.

Quinn was dying of cancer. The doctors said he had less than a week to live. Jim had known Quinn slightly over the last ten years. He was a blunt, outspoken administrator who had totally revamped the department during his term. He fired or suspended hundreds of cops, including station chiefs and detectives. He was a devout Roman Catholic and inflexible on moral issues. He wanted cops to be better than other people, better than they were, better—some people thought—than they could be.

His retirement last Christmas had been abrupt and traumatic. He wouldn't discuss his reasons and the curt, "I cannot continue to do my job under the current conditions" only fueled speculation—he had found some horrendous corruption much higher up in the government than himself. He was being blackmailed. He was ill. When cancer was diagnosed six months later, most of the rumor-mongering stopped. The least interesting theory seemed to have been proved right.

The whole business had troubled Jim. He liked Quinn and Quinn liked good writing. The first time they had ever spoken he had called the paper and said, "I like what you wrote about the mayor's speech yesterday. That he . . . what was it? Oh yeah—he rounded every idea off to the nearest cliché.' Good stuff, Mr. Gramble."

Like most writers, Jim enjoyed few things more than specific compliments, and he didn't get many of them. Most
people didn't remember things in such detail, but Desmond Quinn did—he remembered where a shell-casing
was found on a murder victim's stairway and a precinct
clerk's birthday with the same rigorous precision. It had
made him a legendary homicide detective and a much
beloved station captain before his elevation to chief of
police.

When the news of his illness had been announced, Jim
had called him and they spoke briefly. Quinn was typically
gruff and stoical—the last thing he wanted from anyone
was sympathy. Jim had come to see him in the hospital early
in his stay, but Quinn had discouraged further visits. "I hate
flowers and I want to die in peace," he had growled. There
were a lot of flowers in the room. Jim got rid of them for
him, dumping them into a big garbage bag while the nurse
on duty looked on, horrified, and Quinn laughed the first
laugh he'd had in months.

Jim hated hospitals. He hated the way they looked,
green and sterile, waxed linoleum reflecting fluorescents.
He hated the way they smelled, some banal mixture of disinfectant and dying flesh. He hated the PA systems, calling
the doctors to the dying in code, everything secret, everything STAT. Death was all around him, strangely diminished—monitored, tested, organized; reduced to routine. It
gave him the creeps.

He walked down the busy corridor, dreading his first
sight of Desmond Quinn. There was a cop on guard outside the open door. A nurse was coming out as Jim arrived.

"Please keep it short," she said. "He's very weak."

Jim nodded.

Quinn was sitting up in bed, frail and skeletal, jowls
gone, cheekbones standing out harshly under the tight,
papery skin. Most people with the kind of systemic lym-

phoma that was devouring Quinn's insides would have been
dead already. But Quinn was still fighting.

"I know, I know," he croaked. "I look like a corpse.
They'd love to ship me out of here but I won't give them
the satisfaction. Pull up a chair, take a load off. And thanks
for coming."

Jim pulled a chair up to the bed and sat down heavily.
They stared at each other as the monitors beeped and
gurneys rolled down the hall outside. The PA system
wanted Doctor Kohl In ICU. STAT, of course. The IV
dripped steadily.

"So," Quinn said at last. "They won't talk to you."

"Not a word."

Quinn shrugged. "Well—there's not much that most
of them could tell you. They're afraid. I suppose I would
be, too, but I don't have a whole lot of time left and all I
care about now is making my peace with—I dunno—things
I did. My crazy life."

"Sounds like you need a priest."

"Nah—I gave up on confession years ago, Jim. God doesn't
forgive and forget. He remembers everything. He nails you
for every sin and the good stuff doesn't count. That's okay—
that's the way it should be. Some guy toes the line for 30
years, then he kills his wife. The 30 years mean nothing.
They make him a ticking bomb, that's all. Only crybabies
expect the good stuff to count." He took a few deep breaths.
He was winded. Jim sat forward in concern, but Quinn held
up a hand. There was a residue of immense natural authority
in that gesture and Jim sat back, obeying instinctively, as cops
had been obeying Quinn for decades. He probably bossed his
doctors around, even now, without even thinking about it.

"I have some bad stuff to tell you, Jim. On the record. You
can quote me. Get rid of that cop. And shut the door."

Jim stood and walked out into the corridor. The cop on
duty glanced at him.

"Chief Quinn wants you to take a walk." The cop looked into the room for confirmation and then ambled off towards the nurses' station. Jim pulled out his pen and his notebook, took a few deep breaths and then walked back into Chief Quinn's hospital room, shutting the door behind him.

3

"It's beautiful," said Amy Elwell.

"Wait. It gets better."

Tom was leaning over her to catch the view out the cabin window. Nantucket floated below them, peaceful and remote, a crescent of land flat against the clear blue water, shadowed by shoals.

Apart from Heller and one other agent, they were the only passengers on the Gulfstream jet. At first, traveling with Tom had been a shock for Amy, but she was adjusting fast. A limousine had picked them up in front of Tom's apartment building and driven them to a heliport on the East River just North of the 59th Street Bridge. A helicopter was waiting for them. It flew them to LaGuardia in about ten minutes and set them down next to the jet. No taxis or airport buses, no traffic, no baggage check-in, no slogging through the airport, no flight delays, no plastic seats. No snack-bar coffee.

"It's interesting to see how the other one tenth of one percent lives." she said, as Heller (impeccable in his new role as butler) poured her a second glass of champagne.

Tom shrugged. "We've always been rich. My Dad used to rent a river in Iceland so we could go Salmon fishing. When I was a little kid I sort of assumed everybody did stuff like that. I figured things out eventually, but before I could start to feel guilty about it, my Dad went into politics. He told me he was going to change things. And he did. He still likes the perks, though. The other day he said to me, 'I've been rich and I've been President, and President is better'."

They flew closer to the island as they approached for the landing, over the purple and red moorlands cut by dirt roads, the blue ponds, the gray shingles of old houses and the raw yellow plywood of houses under construction. They crossed the whole width of Nantucket and banked into their final approach over the Atlantic. Heavy surf was pounding on the South Shore.

Amy took Tom's arm. "I'm nervous."

He kissed her forehead. "They're just people. Okay—they're famous people. Powerful people. People who are going to be featured in history books for the next thousand years. That doesn't matter. So what if my Dad could start world war three just by pushing a button? He still puts his pants on one leg at a time. Well, actually, now that I think of it . . . he really doesn't. He has two secret service guys hold his pants and he kind of *jumps into them* . . . just so people won't be able to use that old cliché."

When the plane landed, there was a short walk across the broad, wind-buffeted tarmac to the new terminal building. It wasn't all that new anymore, but it was still white and high-ceilinged and light-flooded with shiny tile and blond-wood benches. It looked like it belonged in Coral Gables, Florida. Tom much preferred the shabby old building it had replaced. But no one had asked him.

As they crossed the wide concourse a deep voice boomed out, "Hey, Tom!"

Tom turned toward a wiry, bearded man behind the Nantucket Airlines counter.

"Hey, Jake—How are you?"

Jake grinned. It was a killer smile. It changed his whole face, made him look impish and predatory at the same time. A demon . . . but a sexy, good-time demon; a party demon. Amy liked him instantly. He said, not quite answering, perhaps commenting on, Tom's generic question: "In general. On the whole. You gonna introduce me?"

"Jake Gritzky, Amy Elwell."

Jake reached over the counter and enclosed her hand in his huge paw. The knuckles were fused and enlarged; they would have identified him instantly as a student of the martial arts to anyone familiar with Budo. Amy thought he might have some disfiguring disease of the joints. He didn't; he just liked breaking cinder blocks with his fists. "Good to meetcha," he said. Then he released her hand and turned back to Tom. "Check out the Secret Service guy outside. I walked up to him yesterday and said 'Wow— the President must be here!' The guy freaked. He couldn't understand how I made him as Secret Service. It was a tough one. He's got the trench coat, the crew cut, the earplug, the wing-tips, the look on his face like he's from another planet and wishes he'd stayed home. So he says, real huffy, 'The President's visit is Top Secret.' And I say. 'Not with you around, Deputy Dawg.' Pissed him off, big time. But you gotta take a peek .on your way out, man—it's hilarious."

"OK. You going to be at the Box tonight?"

"Every night."

"See you there."

"Bring your pool cue—and be prepared to lose some money."

The phone rang on the counter and he picked it up, waving them away.

"Is he a good friend of yours?"

"One of my best friends. Some people think he's dangerously psychotic."

"But not you."

"No. I think he's endearingly psychotic. He's a conspiracy theorist. To him everything is a conspiracy. We were
in Viet Nam for the oil. We're fighting the Medellin drug
cartel because the CIA is in business with their competi-
tion. All the assassinations were conspiracies—even John
Lennon's. Poverty is a conspiracy. AIDS is a conspiracy.
He's certain the CIA developed the virus as a biological
warfare weapon."

"He's not too fond of the CIA, is he?"

"He hates them. He saw them up close in Viet Nam."

They walked out into the cold again, passing the Secret Service man. Jake was right. He was a cartoon. They
both started laughing as they ran to the limousine waiting
at the curb.

It was warm inside the car. The back seat was a pleasant little cave scented with leather. There was a CD player
and a cellular phone, a television, a small refrigerator and
a bar. The driver was sealed away from them by sound-
proof tinted glass.

They drove out of the airport, past the empty parking
lot of the Nantucket Inn, onto Old South Road. Trees and
houses blurred past.

"Why do people say Jake is crazy? Is it just his theories?"

Tom tensed for a moment, then released a breath. "It's
a lot of things. Stuff that happened in 'Nam. Stuff that's
happened since. Lots of stuff."

"Like . . .?'

"Do you really want to hear this?"

"You said he was your friend. You don't seem to have a
lot of friends."

"No."

"So when I meet one I'm interested. What did he do in
Viet Nam?"

"Well . . . there's different sides to the story. He says he saw three officers pulling the clothes off a Vietnamese girl at gun point. This was in Saigon—the summer of sixty eight. He told them to stop and they refused. When it was clear they were going to rape her he . . . intervened."

"Did he have a weapon?"

"He didn't need a weapon. He is a weapon. He disabled two of the officers and killed the third."

"So . . . Jake's a Karate expert like you?"

Tom smiled. "That's a funny way to put it. He's been teaching me since I was eight years old."

"So . . . you believe his side of the story?"

"I'm not the only one. There was a witness. And the officers had been in trouble before. Jake's commanding officer testified for him at the court martial—said he was the best flier and the most reliable man under his command."

"Jake told you this?'

"No—my father did. He was Jake's C.O. That's how they met. Jake got a medical discharge. A lot of people still think he just went nuts that night. After the war he started working for my Dad as his personal pilot . . . and baby-sitter. I saw him breaking cinder blocks one day and said 'I want to do that.' He said. 'It takes time.' I said 'That's okay, I'm only eight years old.' That got a laugh out of him. He's been teaching me ever since."

"But he's not your Dad's pilot any more."

"No . . . when my Dad ran for the Senate, the people who worked for him, the image people, the media people, they said Jake would be an issue. He was always involved in fights— usually breaking them up, but . . . and he was suing the Veterans' Administration over Agent Orange . . . he was just too loud and too big and too angry not to be noticed. They didn't think my Dad should have a private pilot anyway. It made him seem too elitist. So he said, 'Fine. I'll sell the plane and fly

coach from now on. I'll meet more voters that way.' Jake came
up to Nantucket a few months later to visit us. He meant to
stay a week. That was in '82, and he's never left. There are a
lot of people around here like that."

"So . . . there are no hard feelings?"

"As far as Jake is concerned my Dad is still his commanding officer and he always will be. Nothing else matters. I don't think he would have done baby-sitting duty
for anyone else."

Amy hugged herself as if against a sudden chill. "I really am nervous about this. Does that seem silly?"

"No, but . . . it's strange—people expect my Dad to be, I
don't know, part of history already. Not quite alive—like one
of those audioanimatronic statues in the Hall of Presidents
at Disneyland. Then he starts telling fart jokes. And they
don't know what to do."

"I'd know what to do. I like fart jokes."

"Then you're in."

They settled back to look at the scenery. It was beautiful scenery, the long straight stretch of Milestone Road
heading east, cresting the hill at Tom Nevers with the tiny
roofs of 'Sconset in the distance and the standpipe gleam-
ing in the late afternoon sun. Below them to the left, the
cranberry bogs, brown and dormant, stretched away toward Polpis.

"Where are we going?" Amy asked.

Tom shrugged. "I never know. He could be anywhere."

They wound up bouncing down the ungraded dirt of
Pocomo Road, toward Polpis Harbor. Giant, ostentatious
houses loomed on both sides, some still being built. The
car stopped at the public landing. There were three other
cars already there—late model Plymouths and Dodges,
Secret Service standard. Agents milled around aimlessly, looking cold and miserable.

As they climbed out into the chilly, gusting salt air, the

President's golden retriever, Buster, bounded up to them and buried his muzzle in Tom's crotch, tail wagging. Tom bent down and let the big dog lick his face. Thirty feet away two people in waders were bent over in the water, a man and a woman. The man was whistling a complex classical melody. Amy smiled.

"That's Mozart's Fortieth Symphony."

Tom glanced from Amy to his Dad and back. "Some people say, 'You're not just whistling Dixie.' My Dad says, 'You're not just whistling Mozart's Fortieth.' Not too many people can actually whistle Mozart's Fortieth."

"He's on key—I'm impressed."

"Don't be. He was born with perfect pitch."

"So was I."

Then she started whistling. Her music fell into his, filling the gaps, whirling around the melody drifting over to them from the President. Tom stood listening to the bright, stuttering stream of notes, awe-struck and delighted.

"What are you—?" he managed to start.

"Shhh," she said. "It's the obbligato."

She had to pause a moment before she joined in again. The President and the First Lady turned and clumped out of the water holding their dripping scallop boxes. They set the boxes aside and got down to the serious business of hugging and kissing. Tom embraced his Mom while his Dad threw an arm around Amy's shoulders. They finished their duet with a flourish. Everyone applauded, even the Secret Service guys, momentarily startled out of their usual detachment.

Tom said, "That was great!"

Edward Bellamy Jaglom—just like on TV but bigger and more imposing—grinned down at Amy. "A beautiful girl who knows her Mozart. What more could you ask for?"

"Health, money and a sense of humor," his wife shot back instantly.

Jaglom loved rhetorical questions and it had become a family tradition to answer them, to tease into extinction any sign of campaign-trail pomposity. He never got the last word at home.

Tom was next: "Brains, patience and fine motor skills."

Amy was speaking before she had time to stop herself: "Thick hair, real estate and a fast metabolism."

Jaglom sighed. "Great—now I have another smart ass to deal with. You must be Amy."

"How do you do, Mr. President?"

"On Nantucket you can call me Ed. This is my wife, Helen. I guess you've met Buster already."

As they shook hands he turned to Tom. "Come here, kid." He took two steps himself and grabbed his son in a ferocious bear hug, his big hands splayed across Tom's back. At moments like this the rest of the world hurtled away from Tom—everything else was in the wrong end of a telescope, tiny and trivial. He loved these moments, but they scared him, too; it was a relief when his Dad pulled away a little and the world rushed back—the voices, the smell of the sea, the fading light on the water.

"It's great to see you," Jaglom said. "You look happy." He turned to Amy. "You like scallops?"

"I sure do."

"When we get back to the house I'll show you how to shuck them. I can open five pounds an hour."

"And Mom beats him two to one," Tom added.

Helen pursed her lips good humoredly; here eyes turned it into a smile. "Well, yes I do," she admitted. "But I don't like to rub it in."

"Let's go," Jaglom said. "It's getting cold out here."

They trooped back to the cars, twelve people altogether. Amy sat back as they undulated over the washboard ruts of the dirt road, waiting for her reactions to catch up with events. Tom had been right—the President was delightful. The problem was the layers of insulation between him and ordinary reality. Jaglom was like something fragile packed in pounds and pounds of those horrible styrofoam pellets. No wonder presidents lost touch with the world. She was losing touch with it a little bit herself, already.

The scattering of houses and sheds that formed the Presidential compound stood in the dune grass on a low bluff facing the Atlantic. Tom's grandfather had bought the place for five thousand dollars in 1940. There was a main house, two guest houses, a garage and a big storage shed where the Jagloms kept their boats—a pair of canoes, a sunfish, a row boat and a Hobie cat. It was all quite ramshackle and weather-beaten. Ed had resisted all efforts to renovate and 'improve' the property, even the old kitchen which everyone hated but him. He found it "delightfully homey" with its cracked linoleum, sloped floor, lead paint, low ceiling and cramped little pantry room. "This is the real Nantucket," he would gloat. "No cathedral ceiling, pickled floor, French door, fan window, skylight, all-white New York decorator nonsense here. No, sir!"

At the moment he was standing at the kitchen sink, opening scallops with his wife. Tom and Amy were looking on.

"You slip your knife in," he was saying. It was a stubby, rounded little blade; it looked like a sixth finger. "You really have to get up inside that upper shell and sever those muscles. Then you lever it open—it's all in the touch . . . ." the scallop came open in his hand and with another flick of his wrist he had cleaned it of its clinging membranes and muscle tissue. "You peel away the glop and there you are—sashimi." He popped the scallop into his mouth.

Helen, meanwhile, without saying a word, was moving through the same sequence of wrist-flicks with machine-lie precision.

"Save some for dinner, Darling," she said.

Jaglom turned to Tom. "So . . . what's happening with law school?"

"Admissions are up and business is booming."

Jaglom let that comment float away, like a Dixie cup discarded off the side of a boat. He opened some more scallops, tossing them into a big china bowl.

"What are your plans, Tom?"

"I just started my second year of college, Dad. Relax. Besides—there are other jobs."

"It's not just a job. It's a discipline—it's a way of thinking."

"But I don't like the way lawyers think."

"It strengthens the mind—just like Budo strengthens the body. I would have thought that you of all people would understand that."

"I don't know—all the lawyers I talk to want to be something else. Writers, actors, architects, beach bums."

"Not me. I loved the law."

"Dad."

"What?"

"You're the President of the United States, okay? Being a lawyer obviously wasn't enough for you. Being a senator wasn't enough."

"All right, all right—but look at someone like Bill Peller—"

"He wants to be a comedian," Helen said quietly, pressing a smile off her lips, eyes bright with controlled laughter.

"Excuse me . . .?"

"He goes to amateur night at the comedy clubs. He does lawyer jokes—jokes about probate and fiduciary litigation. But nobody laughs—not even the other lawyers. Not even the other lawyers who want to be comedians. And there are quite a few of them. It's really quite sad."

"I'm telling you. Dad—nobody wants to be a lawyer."

"Except me," said Amy.

Everyone turned to her.

"Yeah . . . it drives my parents crazy, but I just like the law. I like to argue. I play violin for fun."

"Speaking of the violin," Jaglom said hesitantly, "Tom mentioned you might bring yours along?"

Amy nodded. "Do you want to play?"

"Well . . . I've been working on the Beethoven sonatas. Maybe after dinner . . .?"

"Sure."

They had an excellent meal—scallops sautéed in butter and white wine, wild rice, a Caesar salad and three bottles of ice-cold white wine. Dessert was Helen's own special recipe cheesecake with sour-cream icing washed down with lots of strong coffee.

As he sat in the living room later, listening to the forceful, intricate, surging beauty of Beethoven's Spring Sonata, it seemed to Tom as if Amy had known his family for years. Both of his parents had decided to like her instantly; his Mom, at least, would have probably insisted on liking her no matter what sort of person she turned out to be. But that wasn't going to be necessary. She was their sort of person. And it was instantly clear to all of them that she had a major talent. Tom could understand her parents chagrin—the world needed fewer lawyers and more great fiddle players.

His mother patted his knee with comfortable, self-congratulatory pride. It embarrassed him, grated on him softly. He turned away from her "You-sure-can-pick-'em" smile and sat back with his eyes closed, listening. It was like her insistence at dinner that he have another slice of cheesecake because he needed to "put on some weight."

Of course the irritations were inevitable, part of the culture of his family, customs too familiar to fight. It was the same way with his Dad. Their arguments about law school and lawyers—sometimes heated, sometimes in fun—had become just one more family ritual.

Before long, these mixed emotions would torment him with guilt and regret. Despite his quibbles, this Christmas would stand out in his mind as the last happy time of his life, the closing days of his innocence, the final unburdened moments before the horror began.

And he didn't appreciate them enough; that would be his final verdict on himself. These days were a gift, and he wasted them. He took everything for granted. But nothing is ever granted. Nothing is ever given freely—everything is on loan, and it can all be foreclosed in a split-second. Of course, that thought never occurred to him. So he let himself be embarrassed, he argued with his Dad, he turned away from his Mom when he should have hugged her.

He would never forgive himself for that.

4

"Want to see how we scared the crap out of those gook farmers?" Jake Gritzky asked with a maniacal grin. "Check it out."

They were flying in one of Nantucket Airlines' Cessnas, a thousand feet above the south shore of the island. Tom and Amy were jammed into the cockpit beside him. Gritzky was a big man, lean with muscle, with big features spread on a wide face. His hands on the throttle were huge, with thick veins standing out over the sharp lines of the bones. Amy could understand why people thought he was crazy: there was a sort of readiness about him. He seemed capable of doing anything any time.

Like now.

They were flying lower, swinging out over the ocean and then back towards land. A man with a big plastic bucket was gleaning surf clams off the beach from the last storm. "Here we go," said Jake. "Of course, to do this right you really need a Huey—one of the big choppers we flew in 'Nam. You cut out those engines and the silence freaks them out before they even see you."

Then, calmly and deliberately, Jake turned the nose of the little plane down and shut down the engines. Tom and Amy felt their stomachs climb tip into their throats as they started to free-fall. The only sound was the vertical gale of air rushing past outside. Jake was staring intently at the beach widening towards them as they dropped.

Tom found his voice—part of it at least. "Jake," he managed.

Gritzky smiled amiably and laced his fingers behind his head, elbows out, as if he belonged on a lawn chair on a summer afternoon.

The clammer looked up. They could see his mouth open in a scream—then he was scrambling up the beach. He tripped and fell face-first into the sand. That was the moment when Amy knew they couldn't pull out of the dive.

She was going to die.

Someone was shrieking. It was her. She grabbed at Tom. He held her. Every muscle in her body was clenched against the impact, every nerve was quivering. Her eyes were jammed shut. Terror engulfed her like black water. She couldn't breathe but somehow she kept on screaming.

Then the engines cut in. Less than fifty feet above the ground the plane leveled off and started climbing again. The little man on the beach was shaking his fist at them— an angry speck in the expanse of sand. Jake laughed and the laugh brought Amy's voice back.

"Jesus Christ! What the hell do you think you're doing? Are you trying to kill us?"

"No, Ma'am. Suicide ain't a party. You don't invite your friends."

"Then what were you—"

"You asked me a few minutes ago what it felt like in 'Nam. That's a fair question but everybody asks it and there's no way to answer them. In words I mean. Because I just gave you an answer. The feeling you just got in your gut when you were sure we were going to crash—that's what it felt like, over there. All the time. And that ain't the movies, kids."

Jake hated the movies. He thought they were boring and sentimental. He despised well-structured stories and happy endings. He was particularly annoyed by the violence in films—not because, as it was fashionable to feel, it was too extreme or exploitative, too brutal or gory. Just the opposite: he thought it was all fake and sanitized, with no relation to reality. He was well-qualified to make these judgments. Jake was a magnet for fights. He didn't start them. They just seemed to break out whenever he was nearby. He and Tom had broken up more of them than he could count—fights in the street, fights in movie theaters and hotel lobbies and locker rooms, fights in elevators and bars and parking garages. They had become expert at the art of non-violent intervention,

Jake had an affinity for dangerous places. That was part of it. He liked bad neighborhoods late at night: he prowled subway stations, deserted parks and barrio playgrounds. In New York he liked the north end of Central Park and the south side of Bedford Stuyvesant.

On Nantucket, he liked the Chicken Box.

It was a working class bar in the middle of the island's modest commercial sprawl, well away from the pretty, historic downtown. It was a place where fights broke out frequently over women and race—it was a favorite spot for blacks and rednecks alike. People would fight over scallop prices, over the Patriots, over a look or a gesture . . . over nothing.

Jake had gradually become the unofficial bouncer for the place. He had curtailed a lot of property damage, saved a lot of people fines, hospital bills and even jail time. Tom would never had considered going there without him—

visits to the box, like smoking Parodi cigars and watching
football games, was one of the customs of their friendship.

They were standing at the bar now, he and Amy, toast-
ing Jake with bottles of Bud, the afternoon's fright not forgotten but set aside. To their left, the stage was empty and
shadowed—no band tonight. Four pool tables lined the
wall to their right, with tacky light fixtures over them. Tom's
favorite was an over-sized bottle of Bud Light resting in a
bed of plastic ice. The bar was crowded, the dart boards
were in use and the place had an amiable insularity that
made Tom think of the bumper sticker Jake wanted to offer islanders during the summer season to replace the
bland and petulant "It used to be nice on Nantucket". Jake's
was rude, but much more to the point: "Fuck you. I live
here."

Jake was still talking about the war. A pair of Secret
Service agents were eavesdropping on one side of them.
On the other side, a beefy housepainter, still in his spat-
tered, caulk-crusty white pants and sweat shirt, still smell-
ing of kerosene and thinner, was drinking shots of Cutty
Sark and watching Amy's legs.

"My shrink says talk about it. My Dad says talk about it.
Even my wife said talk about it. That was the last thing she
said before she walked out on me. So I talk about it now.
Big deal." Jake finished his beer and signaled for another
one.

"I've always wanted to know what happened to you
over there," Tom said gently.

"Okay, kid. I'll tellya. Everybody died. How's that? Everybody I flew with, everybody I knew. Everybody but me
and your Dad. They're all dead now and I'm not. I don't
get it. I can't figure that one out at all."

"There's nothing to figure out, Jake," Amy said. "It's
like winning the lottery. The odds may be against you win-

ning, but it's absolutely certain that someone is going to win, and that someone had the same million to one odds against them as everybody else. This time it was you, that's all. You were just—lucky."

Jake laughed. "Lucky! Now that's an interesting word for it. Lucky. I never thought of that one. Let me tell you about lucky. One morning, in February of '67, I dropped a whole platoon into an ambush just north of An Loc. Forty guys. The VC got half of them in the air—corpses dangling from parachutes. The rest of them bought it on the ground. Nobody survived. And I just kept on flying."

"Were your orders to go back?" Tom asked.

"That's not the point."

"Was your helicopter armed? Were there bombs on board?"

"Nope. This was strictly personnel."

Amy frowned in concentration, assembling the story for herself. "So, you were alone, unarmed, ambushed, facing heavy enemy fire, and you still brought your helicopter back safely." She shook her head, smiling. "It sounds like they should have given you a medal."

"They did—ain't that a laugh? They gave me a goddamn medal. You know, I wanted to re-enlist when Desert Storm happened. I figured it was the last chance I was ever going to get to go down for my country. But they wouldn't take me. Too old. Too unstable."

"Well," said Tom, "I don't know. If you sounded suicidal to them . . ."

"Hold on. You know those Kamikaze pilots in World War Two? The ones who flew their planes right into the American battleships? Do you think they were just committing suicide?"

"They killed themselves, Jake," Amy said softly.

Jake shook his head. "They did a lot more than that. They got the job done. They didn't collect any medals but they went down together and they finished what they started. And that's all that matters. Everything else is just bullshit."

A silence fell between them then, full of clinking glass and jukebox music and other people's conversations. Someone was racking the balls on one of the pool tables. Tom looked at Amy; neither of them knew what to say. But it didn't matter because that was the moment when the evening started to tilt out of control.

The big housepainter put a solvent-stained hand on Amy's knee.

"Can I buy you a drink?" he asked.

Tom watched, knowing Amy would want to handle it herself. Jake watched both of them.

"No thanks," she said, swiveling away from him.

"Wanta dance, then?" he persisted.

"Not with you."

The thick hand was on her shoulder. "Then how about goin' back to my place for some fun?"

She turned to him and smiled politely. "I'd rather have gum surgery," she said.

That was when the women started arguing.

"It's mine and you know it!"

"Like hell it is! You couldn't fit into this sweater with a crowbar!"

They were a female Laurel and Hardy—a weathered, sinewy woman who looked as if she had spent her whole life in the sun, and an obese, pallid monster with a flaring case of acne. They were a grotesque pair, but the anger and violence between them was real. Tom thought of Jake's point about films versus real life. This little scuffle was much more upsetting than all the bodies being blown apart in all the movies he'd ever seen, put together. It made his stomach twist, the way it so often did when he was with Jake—the familiar mixture of anticipation, excitement and dread. There was going to be a fight. And they were going to be in the thick of it.

"Give it back."

"Get away from me, Sally."

"Give it back."

"I'm warning you—"

"Give it back."

"You're drunk."

"Gimme back my goddamn sweater!"

The fat woman jabbed out with the flat of her hand, Tom noticed that the flesh had swallowed the knuckles completely, and the thin woman was forced to stagger back a few steps. The Secret Service guys were looking on, uncertain of what they should do.

The Chicken Box wasn't their world and they didn't know the rules . . . apart from their own rule, of course, which was to remain inconspicuous.

"Give it to me."

"Don't touch me again, fatso—it's my sweater."

But the massive arm snapped out again. This time, the smaller woman dodged inside the blow and flung herself at the mountain of flesh, punching hard at the big woman's throat. Not at the jaw, which would have broken her hand, or that well-padded stomach. The throat. Tom and Jake glanced at each other. This woman knew how to fight, and that meant someone was going to get hurt. Jake inclined his head slightly and Tom nodded millimetrically in response. They each took a deep breath and then they were off their bar stools, Jake headed for the fat lady, Tom closing in on the throat puncher.

By the time they got into the battle zone, the fat woman had one of her opponent's fists in her hand and she was squeezing hard. She caught the other hand as it clawed at her face. There was a sickening crackle of breaking cartilage. The smaller woman screamed in pain, and brought her work boot down hard, stamping on the exposed instep. The fat woman howled and released her grip. Jake grabbed her. Tom grabbed the other one, who was just as strong as she looked.

"Let go of me," she screamed.

"Look, there's no need to fight about this. We can just sit down and—"

But she yanked her arm free and drove an elbow into his ribs.

"Get your goddamn hands off my wife!"

A huge man in brown Carhart overalls and a Marine Lumber cap was charging Jake. Another one, not much smaller, was leaping at Tom.

"Let go of her!"

The husbands.

They hadn't thought about the husbands. The Secret Service guys were off their bar stools now. Tom released the woman, caught her husband easily, used his clumsy haymaker to spin him around and sent him sprawling at the Secret Service agents—rolling him at them like a bowling ball. The group went down in a tangle of stained cotton and gray serge. Jake dropped the fat woman's husband, but she was pounding him, angrier than ever.

Tom was about to dive in and help when he saw Amy out of the corner of his eye. The housepainter had seen his opportunity. Tom was fighting, Amy was alone. He had grabbed her and he was kissing her, smashing his mouth on hers, holding her by the hair with one hand, slipping the other hand under her shirt. She was hitting at him, thrashing from side to side to side, her screams muffled down his throat. She tried to kick at him but he stepped between her legs. Bottles and glasses on the bar went flying. Under her shirt, the bulge of his hand covered her breast.

Something exploded in Tom's brain, white and cold

and soundless. Someone was punching him but he didn't feel it. All he felt was hate, rising inside him, uncontrollable as vomit. The painter had six inches and at least sixty pounds on him, but it wasn't going to help. Height and bulk wouldn't have mattered against a wolf or a pit bull, and Tom—as he launched himself at the bar—was infinitely more dangerous than either of those animals.

He was merciless. His first kick sliced into the side of the painter's knee like a machete into a stalk of sugar cane. The painter released Amy and staggered backwards, but his pulverized knee wouldn't support him. As he toppled sideways, Tom's roundhouse kick shattered his jaw. He hit the bar floor on his back and before he could even assimilate what had happened to him, Tom's knee was dropping down hard into his solar plexus, blasting the air out of his lungs.

Kneeling on top of the immobilized painter, Tom began to batter the man's face, punch after punch, breaking the nose and knocking out teeth in a vile spray of blood and mucus. Amy could only stare. The rest of the bar—including the two bruised and rumpled Secret Service agents—looked on with awe and horror. No one dared to intervene.

Then there was a hand on Tom's shoulder.

"That's enough now, kid."

Tom turned on Jake, still lost in his fury, aiming a brutal punch at the big man's groin. It never landed. Without visible effort, without even seeming to move, Jake took Tom's wrist and bent it, forcing him to stand. The painter was groaning on the floor. There were sirens in the distance. Jake's voice was calm. "The police are coming. We have to get out of here, Tommy. We're going to exit through the kitchen. Right now."

He led the way, his casual wrist grip controlling Tom completely. He nodded at Amy and she hurried after them.

Five minutes later they were heading up the Milestone Road.

"Thanks, Jake," Tom said at last.

Jake grinned into the night. "You did the right thing back there. You just did too much of it."

Amy took his hand and the physical touch brought him back into focus. "Are you all right?' he asked.

"I don't know. I think so."

"That guy—

"It was horrible. I couldn't do anything—he was so big and he just ~-he was if you hadn't been there . . .

"But I was."

She shivered and he held her. They drove on in silence. She was grateful and angry and scared; excited and appalled. She was exhausted but her nerves were screaming. She wanted to kill the man who had made her helpless and violated her; at the same time she hoped he would be okay. The feelings fought and scrambled inside of her. Her stomach ached, she realized she hadn't eaten since lunch. But she was nauseous—she couldn't imagine swallowing anything, even water.

"I thought Nantucket was safe," she said as they turned onto the dirt road to Madequecham and the Presidential compound.

Tom sighed. "No place is safe."

Later, after Jake had dropped them off, Tom and Amy were walking on the beach. The night was clear and cold. The stars were as dense as salt spilled on black silk.

There was a question Amy had to ask. As the tremors in her arms and legs subsided and she forced back the vivid, pulsing memory of a stranger's tongue in her mouth, she organized herself for the interrogation. They were almost at the house when she began. She knew her nerve would fail her inside the well-lit mansion. She needed the darkness.

"What would you have done if Jake hadn't been there?"

"I'm not sure."

"Would you have just . . . gone on hitting him?"

"I'm not sure."

They walked a few more steps. A wave broke with a sound like distant thunder. Foam surged and retreated.

"Would you have killed him?"

Tom put his arm around her and held her tight.

"No," he said.

But he wasn't sure.

5

The man had no trouble getting into Jim Gramble's building. He picked the lock on the front door in less than a minute—forty-two seconds, to be precise. He liked to keep a record of his performance with various tumbler set-ups and diverse field conditions. This particular Schlage was a little rusty; it would have been hard work turning it, even with a key. But the man was strong and his picking tools gave him excellent leverage. Of course, there could have been a problem if anyone had come in or out of the building while he was working. He was prepared to kill if he had to but in his experience, even the cleanest hit created more problems than it solved. That was why he had argued against killing Gramble. A dead reporter was a liability—his death would arouse the interest of other reporters, most of them every bit as inquisitive and dangerous as Gramble himself. And you couldn't kill them all, you just couldn't. It would be like trying to kill all the rats in the New York subway system.

In any case, his specialty was not killing. It was terrorism. As far as he was concerned, the word had been misunderstood and devalued through its random application to events in the Middle East. Terrorism wasn't taking hostages and threatening to kill them if your demands weren't met—that was extortion at best.

Terrorism was the effective management of terror.

Creating and manipulating fear was an art whose oeuvre was drawn not in blood but in blood pressure, not in dead flesh but in the adrenaline that made the live flesh jump. Once a person was crippled with terror, they were yours. "Terror corrupts," he liked to say. "Absolute terror corrupts absolutely."

And it was fun, that was the secret he had never shared with his employers. It was a game and you had to be clever to win. It kept those little trees in your brain healthy. It kept you young—he was the living proof of that. He didn't look fifty; he didn't look much more than thirty five and he knew the reason. He liked his work. Few professional killers could make that statement. The constant proximity to death eroded them—they looked old before their time. Killers died young and often wound up being killed themselves. It was the world they chose to live in. He was too smart to live that way.

The tumblers clicked into place. He eased the door open and stepped into the lobby. The elevator looked unreliable. He trotted past it to the fire door and took the stairs.

Jim Gramble's door had a police lock—a metal bar sunk into a slot in the floor and braced against the door at an angle. It couldn't be forced and the lock itself was said to be 'unpickable'. The man smiled as he sorted through his tools in the dim hallway. All that meant to him was a more interesting challenge. He had opened these locks before; it just took a little more finesse.

He waited a moment before he began. He wanted to savor the feeling of the night's action still ahead of him. Of course, the anticipation was sometimes sweeter than the actual event. He had been disappointed before. Still, the event was always significant: he was about to change forever the landscape of someone else's life.

Humming quietly to himself, he got down to work.

Jim heard nothing at first.

He was totally absorbed in his work, staring at the computer screen, fingers dancing like a five-man chorus line over the softly rattling keys. His notes covered the table but he scarcely glanced at them. He paused only to save his material and he did that at much longer intervals than he should have. If he was stuck for a paragraph lead he would hit the 'save' button while he assembled the proper phrase in his mind. He often had it before the computer was ready for him, and it was in one of those brief, impatient lulls that he realized his back was stiff, his coffee was cold and there was the sound of a key in the lock of his front door.

The computer was ready; the cursor blinked companionably at him. But he didn't see it. Someone was trying to get in, fighting with the key, and there was only one other person who had a key to this apartment. She had never been able to unlock the door without a struggle. He stood awkwardly, pushing his chair back.

Eleanor.

He mastered himself, forced himself to breathe slowly. What could she want now? What purpose could possibly be served by this kind of lunatic surprise attack? Fisk had advised him to change his locks and he had agreed—he just hadn't gotten around to it yet, Well, now he was going to have to pay for his procrastination. He looked down at the dining room table, strewn papers and books and diskettes, littered with full ash-trays and empty plates. Eleanor had always hated the way his work 'took over' a room, the 'squalor' he created around himself. She used debunking animal terminology—he made 'nests,' left 'droppings.'

And of course he had started smoking again. Whatever her purpose in coming, she would take time out to badger him about that.

And he realized that the absence of her carping voice had become a rich physical pleasure for him. It was a specific silence, like the moment when the cicadas stop or the burglar alarm is shut off down the street. Yes, he was still hated—but what an intoxicating pleasure it was to be hated from afar, not to have to feel the coarse grain of Eleanor's hatred chafing against him every day.

He started up the hall to the front door, deciding to unlock it for her, to tell her she should have knocked in the first place. He would be polite but firm.

He was halfway there when the police bar slid over and the door opened. There was a man standing there, about six feet tall, maybe forty years old, wearing jeans and a leather jacket with a Mets cap. He smiled as he slipped his picking tools into a leather case and pulled out a gun.

"Hello, Mr. Gramble. We need to talk."

Jim was speechless. He was startled and frightened, but curiously enough, he was also relieved. Whatever happened to him tonight, at least he wouldn't have to deal with his ex-wife.

The man waved Jim backward with a loose-wristed flick of the gun; they moved through the hall and into the cluttered living room.

"So this is how a Pulitzer Prize winning writer lives," the man mused.

"After his divorce," Jim corrected him.

"Oh yeah—right. Sorry to hear that. How long were you married?"

"Eight years. Look—can we get on with this? Whatever this is. I have a lot of work to do tonight."

But the man didn't seem to be in any hurry. He strolled around the room, glancing at the shelves, the glowing computer screen, the books and papers on the floor. He was careful not to step on anything.

Jim had a gun in his desk drawer, but he knew it was hopeless to try anything. If he had been armed at the moment the door opened . . . but he hadn't been, and it might not have helped him anyway.

The man sighed, cleared some rubble off a chair and sat down. "Look at you," he said. "College man. Journalism school. Big time writer . . . all those prizes. Eyes on the prize, right? So tell me something. How does someone so smart get to be so goddamn stupid?"

"I'm not sure what you—

"You know the real test of high intelligence, Mr. Gramble? The ability to learn—to rearrange your plans and your habits around new information. Flexibility—that's the real test of high intelligence. You're putting yourself in jeopardy, Mr. Gramble. I don't think you've really understood that fact. That's probably our fault—we haven't been sufficiently clear. That's the reason for my little visit tonight. My communication skills are second to none."

As he spoke the man saw the vague anxiety in Gramble's face tightening into fear. Jim knew something was coming but he didn't know what. The man didn't know either; he liked to improvise, he liked to let himself be inspired by the details of a person's home, the information-rich atmosphere of their private space. There was always some message there, some suggestion: a pet he could cripple, a painting he could deface, or in this case . . . He stood up, smiling, and strolled over to the table.

"Nice computer, Mr. Gramble. Laser printer—top of the line. I hope you remembered to save your material lately. You can't be too careful. Hmmm . . . surge suppresser. Uninterruptable power source . . . you're protected from just about everything. Except this."

He turned the gun so that the dark metal caught the

light and Jim suddenly knew what was going to happen. With a furious, agonized wail, he threw himself at the man, who sidestepped the attack casually, and tapped him with the gun butt. Jim crumpled to the carpet. The room tilted around him and gradually righted itself. He was no fighter—his only way out of this was with words.

"Please," he croaked, panting, "It's not just my article in there . . . there's a book—I've been working on it for five years . . . and a novel . . . all my notes, my journals, my tax records . . . everything . . ."

The man smiled. "I was hoping you'd say that. Now be quiet and pay attention. We're about to give new meaning to the phrase, 'crashing your hard drive.'"

Still smiling, he put three silenced shots into the screen of Jim's computer. There were three dull thuds and the mechanism was literally blown to bits in a cascade of sparks. He fired three more shots into the short, wide box that held the hard disk, the memory board—the digitized whole of Jim Gramble's life. Jim could only stare at the sputtering ruins, numb with disbelief.

But the man wasn't finished yet.

"One additional note, Mr. Gramble. Always store your back-up disks in a different location." He swept all the back-up disks off Jim's shelf and there was a moment as he fumbled with them, trying not to drop any, when a person with combat training could have made a move. But Jim wasn't that person. He recalled the story of the man who found one of the terrorists' guns, fully loaded, in the bathroom of a hijacked plane. Of course, the guy had fantasized briefly about saving the day with a few well-placed shots . . . after which he meekly turned the gun over to his captors. Jim understood that failure of nerve very well: after all, what if you started shooting and missed? You wouldn't be given a second chance. When the risks were real, heroism turned foul and cheesy and grotesque. Hunted animals stayed still.

Yeah, Jim goaded himself, even if they were in the headlights of an oncoming car.

So he didn't move.

And the moment passed. The man got the disks under one arm, with the gun safely pointing at Jim in his other hand. "I'll dispose of these for you," he said. "I hope you learned something tonight."

He backed his way out of the hall, struggled with the front door—another vulnerable moment, for what it was worth—and then he was gone.

Jim sat on the floor staring at the sizzling, clicking, smoking mess that had been his Macintosh half an hour ago. The anesthetic of shock was wearing off. He felt as if part of himself had been stolen, some crucial wedge of consciousness deep in his brain. He was less real, now. He had become a sickly hologram of himself, without the writing that had connected him to the world. He was quivering like the steering wheel of a car whose tires aren't aligned properly, shuddering with the velocity of his loss. Was this how you felt when you watched your family house burning out of control, and no firemen in sight? It must be—it was the same holocaust of details, all the small, loved, irreplaceable objects exploding into ash.

Jim had no family house, no heirlooms, no prized possessions—except his words. His thoughts, shaped and cut and polished, rigorously clarified. They were the sum total of what he owned. His collected works. He brought his knees up and rested his head on them, listening to the dying sputters of his computer. He could almost feel the ether that had held his sentences in suspension drifting in tatters around the room like the dangling crepe paper streamers after a child's birthday party.

It was all gone.

The thought weighed him down. It anchored him to the floor. He thought he might stay here, sitting on his rug with his head on his knees, forever. There was no particular reason to get up.

Jim's father had been a family practice doctor in the Bedford-Stuyvesant section of Brooklyn. As the first black in an all-white medical school, in the segregated army during World War II, through his residency in a southern hospital in the early '50s and his fight to build a decent practice in one of the worst neighborhoods in New York City, his struggles had been relentless and heartbreaking. He had known tragedy: after two stillbirths his wife had died of ovarian cancer when Jim was only ten years old. He had raised his son alone, and succeeded in his profession, on his own terms and to his own satisfaction. He never got rich, he charged too little and did too much work for free. But he became a beloved and absolutely essential member of that devastated but still functioning community.

"Ever see weeds growing through cracks in the sidewalk?" he used to say. "That's us."

He was also fond of saying that despair was a virus and healthy people created antibodies for it. Sitting on the floor of his apartment, listening to the sounds of traffic coming through his window, Jim could feel his immune system begin to respond.

It began with a joke.

It wasn't much of a joke, no belly laugh. But it did make him smile. "Well," he thought, "This will certainly simplify my next tax audit."

Then he started thinking practically. He had hard copies, actual printed pages, of at least some of the novel, for instance. There was a third of it sitting in his agent's office right now. Sure, there was a lot he would never recover, but that might be just as well. Most of the other stuff he had printed out at one stage or another. There was damage but it was manageable. Even his note files had begun

with actual notes, scrawled on match-books and paper nap-
kins, before they were logged into the computer. And he
never threw anything away. He would have to do a major—
almost an archaeological—housecleaning, but that wasn't
the end of the world. At least the place would be clean
and tidy if Eleanor ever actually showed up.

The only really devastating loss was the story he was
working on for the *Journal Examiner*. None of it had been
printed yet. And even that wasn't a total loss: he still has all
his notes and source material in his desk drawer at the
paper.

His immune system was charged up now, fueled by a
growing anger and the old outrage that had served him so
well in the past. There was excitement, too—he had managed to throw a scare into his old nemesis Dominic
Nosiglia, and that was better than winning a Pulitzer Prize.
It was fascinating: the Nosiglias were so scared they didn't
want to risk killing him. Their problem had been how to
silence him without injuring him physically or making
news. They must have been proud of themselves when they
thought of wrecking his computer.

But that was their miscalculation. Jim's real computer
was up and running. "They didn't get the mainframe," he
actually said aloud, speaking for the first time in more than
an hour. He jabbed his index finger at his temple. "*This* is
the mainframe."

He pulled himself to his feet.

He didn't even need his notes—he knew the story, he
knew who his sources were, who had told him what, and
when. He even remembered what they'd been wearing
and how the weather was. It just a question of typing it all
out again. All the Mafia had done was make more work
for him. But that was okay—he was a worker.

He strode to the closet where his old Olympia portable was stored, feeling a pure shaft of ruthless mental

energy gathering behind his eyes. It made him cold, drained
all emotion out of him. He needed that. To feel anything
now would ruin him, because even as he pulled out the bulky
black case from behind the litter of shoes and paper bags he
knew he was still wounded, still hurting, still perilously close
to giving up and walking away from the whole senseless catastrophe.

But of course that was unthinkable: the story had to be
told.

In a few minutes he had swept the remains of his computer off the table and set up the Olympia in its place, with a
pile of printer paper stacked beside it, ready for business.

He stepped away from the table and blew out a long
breath, He loved this old machine—he had forgotten that.
He had written a lot of important stories on it, banged away
at it just ahead of a lot of deadlines, carried it with him on
a lot of airplanes. It had been with him at the beginning of
his career and it was still around, like a cart horse when
the fancy tractor breaks down: patient, strong, reliable . . .
unable to hold a grudge.

Jim had read somewhere that you gained ten pounds
in the first year after you shifted from a manual typewriter
to a computer, there was so much less exertion involved.
He believed it—he had definitely gotten heavier since the
changeover. If there was any justice in the world, the process would be reversible.

He smiled grimly to himself: time to lose some weight.

He sat down, rolled in the first sheet of paper, and
began. The first few strokes didn't make much of an impression. This was a manual, you really had to hit the keys.
He started jabbing at them, getting his shoulders into it,
but before he could establish a rhythm the keys jammed.
He pulled them apart and started again. They jammed
again. Again, he pulled them apart.

He typed ten words and they jammed yet again.

He slammed his fist into the table. "Fuck this thing!," he shouted, and pulled the keys apart once more, boiling with impatience. Now it was all coming back: his relationship with the Olympia had always been love-hate at best. It was all right. He'd get used to it.

He made himself pots of coffee and the neighbors heard him hammering at the typewriter, cursing and pacing, long past dawn.

Some of them grumbled about it, but to old Mrs. Byck in 3F it was a wonderful, romantic sound. She had known Jim since his first days at the *Journal Examiner*, when this exasperated clamor always meant there'd be something exciting to read in the newspaper soon.

Jim was after the bad guys again.

She lay in her bed, sipping her red wine, stroking her cat and smiling at the racket coming through the wall.

It was just like the good old days.

6

The old boathouse creaked in the Atlantic gale. It leaned out over the bluff, gray shingles tilting toward the ocean under the milling gray sky. The barren winter landscape made Tom wonder what it must have been like living on Nantucket during the whaling days of the last century, with no heat or electricity. Hard; or maybe he was just spoiled. He pulled the door open against the harsh east wind.

"Go on in," he said.

Amy stepped into the quiet darkness ahead of him. The sudden stillness was like a blow—it made their ears ring. It smelled like Tom's childhood inside, with the mingled aromas of old wood, diesel fuel, mildew and spar varnish. Unused racks for big boats rose into the cobwebs near the ceiling. There were a couple of canoes, a sunfish and a row boats on the lower racks; oars and sails, fishing rods and outboard engines leaning against the unfinished shed walls.

"I hope you don't want to take a boat out today," Amy said.

Tom laughed. "This is the best part of the tour. I promise."

They had been all over the island already. from the Whaling Museum to Sankaty Light, from the Old Mill to the Oldest House. It had been more fun tramping through the moors to Altar Rock and pacing the perimeter of the cranberry bogs. Nantucket had never bothered to devise many tourist attractions. The place itself was the attraction, the wild, sparse, wind-flattened beauty of it. Tom liked the solitary places— the thin barrier beaches that separated the fresh-water ponds from the sea, the deserted dirt roads lined with wild heather and beach plum.

Town was a nightmare these days: since the election, it had been like August all year long. There were twice as many tourists as ever before, and hundreds of press people, who were much more rude and inconsiderate than the tourists had ever been.

Everyone wanted to catch a glimpse of the President, and Tom's father obliged them, stopping on Main Street in front of the Hub or in front of the Something Natural bread rack at the Stop & Shop to sign autographs and argue foreign policy with his constituents. It was good politics, it made for excellent photo opportunities and it came naturally to him. But it was like feeding stray dogs. They didn't go away. They just got more insistent. And their numbers increased. A president who crewed in the Figawi with the contractor who had reshingled his house; who treated local kids to ice-cream cones at the Juice Bar and wrote guest editorials in *The Inquirer & Mirror* was a novelty few could resist.

For Tom it meant only that he had to work that much harder to get some part of his island and his father to himself. Being on Nantucket with Amy silenced most of his gripes, though. There were so many untouched beautiful places to show her, and seeing them with her made them new for him again. Beauty was meant to be shared. These landscapes were melancholy somehow when you were alone,

as if you were trespassing on someone else's life. Today it was
his life and Nantucket was his place.

He hugged Amy in the dim light of the boathouse and
they listened to the wind outside. Her face was cold but
her lips were warm against his neck. He pulled away a little
and said, "Come on, I have to show you this."

He took her hand and led her to the back of the boathouse. There was a pegboard full of dangling tools on one
wall. Tom grabbed a flashlight and they picked their way
through a clutter of lobster traps and scallop boxes, broken chairs and a pile of old mattresses to the far corner of
the little building. He pushed aside a pile of netting and
rubber waders.

There was a trap door in the floor.

The ring handle was rusty, but Tom managed to yank
it open. He set the big wooden square aside as the clay
smell of damp earth billowed up at them. He started climbing down a wood-slat ladder nailed to the shoring planks.
Amy stared down at him.

"You're going in there?"

"You have to see this—come on."

"Is it safe?"

"It's been here for more than a hundred years. Smug-
glers used this house during Prohibition. But the tunnel
was here long before that. They used it to hide slaves before the Civil War. It was one of the last stops on the Underground Railroad. This tunnel leads to the main house."

He took her hand and helped her find the first slat.
Soon they were crouched over in a wood-lined tunnel four
feet high that stretched ahead of them into the gloom. They
ducked down and jogged along until the tunnel opened
up into a narrow, earth-walled room.

"We're below the basement now," Tom said. "There's
a vertical crawl space between the walls. Wait a second—here
it is."

He was whispering but even his whispers seemed to reso-
nate in the cramped space. Amy had caught his mood of
stealth. She followed him up a ladder, through a hole in the
ceiling and into another wood-framed hall. Soon they came
to a tight horizontal passage with just enough room for a slim
person to edge along sideways.

"This living room is right here," Tom said softly.
"There's supposed to be a way in, but no one has ever figured it out."

They pressed their ears to the wall and they could hear
people talking, but they couldn't make out the words.

They moved up to the next level. It was quite warm
now and they were sweating inside their heavy coats. On
the next floor the passage widened to about four feet. Tom
led her along it and they soon came to a section lined with
shelves. Tom let his flashlight play on the book-cases, revealing an arcane and comprehensive collection of por-
nography: *Playboy* from the first issue, but also out-of-print
Chilean bestiality magazines, underground Chinese
group-sex picture books, volumes of obsessive Scandina-
vian breast photography. Amy picked at random and leafed
through a Portuguese foot-fetish newsletter.

"Wow," she said. "Does the Secret Service know about
this?"

"Nobody knows about it. Not even my Mom."

"Don't worry. I won't tell."

"My grandfather started the collection. It's supposed
to be worth quite a lot of money. Kenneth Tynan's first
draft of *O! Calcutta!* is around here somewhere. Erotic letters from Anais Nin . . . things like that. Signed Mapplethorpe
photographs. You name it."

"I'd rather not."

"Here's the best part. Watch."

He pressed a small lever and the wall in front of them
swung inward, revealing Edward Bellamy Jaglom's office.

Tom grinned at her as they blinked in the sudden harsh daylight.

"Cool—or what?"

"You must have had a fun childhood."

"My Dad and I always had 'boy-time'—that's what he called it. Just the two of us. We buried money in Central Park with the pirates chasing us. We surf-cast for bluefish on the south shore. We explored this house together . . . all kinds of stuff."

They slipped into the book-lined room. Tom wiggled an ornamental piece of molding and the wall of law books rotated back. Amy stared at the shelves. They looked permanent and immovable. The room smelled of leather and tobacco. The desk clock was ticking and the wind was whistling in the eaves—A flat, Amy thought to herself automatically, modulating to B natural and in one fierce gust all the way to C sharp. The ocean rumbled steadily.

They stared at each other. The silence between them was more potent than any trite words of affection. Tom wanted to look away—every second he didn't seemed to magnify the intimacy between them. The moment hurtled along under its own power, out of control.

"Amy—"he started

She put her fingers to her lips. "Shhhh,' she said.

Then she was kissing him, her tongue struggling with his, keeping the vital connection between them as she struggled out of her coat, unbuttoned his and pushed it off his shoulders, running her hands up under his shirt and sweater, across his back and his ribs. Her hands were cold but only for a few seconds. The contact of her palms and fingers on his bare skin sizzled through his nerves as his own hands fumbled with her bra strap, feeling absurd adolescent frustration—how did the bra latch, at the front or the back? How could his fingers, which seemed as dexterous as a bundle of sausages, ever hope to unhook them? It was maddening. Amy pulled away from him with a hot sweet tearing as if the very molecules of their mouths had bonded like living Velcro. She was laughing as she unfastened her bra and let him brush the scrap of fabric aside.

Suddenly Tom froze—there were footsteps in the hall, the unmistakable heel-first thumping stride of Edward Bellamy Jaglom.

Tom reared back, panting. "We have to get out of here," he whispered. His eyes were wild. "That's my Dad."

No one was allowed in his father's study. It was a cardinal rule of their house and it always had been. His mind raced. There was no time to go back through the wall. The closet? Same problem—and the hinges creaked. Where else? Under the desk? Too risky. Behind the couch? Behind the curtains?

The knob was turning.

The door opened inward. It was their only chance. He grabbed Amy, swept their coats off the floor and darted to the wall, pushing her ahead of him. They were side by side, backs to the wainscoting, holding hands, holding their breaths, when President Jaglom strode inside.

The door swung three quarters of the way open: they were in plain sight from a little less than half the room. They squeezed closer together as Jaglom rummaged through the desk drawers. Tom caught the door knob and slowly eased it open a little further. Amy let out a long breath and gripped his hand. They waited. A minute passed and then there were more steps. Four fingers of Jaglom's hand curled around their side of the door. One jerk of the invisible arm and it was slamming shut. Tom and Amy were totally exposed, faces flushed, clothes jumbled. Tom couldn't even begin to think of an excuse or an explanation, which would be in itself a serious misdemeanor. How often had his Dad instructed him "Never go anywhere without a plausible cover story"? But his mind was a blank. He braced himself for the inevitable.

But Jaglom still had his back to them. He was walking

toward the hidden door in the wall of books. He hadn't seen them. Now—if nothing made him turn around for the next few seconds . . . .

Neither of them moved or breathed as the book-case swiveled. Jaglom stepped through and the wall started to slide back into place. There wasn't much time. Tom had his hand on the doorknob when they heard the knock.

The sound struck his nerves like a gunshot.

He flinched back.

"Ed?"

The First Lady's voice was unmistakable.

"Doug Connors is downstairs—he has some paper-work to go over with you."

Connors was Secretary of State. He hated travel and detested Nantucket, which he summed up as "Sand, fog, deer ticks and mildew."

If he was here, it was important.

"Just a second, Darling." Jaglom's voice was muffled but audible. "I'll come down with you."

Tom took Amy's hand and moved to the center of the room. He had already broken down every possible per-mutation of action among these four people in this small space and there was only one with any chance of success.

They were at the far side of the bookshelf door when it began to move. Their side turned in toward the secret pas-sages and they followed it carefully as the President thumped towards the closed door of his study, wiggling the molding as he went. When the wall was back in place they fell into each others' arms, giddy with relief and desire. Tom led her back through the tunnel to the boathouse, but they were too fren-zied by then to wait until they got back to the house. There were some old Army blankets stored in a plastic bag; Tom grabbed them, threw them on the top mattress in the pile and climbed under the covers with Amy. Tom was never sure later how they got their clothes off, how he managed to solve the Chinese puzzle of zippers and hooks and buttons that should have turned him into a gibbering lunatic. But it happened and somehow they were naked together under the rough, musty wool. They paused once, staring into each other's eyes, amazed into laughter. It was so natural, after all—so deliciously easy.

They had been cautious physically for a long time, afraid that sex might change things or ruin them, but the tension of holding back had been just as bad. T had gotten to the point where he couldn't handle his school-work any more. In fact, for all intents and purposes, it had ceased to exist. Occasionally he and Amy had studied together, but studying had never lasted long. In the middle of a sentence he would kiss her and the night was lost.

They never did much more than kiss during those frantic sessions, but they didn't hold back out of fear. In fact, they were in a uniquely unclouded position for two twenty-year-olds in the age of AIDS. They were both virgins. They had actually abstained, as all the guidance counselors and politicians and stricken athletes had told them to, though not out of any unusual prudence or religious conviction. It was simpler than that. Neither one of them had ever been in love before and both of them had been raised to think it mattered.

Amy had looked alarmingly like a woman from the age of twelve, and had long accustomed herself to pursuit and cajoling, flattery and whistles and wrestling matches, men turning for that second look; to the arrival of obvious flowers. She had grown to hate roses. Brainless, horny guys sent them to you as proof that they were sensitive and romantic. She had never felt anything back so she had never shown much sympathy for her admirers. She had never understood what it was that would make all those boys and men—some of them twenty years her senior—whimper and bully and beg.

Until now. Now she wanted nothing but Tom. If this was

what those men had felt she pitied them because right now she craved his body the way she craved sunlight and fresh water. Tom was beside her, the whole naked length of him pressed to her, but she needed more, she wanted him inside her.

She whispered, "I'm on the pill,' and found him and guided him to the first touch and felt him shudder.

It was not long after that when Tom realized it might not be as easy as he had thought. In fact, it turned out to be virtually impossible. The torrent of sensation was too much for him, even though he knew he had left her behind.

As Tom subsided above her, Amy was shocked at her own feelings. Sheer physical frustration filled her like black smoke. She actually wanted to hit him for one howling, blood-red second.

She kissed him instead, and began again.

The second time Tom lasted a little longer—just long enough for the fizzled orgasm to sandpaper her nerves and jab a headache into her temple. She controlled the urge to scream, dug her fingernails into her thigh and pulled the anger into her clenched fingers, the five bright spots of pain beneath them.

"Amy?" he said softly. "Are you okay."

"I'm fine."

"You don't sound fine. Look, I'm sorry that—"

"Don't worry about it."

"Amy...."

"We should get back to the house. It's freezing in here." She sat up on the mattress, turned away from him, refusing conversation, wanting to be alone. Tom watched her back. There ought to be something he could do at this moment, some word or gesture that would dismantle her thwarted rage.

It was funny—there was so much he had been trained for in his life: Jake and his father had made him into a superb soldier, but his mother had taught him also. He could sew and cook, baste a dart or a chicken with equal ease. He could iron a pleated skirt, and clean house expertly without being asked, nagged or instructed. So it was strange that no one had prepared him for a moment like this one. His father had always been frank about sex, but he had never really discussed the practical details, the precise application of technique. And the result was that in this essential aspect of life, Tom was untrained. He had always assumed it would just "come naturally" a phrase which had now taken on a distinctly ironic tone.

They dressed and walked sullenly back to the house. They kept their distance at dinner but later that night Tom tried again and failed. Amy's only comment this time was a cool "I don't think we should do this any more." Then she rolled away from him to sleep.

Tom watched her. He was wide awake. He tried to sleep but it was useless. He finally eased himself out of bed, padded across the creaking floor, pulled on his robe and slipped into the hall, shutting the door softly behind him.

He moved through the dark house, down the stairs and along the hall, through the breakfast room and into the kitchen. He saw a light and knew that his father was up. Edward Bellamy Jaglom had been an insomniac all his life, rarely sleeping more than four hours a night and usually much less.

When Tom entered the kitchen his father was making a sandwich—always an entertaining sight. The President took his sandwiches seriously. He was almost finished making this one—slices of turkey, tongue and ham with his own red cabbage cole slaw and Russian dressing. He was just whisking Helen's sweet relish in the ketchup and mayonnaise.

He grinned at Tom. "Hungry?"

"I am now. Can you spare any of that?"

"I'll make you another one. Pumpernickel or rye?"

"Whatever." Tom knew it was hopeless to ask for white. oatmeal or even whole wheat. As far as his father was concerned, rye was the only bread for sandwiches.

Jaglom finished up, scraping the last of the Russian dressing out of the bowl with a rubber spatula, and spreading it on a slab of sourdough rye bread with which he capped Tom's sandwich. He opened each of them a Sam Adams ale and they took their late supper into the living room. Jaglom had stoked the fire and they sat in front of the hearth in worn crushed velvet arm chairs that he would never allow Helen to reupholster. They set their bottles on the floor and balanced their plates on their laps. Jaglom had finally organized himself perfectly when he jumped up again.

"Hold on," he said. "We're forgetting some of the essentials here."

He jogged out to the kitchen and returned with jars of Macedonian peppers and half-sour pickles. He gave Tom a couple of pickle spears and a half dozen of the small, pale green peppers. He kept the jars for himself.

For a while they just ate. They were finishing up the last bites with their last swallows of beer when Jaglom broke the silence.

"I'd ask you how you were doing, but I already know."

"You do?"

"You've slept like you were comatose since you were six weeks old. Nothing keeps you up if you're tired. And you look exhausted. So something must be wrong. You've had a bad jolt to your system, and having watched you and Amy together the last few days, it's not hard to figure out that you lost your virginity tonight and that it didn't go the way you wanted. Or maybe my imagination is just working overtime."

"It is," Tom said. Then, giving up, "Your imagination does very good work, though."

He smiled, blushing. He liked his father's gentle insights. They were like a physical touch, somehow akin to the absent-minded way he would rub Tom's scalp at story-time when Tom was in grade school—effortless, confident, soothing. He had never kept any secrets from his father. He had never believed it was possible. But that wasn't exactly true, was it? He thought guiltily of this afternoon, but before he could decide what to say, Jaglom reached over and patted his knee.

"At least you didn't actually do it in my office."

"You saw—"

"I see everything. It's part of the job. Don't worry about it. That rule was for kids, and you're not a kid anymore. So anyway . . . tell me what happened."

"Well—nothing basically. It was over before it started."

"Did you try again?"

"Sure—right away."

Jaglom chuckled. "Oh, to be twenty again."

"It's not that much fun, believe me. I was just as fast the second time. And the third. If this is twenty, you can have it."

"Come to think of it, twenty wasn't all that great for me, either."

"I wish there was something I could do. I heard you were supposed to think about boring stuff. I tried that, but it didn't work. So then I tried thinking about disgusting stuff. Dead bodies and unflushed toilets. It didn't make any difference, except . . . it's not much fun making love thinking about unflushed toilets."

Jaglom rose and threw another birch log on the fire. The white bark shriveled in a rush of flame. He settled back in his chair. "Thinking isn't the point. You're trying to control a physical response. You have to do it physically."

Tom sat forward. "Okay."

"God—I wish someone had told me this when I was your

age. All I got was double talk and sixth grade botany. But plants don't have these problems."

"So . . . how do you control it?"

"You want to stop the . . . momentum, right?"

Tom nodded.

"Then just stop. When you feel yourself losing control, just stop moving. It will be a jolt—you won't like it much. Everything sort of . . . backs up, inside you. And you get a little numb afterward. Which is really perfect because the last thing you want to be is pleasure-sensitive."

"That's it?"

"That's it, but remember . . . this technique really diminishes things for the man." He smiled. "Women swear by it, though."

Amy was awake when Tom went upstairs.

"I'm sorry," she said. "I didn't mean to be so . . . "

Tom put a finger to his lips. He said, "I want to try something."

He took off his robe. The room was icy. He climbed into the warm bed beside her and kissed her and proved— several times over before dawn—that his father's advice was right on the money as usual.

7

Jim Gramble loved seeing his by-line in the newspaper. But more than that, he loved seeing his words set in type and printed, made public and official, turned into an essential part of the morning for two and a half million people.

He remembered the thrill of his first published article: the glory and the vindication, the delirious Mardi Gras carousing drunkenly inside him while he read the newspaper with a quiet smile. The celebration was soon sobered by a typical combination of clumsy editing and typographical errors—few newspapers were as meticulous as the Journal Examiner, few editors were as respectful and talented as Roy Fisk.

Indeed, it was largely because of Fisk that the feeling still remained, though today would have been special in any case. He bought a paper at a corner newsstand and leaned against a car in the bright December sunshine to check the headlines.

His story wasn't there.

He looked again, checking each column stupidly, as he had searched the street the day his car was stolen. He closed his eyes. No matter how many times he tried to find it, his story wasn't going to be there. Fisk had buried it. Where, though—page two? Page five? And why? Who had put pressure on him to tuck the most significant story of the decade away among the Gristede ads and the Hollywood gossip?

He sighed and started leafing through the paper. He turned every page of the thick tabloid, scanning every column inch.

The story was nowhere.

He crumpled up the paper and threw it away, thinking of Wally Kellerman's prophetic question—What would you do if you wrote a great story and the paper didn't print it? He had answered off the cuff—he'd quit. But he didn't want to quit. Just the opposite. There was a predatory beast inside him that smelled blood. Someone had bought Fisk, or intimidated him, or both. And whoever had done it was now making editorial policy at one of the country's most important newspapers. In a way, it was just as well that Fisk had pulled the story: there was much more to it than Jim had guessed, more than he had dared to suspect.

There were new leads to follow and the first one was his boss.

He found Fisk at his usual table against the back wall of Mahoney's, the bar and grill across the street from the paper. Jim pushed through the early lunch crowd at the bar, breathing in the smoke and beer fumes, the raw tang of sawdust. The room was full of hungry, opinionated reporters, loud with the clatter of dishes and disagreement.

Fisk saw Jim coming and braced himself physically. It was a childish gesture, somehow. He looked like a kid waiting for the stolen firecrackers to go off. But he wasn't hiding, at least—Jim had to give him that.

"What the hell is happening?"

Fisk put down his hamburger. "Jim, listen—"

"Who's running this newspaper?"

"Hey, sit down. We have to talk."

Jim didn't move. "What happened to my story?"

"I'm not at liberty to discuss it—and even if I were, I—"

"'Not at liberty to discuss it? Who wrote that line for you? Because you're starting to sound like all the people you hate. The corporate spokesmen who want you to know that Dioxin isn't nearly as toxic as those crazy environmentalists think."

"Jim, look—you're upset right now, but—"

"Who are you the spokesman for, Roy?"

"That's not fair. But that's fine, that's great. It makes my job easier."

Jim clenched his diaphragm, took a deep breath and let it out slowly.

"What are you talking about?"

"Things aren't working out, Jim. Your material is unusable and your attitude is bad."

"Well, there's an easy connection there, Roy—my attitude is bad because you don't use my material."

"I don't have time to play chicken-and-the-egg with you here. It's all irrelevant, anyway. The paper is letting you go."

"What?"

"It's better this way."

"You're firing me?"

"It's not my decision, Jim."

"Of course it's your decision! What's the problem? What's going on around here, goddamn it?"

"Don't yell—half the reporters in New York are listening."

Jim pulled his voice back down his throat, crushed it to a rasping whisper.

"Why?"

"This is useless, Jim. You know what they say—don't shoot the messenger. I'm just the messenger."

Jim stared down at him. "Too bad. Because you used to be the managing editor."

Jim turned away.

"Hold on—"

He spun on Fisk for the last time. "Well, here's a message for your bosses—they can fire me, but they can't stop me."

"Wrong again. They can stop anyone."

Jim laughed. "That's my lead right there: 'The *Journal Examiner*'s managing editor faced down a gang of terrorists when they invaded his newspaper's city room in 1988. He treats muggers, gang wars and kamikaze taxi drivers with the same fearless disdain. As far as he's concerned, it's only logical—he's a New Yorker. So why does a simple memo on his desk have him cringing with terror?' That ought to grab them."

"Let me give you some advice, my friend. Give this up. You could get dead over this. Nobody's gonna help you. Nobody's on your side. Nobody gives a shit. You're all alone out there."

"No, I'm not, Roy. You're forgetting something. I have friends in high places."

Jim Gramble and The President of the United States had been friends since they were sixteen years old.

Their friendship had survived disagreements and separations, girlfriends and wives; it had finally survived even the fundamental antagonism of their chosen careers.

At twenty-five, newly engaged to the girl of his dreams, Jim had been convinced that love was the single great meal of life. Friendship was just a sort of garnish, tasty but trivial, like mango chutney. He knew better now. Love was a joke and a trap; only friendship really mattered, only friendship really sustained you in the end.

Few marriages could have survived the crises he had been through with Edward Bellamy Jaglom. They had faced some terrible moments together, and the worst moments all had one thing in common: a slouching, slender, pot-bellied man, balding already in his early twenties, with brown teeth and the lumpy complexion of an acne survivor. His name was Dominic Nosiglia, and when they first met him he was heir apparent to the Nosiglia crime family.

He approached them in the soda fountain around the corner from their school. They were seventeen years old and the stars of the city's best varsity basketball team. He introduced himself, bought them each an egg-cream and offered them ten thousand dollars to throw the up-coming championship game with Riverdale.

It was December 10th, 1957. It was late afternoon and the soda fountain was warm and stuffy. There was a freezing rain coming down outside, flayed horizontal by the wind. At first they didn't know what Nosiglia was talking about. He was glad to explain.

"I mean that you would lose the game on purpose, so that those who bet against you could make a profit."

This was Jim's first glimpse of organized crime. He was used to ordinary, relatively disorganized, crime—addicts and muggers, even street gangs. They were part of his world. But this man was part of another world. It was a dark, inhospitable world where you could get lost so easily, where no one would miss you if you vanished forever. It was a world of screams, where your puny little screams would never be heard. It was Jim's vision of Hell.

That was it—this scrawny, greasy little guy was from Hell—possibly he was the Devil himself. Jim could easily imagine the Devil appearing this way, offering bribes and buying egg-creams, with bad posture and a crooked smile. Casual and friendly—yet as frightening as a dark street in the Bronx, as his mother's face in the open casket; as the water-bug that had scuttled into his mouth while he slept.

Jim wanted to run, but Nosiglia was between him and the door.

"This is crazy," Jim said. He looked around for Alan O'Keefe, who worked the soda fountain, but he had moved to the back of the store and was busily unpacking boxes of candy. They were alone.

"We need to think about this," Eddie said.

Jim stared at him, shocked. "No, we don't."

Nosiglia shrugged. "Take your time. I'll be in touch."

He patted Eddie's shoulder, pulled his coat collar tight and walked out into the rain-dark winter evening.

"That guy—he was a gangster," Jim said slowly.

Eddie nodded. "Ten thousand dollars is a lot of money."

"Not to you!"

"Oh yeah—when was the last time I had more than five bucks in my pocket?"

Jim turned away. He had no immediate answer. He pushed his egg-cream around the counter. But his stomach was sour and he wasn't thirsty any more. "You're not thinking straight," he said finally. "You get involved with a guy like that and you're involved forever. You can't just walk away—they won't let you. He scared the hell out of me, man. I wanted to get out of here, just take off running, as soon as he said hello. Didn't you feel that?"

"Yeah," Eddie answered in the watery gloom. "But I liked it."

Until their first meeting with Dominic Nosiglia—and despite their obvious differences in race and class—Jim and Eddie had assumed that in some fundamental way they were the same person. In fact they were drastically different people and everyone knew it except them. Their comic mismatch had been a school joke since the year before.

It had begun the previous September. During the first try-outs for the basketball team. The Dalton School had been recruiting athletes for several years, but Jim wasn't one of them. He had been accepted out of a public high

school in Brooklyn on the strength of his grades and a column he'd written for his school paper called "Check it Out."
He'd written an essay a week for almost two years, on subjects
as diverse as the need for police guards at the front door of
P.S. 231, and the nature of white liberal bigotry; descriptions
of a day-long search for a lost house cat and a long night of
house calls as his father tended to the victims of a Bedford-
Stuyvesant gang war. Even in high school, his writing had
edge and authority. Soon after he arrived at Dalton he was
running the student newspaper, which surprised no one.

The surprise was the way he could dribble a basketball.
He and Eddie developed an immediate rapport on court,
passing to each other, catching each other's rebounds, con-
founding defensive plays with their almost psychic ball-han-
dling.

Eddie was the captain of the team and Jim soon became his star forward. Everyone was pleased except the
coach. A big balding jock named Driscoll whose weight-
lifting muscles were softening into blubber, the coach had
a vulgar, easy-going racism that Jim hated.

"Grab the ball, Sambo!," he'd shout with a jovial grin.
"Good goin'! You people got a talent for the game."

Jim's father had trained him to ignore the Driscolls of
the world. You lost your dignity if you fought with them
and you often lost much more than that. But Eddie Jaglom
had been fighting authority figures all his life, starting with
his own father. Jim would never forget the first night he'd
had dinner in the Jaglom's lavish Beekman Place apartment. The Matisse cut-outs and marble floors had impressed him—so had the food (The Jaglom's chef had
worked for Chiang-Kai-Shek before the Chinese revolution). But the war between Eddie and his father had impressed him most of all. On this night, Eddie had written a
one-page paper that was supposed to be three pages long.
His father was furious.

"I didn't need three pages," Eddie had explained casually.

"It doesn't matter what you needed! The assignment called for three pages!"

"I'm succinct."

"You're lazy!"

"I'm smart."

"You're a goddamn smart-ass is what you are!"

"That, too," Eddie admitted with a smile. He seemed unfazed by his father's mounting wrath.

"Well, here's what you're going to do, smart-ass—you're going to write this paper all over again and it's going to be three pages this time!"

Eddie sighed. "So it's a little short—big deal."

"It is a big deal! It's a very big deal!"

"Okay, okay, so it's a big deal—big deal."

"And that's another thing, goddamn it! Don't use that phrase with me—I don't want to hear any of that 'big deal' stuff at my table. It's disrespectful."

Eddie shrugged. "So it's disrespectful—big deal."

It was as if something was pulling the air between them, stretching it like taffy, making it thin and brittle. Jim and Eddie's mother sat helpless and uncomfortable, unable to intervene.

"I told you not to say 'big deal' to me, goddamn it!," Eddie's father bellowed.

Eddie smiled—this was defiance for its own sake.

"So I said big deal . . . big deal."

"There! You said it again!"

"So I said it again—big deal."

Then his father lunged across the table at him, knocking over two glasses of wine, and Eddie's mom threw herself into the fray, whining 'Robert . . . please . . . we have guests . . .'

Finally Robert Jaglom sat down again, rang for the maid

to clean the spilled wine, took a deep breath and turned to Jim.

"So," he asked. "How are you enjoying Dalton?"

It was a surreal evening, but it helped Jim understand the steel in Eddie's voice that October afternoon in the big gym when Driscoll said "What a nigger move!" and Eddie said "That's enough."

Driscoll turned on him. "What?"

"You heard me. Don't call him nigger any more. Don't call him jig or sambo or rastus. He has a name. Use it."

"Oh yeah? And how are you planning to make me do that, little boy?"

"Easy."

"I don't think so. Because there's no way in the world I'm gonna put up with this kinda crap from you. No such thing. This is my team and I run it my way. Besides sambo don't mind my joking around—do ya, sambo?"

"I'm used to it," Jim said quietly.

"See? So you got a choice, hotshot: shut up during practice or you're off the team."

Everyone was staring at them.

Eddie spoke into the silence. "Sorry coach, but you've got that one all wrong. You're the one with the choice. You learn to behave or I walk. And if I quit the team, Mike and Dennis are coming with me. Right, guys?."

Driscoll stared at Mike Cafferty and Dennis Clark. They were scared but they knew which side they were on. They nodded.

"Cut it out man," Jim had said. "That stuff doesn't bother me.

"Of course it does. You know it does."

Jim looked down. "I can handle it."

"But you shouldn't have to. Understand the situation, coach? Or do I have to spell it out for you? If we quit, Jim will quit, too, and then you'll have no team and you'll have to explain why to a headmaster who feels Civil Rights are the most important issue in America. Which means you'll be out on the street so fast you'll think the building collapsed. Which would suit me just fine."

Driscoll knew when he was beaten. He handled it by pretending nothing had happened. He blew his whistle and shouted "Everybody on the court." Then he made a little mock bow to Jim. "Including you . . . Mr. Gramble." And he called Jim Mr. Gramble for the next two and a half years.

Eddie Jaglom wasn't exactly a rebel—rebellion would have given his oppressors too much credit. He simply didn't believe in their power over him and he was often right. For the obedient and easily intimidated Jim Gramble, this was a revelation. He would never forget the first time he watched Eddie confound a teacher's belief in her own power. It was a white-haired, rock-hard matron named Mrs. Terwilliger. She had been terrifying kids for forty years. She terrified Jim.

"Why?" Eddie had asked. "What can she do to you?"

He found out first hand when he pulled one of his usual stunts: turning in a paper which instead of answering the assignment spent most of its length explaining why the assignment itself was a pointless and insipid waste of time.

Mrs. Terwilliger was not amused.

She made Eddie stay after class and Jim lingered behind to watch. That didn't bother Mrs. Terwilliger, or Eddie—they both enjoyed having an audience.

"This paper is unacceptable," she said tartly, handing it across her desk to Eddie."

"I thought it was a valuable critique."

"You were mistaken."

"In your opinion."

"My opinion is the only one that matters. This class is not a democracy."

"And you weren't elected, so you can't be impeached."

She smiled. "Precisely."

"Still . . . we could organize a coup. That's the best way to get rid of a dictator."

Mrs. Terwilliger was actually beginning to enjoy herself. "Unfortunately," she said, "An army is usually required for that sort of endeavor."

Eddie shrugged. "I don't think recruitment will be a problem."

They stared at each other. The game was over.

"Rewrite this paper properly or I'll flunk you."

It was her ultimate threat.

Eddie grinned his most appealing grin and stuck his hand across the desk. She shook it almost by reflex.

"Deal," he said.

And she flunked him, and the sky didn't fall, and life went on as usual.

Except for Jim's life; that would never be the same.

He'd finally learned something in high school: indifference to power was a form of immunity. Jim had felt an exhilarated sense of liberation at that moment, and it was still with him thirty years later. He never looked at anyone in authority quite the same way again. Even his father, whose sovereignty had always been an absolute fact of his life, like sunlight or gravity. He had never thought about eclipses; never dreamed he could fly. But it was so easy. All you had to do was say "No."

Jim became a pompous, arrogant little rat for a while, under the influence of his new friend. But his Dad didn't mind; he saw the beginnings of self-respect in the defiance, moments of authentic posture amid the posturing.

The Jagloms weren't so happy with the arrangement. Mrs. Jaglom, particularly—a pale, willowy aesthete who painted watercolor still-lifes of her exotic houseplants and yearned quietly for a daughter—seemed to find Jim's very presence distasteful. He ate too much. He talked too loud.

He was undergoing a dangerously awkward growth spurt and
had broken several of her favorite knickknacks. The first time
Eddie had asked if he could sleep over, she had said (and it
was a sentence that still made Jim angry, though with a sort of
amused bitterness now), "I don't want him sleeping on my
Porthault sheets."

It was the kind of statement you formulated answers
to for years. Even today, snappy answers to that appalling
piece of Upper East Side racism would slip into his mind
like wind under a door sill: "I'll sleep in the maid's room,
but I don't do windows," for instance, or: "Feel free to de-
louse me first." Or even: "I'll be glad to bring my own
Negro sheets."

Some were angrier than others: "Don't worry—big-
oted, mealy-mouthed, middle-aged debutantes give me
insomnia, anyway." Others were almost wistful: "You know . . .
if you spent less energy hating everyone who wasn't exactly
like you, you might find the time to lead a reasonably productive life."

Of course he never said any of those things. He hardly
spoke to Eddie's mother at all. Eddie was expert at avoiding his parents.

They spent the summer of their junior year hanging
out together. Jim was working as the new emergency re-
ceptionist in his father's office, but he had nights and week-
ends free. The two lives he led that summer were a shock-
ingly vivid lesson in America's class system and the immense gaps between the truly wealthy and even the relatively well-to-do professional families like his own.

The Jagloms had little contact with reality as Jim knew it.
Mundane tasks didn't exist in their world: food was shopped
for and prepared, served and cleaned up by others; soiled
clothes vanished and reappeared clean and folded in the
proper drawers a day later. It was a life without any of the
normal irritations and impediments, and if not for the curi-

ous fact that Eddie himself got a minuscule allowance and was almost always broke, his life would have been as smooth and frictionless as a stay in the posh mental hospital where apparently his mother spent much of her time.

Eddie was always borrowing money from Jim, who didn't begrudge it; in fact, he was the only one of Eddie's friends who wasn't frustrated by his artificial poverty. No one resented it more than Eddie himself, and he took his revenge by finding many ingenious ways to squander his parents' money.

Wandering through his father's office one day he struck up a mildly flirtatious conversation with a woman who had just been hired as a junior accountant. She handled the family bills and as they chatted she let it slip that her orders were to check any item in the three figures column—anything less was considered petty cash. Eddie let the conversation dawdle past that point, assuring her that she had almost no southern accent left, promising to show her around the city, complimenting her on her short haircut. He left the office a few minutes later feeling like a master spy and soon he was charging ninety-nine dollars in groceries or books or clothes or tools and giving the stuff away with a savage gusto that had little to do with Christian charity.

On one memorable occasion, in the middle of a sweltering New York August, he cranked the air-conditioning up to its maximum power. And when the whole duplex apartment was down to thirty-eight degrees, he built a fire in the living room fireplace and they roasted marshmallows.

Jim thought about that day often—it summed up so perfectly his friend's charming but eerie disconnection from the real world outside where people were sweating through their clothes on the hottest day of the year.

Their parents eventually gave up trying to separate them, hoping that something else, the inevitable advent of girl-friends, for instance, would succeed where they had failed. It was a good thought: both of them did indeed have girl-

friends, and they ignored each other during periods of intense sexual infatuation, with hurt feelings on both sides. But
the girls were always temporary and the friendship endured.

Though they argued constantly, neither of them could
imagine having a real disagreement, or that an issue with
the power to ruin their affections might ever come between them.

But that was before they met Dominic Nosiglia.

A week had passed since that first meeting, and Jim
was hoping the problem had gone away on its own like a
sprain or a twenty-four-hour virus. No such luck: Eddie approached him after practice on Friday afternoon. Everyone else was showered and dressed. They were alone in
the locker room; still, Eddie whispered as if someone might
be listening.

"I did it," he said. "I made the deal."

"No."

Jim sat down on the low bench in front of the lockers.
It was wet but he didn't care.

"I'm gonna do it. But I'm gonna need your help."

"No way."

"Listen to me—I made the deal Jimmy. That's done.
So we have to lose, now. These guys are serious."

"That's what I was trying to tell you last week."

"Yeah—but last week we were arguing about whether
we should take the money or not. Now we're taking it."

"You're taking it. This has nothing to do with me."

"Oh, really? You think they're gonna give you a fair
play award if we win? They'll come after both of us, believe me."

"Then why—? Oh, I get it. You were certain you could
just kind of sweep me along with you . . . between the threat
of getting my damn knees broken and the promise of all that
money and the fact that I've always gone along with your crazy
bullshit before, you figured I'd have to say yes."

Eddie grinned, happily busted. "So say yes."

Jim looked down. "We worked hard for this championship."

"And whenever I got too worked up at half-time when we were trailing by ten points, what did you say to me?"

"It's only a game."

"That's right, Jimmy. It's only a game. It's not global diplomacy or brain surgery. It's not a crusade or a movement; it's just a bunch of guys trying to stuff a ball into a net. It's a way to kill two hours. That's all."

"I don't believe this."

"So we lose the game—So what? Driscoll gets in trouble. That's a bonus, actually. Maybe he'll even get fired."

"What if someone finds out?"

"We get in trouble. We get thrown out of school. Our lives are in the toilet."

"Then why risk it?"

"Risk isn't always bad. Sometimes safe is bad. You stay safe long enough and you're walking in your sleep."

"Eddie . . . it's wrong."

"Does that mean we'll go to hell?"

"You know what it means."

"Do yourself a favor, Jimmy—lighten up a little."

"I can't. I just can't."

Silence pushed between them like another person. Jim forced the words out: "I'm going to the coach."

"He won't believe you.

"Yes he will."

"Come on, Jimmy—you're just a nigger to him. And it would be your word against mine."

"He doesn't like you either."

"He's scared of me. There's a difference."

"He's scared of your father's money, you mean."

"That's right, and he should be scared. My Dad could crush him like a bug."

"You're the one that would get crushed if your father ever found out about this. Maybe I should tell him."

Eddie's face seemed to freeze: the calculating stillness of a threatened animal. "He wouldn't believe you, either."

"There's one way to find out."

"Don't do it, Jimmy. Just don't."

They stared at each other between the banks of lockers. The smells of disinfectant and old sweat hung in the air. A shower was dripping. That was the only sound.

"This is really all about your father, isn't it?" Jim said at last. "That's what's really going on. If your father was a Mafia goon, you'd be the volunteer gopher at the District Attorney's office."

"Sorry, Dr. Freud, this has nothing to do with my father. He's never even going to know about it."

"Sure, like he never knew about your ninety-nine dollar spending sprees or your midsummer marshmallow roasts. You need a shrink, Eddie."

"The hell I do."

"You need something. You need help."

"I'll tell you what I need—I need you to just back off, pal. You don't want to help me? Fine. Then stay out of my way because I'll roll right over you if you don't."

"Look at me shaking. I'm terrified."

"Shut up."

"You know—that's the first good idea you've had in weeks. We've got nothing to say to each other. See you at the game."

They didn't speak to each other again until the championship game ten days later.

It was a strange time for Jim; the whole school was wild with expectation. The cheerleaders staged a pep rally and to Jim's surprise almost the entire school showed up—including dour faculty members who had never before shown any interest in athletics. Driscoll was euphoric, referring to the team, mawkishly, as "my guys" and beaming proudly during routine lay-up drills. Jim and the others were stars. Guys Jim barely knew wanted to be his best friend; girls who had never looked at him before started flirting with him between classes.

It was a nightmare. Jim dreaded the game, but didn't have the will to tell Driscoll or Eddie's father what was really happening. He was confused: allowing the rigged game to happen was wrong, but so was being a stool pigeon. Where were his loyalties? With the school? The team? With some concept of fair play? The law? His friends? He wasn't sure anymore. In the end he decided to just play the best game of basketball he could and ignore everything else.

There was a jubilant party atmosphere the day of the game—not even the teachers were paying attention in class. The stands in the big gym were full an hour before the match began; people who arrived too late to find a seat sat on the floor or stood against the walls. Everyone was talking and laughing. It sounded like a party.

The mood in the locker room was quite different. Despite Driscoll's best efforts to whip them into a predatory, win-or-die frenzy, the team was glum and silent as they prepared for the game. Jim began to suspect that Nosiglia had approached everyone.

They certainly played that way.

They missed lay-ups, they fumbled passes, they wasted foul shots. They walked the ball and dribbled out of bounds. There was a horrified, disbelieving silence from the stands. At the end of the first quarter, they should have been losing by fifty points at least.

But they weren't.

The Riverdale team was playing even worse. It was joke basketball, clown basketball, so painful and embarrassing to watch that the big audience—from both schools—finally just started laughing.

Jim tried to play an honest game, but his own team-mates bumped and tripped him, knocked his re-bounds to the other team . . . who let them bounce off the court. Still, by half-time he had scored the only fifteen points in the game.

Driscoll was furious.

"What the hell is going on out there?" he screamed at them. Jim had noticed Dominic Nosiglia in the stands, looking more and more annoyed; but he had also noticed another group of strangers. And he had a theory. It was bizarre and ludicrous but it fit the facts.

"I'll tell you what's happening," he said to the coach. He got some strange looks but no one tried to stop him from talking. Eddie was staring down at the scuffed floor, apparently fascinated with his sneakers. "A bunch of gangsters are paying us off to lose the game. And we're doing our best. There's just two problems. I'm not part of the deal. And some different gangsters paid off the other team to lose. So the only question now is—who's better at screwing up."

Driscoll looked at the others.

"Is this true?"

They nodded.

Jim was sure Driscoll would start yelling, but his actual response was much worse. There were tears in his eyes. "Excuse me," he said, turning away from them. "Gimme a minute." He rubbed a big hand over his face and looked at them again. "This ain't right," he said. "This ain't supposed to happen. How did this happen?"

No one said anything. Finally Eddie cleared his throat. "If Jim's right, the game is still up in the air. So I say . . . let's go out there and play some basketball."

So they did. After the first fast break, the Riverdale team caught the spirit and soon everyone was playing as hard as they could. It was like a fever breaking—the crowd went wild, and glancing up into the stands Jim noticed that even the mafiosos were on the edge of their seats, cheering and screaming with the friends and teachers and parents of the kids they'd bribed.

At one point, running down court side by side, Jim and Eddie glanced at each other, panting and grinning, knowing they were doing the right thing and that the right thing was sometimes more fun than the wrong thing. It was a swift lesson in practical morality, that exhilarated glance between them, and suddenly they were friends again—for the moment, at least, the last two weeks were forgotten.

The game was tied at 80 in the last few seconds when Eddie feinted and slapped the ball away from the big Riverdale center in mid-dribble. Jim was open, and Eddie bounced a pass between a Riverdale guard's legs. Jim caught the ball, dodged and leapt up for a thirty-foot jump shot that swished a second before the bell.

There was a long gasp of silence, then the gym was full of cheering and shouting and the fans stampeded the court. Carried on the shoulders of a jubilant crowd, Jim was scanning the stands for Dominic Nosiglia, but he was gone.

During the celebration in the locker room, Driscoll made a point of seeking Jim out and shaking his hand.

"You never got a fair shake from me this year," he said. "I feel bad about that, Gramble. You stuck by the team. You did good. So I gotta say—I'm sorry. A man can't help his upbringing."

He moved toward Jim clumsily and Jim found himself hugging the big man, with the coach's whistle digging into his chest.

"That's okay, coach," he said. "We all have our upbringings. I just got lucky with mine."

The coach was in control of himself again. "I'd like to meet your parents some day."

Both of them knew he had conspicuously missed his chance on parents' night, two years in a row. Jim decided not to mention it.

"I'm sure you will," he said.

Then the coach was pulled away into the rush of rowdy basketball players, their friends and admirers. Jim was glad for the chance to escape.

It took an hour for the locker room to clear. Jim and Eddie were the last to leave.

"Everybody thinks we're heroes," Eddie said.

"I can think of one person who doesn't."

Eddie didn't have to answer. Neither of them had any idea how Dominic Nosiglia would respond to their disastrous victory, but they knew there was no point in running away. They felt like prisoners waiting for the dawn trip to the firing squad.

"I got you into this," Eddie said. "I screwed up, big time."

"Yes you did."

"Do you think they're gonna hurt us?"

"I don't know. Probably. They lost money today. They don't like losing money."

The door to the locker room swung open. Dominic Nosiglia and three burly foot soldiers sauntered inside. "Where's the rest of the team?" he asked.

"Avoiding you," Eddie said.

Two of the foot soldiers positioned themselves by the door. The other one accompanied Nosiglia as he strolled along the bench toward them. He was wearing a heavy overcoat with a fur collar, open to reveal a nicely cut suit. He was dressed well but without vanity—no jewelry, no attempt to hide his growing bald spot. He looked like a successful businessman with a second marriage and a third mortgage. He was twenty two years old.

"What am I supposed to do with you guys, huh? I pay you

to lose and you win. Of course . . . with everyone trying to lose
. . . it's an unusual situation. Anyway, the spread was four
points and you only won by two. So it was a push. You know
what I mean?"

"Actually . . . no," Eddie admitted.

"Okay. You can learn something this afternoon. If you
win, but you don't win by more than four points, then we
forget the whole thing. Nobody wins, nobody loses—it's a
push. But I have to tell you something funny. Listen to this—
I've been helping my father with the gambling since I was
fourteen years old. Running numbers, answering the
phone, getting coffee. When I turned twenty one I got my
own bookmaking operation. I figure the spread, deal with
the customers. I handle enforcement myself, just like my
Dad did. I make a lot of money, but I've always wondered—
what makes these crazy bastards tick? You know what I
mean? Why do they do this? They lose money, they get
hurt, and for what? I had no idea because my father never
let me gamble. Not even poker. Not even for matches. Until
today, I'd never been to a sporting event where I didn't
know the outcome ahead of time."

He smiled at them. His teeth were really awful.

"Well . . . today I had all this money riding on the game
and I had absolutely no idea what was going to happen. It
was exciting—I jumping up and down like a kid I turned
to Rocco here and I said—'What a feeling! There's gotta
be some money in this!'—like I just figured that out. It was
a joke."

Jim and Eddie laughed as enthusiastically as they could;
relief was giving them the giggles anyway.

"You played a good game out there—so, no hard feelings, all right? Maybe we can do some real business some
time, what do you say?"

"Uh, sure, I guess," Eddie stammered. Jim didn't trust
himself to speak.

"All right, then. Take it easy. I'll see you around."

He turned and walked out of the room. The foot soldiers followed him. The door to the locker room closed softly, and Jim and Eddie sat on the bench for a few minutes, just breathing.

"We're still alive," Jim said wonderingly.

Eddie was looking at him with a strange, troubled intensity.

"But are we still friends?"

"What are you talking about? Sure we are."

He reached over and squeezed Eddie's arm. But they weren't, really, not in the same way. And they never could be again.

8

That spring, both Jim and Eddie were accepted at Harvard. Eddie chose to attend West Point instead. At first, Jim was astonished. But it made sense—Eddie's father was the black sheep of a military family, a convert to pacifism with a dishonorable discharge in his past. His scathing contempt for military life must have made it attractive to Eddie, who, like most rebels, longed for genuine authority—an order he could obey without reservations, a structure that made sense. Many people were surprised by the success of his military career. Mrs. Terwilliger wasn't one of them.

In the letters he wrote to Jim over the next few years, it was clear that Eddie loved the Army. He went to Viet Nam as one of Kennedy's first 'military advisers' and stayed there through three tours of duty, until 1968. He believed it was a just cause. He believed it was a once-in-a-lifetime opportunity to stop the spread of Communism. But his letters weren't self-serious or jingoistic.

He hated Saigon. "They say Beirut is the Paris of the Middle East. That makes Saigon the Detroit of Southeast Asia. But at least Detroit makes cars. All they make here is heroin and teenage hookers." He also hated the jungle. "I don't even like the forest, Jimmy. Central Park is about the most wilderness I can tolerate."

He ended up a major in the First Cavalry Division, though he disliked planes and detested helicopters. "There are two kinds of helicopters," he wrote to Jim once, quoting a pilot under his command named Jake Gritzky, who had just walked through eighty miles of enemy territory after the Huey he was flying went down in the jungle near Tuc Lo. "Those that have crashed—and those that will."

Eddie's letters became less frequent and finally stopped altogether. Jim was helping to register voters with the Southern Christian Leadership Conference in Mississippi.

"Conscientious Objector" status had kept him out of the military. He was sending occasional freelance dispatches from the front lines of that war to a receptive little New York paper called the *Journal Examiner*.

When Eddie's letters stopped, Jim got worried. He telephoned Eddie's parents, but no letters had arrived from the War Department. They just assumed his work had become top secret.

There was a secret involved, but it was personal.

Eddie had begun to realize that the cause he was fighting for was unjust and futile. He was in a place where everyone hated the United States, where enemies and friends looked exactly alike, where any smiling child could pull a gun at any moment, and drop you in your tracks.

It became clear to him that the communists were winning, and that there wasn't a thing in the world the United States could do about it. We could burn their villages and mine their harbors, torment and inconvenience and even kill them. But we couldn't change their minds. We couldn't turn Viet Nam into a suburb or a theme park. The only way we could win the war would be to annihilate the population and raze the narrow little country, as the "Pave Viet Nam" bumper stickers back home suggested. Which would give us another war with exactly the same choices in Laos or Cambodia or both. Eventually he became aware that Nixon and Kissinger were in fact fighting those wars already—his own men began to bomb Cambodia in a concerted act of amoral, covert brutality whose bloody carnage and total disregard for be Democratic process made the later revelations of Watergate pale by comparison.

And of course it made no difference—all the bombs in the world weren't going to help. We didn't belong: we were the aliens. We were the invaders.

We were wrong.

Every day Eddie became more certain of that, more certain that the hundreds of thousands of American lives being lost were being lost for nothing.

So he stopped writing letters. They would have been censored into gibberish anyway, and he would have been court-martialed for treason. But he kept thinking, and it didn't take much thinking to figure out that this was a politician's war, being carried on by politicians for political purposes. The next war would be the same unless politics changed and the only way to change anything was to pull your shirt off, jump in feet first and get dirty.

He met Helen Perkins when her makeshift hospital was bombed. She was an army nurse. Eddie and some others spent 16 hours pulling still-living soldiers out of the rubble. He bought her a drink afterward and they stayed up all night talking. He told her everything he hadn't been writing to Jim Gramble, and he told her his biggest, craziest secret of all: he wanted to be President.

"Then you will be," she said. "And I'll be the hardest working First Lady since Eleanor Roosevelt."

"But so much prettier."

They touched their glasses one more time and finished

their drinks and he kissed her and they made love so long and hard in the little Saigon hotel room in the August heat that they soaked through the mattress with their sweat.

They returned to the States in 1969. They got married and Eddie went to law school. He graduated with honors and eight different law firms offered him associate positions, but he turned them all down. Instead he ran for Congress in New York City's 14th district. His opponent was an ineffectual Republican incumbent short on funds, with a rodent's face and a droning delivery. By contrast, Eddie had good looks, charisma, passion and unlimited amounts of money to spend on his campaign.

He won in a landslide.

But early in the race he had gotten a frightening phone call.

"Mr. Jaglom?" a vaguely familiar voice had asked him.

"Yes—who is this?"

"My name is Drucker, Mr. Jaglom. I'm with the National High School Athletic Association. Our mandate is to promote fair play and high moral standards among our high school athletes. We reward outstanding sportsmanship and—quite frankly, Mr. Jaglom—we censure poor conduct. We have powerful connections in school boards, police departments and juvenile courts. We are on excellent terms with all three television networks and the major daily newspapers. We have the power to punish those who stray. And we do so with vigor."

"Fine, but I'm not sure what you—

"Even years after the fact, Mr. Jaglom. Time doesn't matter to us. There is no statute of limitations on morality. I'm sure you agree."

Eddie was starting to get nervous. He shooed his campaign manager and two secretaries out of the room. When he was alone he said, "What is this about?"

"I think you know the answer to that question, Mr.

Jaglom. The more important question is how will the voters of your district feel about it? How will they continue to trust a man who bargained his integrity away while still in high school? With corruption scandals breaking out every day, how will they continue to support a man who will clearly do anything, no matter how reprehensible, for the almighty dollar?"

"That's it," Eddie said. "Explain yourself right now."

"Does the name Dominic Nosiglia mean anything to you, Mr. Jaglom"

"What—?"

Eddie went as white as the skin under his wrist-watch. He was gripping the phone so hard his fingers ached. But his sweat made the plastic slither in his hand.

"Does the amount of ten thousand dollars ring a bell, Mr. Jaglom? Does the—does the—"

But the voice could no longer control itself. Eddie listened with dawning relief, surprise, affection and annoyance as Jim Gramble started laughing uncontrollably on the other end of the line.

"Goddamn it, Jim—"

"I had you, Eddie! I really had you going there! National High School Athletic Association—"

But he was laughing again.

They went out to dinner a couple of nights later and it was as if all the time that had separated them was a loop in an otherwise straight string, taking them far out of their way, but depositing them exactly where they left off.

They talked about Viet Nam and the Civil Rights movement, My Lai and Martin Luther King—much had been gunned down since they had last seen each other The carnage had made Jim cynical; it filled Eddie with a ferocious desire to improve the world. Jim liked Eddie's new attitude—it forced him to conjure up the ghosts of a matching idealism.

They saw a lot of each other in those days. Jim was covering the campaign for the *Journal Examiner* and he filed occasional stories on Eddie during his stay on Capitol Hill. Eddie
had a certain novelty value because he actually kept his campaign promises—little ones like re-naming a vest-pocket park
after a local Marine officer killed in the Beirut barracks bombing, and big ones like toxic waste clean-up and Welfare re-
form. He was able to tell the Political Action Committees and
lobbyists that he didn't need their money and didn't want to
see their faces. He spurned perks—he never even wrote any
good checks at the House bank, an institution he fought
without success for years.

During the "War on Drugs" he almost single-handedly
pushed through education programs, early childhood intervention programs, infrastructure work-team programs
for drug offenders, chipping away at the demand side of
the drug economy. "We can't tell these kids to 'just say no',"
he shouted on the House floor as he had shouted on the
stump, "We have to give them a reason to say 'no.'"

By the beginning of Eddie's second term, Jim had
married Eleanor Davis, the smart, tough ACLU lawyer he
had worked with in Mississippi. Miraculously, the two
couples got along. Friendship seemed to get exponentially
more complicated as you got older. Helen put it best when
she said, "If we all have children and the children all like
each other it'll be like winning the lottery."

They were having a picnic lunch in Central Park, at
the time. It was a Saturday afternoon in July. They were
waiting for tickets to the Delacorte Theatre. Eddie took
her hand. "Don't say that—you'll jinx us. I feel like I've
won too many lotteries already."

It was true. Eddie had everything. But he also had a
talent for squandering. He squandered his money, property and time; he even squandered his wife's affections.

He had affairs and Helen found out. She got a phone

call one day from a distraught husband who had just caught
Eddie in bed with his wife. Helen wanted to pack a bag
and leave. She had never been confrontational. She was
like a wounded animal whose instinct was to flee and hide.
Only one thing stopped her: She had found out that morning that she was pregnant.

Jim found himself in the middle, consoling Helen and
taking a firm line with his friend. But all Jim's lectures about
loyalty and fidelity and building a future couldn't compare
to the nerve that was struck by the fact of the baby. The
knowledge of his impending fatherhood was changing
Eddie; Jim was convinced of it and he managed to convince

Helen. So the marriage teetered but stayed upright
and Eddie went to Lamaze classes (they were excellent
photo opportunities, it turned out, for a young congressman who was planning to run for the Senate), and he cut
Tom's umbilical cord when he popped out, right on schedule, June 9, 1979.

Jim and Eleanor remained childless. Jim realized
much later that his marriage had the rhythm of a terminal
disease, with many deceptive periods of remission. They
half-adopted Tom and were easier with each other when
he was around. He allowed them to ignore the loneliness
they had devised together, the sad gusto with which they
embraced any diversion from outside the small, dark room
of their married life. They enjoyed house guests. They
welcomed their in-laws. They liked talking to waiters in
restaurants. At one particularly low moment, he had almost invited a pair of Jehovah's Witnesses to stay for dinner.

The first time Eleanor had said "I like you better when
you're around other people," it had stung him with the
particular, iodine sting of a disinfecting truth. He liked
her better that way, too. If she laughed in the house, it was

because she was talking to friends on the telephone; if she
flirted it was with strangers.

Love failed. It expected too much. It made impossible
demands. Its intimacy was toxic. After a few years he and
Eleanor knew everything about each other. Secrets were
impractical at such close quarters. And passion, he had
come to realize, was nothing more than the sum of a
couple's mutual ignorance. When that anguished curiosity was replaced by the grim knowledge of a thousand mundane, alien and occasionally repellent details, romance
shriveled.

Friendship was easier. It allowed more distance, demanded less . . . and so it survived. It became a kind of ref-
uge, in fact—one small sliver of Jim's life where he could be
himself without fear of violating absurd and incomprehen-
sible female standards.

There was a kind of serenity between him and Eddie—
despite his joke phone calls, they were decades beyond
the kinds of conflicts that had threatened them at school.

Or so it seemed.

And then, during the most difficult days of Eddie's
Senate race, Dominic Nosiglia entered their lives again.

Eddie was running against Bernard Greer, an old-line
six-term Republican who had great power and seniority
on Capitol Hill. He had been rolling over Democratic
hopefuls for more than 20 years, and Eddie Jaglom, despite his glamour and his money, looked like one more
inconsequential road-kill to Greer's re-election committee. Indeed, he was leading in the polls by more than 15
points when he called a press conference to announce that
he was withdrawing from the race. He was retiring, he said,
for unspecified reasons relating to his "health."

Jim's investigation into the matter made him smile
sourly at that word. According to his doctor, Greer was almost alarmingly robust; he never even caught a cold, he

ran five miles every morning, and he had the blood pressure and resting heart rate of an athlete 20 years his junior. Still, his worries about his health were well justified.

Greer had refused all interviews before the press conference, so Jim had been forced to track him down. He kept extensive files on the personal haunts of various politicians and public figures—favorite restaurants and bars, the airlines they flew on, the hotels they preferred. Greer happened to be an avid Knicks fan, and Jim found him at Madison Square Garden during a Bulls game.

He had friends in management at the Garden, and they owed him some favors. He slipped in during the third quarter with Greer's seat number in his pocket, but he didn't need it. He spotted Greer at a concession stand three minutes after he walked in from the street.

Greer was talking to an overweight, balding man with a lumpy complexion. Jim stopped, jostled by the crowd. He eased himself over to the side of the passageway, smelling hot dogs and popcorn, sweat and some residue of the Lestoil the place had been mopped down with that morning. The odors made him sick.

The two men kept talking. The bigger man had his arm around Greer's shoulders in a frightening parody of avuncular good fellowship. Greer cringed away from the embrace but he was trapped. At a casual glance, they looked like two old friends trying on New York Knicks hats. But Jim's glance wasn't casual: he saw the big man's sadistic joviality and Greer's pain all too clearly.

He was witnessing the destruction of man's spirit.

Greer looked old suddenly, much older than his sixty years, and at the same time he looked like a miserable child waiting to be punished.

Jim looked away, at the other man, his stomach still churning. But it was knowledge—and a chilling sense of destiny—that were making him nauseous. It wasn't any

grand destiny, though; it was a squalid one like something
pulpy and rancid at the back of the refrigerator, something
you thought you had thrown away long ago. Destiny: the
man was heavier now, and he had lost the rest of his hair.
But there was no doubt about his identity.

Greer was talking to Dominic Nosiglia.

The senator finally worked himself loose from
Nosiglia's embrace and, looking both ways along the wide,
busy passage, scurried off toward the nearest exit. There
was no dignity in the way he moved, with his coat collar
pulled up and his Knicks hat jammed down low over his
eyes. To Jim he looked like a man trying to leave a porno-
graphic movie unobserved.

He watched until the senator disappeared in the
crowd. A moment later, Dominic Nosiglia was standing
next to him. They were about the same size, two big men
equally overweight, but Jim felt dwarfed by the gangster's
presence. He took a step back and Nosiglia gripped his
arm to stop the retreat.

"Well, well, well," Nosiglia said amiably. "If it ain't the
only honest man in New York City. Looks like you put on a
little weight since I saw you last."

Jim looked him over, letting anger and contempt balance his fear. "You too," he said.

"Yeah—but I never wanted to be a basketball player."

"Me neither. I had a bad experience in high school.
Ruined the game for me."

"Too bad—we coulda made some good money together."

"I don't think so."

"Yeah? Well, maybe not. What the hell—you're doing
okay. You write some good stuff in the newspaper. Don't
gimme that look—you think I don't read? I read everything, pal. Newspapers, books, magazines, you name it. I
like the news—it's interesting. But what happened here today, this wasn't news. This was strictly private."

"You met in public. You're both public figures."

"And that makes it news?"

"I don't know. It depends what you were talking about."

"You'll find out tomorrow. But I still don't want to read about it."

"Sorry, Dominic—a scoop is a scoop."

Nosiglia laughed. He seemed genuinely amused. "Hey—you must think I'm a nice guy."

"And you must think I scare easy."

"There's nothing wrong with being scared.. Sometimes it's smart to be scared. You seem like a smart guy. Be smart."

"Is that a threat? Because threats are actionable in this state."

"Oh no—hold on! I don't want no trouble with the police. I'm just giving you a piece of practical advice. You honest guys tend to be a little impractical. Not to mention annoying. You know that guy Diogenes, with the lamp, wandering around looking for an honest man? He shoulda talked to me first. I coulda told him—forget it. You find your honest man he's gonna be a boring, stuck-up pain in the ass, guaranteed. Ahh—screw it. You can't argue with a Greek. You gotta shoot 'em in the head just to get their attention. See you around, hotshot,"

The next day Bernard Greer withdrew from the Senate race. For health reasons.

Jim was confused and angry when he walked into Eddie Jaglom's living room the next morning. Eddie was standing at the window with a cup of coffee, looking out over Central Park.

"What's going on?" Jim asked quietly.

"Don't you read the papers? I just won an election by default."

Jim took a deep breath and let it out slowly. "If you don't tell me, I'm going to start making guesses in the *Journal Examiner.*"

Eddie turned. He was forty-four years old, but his time in politics had aged him prematurely. He was starting to go gray at the temples. His skin was as dry as old leaves in the morning sunlight.

"I don't get it. Are you saying I had something to do with this?"

"I saw Greer talking to Dominic Nosiglia, Eddie. That was two days ago. Yesterday Greer retired. How does that look to you?"

"It looks like the Nosiglia family forced him out of the race."

"I saw them at a Knicks-Bulls game. That Dominic—he really loves basketball. I should have asked him the final score—I could have made some money."

"Oh. I get it."

Jim just stared at him.

"Dominic Nosiglia came this close to killing both of us. That was almost thirty years ago. I've never seen the guy since and I wouldn't want to."

"Then why is he doing you favors?"

"He wasn't! I don't need that kind of help. I was going to win anyway.."

"Not according to the polls."

Eddie sipped his coffee and winced. It was obviously cold, but he swallowed it. Penance.

"I couldn't care less about the polls. Fifteen percent of the undecided vote would swing the election to me."

"Maybe. Now we'll never know."

"Look, Jim . . . I may be a little reckless, I may act crazy sometimes. But I'm not stupid and I'd have to be brain-damaged to get involved with those people again. Look—they had something against Greer, God knows what, so they turned on him and wrecked his career, just like that. They could do the same to me, or anyone else—don't you think I know that? Why would I have anything to do with them?"

"I don't know."

"I learned my lesson in high school."

"Yeah, but the facts just sit there, man. They ain't going anywhere. This guy was winning until the one mafioso in the world that you happen to know personally stepped in."

"It's just a coincidence! No one even knows I know him."

"The other guys on the team know. Driscoll knows."

"But they have no idea this happened."

"If I write the article, they'll come forward."

"Jim—"

"It's news."

"It's speculation!"

"It's investigative reporting. It's an opportunity for me. No one else could write this story—no other reporter could make all the connections. This would put me in the Woodward and Bernstein league, Eddie. James Earl Jones would play me in the movie."

"If it were true. The Watergate story was true."

"Is this one?"

"No, I'm telling you. Absolutely not. How many times do I have to say it?"

They stared at each other. Jim was thinking of something else Eddie had said—that comment about the thirty years since the big Riverdale game.

By carefully cataloguing the time and the events that filled it, he could intellectually accept that three decades had passed, but in the deep roots of his nervous system he cringed with horror. It was as if something had gone wrong with time itself, as if the hour had been devalued. It was only worth twenty minutes these days, and the slide was continuing.

But even so, he could feel the days and the months in all the years between Eddie and himself. They were a pressure

in his mind, rambling structures of memory like neighborhoods he no longer visited in a much-loved city.

Eddie had never lied to him—that was a fact. They had
argued and disagreed but they had never betrayed each
other. Even at the Riverdale game they had side-stepped
the unforgivable.

To print this story would be to deal their friendship a
blow from which it would never recover, that was certain;
everything else was in doubt. Everything except the wrath
of Dominic Nosiglia. Jim was every bit as smart as Nosiglia
had suggested, and he had seen, over the years, much evidence of Nosiglia's wrath. The shop clerk who had lost
one family member a day until he started paying protection money—including infant twins and an invalid father;
the young man who had gotten his pelvis broken in a parking lot because he made the mistake of dancing one dance
with Ariadne Nosiglia, Dominic's beautiful daughter.

Then there was the case of Aldo Costanza, the hood
who had bribed the Riverdale School team all those years
ago. In the late sixties he had agreed to some kind of truce
with the Nosiglia family, which he apparently violated in
some way. He disappeared for a week or so. Then he was
found in his car, naked, with his throat cut. But that wasn't
even the worst part. There were more than three hundred
separate scorch marks on his body, from his tongue to the
soles of his feet to his genitals and everywhere in between.
No one could ever prove that Nosiglia had been responsible for the lavish brutality of Costanza's death, but gangland informants whispered the rumor of Dominic's only
comment on the incident:

"You burn me, I burn you."

So, yes—Jim was smart enough to be scared, and
though he trusted Eddie Jaglom's eyes, he would never
know for sure how much that trust had been touched with
fear.

Eddie was talking again, making his final pitch:

"If you print that article, it won't matter if you're right or wrong—not to me. My career will be over, no matter what. I'll be ruined. Your paper will eventually print a retraction and fire you, but that won't help me. No one reads retractions. In America you're guilty even after you're proven innocent. Besides, you didn't come here to tell me you were writing the story. You came here looking for a reason not to write it. And you found one. Print this crap and we're both finished. Because it's a goddamn lie."

Jim stuck out his hand. "Okay."

Eddie stared at the big paw jutting toward him for a moment, then laughed. "I swear to God, you're gonna make me crazy, Gramble." He shook the bigger man's hand and then pulled him into a rough hug. "I'm serious about that—my family is full of crazies. My grandfather died in an institution, claiming he was General Steve Lee and that he was due in Jonesboro to lead the Confederate retreat. I could lose it at any moment with all this stress you're giving me."

Jim pulled back, holding his friend at arm's length. The deed was done; he wanted to change the subject.

"What have you got for breakfast?" he asked.

"I got fresh bagels and nova scotia. I got croissants from that new bakery on First Avenue. I got eggs. I got raspberries from New Zealand. I got fresh-squeezed orange juice and hot coffee."

"Then let's eat."

So they ate, and they talked about old times. And Jim buried the story and Eddie won his seat in the Senate. He had a quiet two terms, no longer championing lost causes with quite the same sense of urgency. In the middle of his first term his mother had a stroke and died six months later; the next year his father died of heart failure. Eddie accepted the blows, coped with his grief silently: He just worked harder and focused more of his attention and energy on his son.

Tom was physically and intellectually precocious, and Eddie had a vision of him as some sort of perfect citizen soldier, trained by himself and Helen and Jake Gritzky in all the arts of peace and war, able to concoct a flaky pie crust as easily as he could break a cinder block with his head.

They did wilderness survival courses in the Maine woods: Tom knew every edible plant that grew in the forests of the Northeastern United States by the time he was 12 years old. He could actually start a fire with two sticks. He did everything to please his parents and they were hugely pleased with him. The three of them formed a unit that gave new meaning to the term 'nuclear family'—they were bonded as tightly as the protons and neutrons circling the nucleus of a carbon atom.

Eddie's days were filled completely with Tom and Helen and his work on Capitol Hill. He stuck up for his constituents. He never missed a vote or a committee meeting. But few people outside New York or Washington knew who he was. Jim found this modest behavior baffling and was privately sure that his friend was planning something extraordinary. A low profile had never been Eddie Jaglom's style; it had to be part of his strategy.

No one believed Jim's theory, until Eddie ran for President.

He had a radical platform: By taxing major corporations that paid little or no taxes, he could virtually eliminate personal income tax, while still keeping entitlement programs healthy and the military strong. Eventually, he promised, his plan would reduce and then eliminate the national debt. His position papers were long and complex, filled with cumbersome five-syllable words and higher mathematics. There were many skeptics, among them mathematicians with big

vocabularies. But America embraced his vision of a tax revolution. He was too wealthy to have any ulterior motives, and
too smart to lie. His other policies were equally in tune with
the times—isolationism, protectionism. He vowed to pack
the Supreme Court with liberals again. He wanted health
care universal and abortions safe. Best of all, he could talk.
"Give me a rabble," he had said to Helen one night after a
particularly successful rally. "I'll rouse it."

Jim decided early on not to cover the campaign. He didn't
want his professional life spilling over into Eddie's any more.
Mostly, he didn't want to report on the scandals he was expecting to develop. In an age of dirty politics, when every last
crumb of your personal life was dug out of the crevices and
examined under the public microscope, it seemed impossible to Jim that none of their old teammates would come
forward to describe the Riverdale game with its mafia en-
tanglements. Driscoll was still alive—didn't he have a grudge
against Eddie? If he said anything Eddie would be in the
same spot as every other presidential contender for the last
two decades: Accused, denying, belittling the charges, half-
admitting them, explaining them away, fighting to discuss
'real issues' while the headlines went on and his prospects
crumbled.

And what about the women Eddie had slept with? Jim
was certain there was more than one. Weren't they bitter?
Weren't they looking for revenge? There was no better
way to demolish a front-runner than to tell all to the tabloids.

Yet no one said a word. There weren't even any rumors. Eddie sailed through the convention and a national
campaign devoted to the changes he wanted to make with
no personal attacks. He never wrote speeches or employed
speech writers. He spoke extemporaneously, and slogans
flew out of his mouth as effortlessly as spittle. The simple
phrase "economic democracy" galvanized the voters more

than anything had in decades, but Jim liked some of the
others just as much—"Legalize prostitution, criminalize
pollution" was one of his favorites, and his argument for
both sides of that slogan were compelling. Eddie saw no
point in punishing victimless crimes—the real criminals
were the men who had turned the Niagara River into a
septic tank.

Eddie won an easy victory in November. And then—as
he always had before—he started carrying out his campaign
promises. His first priority was to rush a new tax code through
the Democratic Congress, using the full force of his 'honeymoon' period and his national mandate. That first April,
when people found their tax burden cut in half, Eddie's popu-
larity reached escape velocity and went into orbit.

"For years we've had two economic systems in this country," Eddie said in one of his weekly 'visits'—he spoke to the
nation informally every Sunday morning on the radio. "We've
had free enterprise—for the poor. And state socialism for
the rich. But that's changing now. The big corporations are
paying their share. The fat cats in their corner offices are
howling—and that's good to hear, isn't it? Let them howl.
Some have called me up right here in the Oval Office, and
you know what I say to them—welcome to democracy, my
friend. Democracy always pinches the ones on top—the ones
who deserve it most. I tell them to ride it out and I tell them
what I used to tell my son—'no whining.'"

America loved it.

Even the die-hard skeptics who felt he was too good to
be true were being won over. "Nothing like a little disposable income to brighten a person's disposition," Eddie
gloated over dinner one night with Jim. They still saw each
other a couple of times a year.

"What a rich guy's concept," Jim had said. "You really
think you can buy people's loyalty."

"I know you can. Check the polls some time," Eddie had

laughed. "What a poor guy's concept, anyway. You don't understand money at all. It's not some abstract agent of corruption. It's a brilliant idea. It's a technology of barter. It's the way we value our work. It's the way we live. The only people who resent it are the ones who don't have it and don't know how to get it—bums, in other words."

Jim sat back with a shrug. This was America, after all, where the one thing you could absolutely never argue with was success.

But Eddie's success was tainted. Jim was sure of that now.

It had been a week since he was fired from the *Journal Examiner*. He had used the time well. Fisk's bizarre behavior had given him new leads and he had followed them up relentlessly, calling in favors, working late, sleeping only a couple of hours a night.

Every line of inquiry led him back to Eddie. There were more questions all the time and though most of them illuminated nothing they were helping him indirectly. He was starting to see a sinister presence looming. Its shape was all too familiar—bulky, slouching, pot-bellied. He could almost see the brown teeth of that pock-marked smile.

Jim still didn't know exactly what was going on, but it didn't matter because Eddie did.

Eddie had all the answers.

And Eddie would have to tell him the truth. This time Jim would write it, even if it meant the end of their friendship, even if it meant the end of Eddie's career, even if it meant facing the vengeance of Dominic Nosiglia.

It was Christmas morning.

He had been traveling since the night before, driving the old Volvo from Manhattan to Hyannis, missing the last boat on Christmas Eve, wait-listing himself with Island Airlines, leaving his car at the airport, climbing on a 7 a.m flight to Nantucket.

He had rented a Jeep at the airport, and now he was driving to Madequecham, knowing he would be stopped by the Secret Service, rehearsing what he was going to say to them and preparing himself for what would probably be the last meeting he would ever have with his best friend in the world, President Edward Bellamy Jaglom.

9

Christmas was informal at the Jaglom's: Everyone wore
their jammies, and the press was not invited. Unless there
was a national emergency, the President took no phone
calls. Vice President Crane tried to get through during
breakfast, just as he had the year before, between the election and the inauguration. His feelings had been hurt at
the time, and despite the President's explanations, his feelings would no doubt be hurt again. Lamar Crane did not
learn quickly. As a Southern congressman from a rural
district, he had balanced the ticket, and in fact he was a
decent enough man who had conquered his own bigotry
to become a shrewd and stubborn supporter of the civil-
rights movement. But Eddie had never mistaken Lamar's
political skills, his cunning pragmatism, for real intelligence. They had little in common and rarely saw each
other socially. Eddie's lack of interest in dog racing,
motocross and professional wrestling matched Lamar's indifference to Mozart, scalloping and Japanese cinema.
Lamar's wife had left him shortly after the election (her
parting line baffled Eddie but made Helen nod in recog-

nition: "I've run out of smiles, Lamar"), and now he was lonely during the holidays. At Helen's insistence they had invited him for Thanksgiving dinner—a mistake they were unlikely to repeat.

The 'family only' rule was best, and as far as they were concerned, Amy was already part of the family. Tom had hoped to see his maternal grandmother, but she rarely left Coral Gables these days—especially in the winter.

So there was just the four of them.

They ate their breakfast calmly—that was the family tradition—but when they took their coffee into the living room they launched themselves at the mass of beautifully wrapped presents under the tree like a bunch of 10-year-olds.

Amy was used to a very different kind of Christmas. Her father was the head of the English Department at Bennington College, and he referred to himself as an 'Educator.' He frowned on excessive displays of emotion. Presents were opened quietly, without ruckus or mess; wrappings were preserved for future use. There was no rush—if you received a book, you took an hour or so to read part of it. Clothes were duly tried on. Thank-you notes were written in the afternoon. As young children, Amy and her two younger sisters were purged of the "insipid mythologies" of late December: Santa did not exist, reindeer could not fly and should not be harnessed like sled dogs, no one could live at the North Pole. As for Jesus, Lawrence Elwell delighted in pointing out that the Christ child was born in July.

Even their Christmas tree was a model of taste and decorum—no colored lights, no gunky, sentimental ornaments, no tinsel: just strings of tiny white lights glittering in the boughs like ice crystals.

The Jagloms' tree, Amy thought, staring at the colored bubble lights and the dozens of gaudy eccentric ornaments, all festooned with tinsel and topped by an oversized rhinestone angel, would have made her father physically ill.

She thought it was wonderful.

But what impressed her most were the presents. Some she knew about in advance. She had been with Tom as he poked around in the old 'Sconset dump looking for pieces of glass and the antique bottles his mother collected. She had been with him as he went from dealer to dealer in all five boroughs of New York City piecing together his father's main gift one item at a time. But there were lots of surprises. Somehow Helen had found out that she loved cranberries; there was a box of them from the Nantucket bog under the tree. She and Tom got matching Kryptonite locks which baffled them until their matching Cannondale mountain bikes were unveiled a few minutes later.

Tom gave his mother old cognac and newly remastered Toscanini recordings of Beethoven on CD. There was a tone of affectionate teasing in some of the gifts; every year Helen had to suffer for her eccentric passion: a bright red Austin Healy 3000 mk 3. It had aroused lots of attention in Washington, where the Austin Healy cult was numerous and fanatical. People left notes on the First Lady's car whenever she parked it in public, offering wild sums of money to buy it. A particularly poignant one recently had just begged her for one ride. It was a family joke because the car had a suspension that shook the fillings out of your teeth, and consumed its own weight in oil every month. Still, Helen wouldn't part with it.

Last year, Eddie had given her a gift certificate to her favorite garage; this year Tom gave her a beautiful pair of driving gloves—and a quart of oil.

Tom and Amy together bought the gorgeous, maroon-colored Sage fly-fishing rod with its jet-black solid bar stock aluminum Abel reel that Eddie had never quite gotten

around to buying for himself. He was ecstatic. He hugged
both of them, hefted the rod, hugged them again. "Feel
this," he said. "It's light as a feather. Amazing. A Sage rod.
Wow."

There were a lot of ordinary presents of course—candy
from Sweet Inspirations, toiletries from Crabtree & Evelyn,
and books. New novels by Stephen King, Larry McMurtry
and Martin Amis; new essays by Calvin Trillin and John
McPhee. But the morning didn't come to a screeching halt
so that everyone could read them. They were just gloated
over briefly and then set aside amid the drifts of wrapping
paper.

Tom gave Amy things you could only find on Nantucket—a sweater from the Looms, earrings from Kim
England's shop on Main Street, a set of nesting lightship
baskets. But her favorite gift from him was the least expensive. Months before they had been comparing childhood
Christmas disappointments, and she had described the
time when she was fourteen years old and had specifically
asked her clueless Dad for two records—Elvis Costello's
greatest hits and Neil Young's *Country Roads* album. Young
and Costello were her twin obsessions at that age, and
though her parents frowned on rock music generally, they
were glad to have a specific request from a daughter who
was getting harder and harder to please.

Nevertheless, they managed to get it all wrong. They
gave her Elvis Presley's greatest hits and a Neil Diamond
album. Elvis Presley and Neil Diamond. For a ludicrous
moment she had been on the brink of tears. But crying
would have been 'inappropriate'—one of her father's favorite words—at Christmas. So she thanked them for the
records, opened up a paisley shirt that she was never going to wear and tried to forget about it. She couldn't,
though, because the real disappointment had nothing to
do with music. They didn't really listen to her, that was the

point; her concerns did not concern them. In the ways she
was different from them, she didn't matter.

But Tom listened. The note on the brightly wrapped
package said, "The right guys, finally." She didn't listen to
Neil Young or Elvis Costello much any more, but that didn't
make any difference. As she hugged Tom, she whispered
"It's the thought that counts."

That phrase had changed its meaning over the years,
and degenerated into a euphemism—something nice to
say about some gift you didn't want. It had taken on the
same kiss-of-death quality as "She's got a great personality," that classic description of an ugly blind date.

But the thought did count. Nothing else counted for
much, especially at Christmas. The presents you gave or
bungled told more than you necessarily wanted to reveal
about the level of true intimacy between you and the
people you loved. By that measure, the lavish and meticulously detailed affection she saw represented by the gifts
Tom and his parents gave each other was unique in her
experience. They doted on each others' eccentricities. His
Mom and Dad didn't just know Tom liked old Marvel com-
ics and Stickley furniture; they knew he preferred Jack
Kirby's drawings and Leopold Stickley's chairs, and gave
him presents accordingly. He was sitting on his Leopold-
designed rocker, a pile of 35-year-old *Fantastic Four* com-
ics on his lap, blissfully eating a sweet sloop with his third
cup of coffee when his father started to unwrap his big
present.

This was a real coup of paid attention and hard work.
Eddie Jaglom had never bothered to keep any of the de-
tritus of his many political campaigns. The banners and
buttons and bumper stickers had gone into the trash after
election day. But the buttons especially were collector's
items now, and he made occasional regretful comments
about throwing the stuff away.

Tom had spent six months tracking them all down. from
the first "Jaglom For Congress" button to the "Jaglom for
Change" button of his initial Senate race; from the "We've
Just Begun" button of his re-election campaign to the "Economic Democracy" and "Jaglom/Crane" buttons of his most
recent victory.

Jaglom stared at them all, mounted on canvas in a
simple mahogany frame, seeing his whole career in politics recapitulated. He mumbled "I don't know what to say,"
and hugged Tom and whispered "Thanks, Tommy," in his
ear and then Helen was laughing. "He doesn't know what
to say! The last time that happened was when I told him I
was pregnant."

Helen had bought a present for each of the Secret
Service agents posted at the Madequecham compound.
She thought it was appalling that they had to be away from
home on Christmas, and though the gifts were small—
watches, wallets, Swiss Army knives—the men were touched
and pleased to get them. Helen offered them coffee and
her own refrigerator-dough sticky buns, hustling them inside to warm up. It had gone down to 20 degrees outside
and the wind was scouring the island from the northeast.

One of them said, "Gee. Mrs. Jaglom . . . I didn't get you
anything."

She smiled at him. "Yes you did—you're here."

She patted his arm and poured him another cup of
coffee. She could put anyone at ease, Tom thought, watching her. He didn't even know he was smiling, but Amy was
watching him. She took his arm and kissed him.

Outside, beyond the compound, at the corner of Milestone Road and the Madequecham Road, Jim Gramble
was being stopped by other Secret Service agents. One car
cut him off. The other drove up behind him. Three agents
advanced on his Jeep; one of the drivers remained behind,
talking into a cellular phone. Jim didn't recognize any of

them. They were all clean-cut blond and brown-haired white men in their thirties. They were cordial and pleasant.

"I'm sorry, sir," one of them said. "Unless you have a resident sticker there's no public access on this road at the moment."

"I understand," Jim said. "But I have to see the president." He realized how foolish he sounded even as he was speaking, before the agent chuckled at his effrontery.

"A lot of people feel that way sir," he said. "And the president does his best. But we try to cut him a little slack at Christmas."

Jim smiled back, controlling his impatience. "Look, I'm a friend of President Jaglom's. You have a list somewhere of people who have automatic access. I'm on it. My name is Jim Gramble. Check it out. This is urgent."

"I'm not aware of any such list, sir. And if we let every so-called 'friend' of the president's into see him . . . well, there'd be a couple of million people in line out here every day."

"I don't have time for this, kid. Get Ira Heller on the phone. Tell him Jim Gramble is here—or explain why you didn't and get ready to start job-hunting."

Jim put all his frustration and impatience into a hard, level stare. It was like the old grade-school science experiment of focusing sunlight through a magnifying glass. It didn't take long to burn a hole through the young man's paper-thin official jargon and authoritarian bluster.

"Well—"

"Do it."

Jim eased the tension with a smile. "Make yourself look good. Tell him you know I'm a reporter. Tell him you read my stuff in the *Journal Examiner*. He'll be impressed."

"Uh . . . okay . . . hold on a second."

He walked back to his car, the icy wind ripping at his Burberry raincoat. Jim rolled up his window and turned up

the heater. In a little while the agent came back, holding the
phone. He offered it to Jim through the closed window. Jim
rolled it down.

"He wants to talk to you."

Jim took the phone.

"It's Christmas, Gramble. This better be important."

"It's important. It's Christmas for me, too, Ira."

"Put Larry back on."

Jim handed over the phone. Larry listened, said "Yes,
sir." a few times and then pushed the antenna back in.

"We're going to have to frisk you, sir. And use the metal
detector . . . and check out the car. It may take a few minutes.
I have a Thermos of coffee if you'd like some."

"Thanks." Jim climbed heavily out of the Jeep and the
wind shoved at him. He took the Thermos cap full of weak
coffee gratefully and settled in to wait.

The security procedures took just under an hour. Jim
submitted to the inevitable and then he was driving along
the wide road—paved since the last time he was here—with
Secret Service cars in front of him and behind him.

He had always loved the Jaglom estate, its houses scattered in the dune grass facing the sea. It had always seemed
like a sanctuary to him, set apart from the rest of the world
and untouchable. In the old days, the kids had been given a
guest house all to themselves and were free to stay up as late
as they liked, eat when they wanted, do as they pleased.

In later years, he had brought Eleanor here a few times
and after her initial, pro forma griping about the privileged
classes, she had settled down to thoroughly enjoying each
and every one of the privileges available, from the Chinese
chef to the wine cellar to the maid service and the Jacuzzi
bath.

Thinking about all that made Jim sad.

He was going to miss this place. He drove up the crushed
shell driveway and stopped in front of the main house. He

turned off the engine and sat in the quiet car, listening to the wind. The Jeep rocked gently on its springs.

He was stalling and he knew it. The Secret Service guys were climbing out of the first car. Heller's car was pulling up behind him. Delay was impossible.

Just as well—without Heller's fist rapping on his window, he might have sat in the car, in a warm bubble of memory and procrastination, forever.

He took a breath and climbed out into the wind and the cold and the sharp smell of the sea.

The Jagloms were stuffing wrapping paper into big garbage bags, trying to clear the living room floor while Buster romped in the mess, when the doorbell rang. Jim entered stiffly. He was formally polite, shaking Amy's hand with a murmured "Good to meet you," kissing Helen's cheek. He actually hugged Tom, who managed to whisper "What's wrong?" in his ear. Jim disengaged from the embrace gently, shaking his head and making a low "shhhhh" through clenched teeth. Tom saw an even stronger warning in his eyes. He stepped away and watched Jim and his father go upstairs.

The easy festive mood in the house was broken, like the tray of antique glass tumblers full of egg-nog that Tom had dropped the Christmas when he was 10 years old. He had just stood there, watching the liquid spatter, watching his Mom's favorite glasses disintegrating against the slate floor, too horrified to move, too stunned to cry. Nothing could fix or replace those glasses. They were gone.

This morning was beyond repair now, too.

They would just have to mop up the mess and carry on. It had been like this so often in his life—holidays or family vacations ended abruptly with a phone call or an unexpected visit. There was always some crisis his father had to deal with, something more urgent than opening a birthday present or carving a turkey.

They continued tidying, all of them listening above the crumple of wrapping paper and the snap of plastic for the raised voices, faint and filtered from upstairs.

After an interminable half-hour they heard footsteps in the hall above them. Jim came halfway down with Jaglom just behind him on the landing. Jim turned and shouted up at his friend, "Why don't you just turn on the air conditioning and start a fire? Roast some goddamn marshmallows!"

Then he stomped down the rest of the steps, reached the front door in three strides, let a gust of chill morning air into the house and slammed the door behind him.

Time seemed to stop in the few seconds after that smack of wood on wood. Before anyone could stop him, Tom was sprinting to the front door and pulling it open. When the wind struck him, he remembered he was still wearing only pajamas and his terry-cloth robe. His soft bedroom slippers hit the frozen ground and he knew he was going to ruin them in the race to Jim's rented Jeep.

He shrugged off the thought and ran harder. He had to know what was going on.

Out of the corner of his eye he saw Heller and a few of the Secret Service guys—they were having a good laugh at the way he was dressed. That was fine—as long as they didn't interfere.

He caught up to Jim just as the big man was climbing into the Jeep.

"Wait!," he called out. Jim turned to face him. "What's going on?"

"You don't want to know, Tommy."

"Don't you trust me?"

"You can't help. This has nothing to do with you."

"But Jim—"

"Sorry to wreck your Christmas."

For a second it looked like he wanted to say more. But in

the end he just turned away, swung into the Jeep and closed its flimsy door behind him.

Tom stood shivering as Jim drove off. When the Jeep was about to round the first turn a rabbit darted across the road. Jim swerved; so did the rabbit. A moment later there was a dull thud of impact. It was as if the rabbit wanted to be killed, timing its headlong rush exactly, throwing itself under the wheels. Jim drove on, out of sight. The damp wind surged against Tom's ridiculous clothes. His robe flapped against his legs. He knew he should go inside but instead he walked up to where the rabbit lay dying. It looked up at him as he knelt down beside it, and he saw the last of its life drain out of its eyes.

He wanted to do something for the little animal, but he didn't know what. Bury it? But that would take a long time in frozen ground, assuming he could find a shovel in the shed. In the end he just moved the stiffening body into the grass and started back to the house.

Inside, Amy said, "I don't get it. Who was that guy?"

Tom pushed Amy gently down onto the couch and sat beside her. "Jim and my Dad are old friends. Jim says he's my Dad's 'token'."

Amy's eyes widened. "What?"

Tom laughed. "It's Jim's joke, actually. He says a president ought to have one newspaperman as a close friend. Kennedy had Ben Bradlee; Reagan had George Will. Dad has Jim. But it's more than that. He's like family. We used to spend Easter vacations together. It stopped when Dad was elected. Jim says he'll be damned if he'll go egg-rolling on the White house lawn."

This time they both laughed, but the laughter died when Helen came into the room. Her face was grim. Something had come up. The President was returning to Washington immediately. Air Force One was fueled and waiting at Logan Airport in Boston. The helicopter was even at that moment landing on the front lawn.

Just before he left, Jaglom turned to Tom. "Sometimes I'm not so sure," he said.

"Not sure of what, Dad?"

"That President is better."

Later, after he was gone, the house seemed silent and empty. Christmas was over; it was almost as if it had never happened.

"Don't Presidents wear overcoats?" Amy asked at supper. The image of Jaglom, tie-less in slacks and a green sweater, striding across the lawn to the helicopter, was still clear in her mind.

"Never," Tom said. "It would make them seem effete."

"Or human," Helen added quietly.

There was a sadness in her voice Tom had never heard before.

10

On the last unspoiled day of Tom Jaglom's life, he was awakened by a telephone call from the Secret Service.

"Sorry to wake you up but there's been a change of plans."

For a second or two Tom didn't recognize the sandpapery voice.

"Who is this?"

"It's Ira Heller, kid. I'm calling for your Dad. He's in meetings all day, he doesn't have a second. But he's flying to L.A. tonight—big press conference tomorrow after he meets with President Otani. I have no idea why he needs to call a press conference, so don't ask me. All I know is he wants you on that plane and he wants you beside him there."

"But why, I mean—what did—?"

"Look—I don't have time for a bull session here. It's serious. That's all you need to know. I've never seen him this serious. Calm though . . . like the bad stuff has already happened. You know what I mean?"

"As a matter of fact I do."

His Dad always said: decisions were hard, action was easy.

"Air Force One will be on the ground at Kennedy at 9 sharp. We can only wait fifteen minutes—that's your window. If you need a ride you've got one."

"I can't do it." Tom was wide awake now, sitting tip in bed.

"What are you talking about?"

"This is Amy's birthday. Her parents are coming down from Vermont. We're having dinner at the Waldorf Ballroom. We made the reservation weeks ago."

"I see. Your father needs you but you have a date."

Tom sighed. "If my father needs me he should try giving me a few days' notice. I'm not twelve years old anymore."

"This is an emergency, Tom."

"What?"

"He needs you with him tonight."

"On the plane?"

"He needs you there."

"This is absurd. When is the press conference?"

"Eleven A.M."

"O.K. I'll get a 6 a.m. flight tomorrow, and I'll be in Los Angeles by nine their time. Just have a car meet me at the airport."

"That's not good enough, Tom."

"It's a six-hour flight and a three-hour time difference. I'll be there no problem. Now can we just—

"You're not listening to me. Your father wants you on Air Force One tonight."

"You've been with him on those flights. He sleeps the whole time."

"Not this time. He needs to talk to you."

Tom ran his fingers through his hair and pulled hard. He felt trapped and outmaneuvered. He thought of something Jim Gramble had said on a similar occasion: "Eddie rules people with an iron whim."

Tom was sick of it.

"If he wants to talk to me, I'll be home all day. He can call any time. Otherwise I'll catch the early flight and see him tomorrow. All right?"

"No! It is not all right! It is totally unacceptable! I want you waiting on that runway at 8:45—no gripes and no excuses. Just be there."

Tom squinted at the far wall of his bedroom. Heller had slipped up. "*You* want me?"

There was a pause on the other end of the line. He had broken Heller's momentum.

"This is my job on the line, Tom."

"I thought you hated your job."

"No jokes please. I'm on thin ice, here. You wanta know how thin? All you gotta do is piss on my shoes and I'm in the water."

"Don't get paranoid, Ira. No one's going to fire you. My Dad thinks you're doing a great job."

"Tom—"

"Have him call me. I'll see you tomorrow."

He hung up the phone and stared at it for a few moments, sure it would ring again. But it didn't, and by lunch time he had managed to put the call out of his mind completely.

He and Amy took her parents on a tour of the city, from Coney Island to the Bronx Zoo. Lawrence Elwell wanted to go to the top of the World Trade Center and the Empire State Building; Alice Elwell wanted to climb the stairs inside the Statue of Liberty and walk across the Brooklyn Bridge. They wanted to eat street hot dogs and knishes. They even insisted that Tom find them the "Quint-essential New York soda" to drink. He gave them a Dr. Brown's celery tonic and they loved it.

They were stuffy and bookish, quoting Thomas Wolfe and Garcia-Lorca and Truman Capote on the subject of

the city, debating the fine points of its architecture and social history. But they were having fun and Tom enjoyed being
their guide. For two small, pudgy people, they seemed to
have an unlimited amount of energy and enthusiasm. They
were still going strong at the Waldorf that night.

By 11:15 they had eaten dinner and were out on the
floor, waltzing and fox-trotting to 60-year-old big band
music, watched with glazed indifference by two Secret Service agents at the bar. Tom was doing his best to ignore the
watch dogs, doing a rumba with Amy's mother while Amy
danced with her Dad, silently thanking his parents for forcing him to go to dancing school in seventh grade. He had
just decided he would actually say "thank you" to both of
them the next day, when the announcement came.

In retrospect, the timing of the moment would be grotesque, an irony caustic as Drano.

It happened this way:

In the middle of a song the music stopped. Not all the
instruments together, but within twenty seconds the last strag-
gling notes on the trumpet and the last drum fill had faded
into silence. The maitre d' was standing in front of the band.

"Something terrible has happened," he said. "The
President's plane has crashed."

Tom stared at him. At first the words were detached
from each other, separate and senseless. He could feel the
struggle in his mind to keep them that way. But they were
flowing together against his will, by their own weight and
volume, like pancake batter spreading on a grill, merging
into grim coherency.

Air Force One had crashed.

In Iowa somewhere, the maitre d' was saying. No one
knew exactly what had happened or why, no one knew the
number of survivors or the exact status of—

One of the cooks ran out of the kitchen, waving his Sony
Watchman. The rest of the kitchen staff was following him.

"It's on the news," he said.

He turned up the volume and everyone crowded nearer to the bandstand. Tom was in the middle of the throng, cut off from Amy's mother, Amy herself nowhere in sight. He was dizzy. His heart was battering against his chest. The words coiled through his brain, over and over: "This isn't happening, this isn't happening."

But it was happening; Peter Jennings said so. The miniature face on the tiny TV made the nightmare real.

"We now have confirmation that Air Force One has crash-landed just outside the small farming community of Alleman, Iowa. Lou Steadman is in Des Moines. Lou?"

"We have no word yet on the status of the crash survivors, Peter," Steadman said. "But they were rushed here, to the trauma center at Iowa Methodist Hospital in Des Moines. Both the President and the First Lady were on board, as were some members of the press corps and a working crew of seven. Vice President Lamar Crane has assumed emergency powers until the situation clarifies."

"Is there any word on the President's condition?"

No, no—he already said no, you fucking ghoul, Tom thought.

"Not as yet, Peter. There's an enormous response to this accident, and we're not likely to hear any details for awhile. But we'll be staying at the hospital through the night to update the situation for you as frequently as possible. For now, all we can do is wait—and pray."

"Thanks, Lou. Once again. Air Force One has crash-landed about 30 miles outside of Des Moines, Iowa. The condition of the President and First Lady are not yet known."

They knew nothing.

How could they know nothing? It was a cover-up. Everyone was dead. They were keeping it a secret until the last possible moment. No, that was ridiculous. That was just fear talking. People survived plane crashes. Air Force One had many unique safety features. This could all be a false alarm. No one knew yet. Or maybe they knew too much, maybe—

Tom's brain was spinning out of control. He stopped it with a giant, painful act of will—like jamming his hand into the blades of a fan. In the stillness it was obvious.

He had to be there. He had to go there now.

He had to get out of this room full of strangers and get to the airport. That meant fighting his way to the elevators, getting downstairs, finding a cab, making it out to— was it Kennedy or LaGuardia? He had never flown to Des Moines. Kennedy probably. The cab driver would know. If he could get a flight he'd have to change planes in Chicago. You always had to change planes in Chicago. And then he'd have to wait around O'Hare airport until—

No—there was a better way.

For the first time since his father's inauguration, he was happy to have the Secret Service nearby. He could finally put them to good use.

They were standing on the edge of the empty dance floor, one of them talking quietly into a cellular phone, the other one keeping an eye on the group clustered around the TV. Amy broke out of the throng and reached them at the same moment that Tom did.

She took his hand as he walked up to the two agents. When he said "Get us to Des Moines," that simple plural made her release a breath she hadn't even known she was holding.

The agent closed his phone and nodded.

"Those are our orders," he said. "But the girl stays here."

"What?"

"Our orders are to bring you to Des Moines. Just you."

"Disobey your orders then. She's coming."

The agent smiled gently. "Can't do that, son."

"Then get out of our way."

He pulled Amy past the two big men and started for the far side of the dining room. The agent with the phone grabbed his shoulder.

"I mean it, kid."

Tom let himself be turned around. He was on the edge, Amy could feel it. But when he spoke his voice was calm.

"Don't try this now. Your timing is lousy."

"I have the authority—

"No you don't."

"We can take you by force, if necessary."

Tom smiled. "Try it."

He released Amy's hand and shifted into a loose fighting stance.

Amy said "Tom . . . " but the plea died in the poisoned air between those two sets of eyes. Tom was ready. Sheer animal danger fumed off him like some rank body odor. These men were trained; they had to sense it, they had to know the risk they were taking. Amy stepped backward, cowering in anticipation.

But the agent backed down.

"What the hell," he said. "All right—bring the girl if you want."

Tom let out a breath through his teeth. "Thank you," he said.

Then the four of them were sprinting for the elevators.

The trip to Des Moines was a torment of delay. The Secret Service helicopter had engine trouble and they were forced to drive to the airport. There was a traffic jam that started at the Triboro Bridge, and while their siren pushed them through it at first, eventually they were stuck with everyone else as four lanes merged into one around at a three-car crash. As they inched past the site of the accident, there were ambulances with their lights flashing and police cars pulled up in a tide of broken glass. One car was crumpled into a ball. They had cut the metal apart and were pulling out a woman. Her clothes were soaked and lines of blood fissured her face. She didn't move. Tom looked away as darkness bubbled up behind his eyes. Death was everywhere. For a second he was sure he was going to throw up. He forced himself to sit back. He shut his eyes.

Half an hour later they arrived at the terminal. But they had a problem there, too—apparently a different Secret Service unit had already taken the Agency jet. They had left for Des Moines an hour ago.

The agents flashed their badges and had four people bumped off the next flight to O'Hare. Tom got the people's names and addresses from the woman behind the ticket counter. The Secret Service men were baffled.

"My Dad will want to thank them," he explained. "I mean, if he—"

The rest of the sentence stopped halfway up his throat. He swallowed it.

"That's a good idea," the agent said with a cautious smile; Tom realized they were almost the same age. "I should have thought of it myself."

"If he were your Dad, you would have."

Ten minutes later they were on the plane, waiting on the runway. Thinking they were in line to take off, the agents went up to the cockpit to demand priority status from the tower. But that wasn't the problem. Ground crews were checking the fuel lines.

It was full hour before the plane was determined to be unsafe. Everyone filed out and waited another two hours while the airline located another plane and transferred all the luggage. By way of compensation, they offered free coffee and food to nibble on. Tom tried to laugh but the sound that came out wasn't laughter. When a flight attendant shoved a tray at him, her cheerful insistence snapped a few more wires.

Amy was afraid he might kill the woman. But he spoke softly.

"My parents are dying. I need to be with them. Beer nuts won't help."

The flat, venomous contempt with which he named that innocent snack made Amy cringe. She had always rather liked the salty sweetness of beer nuts—she was chewing a mouthful of them even as he spoke—but she knew she would never be able to eat them again. They would always taste like this endless, horrific night. Tom's tension had leeched into her, slimed her own nerve endings. She was seething with his frustration; she was cold with his fear.

It was almost dawn—soon another bland airline robot would appear, offering them breakfast. She thought she might kill the next one herself.

But things started to go more smoothly after that. They got on a plane, flew to Chicago uneventfully, landed with no problem and were rushed onto a connecting flight to Des Moines by an efficient and sympathetic Secret Service escort. Tom began to calm down a little—or at least he drew deeper into himself. He didn't want to talk, so Amy kept quiet, fending off the cabin attendant on the old two-engine commuter plane. The flight was just over an hour, but the man still managed to offer coffee, soft-drinks, pillows and the dreaded beer nuts.

She was just starting to relax herself when for the insane, impossible third time in one trip, their aircraft developed mechanical problems. The pilot announced that they would be making an emergency landing in Cedar Rapids.

Tom gaped at her. He was holding his arms straight, fists clenched, clamped between his legs. There was a light sheen of fever sweat on his face. He had a glistening, soap-bubble fragility at that moment—he was all trapped air and surface tension. It seemed that even the lightest touch would puncture him, make him vanish in a flick of spray. But she didn't know what else to do. Desperately, she twisted sideways, digging her right arm between the seat and his back, grabbing his shoulder with her left hand and pulling him towards her. For a second he resisted, but only for a second. He hugged her, but he was shaking. "We're not going to make it," he kept saying. "We're not going to make it."

"Yes we will," she whispered to him. "It's going to be okay now. It can't get any worse than this.'

But it did.

There was a four-hour wait for the next flight to Des Moines. It had started to snow and the worsening weather had delayed everyone. There was even a chance that the airport would be closed altogether. "Occasional snow showers" predicted to cause a "light dusting" by midnight had turned into a blizzard by morning.

Tom touched the airport manager's shoulder. He seemed supernaturally calm, reduced to a sort of zombie indifference by shock and stress. "How far is the bus station?" he asked.

"It's right in the center of town, son. But I wouldn't want to be out on the road in this weather. If I were you—"

But Tom had already turned away. He was walking to the exit. Amy hurried after him.

Outside it was frigid and snow was swirling down out of a solid gray sky. The wind made their eyes water and the air burned in their lungs. There was one cab at the stand in front of the terminal. They trotted over, skidding on the slippery sidewalk, and climbed in.

Fifteen minutes later they were cruising through downtown Cedar Rapids. The snowplows had been out already and the roads were relatively clear. Tom sat staring straight ahead. "The buses better be running," was all said.

"They will be," Amy answered.

And they were.

By 10 a.m. they were sitting on wide, plush seats in a warm, comfortable bus, heading west. The Secret Service agents were still at the airport, waiting for a flight. The passenger across the aisle assured Amy it was a short trip and that the Des Moines bus station was near the hospital, downtown.

Everything would have been fine if not for the patch of black ice ten miles east of Grinnell. The bus was going too fast anyway and when it hit the ice it started skating sideways across the highway. Tom felt the skid begin and reached across, pressing Amy back against her seat. The bus spun all the way around twice and then slid off the road backward into a snow bank. They jolted to a stop; Tom's arm kept Amy from doubling over around her seat belt.

Passengers were crying and screaming. Some were just pissed off and cursing. The driver tried to muscle out of the snow, but the wheels spun uselessly. The engine whined and finally stalled. He couldn't get it started again. It sounded to Tom like he flooded it trying.

Amy glanced over at Tom, afraid this final outrage might have broken him—but he was laughing. She started laughing, too. The pure, mindless impossibility of getting from New York to Des Moines suddenly seemed hilarious.

Tom stood up, catching his breath. "Come on," he said. "Let's hitch-hike."

She didn't argue with the idea, despite the cold and the snow. There was nothing else to do now except walk, and the way things were going one of them would break an ankle if they tried. She was giggling again.

"We'll probably be picked up by some lunatic."

"Or worse—someone who knows a 'shortcut.'"

"Or even worse than that—Secret Service guys!"

They were actually picked up a few minutes later by an English professor from Grinnell College named Noah

PARANOID   161

Mellman. His old Saab was rusty but it had the essentials—
snow chains and a good heater.

Amy chatted with him and soon had him chuckling
over their bizarre odyssey. Tom said nothing. The laughter had lifted his spirits only to drop them lower. It was
like eating a candy bar when you were really hungry; when
you burned the last of the sugar you could feel the bottom
of your stomach fall out.

He was just glad to be moving again.

"This is like something out of Kafka," Mellman was
saying. "Did you ever read *The Hunger Artist*? People take
that story so seriously. Kafka thought it was funny. He
couldn't read it aloud without cracking up. Of course . . .
Kafka was kind of a weird guy."

It was New Year's Day and traffic was light heading into
Des Moines. Mellman put on his car radio and they listened to the latest news. The President was in stable but
critical condition. All the reporters and most of the flight
crew had died instantly. Two cabin attendants and a pair of
Secret Service agents were hospitalized. They had recovered the black box and would soon know more about the
last moments of the flight. For now, no one knew what had
caused the disaster, and the officials interviewed were careful not to speculate.

There was no word about Tom's mother.

He wanted to say something about that strange omission
but his vocal cords were knotted too tightly. He was mute with
an emotion bigger than fear. Fear shared space inside you
with other feelings—anger, excitement, shame—but this left
no room for anything else. It filled up every part of him. This
was primal. This was about killing and fleeing and burrow-
ing yourself into the ground to hide. This was where you
parted company from any memory of your rational self and
just started howling at the moon and clawing your face with
your nails.

Knowledge scourged him as he sat trembling in the little car. And hope scourged him just as badly.

Hope kept him conscious. Hope held him in place, bound him to the this unbearable procession of moments leading to the unbearable truth. Despair would be better. It would be a relief to know the worst, to stop falling and hit bottom.

If anyone tried to coddle or comfort him he would— what? He had no strength left to fight or even scold. Perhaps he would just start crying like a child. He didn't know.

The streets around the hospital were jammed with press vans and trucks, snaking cables, lighting set-ups. Local TV stations, CNN, all the networks, foreign press working off satellite hook-ups—a surging chaos of reporters ravenous for information. Still, the majority of the huge crowd gathered around the hospital were ordinary people, thousands of them, keeping a vigil for their President and their First Lady.

It didn't take long for Mellman's car to get hopelessly stuck in the grid-locked traffic. The radio babbled on. The doctors talked about the world-class level of care at the trauma center. They discussed various treatments and praised the President's will to live. Pundits discussed the vice-president's takeover under the Emergency Powers Act. They talked about the chief surgeon's qualifications and the crowds outside and even the weather. Anything but the First Lady.

Amy knew what he was thinking. She was thinking it herself.

"She can't be dead, Tom. They'd have to announce it if she were dead. Even if they didn't want to, word would leak out. She has to be alive. She has to be fighting. She needs you. Come on—we have to run."

Tom realized she was right. It was like waking up from a

dream, the frantic way you wake up when the alarm didn't go off and you have a plane to catch. She was opening the car door. "Thanks, Professor Mellman," she said. "We wouldn't have made it without you." She climbed out of the car and Tom scrambled after her. They pushed their way through the crowd in the street. Tom's took the lead and cleared a path for Amy. He wasn't gentle, though he tried to be polite. He made a few people stumble, but the streets were packed too tightly to allow anyone to fall. At first people were angry; but then someone recognized him.

"That's the President's son!" a voice bellowed. "It's Tom Jaglom," someone else cried out. "Let him through!"

Then an extraordinary thing happened. The crowd parted. People stepped backward all at once, crushing against each other to make an open corridor.

They wanted to help, they wanted to do something. This was all they had been given to do, so they did it extravagantly. The sidewalk was clear all the way to the hospital door. Tom and Amy stared at each other, startled by the moment, enchanted by the silent good will of the people around them. Then Tom took Amy's hand and they started running.

The first person they saw inside the hospital lobby was Ira Heller. He looked rumpled and bored as usual—but tired also, this morning. There were dark circles under his eyes. He walked up to Tom and gripped his shoulders. He stared into Tom's eyes. You couldn't soften the news, and delay just made things worse.

He spoke softly but clearly. "Your mother died fifteen minutes ago."

Tom screamed.

He tried to twist away from Heller, but his legs had turned into pudding. Black algae floated in front of his eyes and he fainted. Heller caught him and dragged him to a plastic chair against the wall.

When he regained consciousness a few minutes later, there was a tall doctor with granny glasses and a bald spot standing over him, between Amy and Ira Heller. Tom looked at them all in a space of pure consciousness, aware of physical facts only—the texture of his clothes, the melting snow under his collar, the hard plastic seat, the concerned faces looking down.

Then awareness rushed back. He was in a hospital. He was in the Midwest. His mother was dead.

He had failed by fifteen minutes.

There was nothing and no one to be angry at except God, and he didn't believe in God. Religion must be wonderful, he thought. What a luxury—having someone to blame. But even now, he couldn't pretend to believe. The old saying was wrong—there were atheists in foxholes, and in hospital corridors. Religion was invented to shut out this one fact: life was a series of accidents. Even the fact that he was alive right now was an accident. After all, if it hadn't been Amy's birthday, he would have been on the plane himself. He was lucky—the way Jake had been lucky in Viet Nam.

Lucky.

The doctor was talking. "Your father is doing well, surprisingly well, given the circumstances. He should be out of intensive care within a week and then we can start—"

"What happened to my mother?"

The doctor smiled gently. He had obviously practiced this serene, controlling look in front of the mirror. Tom was not impressed.

"I don't think it's appropriate to discuss the details right now, Mr. Jaglom," he said gently. "This has been a terrible shock and I don't think you're ready—"

Tom stood. "You don't get to decide that."

Tragedy had given him a kind of authority, set him above this self-important circle of his elders. This wasn't happening to them. It was happening to him.

He stared at the doctor. "What happened to my mother?"

"All right. If you insist. She had third-degree burns over 90 percent of her body, Mr. Jaglom. She had lost a great deal of blood. The structural damage to the aircraft and the weather conditions delayed treatment—it took a while to get her out of that plane, and the ambulance drove most of the way here behind the snow plow. We did everything we could, but . . ."

Tom sat down again.

"I'm sorry," he said to the doctor. "I'm sure you did. Thank you. I didn't mean . . ."

"Would you like to see your Dad?"

Tom looked up gratefully and nodded. The doctor helped him to stand and Amy put her arm around his waist as they started toward the elevators. "My name is Jerome Clifford. I'm a plastic surgeon. I'll be doing the reconstructive work on your father. It's going to require more than one operation. It's going to take a while. But I believe we can do it. He's very strong and very stubborn . . . as I'm sure you know. That happens to be the ideal combination of characteristics, in terms of a recovery profile."

He smiled as the elevator doors opened and they walked into the long compartment obviously designed to carry stretchers and gurneys. "Actually," Clifford went on as the doors closed and they started up, "physical strength isn't even that important. The essential thing is that intangible quality of will which somehow—

Heller cut him off. "In other words, he's a goddamn stubborn pain in the ass—lucky for us."

The doctor chuckled. "Well put, Mr. Heller."

Tom smiled weakly. He was beginning to feel a dog-like affection for the big balding doctor.

A few minutes later, after donning surgical masks, they walked into the intensive care ward and stood in over Edward Bellamy Jaglom's bed. He was swathed in bandages, under an oxygen tent, with tubes snaking out of him and IVs dripping and monitors registering his every breath and heartbeat. The breathing was regular; the heartbeat was strong. But medical technology had rendered his father anonymous. It could have been anyone under there.

In the hallway, Dr. Jerome said, "There's really no point in you staying at the hospital now. Eventually it will be important for him to see you. Until then . . . and I know this seems impossible, or even disrespectful . . . you should try to carry on with your life. Your girl, your studies. There's not a lot you can control right now. But your school work doesn't have to suffer. If you took charge of your own life, I'm sure your Dad would be proud of you."

Tom nodded. It was all valid, but he couldn't deal with it. The thought of finishing the Emile Durkheim essay he had been reading on New Year's Eve, or starting the paper on Emmanuel Kant that was due in February made him laugh.

He couldn't read a newspaper at this point. He couldn't write a shopping list. But he nodded in agreement because it was easier than trying to explain.

When they returned to the waiting room, Someone took a picture of them, and sold it to UPI. In years to come that photograph of Tom and Amy—he in a dinner jacket, she in a ball gown—slumped in the lobby of Iowa Methodist Hospital, would fix itself in America's memory as firmly as the image of Jacqueline Kennedy in her blood-stained skirt.

Tom's grandmother arrived an hour later. Her coat was dusted with snow and she smelled of the cold.

"Is it true?" she asked.

Tom nodded wordlessly and hugged her.

Ruth Perkins was Helen's mother and the only one of his grandparents still alive. She had been a harsh and difficult woman when she was younger. She disapproved of her son-in-law. She was certain he was marrying Helen for her family's modest fortune, until she saw the Beekman Place apartment. When she realized how wealthy the Jagloms were, she remained true to her own prickly, impartial cynicism and immediately began doubting her daughter's motives. She was intolerant of anyone who disagreed with her conservative political views, and had once called Eddie "That spoiled, ambitious, two-faced little pinko."

But that dragon lady was a matter of legend for Tom. Old age had mellowed her. At some point in her sixties she had begun to question all her values and opinions. Around that time she moved from her big old house into a small apartment. She had been forced to 'sort and chuck' all her possessions, discarding the mountains of unessential rubbish she had collected over the years. She found it invigorating and started on a similar project with her accumulated beliefs. There were black ladies in her building and two of them turned out to be excellent bridge players. In a month the habitual racism that had tainted her conversations for years vanished completely. Other transformations followed: She finally understood that you could be both anti-abortion and pro-choice. She started listening to rock and roll; she became a vegetarian. And she started reading novels, which she had always scorned as frivolous.

She was still shrewd, her wit was still biting, but her daughter had summed up the change in her best when she said, simply, "Granny doesn't hold grudges any more."

Tom sat down beside her. She and Amy had met once, but there were no amenities this morning. Ruth's eyes were dry but her face was grim.

"I want you to do me a favor, Tom."

"Anything."

"I want you to deliver the eulogy at your mother's funeral."

Tom stared at her. "No, I mean—I don't think I—"

"Please, Tom. Your father obviously can't do it. I could never do it, I'd just start crying in front of all those people. But I don't want some priest who barely knew her talking about her good works and her loving family and saying nothing. She deserves better than that. Please, Tom . . . I know you can do it."

Tom hugged her again. "Okay."

Amy had moved away to talk with Heller. Now she helped Tom up and they started walking towards the front door. "That's strange," She said.

"What?"

"After all his bullying about getting you on Air Force One last night, Heller wasn't on the flight himself. He took that Secret Service jet to Des Moines—the one we missed by an hour."

"He probably had things to do in New York."

"I guess. It just seems so . . . I don't know . . ."

"Lucky. He's a lucky guy. Just like me."

Tom's face was tight. She dropped the subject.

But both of them remembered.

11

The funeral was three days later. Tom was standing in a black suit, facing a full house in the Tobias Cahoon Funeral Home on East 65th Street. Outside, thousands of grief-stricken New Yorkers along with reporters and cameras and trucks of video equipment had virtually stopped traffic on Madison Avenue. The service itself was strictly private—perhaps a hundred and fifty people. Tom had known most of them all his life. His grandmother had been right. He could see it in their faces; they wanted to hear what he was going to say. He took a breath and began.

"One day, almost thirty-five years ago, a landlord named Raymond DeRensis threw a glass paperweight at my mother. But she was quick. She ducked. She had just forced him to allow a black family into one of the apartments in his building. She did it by presenting herself as the same in every way as a black woman he had rejected the day before—same size family, same income, same seniority in the same type of job. He had told the lady there was nothing available. But he showed my mother four different apartments, including the penthouse. So she, and the organization she worked for, which was formed to help enforce the open-housing laws in this city, nailed Mr. DeRensis. They caught him in a lie that happened to be illegal and they forced him to do the right thing. He wasn't happy about it. He called my Mom a "traitor to her race" and a lot of other worse things. But he integrated his building and one black family had a decent place to live.

"My mom did that for more than fifty black families during the 'sixties. She remembered every family and kept in touch with most of them.

"That's the kind of person she was.

"She had a relaxed attitude about parenting. When I was little, she let me climb some hair-raising rock formations in Central Park, and let me fall down when I lost my grip. She despised the coddling, over-protective parents—the 'watch-out-sayers' she called them. But she could be ferociously protective when she needed to be.

"She didn't make a big deal out it. She'd just shrug and say "Parents are a service organization."

"She told me once . . . 'you'll never know how much I love you until you have your own kids.' But it wasn't an indiscriminate love. If she thought I'd done something wrong, been rude or inconsiderate, she'd tell me—but I could see it in her eyes before she said a single word. Am I talking too much right now? I could see her frowning just a little and know I should shut up. My Dad felt the same way. She kept him honest. She demanded the best from him and most of the time she got it. They say Dad's going to be okay. He's going to live. But he has much less to live for now. That's something we share. My mother will never see me graduate from college, never meet her grandchildren. And I realize that each thing in my life was made special, made more real, because I could share it with her. Everything is less now. Everything will always be less."

He looked down at the podium, waiting for the tears to recede. He had a little more to say.

"The last thing I ever said to my mother was, "Come on, give me a break! When have I ever not called?" Then I squirmed when she hugged me. That was our last moment together. And that stinks. I have to live with that forever.

"So if this week has taught me anything it's just this— treat your family as if they might die in a plane crash tomorrow. Because they might. Don't be embarrassed when your mom hugs you. Hug her back. Say 'I love you.' Say 'Thanks.' Say everything you feel. Because I didn't and I learned the hard way that nothing else matters."

He paused again. He was almost done and now he was sure he could make it to the end.

"This is strange—my Mom was never much for funerals. She wasn't morbid. She'd want us to remember the good things about her and the good times we had with her and be happy. She expected a lot from the people she loved. She made some tough demands. This may be the toughest one of all. But as usual, she's right.

"So we have to try.

"Thank you."

As he stepped down, there was a rustling in the crowd and he could see that many people were crying. For the moment his own eyes were dry. His grandmother embraced him and said "Thank you"—just as he'd told her to from the podium. Uncles and cousins and friends of the family shook his hand and hugged him. Of course it was a somber moment, but it seemed a little less so, now—as if he had conjured his mother's bright spirit as he spoke.

Halfway up the aisle, Jim Gramble pulled him into a bear hug. They hadn't seen each other since Christmas morning, though both of them had been at the hospital in Des Moines the day after the crash. It had taken Jim a long time to separate himself from the mob of reporters and the effort had proved useless anyway. Only family members were allowed to see Jaglom, and in any case he was still unconscious.

"That was beautiful," he said to Tom now, amid the crush of mourners. "No one else could have done it, Tommy. No one else knew her like you did."

Tom smiled at him as he was pulled away by someone else, but he said nothing. To Jim he seemed over-whelmed—delicate, baby-faced, pathetically young. It was odd, because he had appeared so much older than his years on the podium a few moments before. The effort had clearly sucked him dry and the day wasn't over yet. They still had to travel to the cemetery on Long Island for the burial.

It was after that half-hour drive (With the twenty cars in the funeral procession surrounded by more than twice that many press cars and TV news vans), after the walk through the graveyard (just the mourners; the press were locked out at the gate), after the quiet reading from the Bible, the ashes to ashes, the dust to dust, after Tom had dropped flowers on the casket and shoveled the first dirt into the grave (it rattled like dry rain on the mahogany lid), after the group broke up and started walking to their cars, that Jim finally saw Tom Jaglom cry.

He and Amy had moved away from the others, toward a stand of elm trees. Tom seemed to stumble, as if he had tripped over an exposed root, and Amy grabbed his arm to steady him. He threw his arms around her and the tears began. Jim could hear him sobbing thirty yards away.

Jim stood for a moment in the windless air, the pale winter sunlight, wishing there was something he could do to help. But he felt a quick stab of self-disgust at that thought. He wasn't going to help; just the opposite, in fact. He had worked very hard to make things much, much worse.

Jim Gramble had only gone back to the *Journal Examiner* office once since he was fired, to pick up his files and clean out the last personal effects from his cubicle in the newsroom. His true personal effect could be measured in the faces of the men he'd worked with for the last fifteen years. They were baffled and outraged. Some talked of quitting in protest, some talked of going on strike. Jim discouraged them: the farther away from him and his predicament they stayed the safer they were. Sam Crawley gestured him over to the city desk.

"It was that story, wasn't it?"

"Sam—"

"In all the years you've been here, Jimmy, that was the only story of yours I never got to look at. Nobody saw it but Fisk. He never ran it and now you're gone. So what the hell was it? That's what I wanna know—what the hell were you writing about?"

Jim patted him on the shoulder—Sam was still sitting down. Jim realized suddenly that he had never seen Sam Crawley standing up.

"Keep reading the *New York Times*, Sam. You'll see."

No one had much time to talk—they were three hours away from deadline. By 6 P.M. the evening edition of the *Journal Examiner* would be on the streets, as it was every day of the year including Christmas.

Jim looked around at the writers on the phone or banging out their stories, the desk-men fixing leads and writing headlines, the copy-boys running.

He was the only one there with nothing to do.

But he didn't want to leave. This was his place. It was his home, more of a home than his apartment had ever been. He belonged here. He was respected here. The grizzled reporters around him would wince at the word, but he was loved here, too. He was needed—there was work to be done.

It wasn't fair: he was being punished for doing a good job.

But the fact remained: he would never be here again.

Fisk wouldn't allow it. The guard in the lobby would stop him if he tried to come upstairs. He had tried to laugh off the loss, bury it in work, cauterize it in the heat of righteous anger. But none of that had worked. He felt a ghastly prickle of tears and clenched his whole body against them. He refused to cry—not now, and certainly not here.

He had things to do. He had come back for a reason.

He walked to his desk and stuck his clock, a coffee mug, some pens and pencils into a paper bag. What he had really come for were the rest of his files on the Blasi story—clippings, notes, transcripts of interviews, source material, deep background, phone numbers, addresses . . . everything he couldn't or wouldn't trust to his now defunct computer. There were three file folders in all, bulging and held together with rubber bands.

He wasn't really surprised when he pulled open the empty drawer. He didn't have to ask if Fisk had been at his desk—it was obvious. Jim looked around. Fisk was at lunch, but he'd be back any minute. No time to waste.

Jim strode into the managing editor's office and slammed the door behind him. This was a fundamental violation of the newspaper's laws and mores. No one went into Fisk's office if he wasn't there. Half a dozen people should have been rushing over to stop him, but no one moved. They had all seen Fisk pilfering his desk. Everyone was rooting for Jim today

No one was going to interfere.

There was a file cabinet in the office, near the window. It was open, as always. Jim didn't bother to check it. He had a feeling that the Blasi file would be stowed away securely, and the deep bottom drawer of Fisk's desk was in fact locked. It didn't budge when he pulled the handle.

Now what? He was running out of time.

He jogged out of the office, through the controlled frenzy of the City Room. No one seemed to notice him. He rang for the elevator but decided not to wait. He took the stairs down to the basement and he was panting by the time he got to the maintenance department.

A Jamaican handyman named Tiko was drinking a cup of herbal tea in the doorway.

"Do you have a really big screwdriver I can borrow for a couple of minutes, Tiko?" Jim asked.

"Sure, man—straight or phillips?"

"Straight. And a hammer."

"You need some help?"

Jim laughed. "All the help I can get.'

Tiko crumpled his paper cup. "Let's go.

"No, no—not right now. I don't want to get you in trouble."

"Trouble? What do you mean, trouble? You in trouble, man?"

Jim nodded.

"Big trouble?"

Jim nodded again.

"What can I do?"

"Just get me the tools, Tiko. And tell anyone who asks that I stole them."

Jim took the hammer and the screwdriver hack upstairs, once again ignoring the elevator. He had to pause twice to get his breath back. But the office was still empty, the door still standing open.

He shut it behind him and began systematically vandalizing Roy Fisk's desk. At first he tried to lever the drawer open with the screwdriver but that didn't work. He wound up driving the point into the wood next to the lock mechanism with the hammer and tearing the top third of the facing apart. He worked frantically—Fisk was already late. "Have one more cup of coffee, Roy," Jim muttered to himself.

At last he levered open the drawer. It slid out so quickly and easily that Jim lost his balance. But the files were in there, all three of them, still bound with rubber bands. Jim put the tools down and let himself sit on the floor. His heart was pounding like hooves on packed dirt, as if he was strapped to the back of a terrified horse. When the gallop slowed to a canter he stood and lifted out his files. He jammed them in the paper bag. Still no Fisk.

He stumbled out of the office and across the City Room. He heard Sam Crawley say "Good luck, Jimmy," but he didn't turn or answer. He felt like a soldier who had pulled the pin on a hand grenade and then lost count. Something was going to blow up soon, that was for sure.

He was still winded and the bag was heavy. He didn't want to struggle with the stairs again, and as it turned out he didn't have to. The elevator doors opened as he was lurching past them. He turned and found himself face to face with Roy Fisk.

Jim walked into the elevator with a sigh of disgusted resignation. He pushed the 'lobby' button and faced forward.

"What are you doing here?" Fisk's voice was cold and impersonal—as if Jim were just some trespassing nobody off the street.

"This stinks, Roy. We were friends."

"Yeah, well—life stinks. But we were never friends, Jim. I don't have friends. Just colleagues. So what are you doing here?"

"I came to clean out my desk. But someone beat me to it.

"Then why the bag?"

"I cleaned out your desk, Roy."

"What the hell—"

"And you'll never guess what I found."

The elevator stopped. The doors groaned open. People were waiting to get on. Fisk glared at them and shook his head. The doors closed again.

"It sounds like you just committed a class A felony, Jim. Breaking and entering. Criminal trespass—

"I don't think so."

"Those files belong to this newspaper."

"The hell they do."

"Come on upstairs. Let's call the cops and ask them."

"I'd like that. I want to hear you explain what my papers were doing in your office and why you never ran the story in the first place."

"That's a laugh. According to you, the police don't give a shit, remember?"

"There's a lot of good cops out there. Chances are you'll get one of them."

Fisk cleared his sinuses, shaking his head. The gesture was contemptuous, but it meant he was backing down. "Ahh, the hell with it. You'll never get that crap published anywhere."

"We'll see."

"Just remember—until it happens . . . it didn't."

Silence dropped between them. They reached the lobby again and the doors opened.

"It sounds like you owe me for my desk."

"Send me a bill."

Fisk smiled at him, an ugly little smile of superior knowledge. "I may not be able to find you."

Jim didn't bother to answer. He just pushed past the waiting passengers and started across the lobby. There was nothing to do with Fisk's implied threat but ignore it, so Jim did his best.

He took the precaution of storing the bag full of file folders in a friend's apartment on the upper east side. It was a perfect hiding place, for several reasons. Gary Meredith was an old schoolmate who had grown up to make a fortune producing hip-hop records for a growing uptown label. He kept the apartment a secret himself—he used it for his af-

fairs and paid for it out of the miscellaneous and petty cash
accounts. Officially it didn't exist. Gary was in Los Angeles
for a few months, so that even if the material was discovered
somehow, he would be in no danger.

He had helped Jim before, in much riskier situations
than this one. He liked the adventure of investigative reporting. He liked any kind of adventure, even the high
stakes, semi-suicidal thrill-chasing of his rampant promis-
cuity during a virtual plague of sexually transmitted dis-
eases.

Still, Jim felt uneasy about involving Gary—without his
consent—in this extremely dangerous business. But Gary
was actually safer knowing nothing. And the other choices
scared him more. Safe deposit boxes left paper trails, airport lockers were too easy to force and it was too easy to
follow someone in a crowded airport. Jim preferred the
wide, empty sidewalks of what Gary always called 'the ken-
nel'—the eastern end of the east side, cut off from the
Lexington Avenue subway and the rest of the city by those
long drab cross-town blocks, islanded north and south away
from anything lively or dangerous or fun. It was as close as
you could get, in Manhattan, to the middle of nowhere.
That was what Gary liked best about it. The anonymous
red-brick, post-war apartment buildings all had the same
awnings and terraces and lazy doormen and grandiose
names (Gary's was called "The Monarch"); they were filled
with a tidily integrated population of white and black and
Asian and Puerto Rican executives and executive secretaries; they were bland and interchangeable and they were
perfect for keeping secrets.

Jim had a secret he needed to keep now and he felt
much better with his files stored in Gary Meredith's closet on
the twentieth floor.

The day before Air Force One went down, Jim had submitted the actual story to an old friend of his at the *New York*

Times. Doug Baird had been excited to receive it, though he was in the middle of organizing his famous New Year's Eve party, frantic with last-minute details.

"Chill all the glasses," he had been saying to one of the caterers, and then, to his wife: "As long as we remember to serve the good stuff first, we'll be fine, darling. Nobody cares what their fourth glass of champagne tastes like."

He hefted the manila envelope, turning back to Jim. "This is all rather cloak and dagger, isn't it? I feel like we're a pair of spies. Or drug dealers."

"We're much more dangerous than spies or drug dealers."

"What an alarming thought!"

He had promised to get in touch after the first of the year, but it was January 4th and Jim still hadn't heard anything. He wasn't worried. He knew there was a lot of material to wade through, a lot of facts to check. But he was impatient. He wasn't going to feel safe again until the story was printed.

Two days after the funeral he called Doug's house. He didn't mean to badger his friend but the waiting had immobilized him. He was sitting around his apartment watching C Span, eating bologna and drinking beer, waiting for the phone to ring. There was a question (possibly of some scientific interest) about how long a normal person could survive on bologna and beer, but Jim didn't want to volunteer for that experiment just yet.

And so, despite his best intentions to the contrary, at seven-thirty on the evening of January 6th, he wound up calling Doug Baird.

A male voice answered the phone.

It wasn't Doug, or either one of his two boys. But the voice was familiar.

"Hello," Jim began. "This is Jim Gramble. Is Douglas Baird there? I need to talk to him for a minute."

"Sorry, Mr. Gramble. 'that won't be possible. Your friend is the city's newest homicide victim. Someone cut his throat. Severed every artery in his neck. Hell of a mess. Everything's soaked . . . even this manuscript he was reading. It's nothing but red paste now."

Jim gagged as if he could see the spatters of arterial blood, and smell the coppery stench. He knew what blood smelled like—he remembered Stan Polidakis.

Then with a different kind of shock, he recognized the voice on the other end of the line.

It was Armand Taliafero.

"You know what the only legible words on this soggy red mess are? Jim. And Gramble. You're bad luck for people. Death follows you around, Mr. Gramble. Take my advice—keep moving. Because it's catching up with you fast."

There was a click. Then Jim was listening to a dial tone.

Jim hung up the phone feeling a bitter contempt for himself. He had just killed his friend as surely as if he had held the knife.

Stupidity kills, arrogance kills, ignorance kills.

Why had he gone up against these people in the first place? Why had he put his friend into the line of their fire? What had he imagined might protect either one of them— their stature as journalists? The power of the press? The First Amendment? He wondered if they tortured people before they killed them. If so Jim might have time him- self, as they attached the electrodes to his testicles or heated the poker on his electric stove, to contemplate the power of the press and the sanctity of his First Amendment rights.

He was a fool. A dangerous fool.

And he was in danger himself. Everything had twisted out of control—they had killed Doug just for *reading* the story.

Jim had written it.

They had drowned one copy in blood, but they had to

know there were others. They would come for him now, and torture him for the other copies and kill him as they had killed Alfredo Blasi and Stan Polidakis and Douglas Baird. Someone somewhere had lost their patience; someone's temper had snapped, and Jim had a very good idea who it was.

The thought of Dominic Nosiglia produced the same response that the man's physical presence always did—a gibbering rabbit-panic, a brainless need to run and to keep on running until he dropped. But that would be more foolishness—tearing off without a plan or a direction while bored professional killers lined him in their gunsights.

He walked over to his desk and pulled out the .38 Police Special that he had been unable to use the night they destroyed his computer. He knew he wasn't much of a shot and he might not be able to pull the trigger anyway. But the heft of the gun was still comforting.

He had to think clearly, if he was going to organize an effective vanishing act. He didn't need to pack much. The less he took with him, the better; the longer it took them to figure out he was gone, the more the odds in his favor increased. He could bring a copy of the story, but not the only one. He had to hide a copy here in the apartment. A note with the manuscript could explain that corroborating materials were in Gary's closet.

The only problem was the hiding place itself. The solution had to be rooted in his relationship with someone he trusted, based on some private understanding—a encryption of shared history. So where he hid it depended on whom he hid it for.

Who?—That was the question. Was there anyone he could still trust? Anyone he could bear to put at risk? He couldn't jeopardize the lives of his friends any more. His ex-wife would just laugh at him and tell him to get some therapy. No, there was really only one person in the world he could contact now, only one tough, reliable person who could hold his own against these killers, who was actually involved, however indirectly; only one person who had actually offered to help.

Jim picked up the phone and dialed Tom Jaglom's number.

With Tom's name came the memory of an Easter holiday the boy had spent with Jim and Eleanor. Jim had outdone himself that year, hiding Easter baskets. Before the phone had rung twice, Jim knew the perfect hiding place; and the code to describe it.

The answering machine picked up.

"Hi, this is Tom. I know you want to talk about what's bothering you. But a two-way conversation would just slow you down. So tell me all about it—if I have any brilliant insights, I'll get back to you."

Jim had to smile. He could use some of Tom's brilliant insights right now. A little of his sense of humor wouldn't hurt either; nor would his expert body-guarding skills. But he was happy to get the recording. He didn't want to explain or elaborate.

Suddenly he pushed the plastic buttons down, breaking the connection. You didn't have to be a master spy to know that leaving a message on a tape machine in someone's house was the ultimate in unsecured communications. Anyone could play that tape—anyone at all. A cleaning lady, a cop like Taliafero, even Dominic Nosiglia himself. If Tom's phone was bugged they could trace the call easily. He thought of calling from a booth, but he was caught by a jittery squeeze of cabin fever: he didn't want to hit the street until he absolutely had to. Someone could be out there right now, waiting for him. Was that crazy? He thought of Taliafero's voice on the telephone. No, that wasn't crazy—crazy was being careless and over-confident.

He thought the situation over as calmly as he could. It had to be all right—their 'code' should be unbreakable and even if Tom's line was bugged and the call was traced somehow anyone who was looking for him already knew where he was.

That was the whole problem.

Quickly he punched in the number again, waited for the beep and said, "Tom, this is Jim Gramble. At Christmas you said you wanted to help me. I'm going underground for a while. My life is in danger. I'll be in touch when I can. If anything happens to me there are some papers in my apartment that have to be published. I hid them Easter style, so don't let the Bunny stump you again. Wish me luck."

Now all he had to do was sleep, if he could. He desperately needed rest, but he set the alarm for five A.M. With any luck he could be out on the street, free and clear, by dawn. He fell onto the bed fully dressed and let sleep suck him under.

The two boys were named Lincoln and Jefferson.

They were sixteen years old. They had been stealing cars together for three years and proudly thought of themselves as professionals. They could jimmy a door lock, break open an ignition cylinder and get an engine running in less than ninety seconds, and if a car needed to be broken down to parts, they had their own small garage where they could do the work.

The tragedy of this particular January morning on the upper west side of Manhattan was that these two boys were not just a pair of teen-age felons. They didn't fit the statistical profile. They didn't come from broken homes; they weren't drug addicts. And they weren't stupid—they weren't even underachievers. They were both doing well in school and they had ambitions beyond the criminal.

Lincoln Graves was a gifted poet and a dancer. He had started his own rap group the year before. They worked clubs and parties and were getting a reputation in the 'hood. A couple of record labels were sniffing around, showing careful interest.

Jefferson Carswell was doing college level biology and chemistry with tutors he paid for by stealing cars. He wanted to go into some area of medical research. But what the police referred to as grand theft auto did more than finance his education. It gave him a status with his friends that even his 'bookworm' reputation couldn't damage. More importantly, it allowed both boys to carry on a kind of guerrilla war against rich white America.

It felt like a little revolution every time they dismantled a Lexus or a Cadillac. One of Lincoln's rap songs began, "Hey, hey sucker—whatdyou say? Some pasty-faced motherfucker's walking today."

They'd had some bad experiences with top of the line cars recently, though. The electronic alarm systems were getting more complicated all the time, and you needed a degree in electronic engineering to disarm them. They had decided to go for the older models from solid, dependable makers—Saabs, Volvos, Honda Accords, Isuzu troopers. The money wasn't as good but neither of them had ever spent a night in jail and they didn't want to start now. Neither of them planned to ply this trade much longer.

Everything might have worked out fine for them if they hadn't seen the old Volvo station wagon parked near the corner of 88th Street and West End Avenue. One of their contacts had just been asking them about the rear-end crash resistant seat-backs in Volvos and the two front seats could make the morning worthwhile all by themselves.

They were chatting and singing as they went to work on the door. They felt good. They were young, they were healthy, they were beating the system.

And they had two minutes left to live.

As the boys snapped the door and slid into the Volvo,

Jim Gramble was walking down the fire stairs of his building, jogging through the basement to the service entrance. He had gotten exactly the right amount of sleep. He was refreshed and alert—none of the usual morning grogginess. Fear was better than three cups of coffee; he'd take his home-made adrenaline over store-bought caffeine any time.

He paused at the service entrance, breathing shallowly, as if someone might hear him. They were out there. He knew it. Slowly, millimeter by millimeter, he craned his neck around and peeked into the street. A cold dry wind blew grit into his eyes. The surveillance car was parked twenty feet away, directly between him and the corner. He would have to pass it to reach his car. Had he really imagined they wouldn't be watching the service entrance? What an idiot. In fact, from their position, they could see the front of the building, too, along with his car, parked on West End Avenue. They were perfectly located. They knew their business. But even as he was cursing himself out he noticed that at least one of the men seemed to be dozing. Five A.M. was a sleepy time of day for most people. If he could just—

But all of a sudden the other man was shaking his partner, yelling silently behind closed windows, pointing frantically and lunging for the door.

Jim clutched his gun. They'd seen him. He didn't know how they'd seen him or why they had reacted with such apparent panic, but—

The car doors slammed. Jim heard footfalls and braced himself for another look. He had cover and they didn't— finally the mistakes were falling his way. He could pick them off as they ran. But even as that thought occurred to him he knew that he couldn't fire the gun, that he could never shoot at the men running towards him, or at anyone, ever.

He dropped the revolver and it clattered down the short stairway to the basement, sounding loud enough to wake up the whole neighborhood. He still hadn't glanced into the street and he didn't now. He listened instead.

The footsteps were getting fainter. The men weren't running towards him. He looked out again.

They were gone.

Around the corner, Jefferson Carswell was just touching the ignition wires together when the two men came pounding up the sidewalk, guns drawn, shouting "Stop! Get out of that car! move it! Don't—"

But he never finished his sentence.

Jefferson sparked the ignition on Jim Gramble's Volvo and the bomb wired under the hood went off, mashing him and his friend Lincoln Graves, along with the two Mafia foot-soldiers into a burning, unrecognizable batter of blood and flesh and pulverized bone. A second later, the car's gas tank ripped the rear-end apart and windows shattered and glass rained down on the street

Jim heard the two explosions, felt them hammering his body as if the air had stiffened—hardened like water when you belly flop from the high dive. He was slammed against the far wall of the little stairwell by the first blast. The second one snapped his head against the bricks.

He didn't know what had happened—all he knew was that by some miracle the surveillance on him had broken down. He had to run for it while he could.

Head and body still jangling, he grabbed his suitcase and stumbled up the street. He wanted to be gone before the first cops or paramedics arrived. Hundreds of windows had been blown out by the explosions—glass crunched underfoot. He could hear the roaring of a fire, smell the burning fabric and plastic and metal—and something else. Flesh probably. That sickly sweet tang in the air was the stink of skin on fire.

He turned the corner and stopped so suddenly he almost fell forward over his own feet. His old Volvo was a red storm of flame, lighting the street with a flickering lurid glare. It was a scene out of Ulster or Beirut. It didn't belong on West End Avenue.

Jim could hear the ambulances and police cars now, faintly, coming from all directions. He couldn't think—all words and ideas and plans had been smashed out of his mind, torched in the street.

All he could do was run.

So he did, stumbling across the avenue, toward Broadway, away from the garish death-light of the flaming car and the rising shriek of sirens.

12

For the next month, Tom visited the cemetery on Long Island every day. He commuted, leaving the city in the morning, returning in the afternoon, with rush hour traffic stalled on the other side of the road both ways. It seemed appropriate to him: he was in his own world, opposite to everyone.

He told Amy that he talked to his mother, but he didn't talk to anyone else. He kept his answering machine on to avoid phone calls, and ignored all of them except one. Jim Gramble's chilling and cryptic message galvanized him briefly. But there was no answer at Jim's apartment, the news item the next day about the car-bombing in front of Jim's building confirmed Tom's fears. He almost went over to look for the papers. At any other time he would have, despite Jim's apparent escape and his instructions to wait. But Tom didn't have the energy to start poking around in someone else's life right now.

His own was more than he could handle.

There was a reading of his mother's will, but he didn't attend. The lawyers sent him a note about bequests and

probate, but he never even read it. Amy understood his grieving silences and his emotional withdrawal, but she knew they
weren't helping and they made her mad.

One day in February she shouted at him, "If I die, will
you talk to me, too?" And he had talked then, a little.

Amy's sunny life, so devoid of tragedy or drama (Her
large family was basically happy, and she hadn't even lost a
grandparent yet) left her ill-equipped to help Tom at this
moment and both of them knew it. He needed someone
who could say "I know how you feel" and mean it. Amy
had no idea how he felt. That was what made her think of
Jake Gritzky. Jake would understand this loss—his life had
been defined by loss for more than twenty years. Tom's
school-work was disintegrating anyway, so there was no
academic reason to stay in the city.

She told him to visit Jake.

It was a good idea. Tom wound up staying Nantucket
for almost three weeks. It was good for Jake, too—Tom suddenly had a way to understand at least a part of Jake's experience: he was suffering from his own case of survivor guilt.

"I should have been on that plane," he said one night.
They were shooting pool. The Chicken Box was half-empty
and peaceful. Everyone knew everyone else, everyone was
drunk. The band was goofing around, playing a few last
requests and letting customers sit in as they started packing up. It felt like the tail end of a blue-collar wedding
reception. Jake was clearing the table as they spoke.

"Fourteen ball, corner pocket. Remember what Amy
said to me when we were talking about this stuff, Tommy?
Six ball in the side. I was lucky, she said. Eleven ball, left
corner."

"No way!"

"Watch and learn, sonny." Jake sank the shot, walked
around the table, chalking his cue. "Nine in the side. Well,
you're one of the lucky ones now. How does it feel?"

"It feels like I cheated. It feels like I don't belong. It feels like shit."

Jake laughed. "Weird stuff, luck."

They kept coming back to the subject. After a silent dinner at The Brotherhood, which Jake still patronized despite what he felt was a gradual decline in quality (To Jake, the whole world was suffering a gradual decline in quality), it came up again.

"So . . . this is what you felt after the war?"

"Close enough.'

"How do you stop feeling it?"

"You don't."

"Then how did you manage to—

"Everybody manages a different way, Tommy. My way wouldn't help you. After the war I was alone. You're not alone. You've got Amy. And your Dad's alive. He's gonna need you. That's a good reason to stick it out."

"I know. I just wish they'd let me see him."

He called the hospital every day and always got the same soothing, anodyne responses from the doctors there. His Dad was doing fine, was as strong as a horse but required several more operations and couldn't have visitors yet. When Tom lost his patience they sympathized in a kindly, institutional way that just made him angrier.

But it was no use. He had to wait.

Meanwhile, it seemed that death followed him everywhere: during the second week of his visit, his father's golden retriever, Buster, was run over and killed on the Madequecham Road. Tom had loved Buster, too, and this extra death was just one thing too many. He cried as he had cried at the funeral. Jake left him alone then, but afterwards he helped. Not with words but with rituals. They cremated the body and scattered the ashes over Sesacacha Pond.

Tom went back to the city a few days later, but he no

longer visited his mother's grave. "It was getting a little weird," was the extent of his explanation to Amy, but it was enough— the visits had started to strike her as weird weeks before.

Finally, toward the end of February, they had a count-down. Tom's father would be ready for visitors in 10 days. Tom organized their trip to Des Moines with the Secret Service and started to relax. He spent a week of all-nighters, reading textbooks and writing term-papers. He knew Dr. Jerome was right: good grades would cheer up his Dad.

He took Amy out to the movies and out to dinner and they started talking again. They talked about his mother and the absurd small details that rose up to ambush him out of the innocent sunny afternoons: the evening bike rides they took through Central Park in the springtime when he was little; watching her make a delicious soup from some chopped raw vegetables and a can of peeled tomatoes. He talked about the morning run she took ev-ery day of her life, no matter where she was, at home or on the campaign trail; the pile of New Yorker magazines she never caught up with. But most of all he tried to describe the way she could simultaneously mock, summarize and clarify his confused emotions, often at a tangent to what he was feeling so that he didn't quite understand what she meant for a while. Once, in high school, he had com-plained that his beautiful date's face got ugly when a sad movie made her cry. His Mom had said, "I know—dream girls don't go to the bathroom."

Tom had just stared at her; but he figured it out even-tually.

Amy laughed when she heard that story, from recog-nition but also from relief. Tom was himself again, scarred but surviving.

The day they left for Des Moines it became clear that someone at the hospital had leaked the news. Everyone knew the President was having his first visitor and there were reporters in front of Tom's apartment building, at the 61st Street heliport—they even rushed the tarmac at Kennedy, and some of them got close enough to the plane to shout questions, the same ones Tom had been hearing all morning—"How does it feel?" they wanted to know. They wanted a tidy sound-bite but he didn't have one for them. In fact he was nervous. He knew he looked haggard and he didn't want his worry to show so obviously on his face. He wasn't sure what he was going to say to his Dad, or how to begin.

Amy said, "Don't worry, your Dad's good at making things easy for people."

But would he still be? And did Tom even want that? Making things easy for a grieving son shouldn't be his job right now. Tom should be the one making things easier. The potential reversal of roles was scary. Would his Dad be reduced to some sort of drooling second childhood by the tubes and monitors and bossy nurses? Would he have bed-pans? Or would they give him those giant diapers to wear? Tom didn't think he could endure the sight of his father in a giant diaper.

Still the fact that he was alive and ready for visitors kept bobbing up to the surface, buoyant as a Ping-Pong ball. The waiting was over. That was the main thing Tom felt, a simple physical relief, the way he felt when a cramp relaxed or the aspirin started pushing back the headache.

Finally, the waiting was over.

The Des Moines airport was crowded with reporters, but Tom saw them only from the air, as the helicopter lifted off and banked over the sprawling terminal building. To the East behind them, the heavy clouds were still threatening snow, but they were flying toward bright blue sky to the West. Directly above them the sunlight was pouring through the clouds in great vertical beams. It was satisfyingly dramatic and Tom was content to turn his brain off and watch it like a movie. Amy's hand was resting on his thigh.

Ira Heller was sitting shot-gun up front. He turned around and said, "You're a celebrity, kid. *People* Magazine wants to put you on their cover. What do you think of that?"

Tom sighed. "I'd prefer not to think of that right now, Ira."

They landed on the roof of the hospital. Dr. Jerome strode under the rotors without ducking, which Tom noticed with an appreciation he had learned from Jake Gritzky who was always irked by the sight of people hunching irrationally under helicopter blades revolving at least two feet over their heads.

The Doctor shook hands with Tom, helped Amy down from the helicopter and walked across the gusty roof to the door leading downstairs at the far side. No one bothered to speak above the chopper engines and the wind.

Inside, Dr. Jerome turned to Tom. "I know this is a big day for you. It's a big day for your Dad as well. He's been through fifteen different surgical operations since you saw him last—orthopedic surgery, brain surgery, plastic surgery, joint surgery . . . not to mention burn treatments, skin grafts and a physical rehab program that makes Marine boot camp look like Disney World." They were walking downstairs. They pushed through a door into the fifth floor corridor. "What I'm trying to say," the Doctor continued, "Is go slowly in there. Take it easy at first. Don't expect too much, don't demand too much. Let him lead the way."

They had reached a set of doors marked **SECURITY AREA, AUTHORIZED PERSONNEL ONLY**.

Dr. Jerome turned to Amy. "I'm sorry, my dear . . . but this has to be family only. At least until things stabilize a bit more. Mr. Heller has arranged rooms for you at the Des Moines Hotel. Perhaps you could organize you visit and start unpacking while Tom is with his father?"

"Sure, I guess—okay. Tom, will you—

"I'll be fine."

Amy kissed him, and hugged him a little longer than was necessary, then walked away with Heller.

"You're on your own now, Tom," the Doctor said. "It's the third door down on your left."

Tom nodded and pushed through into the corridor beyond. His sneakers squeaked on the waxed linoleum as he walked.

Nothing could have prepared him for what he was going to see in his father's hospital room. It was too horrible, too insane—the impossible, smiling blandly, mundane as Monday morning traffic, but all the worse because of that, a thousand times worse without the Hollywood thunderstorm and the spooky music.

When he opened the door to the hospital room, his years of training took over. A close observer—and there were several that morning—could have seen nothing but a tiny tremor in the muscles of Tom's face, an instant's hesitation in his stride, easily attributable to the first sight, after months of waiting and uncertainty, of a badly battered but much-loved father.

But those first few seconds were the most difficult ones of Tom's life because in one look, in one instant, he knew absolutely—as only a son could know it—that the man sitting up in the hospital bed grinning at him was not his father.

This man was a stranger. Tom didn't know how it had been done, or who could have done it or why, but somehow, lunatic and unthinkable as it seemed, The President of the United States had been replaced by an impostor.

PART TWO: SPIES

13

FROM TOM JAGLOM'S JOURNAL:

3/10/98

My Dad is dead.

There's some stranger in his hospital bed pretending to be him and that means they murdered him, someone killed my Dad and I want to scream and cry I'm crying now while I'm writing this, I can't even read my own handwriting. I don't care I just want to tell everyone he's gone, they took my Dad away from me, but I can't do that. I can't go to the newspapers. I can't do anything.

I feel like I'm losing my mind. Maybe I am. Isn't this what being crazy is supposed to be like—when you can't believe the evidence of your senses, when impossible things are happening and no one sees them except you?

But I knew him. I knew my Dad. None of these other people really knew him. So I'm the one they have to fool. They must be watching me every second I'm with him, to see if it's working.

I remember thinking as I walked into the hospital room, it was like an alarm going off in my head—if they even suspect you know the truth, they'll kill you. This is a conspiracy and the conspirators are all around you, watching you at this very moment, studying your responses.

Your life depends on the sincerity of your smile.

So I can't even grieve. I want him to have a funeral. My Mom got a funeral at least. I want a grave to visit. I want a will to be read, I want some of his stuff to keep. That old dufflecoat that he could never bear to part with—he said he'd leave me that. He was only kidding around but I want it now. It still smells like him, it's still part of him.

And he was more than just my Dad. I want to see the sorrow and the outrage of the whole country and the whole world rising up at his death. It should be like the Kennedy assassination. People loved him as much as they loved Kennedy. Everyone would remember where they were when they first heard the news, it would mark everyone's life forever.

It should. There should be news specials and a State funeral and every flag in America at half-mast. There should be days of mourning and candle-light vigils and I know all the publicity would make things worse but it would help, too. It would be everybody's tragedy, and I'd resent that, but at least I wouldn't be alone.

Because right now I am totally alone.

I feel like a guy on Death Row when the cell door slams shut. I feel like a little kid lost in an airport. I feel like I'm dying myself and my illness puts me in another world from all the healthy commiserating friends who aren't being eaten from the inside, who will be alive next month to talk about the tragedy of it all.

That's why I have to write this stuff down.

I can't say it, I can't show it, but it has to come out somehow. I have to stay in control, and even more important, I have to keep an accurate record. I need to document the details. Details are the heart of the game they're playing and details are going to be their downfall. I see the details. I put the details together and they add up, they become significant.

They become evidence, they become proof.

So I have to explain exactly what happened today.

It began with the hug. The hug is a perfect example— they never taught this guy how my Dad actually hugged me. They probably never noticed. They probably don't put much store by hugs anyway. This guy put his arms around me and he grabbed his left wrist with his right hand, so that he was touching himself more than me. Unemotional people hug like that; cold fish hug like that. But my Dad never did, ever. And that's not the kind of thing that's changed by a plane crash.

It was just wrong. It was so wrong, I started crying. I had the urge to twist away but I knew this was the most important moment of my life.

This was the crisis I had spent my life preparing for. This was my first, my best—maybe my only—chance to convince them, to save my own life, to avenge my father's death, to beat them.

To win.

But I didn't have the strength. I couldn't do it. I needed a real embrace, I needed to feel my real father's fingers pressed against my back, I needed to be with him, to talk about everything, to talk about Mom, he could help me, together we could find some way to go on living without her.

But it's hopeless. That's what death is. Hopelessness. When people die hope dies with them.

But the worst part was that I was going to have to talk about Mom with this guy. I had to.

Private things I'd have trouble saying to Amy I was going

to have to say to him, because if I didn't, they'd know instantly that something was wrong.

That thought made me angry, and the anger got me through. It clarified things and I could see that the emotions I didn't want to share were really my best weapon— my only weapon, at that moment. They were my only way to survive this first encounter and start planning my counter-attack.

So I closed my eyes, hugged the guy tighter, and said "I miss Mom so much."

"Me too, son."

But My Dad wouldn't have said anything at that moment—and he never called me 'son'. I wonder whose idea that was.

It was peculiar though—the guy actually wound up saying some pretty smart things to me: that we have to keep remembering her even if it hurts, because that's how people who have died keep a living presence in the world. And he said, "You're angry and you have a right to be angry. Scream. Break something—you'll feel better."

He really surprised me with that one. And I have to admit, they did a good job. They briefed the guy thoroughly. I came away from that first encounter respecting my enemy. The plastic surgery is state-of-the-art. He must have looked a little like my Dad to begin with. He even sounds right: the dry timbre of the voice, the staccato rhythms . . . It was like watching yourself lip-synch in the bathroom mirror—for a couple of seconds at a time you almost believe it.

Rich Little did a perfect impression of my Dad—right down to the hand gestures and the glottal stops. He fooled Lamar Cram, he fooled Ted Koppel, he even fooled my Mom once, when the TV was on and she was in the next room. I was with her at that moment. He didn't fool me.

Not for one second.

And neither did this guy—he wasn't even as good as Rich Little. He wouldn't have fooled my Mom. She would have

Wait a second.

Hold it.

Jesus Christ, my hand is shaking again.

This makes sense:

My Mom would have known this guy is a fake.

She died when Air Force One went down. Was that part of the plan? In the confusion of the wreckage they could remove all liabilities with no questions asked, do what had to be done with the perfect cover story. But that would mean the Secret Service was involved, they would have to be if

Oh God. Ira Heller.

He wasn't on the plane. He took the other flight.

He knew.

That phone call on New Year's Eve. He was so insistent I be with my Dad. Of course—if both my Mom and I were dead there would be no one left who could see through the deception. I mean—who else was there? Who else would have that visceral, instinctive knowledge of him? Friends might suspect for a moment or two, but without that basic animal response

Oh, Jesus Christ, my head is splitting.

This is nuts, this is just crazy.

And the craziest part is it all fits, Everything is connected—even things I didn't notice or didn't think were important.

Buster, for instance.

My Dad's dog, Buster.

Buster, who was run over on the Madequecham Road just three weeks ago. Buster, who would have known in the same way I did, in more ways than I did, that this guy is a phony. I bet he doesn't smell right, for one thing. You can't fake that. Whoever these conspirators are and whatever they're planning with this impersonation, they can't afford to have their plans wrecked by a growling dog.

That meant one more detail to manage and they did it in their usual way.

Murder is easy. Death is a guarantee.

But I'm still alive. That means they think they're fooling me. But I'm fooling them and that means I'm winning, at least for now. I know; and they don't know it. I have that advantage over them. It isn't much.

But it's a start.

3/11/98

I did some research today. I went to the main branch of the Des Moines public library and spent five hours there working. I told Heller I had stuff to do for school. "Dad would be heartbroken if I flunked out of college because of all this," I said, and I reminded him of my Dad's warning—that only a death in the family was a good excuse . . . *your own.* "Forget a note from the Doctor. I want to see a death certificate." And he was only half joking—kidding on the square, that's what he used to call it. It was interesting to study Heller's face when I said that—to see the little predatory squint of sharpened attention. This was something he could use. This was the reason I was worth keeping alive. It will be interesting to see if that phrase turns up in a press conference some time.

Anyway, the library is an ancient looking stone pile that still uses card catalogues. That's important. I didn't want anything recorded on a computer. I didn't even want to ask the librarian for help.

This little research trip had to be private.

I was looking for some historical evidence for the idea of using doubles and impostors. And I found quite a lot.

The Pharohs did it; Roman Emperors did it. The Borgias did it. Mussolini and John Gotti did it.

In general it was done for protection, the double serving as a decoy. It was done for convenience sometimes also—if a dignitary needed to be in two places at once in the millennia before television and the internet, when you could get away with stuff like that.

I didn't dig up any historical precedent for exactly what's happening right now, but it's the next logical step, given the advances in medical technology in the last fifty years. People routinely go into the plastic surgeon's office and ask for Michelle Pfeiffer's cheek bones or Angelina Jolie's lips. If you had a guy with a basic resemblance there's no reason why it couldn't be done. But I keep coming back to the question of why? What horrible thing could my Dad have been involved with that required such a drastic cover-up? And who? Who could summon the resources to accomplish a project of this magnitude? I have the find those answers without causing any suspicions, somehow. I don't know how I'm going to do that, but I know I can't do it alone.

I have to tell Amy. I need her on my side. But it's dangerous. First of all, she might not believe me and if I can't convince her she'll become a threat and I have no idea how I could handle that. I'd be at her mercy. If she thought I was crazy, she'd have no choice but to turn me in.

But if she believes me, then she's in as much danger as I am. I don't want to put her in jeopardy but I need her. I need to convince and her, I need to protect her, I need to teach her how to protect herself.

And I need to do it soon.

Later

They're letting me visit with "Dad" tomorrow fitting me in between physical therapy sessions. I have to use the time. I have to trick some piece of evidence from him, something I can use to convince Amy. There are so many ways I could trip him up; so many questions I could ask that he couldn't answer, so many old family jokes that would mystify him, so many references he wouldn't get.

It would be easy. It would be fun.

It would also be suicidally stupid. Pulling his mask off with questions he can't answer reveals *me*, not him. Any overt move gives me away. Somehow I have to make him screw up without arousing anyone's suspicions.

But how?

First of all: it has to seem inadvertent. I have to put his credibility in peril in a way I wouldn't even be aware of myself, if I didn't know the truth. I have to make some statement, ask some question that forces him to gamble with his ignorance.

They must be waiting for a moment like that. They have to know that those moments will come. However well-trained and comprehensively briefed the guy is, there's no way he can be fully prepared for this performance. He can't know everything about us and so he can't escape the need to improvise.

All I have to do is make him guess; and then convince him that his guess was right.

3/12

"You know, Dad," I said, "I was thinking last night about the money we buried in Central Park, when we were pretending the pirates were chasing us to get their treasure back. How old was I then? Nine or ten?"

"Something like that," he said.

"There's a lot of money stashed away around the Park," I went on. "Unless the pirates found it."

He nodded cautiously. This was the moment he had been dreading. I pushed on, apparently oblivious to his tension. "It sure seemed like a lot of money back then," I said.

I let the silence gather between us. He had to commit now: he had to say something about that day and he knew it. But I was impressed with the calm assurance in his voice. He didn't even hesitate.

The guy was good.

"Well," he said, "That's part of the sadness of growing up. Everything seems smaller when you look back on it. You know . . . 10 dollars probably seemed like a thousand to you then. Of course, inflation hasn't helped matters any."

I almost had him, but that last comment was still open to interpretation. So I had to continue . . . in a suitably aimless and casual way. Sweet little Tommy Jaglom, sharing a nostalgic moment with his dear old Dad.

"I wonder what all that money put together would buy right now."

"Hmmm . . . let me see . . ."

He was stalling for time, hoping I'd answer my own question and let him off the hook. So I did:

"What do you think, maybe one good meal at The Russian Tea Room?"

He nodded, "Just about . . . if you skip the White Russians and the champagne."

"Maybe I'll dig it up sometime, and take you out to dinner."

"Sounds great. I'll buy the champagne. We'll drink a toast to those dim-witted pirates."

A nice touch at the end, there—just the kind of thing my Dad would have said. I gave him a big hug before I left a few minutes later and I'm sure he thought he had pulled off his first major coup, venturing into the private life of my family and emerging with more confidence and credibility than ever.

As for me, I could barely contain a childish desire to leap up, jab my fist into the air and shout "Yes!"

I was jubilant, I was delighted with myself.

I had won my first battle. It was a small one but it wasn't trivial. I set my trap and he blundered right into it. He gave himself away, as blatantly as if he'd shown me the before and after photographs of his plastic surgery.

And he doesn't even know it.

3/13

I told Amy this morning.

We took a long walk through downtown Des Moines. It was snowing hard and the drab streets were empty. We had a Secret Service tail but we managed to keep him out of earshot. I was trying to decide how to begin, when she did it for me.

"What's wrong, Tom? What's happening? You've been acting so strange for the last couple of days."

I nodded—of course she had sensed something when no one else had.

That was my way in.

"Ira Heller thinks I'm fine," I said. "Everyone is impressed by how healthy and resilient I am."

She looked at me with a kind of annoyed, questioning squint. "But I know you. They don't."

"Exactly. That's exactly my point."

"I don't understand."

I put my arm around her while we waited for a light to change. "Who in the world knows my Dad as well as I do?"

"His parents?"

"They're dead."

"Brothers? Sisters?"

"He was an only child. There was just my Mom . . . and maybe his dog. And me. But Mom and Buster are dead now, too. I'm the sole living authority on my father's identity."

"Well, Okay, but—"

"Think about your own Dad. If he . . . wasn't himself, for some reason, you'd know, wouldn't you?"

"Sure."

"But you have sisters—you could talk it over with them, you could compare notes. I don't have that option."

"Is something wrong with your Dad?"

"Everything's wrong with him."

"Tom . . . he's been in a terrible accident. He was in intensive care for weeks, he had all those operations . . . he's not going to be his old self for quite a while. I mean, you have to expect that."

I stopped walking and turned on her, drilled it into her eyes.

"It's not him, Amy."

"What? I don't, I mean—how—?"

"That's not my father in there. Just—just listen to me for a minute."

I told her everything, all the wrong notes, starting with the bogus hug and ending with yesterday's conversation. I described it pretty much as it happened and let her make the logical response.

"I don't see how that proves anything, one way or the other."

I told myself, go slow. Take it easy. Breathe.

We walked on a few steps before I answered her. "My Dad was an eccentric person. He was not like other people, especially about money. When I look back on my childhood, that afternoon burying treasure seems like one of the strangest

days of my life. We buried treasure, Amy. We didn't stuff coffee cans with amounts that would wow an eight year old kid.
My Dad wasn't interested in the most cost-effective way to
impress me. He was interested in verisimilitude."

I had her interest now. "How much did you bury?"

"He had a roll of hundred dollar bills. They were his
favorite item of currency. He liked to give them away. 'Stok-
ing people's fires,' that's the way he put it. He gave homeless people hundred dollar bills. We were walking on Broadway one night and he gave one to a hooker who looked exhausted. He said "Take the night off." A friend of mine was
waiting tables at P.J. Clark's. My Dad went in for dinner and
gave him a hundred dollar tip. That was his style. Anyway . . .
we buried five cans that day. There was five or six hundred
dollars in each can. It comes out to something like three
thousand dollars, Amy. That would buy a lot more than one
meal at the Russian Tea Room."

We walked along. I helped her over a huge lake of
slush at a curb.

"He might not have remembered . . . ."

"That's not something you remember, Amy. That's
something you know. That's who you are."

We turned a corner and the wind was in our faces. The
snow sparkled on her hair. She obviously had no idea what
to say. I was happy with the silence; I let it work for me.

Three blocks later, she said, "Tom, you're exhausted.
The stress of all this has been unbelievable. You could be—"

"Hallucinating?"

"No but . . . It's like some fantastic science fiction movie,
it's like *The Invasion of The Body Snatchers*—"

"That's what it feels like."

"So he's . . . a pod person?"

"Amy, please. This isn't science fiction. I'm not hallucinating. I spent most of yesterday in the library research-
ing this. People have used doubles for thousands of years.

Then purpose is different here. Then scale is bigger. But that's all. Amy, listen to me. That man in there is an actor. He's been brilliantly coached, he's had plastic surgery, and he's the front man for some kind of conspiracy that—"

She looked away. "I think I prefer the pod person theory."

Go slow. Back it up. Breathe.

"My Dad was about to reverse himself on some major policy—that's why he was flying to Los Angeles. There was going to be a press conference New Year's Day. He told me that before he died. He knew the announcement would be a calamity of some kind. He thought it might end his career. Someone else knew what he was planning. And they weren't going to let it happen."

"Tom—"

"Think back to Christmas Day, when Jim Gramble showed up after breakfast. He had some kind of argument with my Dad. Whatever was going on, Jim had figured it out. He knew. That's why he was there. On the way out he said, 'Turn on the air conditioning and build a fire—roast some god damn marshmallows.' Do you remember that?"

"I remember, but I never understood what he meant."

"Jim and my Dad went to high school together. Once on a really hot day in August when my Grandparents were away, Dad turned the air-conditioning in the Beekman Place apartment on full force until it was freezing cold inside. Then they built a fire and roasted marshmallows while the whole city was sweltering around them. He invited Jim over to the White House for dinner last summer and did it again. As a kind of prank. For old times' sake. He used to kid around about it—hoping the Republicans never got their hands on the White House electric bill."

"So . . . Jim thought that was a little strange?"

"My Dad *was* a little strange . . . there's no doubt about it.

But Jim told me later—he said he thought the whole business revealed something about my Dad. He was so rich he was able to, I don't know . . . live in his own world? In his own head. Jim often felt he was sort of . . . out of touch. In an attractive way, and yet . . ."

"Strange."

"Strange. Anyway, I asked Dad about that last argument with Jim at Christmas. He didn't tell me any details, but he said one thing that seems important now. It was the last conversation we ever had. Dad said . . .'Jim made me doubt things.' I asked him, 'Which things?' and he said, 'Everything.' He seemed old to me at that moment. Sad and lonely. As if he'd failed in his life, as if he hadn't really accomplished anything. The last thing he said was 'It's time to make some changes.' But he never got a chance to do that."

Amy stared at me. "Is this really happening?"

"It's already happened. I know it's incredible but that's their best defense. Can you imagine me going to the FBI and saying this stuff? They'd lock me away, if Heller's goons didn't kill me first."

"Heller?"

"He's part of it. He has to be. The day of the crash he did everything but actually put a gun at my head to get me on that plane. And he took a different flight. As you pointed out."

"You said he was just lucky."

"That was a long time ago."

She took my arm. I could see her thinking and I knew I'd done the right thing. I needed her particular unflinching intelligence focused on this problem.

"Why hasn't he tried to kill you since then?" she asked.

"I've wondered about that. There's a lot of possible reasons. For one thing, I'm not that easy to kill, and a slip-up could be disastrous for them. But I also think they're cocky. They like the idea that they've fooled me. I mean . . . if they can fool me they can fool anyone. And I sort of become the spokesman for them. I'm their final seal of approval. That's what they were hoping for, and it's too late to change their minds now. I'm getting too famous. *Time* and *Newsweek* and *Us* and *People* and *Today* and *Good Morning America* and Oprah and everyone else have been calling and asking for interviews. Heller's advice is—talk to the media. 'Reassure the country'. Thoughtful of him, don't you think?"

"Tom—"

"What?"

"It just occurs to me . . . they'd be silly to kill you now, anyway. It would be much better to interrogate you. Or hypnotize you or something, and find out what their mistakes were. They could fine-tune his performance to perfection if they had you drugged up somewhere critiquing it."

I shuddered. She was right. But I was becoming a public figure. My disappearance now would complicate things for them. I had been taken yet; that meant I probably wouldn't be. Not for a while anyway. Not unless I made a mistake.

We kicked through the snow. "So . . . you believe me a little bit?"

"That's like being a little bit pregnant, Tom."

"Amy . . . ."

She stopped walking and took both my hands.

"Yes. I believe you. I love you. I want to help."

It was amazing. The relief was so strong I just kind of fell into her arms. I wasn't sure I could stand by myself. After a few seconds I got my legs back under me and kissed her neck.

"Thank you," I said.

But she was all business.

"What can we do now?"

"There are a few things. But we don't have much time and we have to be careful. We can't fool them forever. The most important thing is to find Jim Gramble. He has the rest of the story. I know how. He knows why. Together we can stop them."

"If he's still alive."

A fresh gust of damp, freezing wind cut through my coat. It was true. He might be dead—in fact it would be a miracle if he wasn't. But it's pointless to think that way.

I said, "We have to assume he's alive. It gives us something to do. There are some papers hidden in his apartment—Easter Bunny style, he said on the answering machine."

"Do you know what he meant?"

I shrugged. "I have no idea."

We had walked past the hospital now. Amy seemed more and more subdued—bleak and colorless, like the city streets around us.

"What?" I said.

"It just seems so hopeless. Any move we make will give us away and there's just us. Just you, really. I'm not going to be much help and—"

"Don't say that. You're going to be a huge help. If I get caught you may have to fight them without me."

"I don't even want to think about that."

"Well . . . it's not strictly true, anyway. We'll have Jim on our side—if we can find him . . . and Jake."

Amy smiled. "Now that makes me feel better! Oh, Tom—he'll love this! He loves conspiracies. This will be Heaven for him."

"It's true. And I'll tell you the first thing he'd say: you need some training. I need to get you comfortable and accurate with hand-guns. We can use the Secret Service range in Brooklyn."

"Tom—"

"It's not even a question, Amy. You have to be able to defend yourself."

"But won't they be suspicious if—"

"No way. I've talked to Heller about this before. He thinks every woman in New York City should be competent with guns. If we act suspiciously, they'll get suspicious. So we won't act suspiciously. I'll get permission from Heller and we'll just do it. That incident in the Park gives us more than enough justification."

"I hate this."

"Me too."

"I just wish . . ."

"We can't go back. We have to go forward. But sometimes having no choice makes things easier."

We talked for a long time. I don't know if anything I said really helped, but she seemed to pull herself together. I know she's feeling daunted. She's a practical person and the odds against us are so high that any self-respecting bookie would just laugh.

But it's us now, just as she said. We can face it together. Together, we might even win.

3/15/98

I shouldn't be keeping this journal—that's what Jake would say. It's a liability. It's potential evidence against me . . . and Amy. But I have to do it. I think best with a pen in my hand; it connects to some essential nerve in my brain.

This book itself, blue cover, spiral-bound, five-by-seven-inch, college ruled, is small enough to carry with me, easy enough to tuck away in the cut-out center of some larger book; my World Atlas, maybe. It's outdated now in any case with its maps of the Soviet Union and Yugoslavia; I've been meaning to buy a new one for years. Now at least I'll be able to put it to good use.

Tomorrow we head back to New York, back to school, back to our 'normal' lives. Any plan we make has to be woven into those routines. My first thought was to snoop in the White House itself, in my Dad's office and our living quarters. I thought I might find papers or memos, or some other incriminating material. Hard evidence. I have the access, and I think I could pull it off. But the risks are too great. There's no way I could ever get into the Oval Office alone now. Besides, this isn't a movie. The bad guys don't leave incriminating documents around for the intrepid hero to find. All I'd do is jeopardize our one slim advantage, for nothing.

3/18/93

A guy from People Magazine cornered me in a restaurant bathroom yesterday. He stood at the next urinal and said, "I'm prepared to offer you a hundred thousand dollars for an exclusive interview."

"You know," I said, "It's scary, but if I was broke, if I desperately needed money for gambling debts or a liver transplant operation, I might actually think about taking you up on your offer. What a despicable little rat! I make myself sick sometimes."

He didn't quite get the message.

"Does that mean 'Yes' or 'No?'"

"This is really boring, but that makes sense. Your magazine specializes in telling the boring stuff about interesting people."

"We have millions of readers and they think it's the interesting stuff."

"That some Nobel Prize winner does needlepoint? That some great film director lets his dog eat at the table? Give me a break."

"We're off the point here, Mr. Jaglom. The point is— do you want to be on the cover of the most popular magazine in America? If you want, we can get that cute girlfriend of yours up there next to you. What do you say?"

I walked over to the sink and washed my hands. He didn't get the symbolism.

"Look," I said. "I'm rich. My family is one of the twenty richest families in America. My Dad once considered buying your magazine just so he could have the pleasure of closing it down. His accountants talked him out of it, which I think is a real shame."

"Now, Mr. Jaglom—you don't have to—"

"Listen to me. I could never, ever, be desperate or hopeless enough to cooperate with your magazine. If you keep bothering me I'll sic the Secret Service on you. And in case you were still wondering—that's a 'no'."

There's not much satisfaction in a conversation like that. I ventilated some anger but it didn't do any good. I bet I didn't even really discourage the guy and there are dozens more just like him. It was probably a mistake to talk to him at all, now that I think about it. In effect I gave the guy an interview.

And he was back on the street in front of my apartment today. I went down stairs and put him in a simple wrist lock that forced him to his knees. I said, "If you move in any direction but down, any way but the way I'm pushing you, your wrist will break. Can you feel that? Wiggle a little bit. Try to move left or right." He did, but of course he stopped, grimacing in pain. "OK—that's your situation with me. Any move you make is going to hurt you. Understand?" He nodded and I released his wrist. I looked him in the eye as he straightened up and said slowly, as if to a dog, "Go away."

He took off running.

I heard someone clapping—Heller was standing across the street, grinning in that snide, twisted way of his. He crossed over against the light with the effortless dignity of a life-time jaywalker.

"Nice work, kid—you're the only person I know who can

beat the crap out of someone without even fighting them."

"Musashi says, 'The greatest warrior isn't the one who wins a thousand battles; it's the one who wins a thousand battles without fighting them.'"

Heller grunted. He's too practical for these little gems of samurai wisdom. "Sounds good," he said. "But I bet he had to kick a lot of ass anyway."

This was the opening I'd been waiting for. I told him I'd been thinking about the attack in Central Park and that I wanted to start training Amy in small arms. He agreed instantly and promised to set up some time for us at the Brooklyn firing range.

It was that easy.

3/20

I'm teaching Amy just the way Jake taught me—saying so many of the things he told me so long ago. A lot of talk about guns on the subway ride. She's managed to absorb most of the media's misinformation from watching movies and TV over the last decade. She asked if I was going to train her with "one of those 9mm semi-automatic assault rifles."

I blew out a breath, took her hand and began her education, explaining that there's no such thing as a 'semi-automatic' weapon. It's a meaningless phrase. Assault weapons are fully automatic: they keep spraying rounds as long as you press the trigger. She was talking about auto-loaders—guns where you have to squeeze the trigger for each shot, although the gun pumps the next round into the chamber for you. Anyway, the 9mm is wildly overrated, at least for our purposes. It's a sharp, narrow little bullet designed for penetration—for firing through walls and car doors.

Jake showed me a police video once—two cops pouring gunfire from their 9mm pistols into some rampaging drug addict. They must have shot three or four magazines into the guy, forty rounds at least, and he kept coming at them. They finally dropped him right at their feet, after a thirty-foot charge.

Part of the problem was the cops had no idea how to shoot. If they had picked a spot—head or neck, say—and been able to group their shots, they could have done much better. But the 9mm just doesn't have the stopping power they needed.

"What does that mean?" Amy asked. "I hear people say that all the time—'stopping power.'"

"The kind of gun you're going to be using—the .45 ACP . . . it's like a big hand, pushing against someone. It fires a hollow-point round that can take a running 250-pound man and just knock him backward—blow him off his feet. It keeps him away from you. That's the important thing."

"This is horrible."

"Yeah. So is that 250-pound man if he catches you."

She waited until the next station before she spoke again; three ladies carrying big shopping bags sat down across from us, smiling. We obviously made a very nice couple. Amy sighed.

"When we started seeing each other, my big fear was that I'd get sucked up into your father's world somehow. Those Secret Service guys following us all the time . . . It was so . . . I don't know—so grim. So unlike you. And now I just—"

"We're both in it now, Amy."

"I know, but—"

"All we can do is try to get out of it alive."

We rode along in silence for a while—as much silence as you can find in the pounding racket of an IND train lurching through the New York subway system. We were jolted against each other, jolted apart.

She took my arm. "I chose you," she said, "so I guess I chose this."

"Thanks, but you didn't—no one would choose this. You were drafted. And now you're on your way to boot camp."

I pressed my hand against hers as we rumbled through the dark, that one sentence running through my head again and again; the simple, unambiguous truth, like a caress.

Three words—"I chose you."

I knew it, but knowing it is a very pale and flimsy thing compared to hearing it, compared to her voice, saying the words.

So I found myself shouting over the clatter of the train. "I love you."

"I love you," she shouted right back.

And the three ladies beamed at each other, pleased to see a flicker of romance amid the grime and the graffiti. We got off the train two stops later and strolled away arm in arm, storybook lovers in the mild spring air, to study the techniques of killing efficiently with a Colt .45 Automatic Caliber Pistol.

Later

This is the standard lecture:

The person teaching you is the Range Master. In this case me. The Range Master must be treated with instant, absolute obedience. The firing range is a dangerous place and has to be regarded as a combat situation. Your life is at stake. Other people's lives are at stake. These aren't water pistols or cap guns; you aren't firing blanks. These are live rounds. One mistake, one misfire, and someone is critically injured or someone dies. Guns are unforgiving. You can't take a round back once it's out of the muzzle.

And Jake always added:

"There are no accidents on the shooting range—only mistakes. An injury isn't 'no one's fault', it isn't 'the gun's fault'.

"It's your fault. You are responsible. If you can't handle that, go home."

Amy said, "I can handle it."

More of the standard lecture:

A gun is a tool, like a bandsaw: it can cut lengths of timber all day, or it can take your arm off in a split second. People say "The Walther is the best gun" or "The Glock is the best gun". It's all bull. The best gun for what? Every gun and every type of round does a different job. Since 1911, the Colt ACP was the standard American military side-arm—until about 15 years ago, when they shifted over to 9mm weapons. for the sake of NATO compatibility. Jake is certain that someone is getting rich manufacturing the inferior Beretta (It actually blows up in your hands sometimes) that has become the standard sidearm of the Western Alliance.

By the time we got to the range Amy's interest was piqued and she expected to start shooting right away. But first she had to learn the gun—each part, from the barrel bushing to the magazine well, from the grips to the rear sight hammer, bobbed so it won't dig a hole in your thumb when you start to fire. Jake always insisted on this point: know your gun before you use it. Amy asked how many bullets were in a clip . . .another phrase from the media world. A 'clip' attaches your holster to your belt; the package of rounds you shoot with is called a magazine and that's all it's ever called.

Amy wasn't really delighted to be learning all this stuff. It just felt like delay to her. But there was still a long way to go. We spent the rest of the day talking about guns while taking apart, oiling, cleaning and reassembling a Colt. At the end she said, "Do I get to shoot tomorrow?"

I shook my head. "Tomorrow you get to learn how to hold a gun."

"I know how already." She took up the classic TV stance, one hand bracing the other, both arms straight out in front of her. She frowned dangerously, squinting into imaginary gun sights.

"The Angie Dickinson stance!," I laughed. "Looks great."

"But it doesn't work?"

"Well . . . it depends if you want to hit anything."

She dropped her arms, drooped her shoulders. "Rats."

"I'll show you the real thing tomorrow."

"Show me now."

"I thought guns gave you the creeps."

"You got me interested. You're a great teacher."

"And you're a con-artist."

She grinned

"Does that kind of simple minded transparent flattery always work on guys?"

"Most of the time, yeah."

"How good a teacher am I again?"

"The best. And good-looking, too."

It took another hour to get her into the Weaver stance and at the end we both agreed we should have waited until she was fresh. It's a difficult thing to get exactly right, and it has to be exactly right or it won't work at all.

I got her standing with her feet shoulder width apart and had her step backward with her right foot—a small step, eight inches or so, turning her on an oblique angle. She raised her left—or 'non-shooting'—arm straight up from the waist, pointing at the target, and I turned her head gently the same way. Then she brought her right arm across her body, parallel with her left arm. Her hips started to turn—big mistake. I straightened them out with my hands and she giggled and said "This is the fun part". I had her drop her left elbow as if it was weighted—that brought her left hand level with her right. She made a fist with the right hand and enclosed it with the left, so that the heels of the palms were touching.

Shooting arm rigid.

Hips straight.

Left elbow clear of the body.

Shoulders extended fully—triceps separated from the ribs, no scapula projecting . . . shoulder blades smooth.

The line you're toeing with your feet should make a cross with the line of your shoulders—a big X. That's what stabilizes you.

It's a lot to remember, all at once.

You have to be able to see your left shoulder in the peripheral vision of your left eye—if you can't your shoulders aren't extended far enough.

Amy got her shoulders right—and then rotated her hips; fixed her hips, aligned them with her shoulders properly . . . and then let her right arm ease up.

She started to lose it.

We tried one more time and I showed her the most complicated part—you have to push with your right hand, pull with the fingers of your left and at the same time press your palms together, while holding the rest of your body correctly.

"I like the TV way better," she said. "I've studied Graham technique. It's easier than this."

"Ah, but could Martha Graham shoot straight?"

"I don't think it was a big priority for her, Tom."

A few minutes later we quit for the night. Fourteen hours is enough.

More tomorrow.

3/21

It took three more hours but she finally got it. She was a rock. I couldn't yank her wrists apart, up, down or sideways. I lifted her up and carried her around the floor by her arms—

without breaking her stance. It was like hauling a statue. The most important test was slamming my palms down on her wrist on a diagonal that ran right through her center of gravity to a spot just behind her heels: the angle of recoil. The extension of that line upwards is the path Angie Dickinson's gun would follow if she ever fired a real gun from that ridiculous stance. Not that the Weaver stance stops recoil; nothing could do that; instead it brings the muzzle of the gun back to the same exact position after each shot. It controls recoil; with Amy in the stance, and I couldn't budge her.

We were both excited. We went out for lunch and when we came back I handed her the .45 ACP we had field-stripped so many times the day before.

"It feels like a different gun, now," Amy said. "I guess that makes sense—it's loaded."

I took a breath. This was one of the most important lessons I had to teach her. "I know what you mean," I said. "But you have to think and act as if there's no such thing as an unloaded gun. I mean it. Never point a gun at someone unless you're willing to kill them. Don't even point it at an inanimate object unless you're willing to destroy it. That's a standard safety precaution but it's also a practical truth: even after you remove the empty magazine, there's can still be a round left in the chamber. You can't ever forget that."

There was a tremor in Amy's wrist. "It's so heavy," she said. "It feels like death."

I nodded. "Exactly. That's exactly what it is."

About three hundred rounds later, she was used to firing the gun. Buy the end of the day she was shooting from seven feet (Amy was surprised to learn that 75% of fire fights in civilian life occur with the shooters no more than twelve feet apart—and most people can't hit what they're aiming at, even at such close range); grouping fifty rounds into an area the size of a silver dollar. And loving every minute of it.

There's a lot more to do, she has a lot more to learn; she
needs practice and lots of it. But she's already a dangerous
person and that's what I need with me right now—the more
dangerous the better.

3/22

After seven hours of practice yesterday, when her hands
should have been cramping and her arms hanging dead
from her shoulders, Amy looked as if she was ready to start all
over again. She broke the gun down expertly, but she was
reluctant to hand over the Colt when she was finished.

"This sounds crazy, but . . . I'm really getting attached to
this gun. It makes me feel safe"

"Well, that's good, but don't get feeling too safe. A gun
can be too slow coming out of your purse, you can miss
the person behind you, the sun can get in your eyes, you can
forget to take the safety off. You gun can be taken away from
you. People get shot with their own guns all the time."

"Thanks a lot."

"I'm sorry, but it's the truth. When I was at just about this
stage, Jake said to me, 'Look out kid, now you know just
enough to get yourself killed."

"So what should I do?"

"You should be careful. You are more powerful now.
You're safer—unless you get careless. Remember what you
said—the gun feels like death. You can actually kill people
now. That ought to scare the hell out of you."

When we made love later she was wild, almost desperate.
She hugged me tight afterward and when I finally slipped
out of her, the physical separation seemed to cause her real
pain. She bit my shoulder, hard. After a while she rolled off
me and said, as if seven hours, a dozen other discussions, a
meal, a long walk and forty minutes of passionate love-mak-

ing hadn't interrupted our conversation, "Have you ever shot anyone?"

"What?"

I don't know what I expected her to say. Some sweet nothing? But this was something—the main thing, in fact—and it was bitter on the tongue. She stared at me and I shook my head.

"No. Not yet."

She looked relieved; but more afraid than ever. "Do you think you could?"

"I don't know. I was ready to pull the trigger on that kid in the Park."

She flopped down on the pillows. "Oh, God."

"Amy?"

"It's just so hopeless."

I sighed—my pep talk in Des Moines hadn't really worked after all. I should have known it wouldn't—Amy's too smart for that. She went on: "When I think about the two of us against this gigantic conspiracy and we don't even know who we're fighting, or what they're trying to do, or how to find out and here we are with our guns and neither of us has even ever used one, really used one I mean, I don't . . . I mean, we're just kids. Two kids. It's ridiculous."

"But it's not just us."

I know, I know—you want to find Jim Gramble. But it's not that easy. As soon as you start looking for him Heller's going to get suspicious. As soon as you do anything, Heller's going to get suspicious."

"Heller would be suspicious if I did nothing. That's what he's paid for. But I can handle him, Amy—all I need is a cover story."

"He can check any story you make up and when he finds out you were lying, we're finished."

"I can do it in secret. I can ditch the Secret Service, you know that."

"It doesn't matter, Tom. They probably have everyone Jim's ever known under surveillance, too. As soon as you talk to anyone, they'll know."

"I don't have to do it as me. I can be an IRS investigator with one person, a corporate headhunter with another, or—"

"But you're famous. You can't pretend to be anyone else. Not any more."

She pulled the new issue of People Magazine off the floor. I was on the cover—the guy had done his story on me anyway.

They didn't need my cooperation. "I hadn't seen that yet."

"I wasn't going to show it to you."

"I would have seen it, eventually."

"I know."

A dispirited silence fell between us, textured with the sound of traffic.

"I could use a disguise," I offered lamely.

"That only works in the movies."

I nodded.

After a while she said, "Maybe we'll think of something in the morning. We're both exhausted."

I kissed her and said okay and 10 minutes later she was asleep. I read the article in People—which was actually quite well-written, though I have no idea where they got the information or the photographs.

I've been writing since then.

Maybe Amy's right and we'll get some new ideas tomorrow. I certainly hope so because as of right now, I have no idea what to do and we have to do something, even if it's the wrong thing.

Soon it's going to be too late.

I read that over and it sounds like melodramatic crap. But it's true. Unfortunately that doesn't disqualify it from being melodramatic crap. My life has turned into melodramatic crap. It's like I'm living in one of those trashy thrillers I used to read all the time. I always wanted to be the hero of a Ludlum novel, to be Robert Redford in *Three Days of The Condor* . . . a glamorous fugitive, saving the world from evil conspirators. Well . . . now it's actually happening and it stinks.

Suspense is fun in movies, but real suspense, not knowing if you're going to be killed, not knowing what's coming next or if you'll be able to handle it—that doesn't make you suave and debonair. It makes you weak. It makes you want to climb in bed next to your girlfriend, pull the covers over your head and stay there forever.

Well . . . for eight hours, anyway.

Maybe I'll wake up and realize this was all a dream. Or maybe I'll just be dreaming I'm awake. Or maybe it doesn't make any difference. They say if you're murdered in your dreams you really die—murder is murder.

Dead is dead.

A good thought to sleep on.

14

3/23

I don't believe in ghosts, but this morning made me wonder. I held a letter in my hand, a sheet of paper that solved so many problems at once, and I felt my mother's presence so strongly I turned around as if I might actually see her standing across the room, vanishing in the morning light.

She wasn't there of course. And the timing of the letter was just coincidence. But if Mom had wanted to help me from the grave, she could hardly have done a better job.

The letter was from Norman Richards, our family's lawyer. There was a check enclosed. The will was out of probate and her bequest to me was two hundred thousand dollars. Norman warned me that I could expect to see that amount cut in half by taxes and death duties. Still, it was more than I needed for a war chest. I could cash the check and put the money in a safe deposit box until I needed it. My concerns about weapons, ammunition, materiel, transportation and a thousand other problems vanished instantly. I can finance the battle now, if there has to be a battle, without touching my own bank account, which I have to assume is being watched.

Thanks, Mom.

But there's more. Norman asked me for a favor. Apparently Mom left Jim the bulk of her library, including many volumes he had been borrowing and returning reluctantly for years. Letters and phone calls had failed to locate Jim and they were hoping that I—as a personal friend—might have better luck tracking him down. "As we wish to clear up the estate in a timely manner, any help in this matter would be greatly appreciated."

A real warm guy, Norman. I read the letter over, starched passive voice and all, and then sat down, winded with good fortune. Now I not only had all the money I needed, I had an excuse to search for Jim, a cover story that Heller could check as much as he wanted—the perfect cover story.

The truth.

Amy came in with two cups of coffee. I took mine and handed her Norman's letter. I watched as she read it. Her face moved from a sort of neutral attentiveness to a smile and then a wide-eyed grin. She took in a breath so sharp it sounded like a croak, and clapped her hand over her mouth as she read the rest. Then she was in my lap. Somehow her coffee made it onto the end-table next to mine. She hugged me like a pro wrestler and then took my face in her hands and kissed me.

"See?" she said. "I told you so."

"Hey—we didn't think of this. It just happened."

"Don't get technical," she said, and kissed me again.

3/24

Our first day in the field.

First stop: the New York Journal Examiner. We got in to
see Jim's editor, Roy Fisk, mainly on the strength of my new-
found celebrity. Maybe he thought he was going to interview
me.

He's a physical type I detest. I could almost hear Jake
sneering, "Skip a few meals, pal." Fat and soft and chinless;
skimpy beard cut sharp with a razor marking the line
where his jaw bone is buried under rolls of pink flesh. What
else? Hard, close-set eyes and the kind of voice you get
from three decades of unfiltered cigarettes.

He met us in the lobby, offered some brusque condo-
lences and said "How can I help you?"

"We're trying to find Jim Gramble, "I began.

"He no longer works here."

I didn't get it. "You mean—in this building? Is he on
assignment or something? Because—"

"He's gone, Mr. Jaglom. The paper let him go."

"But why? I thought—"

"He was becoming a problem. He was unstable. He
was drinking heavily. He was no longer an asset to this organization."

"Do you know where he is now?" Amy asked.

"No one does. The Mafia blew up his car a coupla
months ago. He oughtta be dead. Maybe he is dead."

"Wait a second." Amy took a step closer to him and he
backed up. It looked like the beginning of some new dance.

"Jim is an investigative reporter. If the Mafia is trying
to kill him, isn't possible that he wrote some sort of story
that—"

"Right—an expose that could bring organized crime
to its knees. All you need is someone shouting 'stop the
presses!'."

"But—"

"I'll tell you something, honey. He could have written a
story like that and I could have printed it. Wouldn't matter—

nobody would notice. Nobody would give a shit. Nobody reads."

"Sure they do—"

"Hey, most people can't even read a STOP sign—and that's just one word."

"Sounds like you're in the wrong business," I said.

"I put out a good paper. That's all I care about. I get it right and I go home. You wanta wrap fish with it? Fuck you."

So that was that. We both knew he was lying, but it was pointless to confront him. All we would have done was wreck our cover. We went upstairs and talked to some of the other reporters in the City Room, and the men at the Copy Desk. Fisk called Security and two rent-a-cops escorted us out of the building. It didn't matter. No one knew anything anyway. Neither did Jim's neighbors. A couple of old friends we contacted were used to not hearing from Jim—months and sometimes years would go by between visits or phone calls. They never knew when he was going to show up and they liked it that way; it kept him present in their lives. But it didn't help us much.

Next: Jim's ex-wife, Eleanor.

We just missed her at work. She's a partner in a law firm on Third Avenue in the forties. But we caught up to her at her health club. She was on the stair master, *U.S. News and World Report* propped up in front of her while she worked out.

Eleanor was painfully thin, all fat rendered off her by a vegetarian diet and this punishing exercise regimen. She was the precise opposite of Roy Fisk, the other side of the same craziness. I wondered idly if she was bulimic and when she had changed. She had been a lot more substantial in the old days. It was hard to imagine her with a bulky guy like Jim Gramble, now. Maybe that was the point.

She was glad to see me. "I was so sorry to hear about

your mother, Tom." after the introductions were complete. "Are you holding up all right?"

"I guess so. She left Jim some books in her will but no one seems to know where he is right now."

"I haven't seen Jim in more than a year—a statement which still astonishes me. I keep thinking someone is going to tell me it's all been a hoax and I really have to go back and start cleaning out his crusty cereal bowls again. Who would do such a thing to me? The Divorce Police? Or maybe my parents. They're still furious at me for walking out on him. But so far so good. If I hear from him I'll call you."

I thanked her and we started to go, but Eleanor said "Wait," and turned to Amy. "You hold onto this boy, my dear," she said. "You have no idea how lucky you are. His parents actually trained him to be a fully functioning human being. You'll never be his servant. He actually pulls his own weight. That doesn't seem like a lot to ask, does it? But I've never met another man who did—Jim included."

"Jim may not have been a good husband," I said. "But the Mafia is trying to kill him now. He's—"

"He's a world champion at self-dramatization. Too bad it's not an Olympic event. He'd win the gold for his country. Can't you just see him on the Wheaties box? Or in Jim's case, perhaps a Maalox package would be more appropriate."

"His car was blown up," Amy said angrily. "Aren't you even worried that—"

"I stopped worrying about Jim a long time ago. It's exhausting and I just wasn't up to it any more. I couldn't pass the physical. You feel free though—it's an ideal recreational activity for young people. Kind of like drinking too much and staying out all night. As you age you try to find better things to do with your time."

Strange—I had always assumed Jim and Eleanor had a

happy marriage. They seemed so happy; but this was years of accumulated bitterness and disappointment talking. Is happiness that easy to fake? Or do we just not pay that much attention to each other? It makes you wonder how many happy marriages there really are. I mean—what if there aren't any? What if it's a whole world full of miserable angry couples faking it? The new happy ending: "The Prince and the Princess were married and pretended to live happily ever after."

I said to Amy, "Will we wind up like that?"

She hugged me. "Absolutely not."

"You're sure?"

"Absolutely."

"What will we be like?"

She thought for a few seconds and then spoke very carefully, working it out as she went along. It was wonderful and I want to put it down exactly as she said it:

"We'll say whatever we feel, and talk about everything for hours and not let each other get away with anything and that means we'll fight a and scream and throw things at each other and then make up and then make love and then make pop-corn and watch old movies and cuddle and never get lazy or take each other for granted and always wake up in the morning amazed at our luck, and hug and kiss each other whenever we want and need to sneak away and be by ourselves even when we're eighty years old and scandalize our family by dying in bed, in each other's arms screwing our brains out one last time. No separate beds. no separate tables, no separate vacations. No secrets. We'll never know each other well enough and we'll always want to know more."

"You won't get sick of me?"

"I can't imagine that."

"But everyone else is so unhappy."

"Not everyone. My parents are happy. So were yours."

I thought about that. It was true.

"So we can really live happily ever after?"

"No. I don't want to live happily ever after. That's boring. I want to live interestingly ever after, curiously ever after, passionately ever after."

"Then let's get married." I said it before I even knew what I was saying

She stared at me and it was like—this is impossible to write down. How do you explain the nakedness and vulnerability of actual human experience? Realizing what I'd just said made me dizzy—like leaning out over a height. A long way to fall.

Or jump.

Wild thoughts, as I looked into her eyes, face to face with a woman but also with a living breathing split second on the planet earth—the unknown, the uncertain.

She kissed me, a long deep slow kiss and when she pulled her mouth away from mine she said, "When this is over."

She was right. By this time tomorrow we could both be dead. The whole idea of an 'ever after' longer than a week is just a fantasy, fantasies are distractions, and we can't afford to be distracted right now. If we survive we can celebrate; if we live we can live together. After all, marriages are one of the two traditional, all-purpose endings for a story.

But funerals are the other one.

3/25

Amy woke up with the idea this morning.

"What about Jim's parents?"

I told her his mother had died when he was very young. But as far I knew, his Dad was still living in Bedford Stuyvesant.

She said: "Let's go."

The only problem was the entourage . . . that's what I'm calling them these days. It's not just the Secret Service any more; now it's the press, too. Camera vans parked outside, reporters trailing us everywhere, asking insipid questions. I'd be so happy to hear a smart question, I might even answer it. But there's not much chance of that. As for the Secret Service, they've given up on their usual discretion. There's a three-man team on us all the time, including this six-foot five three hundred and eighty pound ex-linebacker named Duane Claassen. The other agents call him the Hulk. But probably not to his face.

At first I thought the Secret Service might be able to keep the reporters away from us, but all they did was check people's credentials, to be sure no would-be killers and kidnappers were posing as members of the press corps. After dealing with the press for a month or two the thought of a regular old killer or kidnapper is starting to sound very appealing.

They make an odd bunch, these two groups. They're very different—the passive surveillance force and the aggressive, information-mongering media. There's a kind of opposition built into their roles. I have to use that if I can, because I don't want to lead them to Amos Gramble. My thinking took me this far: the only way to beat both groups is to set them against each other. I told Amy and confessed I was stumped. She said, "Do what the press does when they want to generate some action."

I looked at her blankly.

She said: "Lie."

She can be quite cynical sometimes.

The set up was the same as usual when we came downstairs—press people bunched around the front door of the building, Secret Service guys half a block away. I could feel Amy cringing at the sight of the crowd.

We pushed outside and I saw the writer from *People* Magazine. You have to give this guy points for sheer persistence.
Of course, he probably assumed there was safety in numbers.
He tried to wiggle through the packed bodies when he saw
me coming, but he had nowhere to go. I grabbed his arm and
smiled.

"Brad Killen—right?"

"Uh, yeah—"

"Hey, listen—that was a great article you wrote, Brad. No
thanks to me. You deserve a break. Amy was just saying to me
this morning . . . 'these guys aren't your enemies. Tell them
about Duane.' And you know what? I think she's right."

The others were crowding around, listening. The surveillance team was obviously wondering what the hell was
going on—I had never paused for one second to talk to
reporters before.

"Duane?' Brad prompted me.

"Duane Claassen—that big Secret Service agent over
there by the car. Then huge guy with the crew cut. See
him? I heard him bragging about his inside information
on the Air Force One crash. You know the investigation
has been Top Secret. Well . . . apparently there was something important in the black box recordings from the cockpit, the kind of information you could cash in on big time,
if you didn't mind taking a little heat from the government.
'It's gonna be early retirement for ole Duane,' that's what
he said. But he wouldn't say any more. 'Read about it in the
papers, kid.' That was all he told me. So I asked him—which
papers? And he said, 'That depends on who pays the most.'"

The result was wonderful. First Brad started elbowing
his way back through the crowd. But people started moving with him. Enough of them had heard enough of what
I'd said to start a stampede. In less than a minute, Duane and
the others were surrounded by jabbering reporters, making

phony-sounding denials, just like the men they were usually assigned to protect. I stayed and watched for a few seconds.

"You're gloating," Amy said, and then—"Gloating is okay . . . f you can gloat and run at the same time."

"No, no—it's like drinking water when you run. I always get a stitch."

She pushed me.

I caught Duane's eye and waved at him, just before we turned the corner.

An hour later we were standing in front of Amos Gramble's front door. I rang the bell and heard brisk footsteps. He opened the door—a tall, very black man with a full head of gray hair. He was clean-shaven. His huge eyes were made even bigger by the thick lenses of his horn-rimmed glasses. He frowned at us suspiciously for a moment, then smiled.

"You must be Tom Jaglom," he said. "And this is Amy Elwell?" He shook our hands. "Jim said you'd be coming."

He stepped aside to let us in. After the unseasonably chill street outside, Dr. Gramble's front hall was as comforting as a warm towel after a cold shower. The house smelled of baking bread and frying garlic.

"You have to stay for dinner. I'm making Bouillabaisse and a little salade Nicoise and some French bread just out of the oven. I finally lined my oven with ceramic tiles and I put a bowl of boiling water in there with the loaves. Steam is the secret of a good crust."

I pointed out that it was only one in the afternoon, but he reminded me that Bouillabase took time. And in the meanwhile, would we like some lunch? We pieced together a delicious meal from cold rack of lamb, sour dough rye bread and marinated artichoke hearts while the fish stew simmered on the stove behind us.

"People have been looking for Jim since the morning he disappeared," Dr. Gramble said when we were settled. "Press people, men in cheap suits who looked like government men. Men in expensive suits who looked like criminals. It was actually amusing to try and detect any difference in their tactics and attitudes. On the whole, I'd say the criminals were more polite. My house is being watched. My phones are tapped, though apparently to no avail. The criminals say they want to 'talk to' Jim. The government people say they want to 'help' him. I suppose they think they can just kind of stroll in and pull the wool over the eyes of this old colored man, easy as pie. Whereas in fact an old colored man like myself—well-educated in every way—is very difficult to hoodwink. Difficult as pie crust, if you like. And if you've ever tried to make as nice flaky pie crust, I'm sure you know what I mean." He took a bite of lamb, chewed it slowly, swallowed. "I shall be direct with you, Tom Jaglom. They want to kill my son. I know that and I grieve in advance because I don't see how he can escape them much longer. He's not a soldier. He's a writer."

Then he turned on me, all kitchen chit-chat forgotten, my privileged status as Jim's friend irrelevant and those dark brown eyes caught me and held me still, unblinking.

"Are you going to help Jim?"

I stared back. "I was hoping he could help me."

His mouth twisted down a little and his eyes narrowed. It was an assessing look—not quite a smile.

"So . . . you're honest at least. That's good. But Jim is no position to help anybody."

"He wrote an article, Dr. Gramble. That's why everyone is chasing him. That's why he was fired from the newspaper. If we can make that story public it will help both of us."

Dr. Gramble sat back and laughed. "Yes. That sounds like Jim. He has always thought he could somehow change things, fix things . . . remedy the world."

"You don't think that's possible?" Amy asked.

"Look around you. For all the efforts of Jim and those like him, things continue to get worse and worse.

"I can't believe you can say that, after living through the civil rights movement."

He smiled at her, a tired, tolerant smile.

"The Civil Rights movement. A lovely historical moment. It made white people feel so much better. But make no mistake, this is still a virulently racist country. Bigotry is embedded in every detail of American life. We live under the rule of Apartheid—in New York City far more than in Johannesburg, these days. Their Mandela is a free man, helping to re-shape his country. Ours was murdered more than thirty years ago. We spent most of that time furiously denouncing South Africa. Perhaps they will denounce us now. That would be ironic—if you like irony. I myself have always detested irony. But there you are. Another artichoke heart?"

Amy was smart enough not to argue the point. Dr. Gramble may not have been completely right; but he had the right to be wrong, and we didn't.

The most interesting thing about his beliefs is that they haven't made him bitter. His expectations for the human race are quite low and his judgments are tempered with a tolerant gentleness. "We're none of us down very long from the trees," he said at one point. And, later, "You mustn't forget, it's very hard just getting up in the morning and going about the business of being human. It's more than most people can manage."

3/28

Dr. Gramble suggested we camp out and wait for Jim to call, so we've spent most of the last three days cooking elaborate meals, eating them, cleaning up after them, while arguing about everything from why the French use so many sauces to why they were in Viet Nam, to why we were in Viet Nam to the nature of war itself ("Primates like to fight.")

At first Amy was nervous about the two of us vanishing together this way, but having her with me actually makes justifying my disappearance much easier. This way it looks like a simple romantic escape, which we certainly deserve.

I took some time to set up basic security procedures with Amy—some basic codes in case we have to talk and can't speak freely. Simple ones, like "tutoring" (Which means "help") or "flunk" (Which means "terminate the conversation") to more complex ones like "cram" (Which means "These people are pointing guns at me") and even "final exam" (Which means "Meet me at the Alice in Wonderland statue in Central Park. Be there at 10 A.M. on each of the next three days.")

We drilled them—maybe 10 phrases in all—until she had them solid. I also taught her a few simple hand-to-hand techniques: simple ways to stun an attacker or break a stranglehold. It's a productive way to kill time, but that's all we're doing and it's making all of us a little crazy.

Jim just called.

He's alive. He's okay. I'm going to call him back in a few minutes.

The way they do it is—Jim leaves a jumbled phone number and Dr. Gramble decodes it; then he calls back from another pay phone. It's as close as they've been able to get to secure communications. And so far at least, it's worked. I'll finish this entry after I've talked to him.

It was good to hear Jim's voice, but we didn't have time to say much.

"Tom. Thank God."

"Where are you?"

"I'm moving around. We need to talk, but not on the phone."

"We should have talked at Christmas." There was a pause on the line.

"I know."

"It's okay—we'll talk now. We'll meet somewhere."

"That sounds good. Washington Square Park. Under the arch."

"When?"

"Tomorrow at noon."

"Great."

"Thanks, Tom."

He hung up.

Twenty hours until the meeting. Nothing to do until then but eat and talk and make love.

Sleep is out of the question.

3/29

I finally know the truth.

I know what's happening and I know why. Jim gave me all the answers. Now I just have to write it down exactly as I heard it, one word at a time, and let the truth sink in.

I was early. I had given myself extra time to dodge the Secret Service. But I forgot: we lost them three days ago. When I stepped outside, I was alone in the street. It was a startling moment, something out of a lost childhood— walking out of school for the last time on a warm June afternoon, with a summer of freedom in front of me. Freedom: as if I could just take Amy, walk away and disappear into a new life. As if I could turn my back on everything that's happened, just grieve for my parents and let the men who killed them win.

But that's impossible.

Forgive and forget?

Just the opposite: rage and remember.

And don't for one second fool yourself that you're free.

I saw Jim first.

I was standing in the granular East wind, listening to an A Capella group singing "Heard It Through The Grapevine" watching two old men playing chess. Two women walked past pushing expensive German baby-carriages.

Jim was hurrying, hunched over. He stopped to give some change to a homeless man. I circled around and fell into step beside him. He jumped when he finally noticed me.

"I never see you coming," he said. He looked terrible: sick and tired.

"How are you?'

"Alive. That puts me way ahead of the game. Let's get out of the cold."

We wound up in Caffe Reggio, under the dark, pressed-tin ceiling, against the wall in the back, well away from the windows and the door. We ordered two double espressos. Jim took a sip, set the cup down and began.

This is what he said:

"Back in November, a Mafia informant named Alfredo Blasi was killed before he could testify against the Nosiglia crime family. I was there. I saw it go down. It looked like a set-up to me. I started investigating it. Everybody was scared. The one cop who was willing to talk to me got killed. I was getting nowhere and I was about to give up when I got a call from ex-police chief Quinn. He was dying. He passed away in January. I should have gone to the funeral but I was scared. Anyway . . .he told me the order had come from the top—from the State Attorney General's office, from the Justice Department—to lay off. 'Throw the big fish back'—that was the phrase they used.

"High-level law enforcement has more or less ceased to exist, Tom. No more major drug interdictions, no more major investigations. They've all been 'suspended indefinitely'. Undercover guys have been yanked from long running operations. As far as Quinn could tell, the Federal Government was involved in some kind of complex negotiation with the prominent crime families. U.S. Attorney General Michael

Cafferty was supposed to be behind it. Though what 'it' was Quinn didn't know. All he knew for sure was that the 'hands off' policy led directly to the kind of purposeful negligence that would allow a man like Blasi to be killed under the noses of thirty policemen and FBI agents.

"I was gasping. I literally couldn't catch my breath. I was shivering too. I turned around to see if the window was open, but there wasn't any draft, there was just that name, Michael Cafferty.

"You see, I went to school with Mike Cafferty. So did your father. We were all on the same basketball team. So was the White House Chief of Staff Dennis Clark. And in the winter of 1957, a young Mafioso named Dominic Nosiglia tried to bribe us into dumping the inter-mural championship."

"Did you do it?"

"No. Your father wanted to. So did Mike and the others. But a different bunch of gangsters had bribed the other team. So everyone was trying to lose. We finally decided to just play. We wound up winning, but fortunately for us we hit the point spread exactly. Nobody lost any money so we didn't get our knees broken. Years later, when your father was running for the Senate, I was sure he was still involved with the Nosiglias. Dominic forced his opponent to retire just a few weeks before the election. I saw Dominic talking to Senator Greer, Tom. And Dominic saw me. He threatened me. A day later, Greer was gone—for 'health' reasons. I liked the choice of words. I confronted your Dad."

"What did he say?"

"He admitted that Greer quitting helped him. But he didn't know why the mob had done it and he swore it was a coincidence. He was very persuasive. I guess that's how you get to be President. I was happy to be persuaded— Dominic had gotten me worried about my own health.

"When your Dad was choosing his cabinet last year, he

made Mike Cafferty Attorney General, which made sense. The man was an accomplished trial lawyer, he'd been New York District Attorney and spent five years as a Federal prosecutor. He was qualified.

"But he had done business with Dominic Nosiglia.

"And he still was.

"He still is.

"Quinn said 'Is this too much for you, Jim?' I couldn't talk, I just shook my head. I felt sea sick and I must have looked that way. Quinn finished his story: small time criminals are still being arrested. the machinery of the law creaks along, a little slower than usual, maybe. But men like Dominic Nosiglia are invulnerable now. Gotti would be invulnerable now. And everyone knows it."

Jim swallowed the rest of his espresso and winced, setting the cup down.

"Quinn said the new guidelines were frustrating the brass: guys like himself and the new chief and the Police Commissioner. But they all have a 'wait and see' attitude. You know . . .maybe there's some large plan. Maybe somebody somewhere knows what the hell they're doing. They all love your Dad, Tom—and Cafferty made it clear that the orders were coming from the White House. Most of them think it's some kind of elaborate sting operation. The prelude to the biggest bust in history, something like that. Since the actual crime rate isn't going up, they're not panicking.

"But on the street it's different. That's what was worrying Quinn. That was why he wanted to see me. Good cops are quitting. They're drinking and smoking. They're snorting and shooting up. They're taking early retirement, getting divorced, committing suicide. Police brutality is up—police shootings have tripled in the last nine months. And this isn't just New York. Quinn knows law enforcement people all over the country. One of his friends, a prosecutor in Denver, put it best. He said 'Street justice is the only justice left.'

"Whatever this plan is—it isn't working. That was what Quinn wanted to tell me."

Jim ordered another double espresso and a slice of chocolate cake.

"Some people can't eat when they're scared or nervous," he said with a crooked little smile. "I envy those people."

The food came. Jim took a bite.

"Quinn told me this was all on the record—he let me quote him and use his name. He didn't want to be deep throat. He wanted the full force of his reputation behind the allegations. That made it an important story, maybe the most important story, at least in my career. When I was writing it, a Mafia hit man came to my apartment, pulled out a gun and—"

"He shot you?"

Jim smiled. "No. He shot my computer. And he stole my back-up copies. Ever lose a few pages of something you were writing at a computer when the power went out and you'd forgotten to save your material?"

I nodded.

Well, I lost everything. Hundreds and hundreds of pages.

Parts of three different books, notes, tax records, journals . . . and the Quinn story."

"So what did you do?"

"I couldn't walk away from the story, so I pulled out my old Olympia and started pounding away. I had a funny moment with Roy Fisk when I turned in the article. He said, 'Something happen to your printer? This looks like shit.' I just laughed—the printer was the one piece of equipment I still had left. Fisk never ran the story—you know that. When I complained, he fired me. So I started investigating the *Journal Examiner* itself. I wanted to find out who owned it— who was giving Fisk his orders. I had to do a lot of foot-work and call in a lot of favors. There were false fronts and dummy corporations out of Delaware . . . a real maze. But I found out what I wanted to know. "Care to guess who owns the company that holds a majority position in the media conglomerate that controls the company that owns the *Journal Examiner*?"

I shrugged. He watched me. It was gloomy in the cafe, but I could feel that look, the concentration of his personality. His will.

Then he said two words:

"Your father."

Jim grabbed my forearm, pressed it to the table.

"That's why I came to Nantucket. That was why I had to see your father . . . Christmas or not. I needed answers and I got them."

"Jim—"

"You have to hear this."

He released my arm, and I sat back.

He was right.

"I included our conversation verbatim in the revised version of my article. You could just read it but I want you to hear it from me. You deserve that. You deserve more than the words. I want you to know how it felt. Your father is the closest thing I ever had to a brother. Tom?"

I just nodded again. Jim went on:

"I said to him, 'You had me fired from the paper. Why?'"

"He said 'Merry Christmas, Jim. Care for a sticky bun or some coffee?'

"I said, 'Why did you do it, Eddie?'

"He put his coffee down. He'd never seen me this way before. I'd been angry other times but this . . . this was the sum of all those other times, this was the end-point of everything I'd ever been angry about, going all the way back to high school.

"' I'm sorry, Jim,' he said. 'That was a terrible mistake.

That was wrong. But you were about to ruin everything. And I couldn't let that happen.'

"This was all coming at me too fast, Tommy—"

"I know the feeling."

"I'm sorry. But I had a job to do. And so do you. That should help you a little. It helped me. I remembered I was a reporter. I said, 'It's illegal for a President to own a newspaper, Eddie. Besides, all your assets are supposed to be in a blind trust. How could you—'

"He cut me off. 'It's easy, Jim. It's like I used to tell you in high school—you can do whatever you want in life as long as you don't wear a sandwich sign telling people you're doing it. Don't ask permission. If you ask they'll say no . . . whether it's old Mrs. Terwilliger or the SEC.'

"Tom, I just shook my head and said 'Rich guys.'

"He shrugged. He said 'Poor guys.'

"'No,' I said. 'Middle class guys.'

"He laughed—I could always make him laugh. 'You're right,' he said. 'Poor guys understand this stuff. God save me from the bourgeoisie.'

"He looked at me and we both felt it. The friendship was still there. We just . . . we enjoyed each other. Even that morning, there were these moments of, I don't know . . . pleasure, privilege, gratitude. Despite everything I was glad to know your father. I still am, even if I never see him again."

"You won't," I said softly.

Jim looked at me, confused. I just said, "Go on."

He raised his cup but it was empty. He set it down again, There was no cake left either. He had nothing to do but talk. He cleared his throat.

"I said to him, 'What was I going to ruin, Eddie?'

"'My plans. My career. The economic recovery. The people's faith in their government. Maybe even the structure of Government itself.'

"'With one article?'"

"'No, you're article couldn't have done it alone. But it would have been a start. There would have been other articles, Congressional investigations, impeachment hearings . . . It wouldn't have taken long. You made the basic connection.'

"'Mike Cafferty? And Dennis Clark?'"He nodded.

"'They were in with the mob.'

"He nodded again.

"'But the orders don't come from them.'

"'No.'

"I had to say it. 'You're dealing with Dominic Nosiglia again.'

"He didn't say anything. So I pushed. 'I told you forty years ago that you could never walk away from Nosiglia, that you'd be stuck with him for life. And I was right, wasn't I?'

"He still didn't say anything. So I pushed harder. 'When you ran for the Senate, you knew about Greer and Nosiglia. Dominic destroyed him for you, didn't he? I bet he never owned his own Senator before. What do you give to the man who has everything?'

"'Jim—'

"'It's true, isn't it?'

"'Yes.'

"'So you lied to me.'

"Again: 'Yes.'

"'Because you were scared of him. Because you were in too deep. Because you were ashamed.'

"'Once more, almost inaudible now: 'Yes.'

"'So now he owns the President. Now he's running the country. And you're his puppet—just like some sleazy Third World strong man, propped up by the CIA. It's poetic justice, Eddie—you've turned yourself into one of the Pinochets and Noriegas that you've always hated. Well you should have learned a lesson from Saddam Hussein and

Khadaffi. It's an easy lesson—push it too far and this country turns on you. They'll destroy you when they find out. Impeachment is going to start looking good. And I'll tell you something. When this comes out it's going to reaffirm everything people love about America. They won't despise anyone or anything—except you.

"And do you know what he did then? He smiled at me, Tommy. He smiled and shook his head.

"'Nice speech,' he said. 'But you have no idea what you're talking about. You don't know what I've done. Nobody does. They will someday, though. I want them to. Not now—not until the benefits are planted so deeply in the economy, rooted so deeply in people's day-to-day lives that there's no going back.'

"'Don't tell them it's heroin until they're really hooked?'

"'You're cruel, Jim.'

"'What have you done?'

"'Excuse me?'

"'You said no one has any idea what you've done. That's why I'm here, Eddie. Tell me what you've done."

"'All right, Jim. I'll tell you.'

"He paused. He was enjoying the moment.

" Then he said: 'I'm taxing the Mafia.'

"His campaign promises were a con-game. Oh yes—he was planning to tax the big corporations, all right, and he did. But that was just a cover. The real money comes from Mafia front companies. Some are real—they've been laundering money for the Nosiglias and the other New York Families for years. Others were created for this specific purpose. You have to remember, Tom, they've been developing this plan for decades. It started before your father ran for the Senate. There are hundreds of companies that have been posting low earnings since they were incorporated which suddenly started showing huge profits. The companies don't produce

anything, the profits aren't connected to anything. Allied
Widget never made widgets and still doesn't. It used to be a
place to hide money; now it's a place to transfer money to the
IRS. The sales and capitalization reports are total fiction. But
that doesn't matter. It's all happening in cyber-space. No one
was ever audited for declaring too much money on a tax
return. And of course your Dad also more or less abolished
corporate welfare. There were a lot of real loop-holes that he
closed. Dow and GM and Microsoft needed to be authenti-
cally pissed off and they are. But their money is nothing compared to what the Mafia has been funneling through the hundreds of dummy corporations, established firms, and start-ups-
-not to mention the casinos. These places are opening their
books for the first time ever. It's complicated. You should see
the new tax code. It's a six hundred page book that would
give an accountant a migraine. I tried to go though some of
it. It's all GAO jargon–fiduciary liabilities and ancillary prime
rate depletion allowances. What it comes down to is this: the
Federal Government is now taking a deep cut—something
like twenty eight percent off the top—from every profit center
in organized crime. Prostitution, protection, numbers, loan
sharking, gambling casinos . . . and drugs."

"How can he trust them?"

"That was my question. But your Dad didn't get it. He
was sure it was too good a deal for them to screw up. Dealing with law enforcement was costing them close to fifty
percent of their annual gross. They were spending billions
fighting the cops; we were spending billions fighting back.
And all we had to show for it was a high crime rate and a
net loss of billions of dollars. We weren't controlling crime.
We weren't winning the war on drugs. We were getting
nowhere. So it occurred to your father, that we might be better off if we simply . . . co-opted the Mafia.

"He talked it over with Dominic Nosiglia and they agreed
on a kind of merger, a business relationship that would put

all the money both sides had been throwing away to some good use. The idea wasn't to change the patterns of crime in America. But rather to spread the benefits of that criminal activity to the average hard-working middle-class American. It's interesting—the patterns of crime haven't really changed since your father took office. But now we're ending personal income tax and paying off the National Debt. We've turned our greatest liability into our greatest asset."

I took a breath. "In other words—if you can't beat 'em, join 'em."

Jim nodded. "Yes—that's exactly what I told your father. And he said, 'The line between crime and venture capitalism has always been a little hazy. They didn't call guys like Andrew Carnegie robber barons for nothing.'

"And I said. 'Andrew Carnegie didn't sell crack to children. The Mafia sells crack to children.'"

"What did he say? What could he say to that?"

"He said 'They have and they will, no matter what we do. But now someone besides the hoods are getting the benefits.' It's not a bad point, Tom. In 10 or twelve years, with the deficit paid off and the country's infrastructure repaired and the inner cities revitalized and the educational system recharged with the kind of money that could make every school into a 'magnet' school and attract the best people into the teaching profession . . . with national health care in place and people disposing of their disposable incomes creating the biggest economic boom since World War II . . . well, at that point, in that kind of world, there wouldn't be much of a place for the Mafia. If you give the inner city kids good nutrition and first class educations and meaningful jobs and a sense of hope . . . they won't need crack. That's your father's long-term plan. He wants to make the Mafia obsolete. And in the meanwhile, he finances the rebuilding of America. No one else has done that. No one has even come close." ,

"So the end justifies the means."

This time Jim laughed out loud, a short, bitter laugh. "I guess I made all the obvious points, didn't I? But he must have been expecting that one. He said 'Yes! This end justifies these means. I'm not making things worse in the short term for some idealistic, dreamy goal in the future. I'm making things better from the very beginning. Things are better now. People have money in their pockets, extra money, for the first time in their adult lives, some of them. They're giddy. At first they didn't believe it, but it's starting to sink in. And there hasn't been a crime wave. Crime just goes on as usual. It's like a river, Jim. It flows on, regardless. You can drown yourself in it—or you can build a dam.'

"He worked out the details with Dominic Nosiglia, but took years to get the treaties written with the other families. Still, everything was on paper and most of the corporate entities they were going to use to move money around were in place before your father ran for President. That was why they made sure he won the election."

"How do you mean?"

"Well . . . there were a number of scandals that could have come out. I shouldn't go into the details, Tom. I don't even know all the details. But a number of people could have come forward and destroyed your father's campaign. Nothing happened, though. It struck me as odd at the time. But now I understand. Some of them retired to Florida. Some of them just had nightmares. Others had accidents. When Dominic Nosiglia asks you to be quiet, you shut up. You have your vocal cords removed in case you talk in your sleep."

"He's that bad?"

"He's worse than that. The first time I ever saw him I thought—this man is the Devil. And I haven't had any reason to change my mind since then. That was what I tried to explain to your father. However noble his goal was, however ingenious his plan was . . . he's effectively turned the government of the United States over to Dominic Nosiglia. As long as wants their deal to be secret, Dominic has the power of blackmail over the Oval Office."

"But he likes the deal. He doesn't want to blow it. So it's like a Mexican stand-off, isn't it?"

"I wish it was. But your father has much more to lose. So the Mafia controls the President. When you put that together with the number of Congressmen and Judges already on salary for the mob, the government begins to look like a wholly-owned subsidiary. The ultimate front. No one can stop Dominic Nosiglia now. Who's even going to try? The Justice Department? The FBI? They're on his side.

"That was my final moral plea. From now on, every time some little guy gets his grocery store burned down because he can't pay the protection money, every time someone gets their knees broken because they don't have the vigorish on their loan, every time a kid ODs on heroin or PCP every time one kid shoots another with a black market 9mm pistol . . . that's going to be the policy of the Jaglom Administration. And that's going to destroy this country long before his new prosperity can fix it.

"I could see I still hadn't gotten through. I couldn't make it real for him. So my last ditch effort was to attack the actual logistics of the thing. It's impractical, Tom. It's unworkable on so many levels. He was like a man who'd built a house of cards and was actually talking about moving in. Where to put the sectional couch and the dining room credenza. *In a house of cards.* It was just so crazy. There's no way you can buy enough people and scare enough people to keep something this big quiet. And that's just the Government side of it. I tried to make him think about the Mafia itself. There are big changes going on because of this. They don't need the man-power they used to. They're downsizing, just like any other big corporation. These Mafia guys are learning what it's like in the real world. People are being laid off. And they don't qualify for unemployment. So what are all those out of work leg-breakers and hit men supposed to do now? Re-train themselves for jobs in high technology? Go to Beauty School? Work at MacDonald's? No—these guys are breaking off and forming new gangs, with no allegiance to the government. Nosiglia is losing control. And there's another problem. What on earth makes him think these guys are actually going to *pay their taxes?* They've been cheating on their taxes since Al Capone. It's what they do. That's what I was trying to make him see, Tom—the thing is falling apart from both sides. There are too many moving parts. He built this weird contraption and it's breaking down. Even the cops on the street know that something is wrong. You can't disable your whole law enforcement system without *someone noticing.* And believe me, they are. They see it and they don't understand it and it's killing them.

"So I told him—come clean while you can. Admit it before everyone finds out. America might forgive you if you confess and say you're sorry. But if they catch you red-handed turning over the country to a bunch of gangsters, they'll destroy you. They'll burn your pictures and hang you in effigy and throw you in jail and hate you forever. It'll make impeachment look like summer camp. And they'll be right. No one will defend you. Not even me."

Jim sat back and rubbed his face with his hands. He looked spent by that final diatribe. He was back on Nantucket, going through that Christmas morning one more time. For myself, I wasn't quite as horrified or surprised as Jim had been. The plan sounded like my Dad, you could see him in it the way you could see Nixon in Watergate or Reagan in Iran Contra. Each of them had his own special craziness. You can hear Nixon saying "Let's just bug the Democratic headquarters!" and Reagan chortling "Then we'll give the money we make to the Contras! And we won't have to tell anybody!". In the same way I can hear my Dad explaining patiently "Fighting crime misses the point . . ."

But I felt good because I knew something Jim didn't. He assumed that nothing he said had connected, that the whole meeting had been futile.

I knew better.

Dad made it clear before he died: Jim had changed his mind. Jim was probably the only person on Earth who could have done it. He had always depended on Jim's basic down-to-earth practicality. I told him that Dad was planning to come clean at a Press Conference on New Year's Day.

Jim looked at me curiously. "Has he rescheduled?"

This was the part I had been dreading.

There was only one way to tell him: just tell him.

"He's dead, Jim. They killed him."

"I told him everything then. Everything I'd told Amy and more, stuff I'd figured out since then. My Dad must have told other people about his change of heart, people he trusted the most. Dennis Clark? I don't know. But obviously he trusted the wrong people. He turned himself into an enemy and the people he was up against had unlimited amounts of money and no scruples. They also had a contingency plan to protect themselves. And it's working. They've replaced my father and no but me can tell the difference. Everything is going smoothly.

"Amy and I are fighting it as best we can, without giving ourselves away," I told Jim. "But there are just two of us."

Jim clasped my shoulder and squeezed.

"Three," he said.

That's one of the best things about having a friend who's also a writer—he always knows the perfect words to say.

Or in this case—the perfect word.

I grabbed him awkwardly; he's a big man, not easy to

hug. And we sat there, like two refugees on an open boat and just let the truth fall on us like rain.

We both knew what we had to do next: publish Jim's article.

"You have to do it," he said. "I can't. All my contacts are being watched. Everyone who gets near me dies. I can't put any more of my friends at risk. And I won't send it over the transom like some stranger. The press follow you everywhere—choose a reporter and give it to him. No one knows we're meeting. If we can manage this one more time, no one will have any reason to suspect you.

"One more time?"

"I don't have the story with me."

"Why not? Weren't you planning to give it to me?"

"Well . . ."

"What?"

He looked away. He was actually embarrassed.

"I wasn't . . . I didn't . . . I don't know, Tom. I guess I'm suspicious of everyone these days. For all I knew, maybe you were . . . maybe someone had . . ."

"Bought me? Threatened me? Manipulated me?"

"Or just convinced you. I didn't know your side of the story. That's why I had to see you first I had to be sure."

"Well—it worked. You're sure now."

"I guess I was getting a little paranoid."

"It's OK. I know the feeling, believe me. Where do you want to meet?"

"Someplace public—outdoors."

"The sailboat pond in Central Park?"

"10 o'clock in the morning?"

"Okay."

"We're really going to do this?"

"We better!"

He shook his head. "I don't know, Tom. I'm scared."

"Of course you are—that's why you called me. It's like a

relay race. You've done your part and you did great. You dug up the story, you wrote it and you found me. Now you give it to me and my laps begin. My part is easy—ditch the Secret Service, jump on the shuttle to D.C., walk into the Washington Post . . . and the rest is history."

We paid and left. Outside in the street the wind had died out. The air was still and cool. It seemed to amplify sound. We could hear the traffic on Fifth Avenue, raucous hip hop from a distant boom box, kids squealing. A couple of cars passed on MacDougal Street.

We hugged one more time and I said, "10 A.M.—by the pond."

He nodded and hailed a cab. Its off-duty lights were on but it stopped anyway. He climbed half-way in, and after a brief conversation he sat down and shut the door. I guess he and the cabbie were going in the same direction. I watched them drive off toward Waverly Place and then started walking in the opposite direction, toward Seventh Avenue and the Houston Street subway station.

I don't blame Jim for being scared, but I feel good tonight. I wish I could do more, but I've done all I could. By next week Jim's article will be published and this whole horror will be over. If all goes well.

For now, all I can do is wait.

But I'm good at that.

15

Ira Heller closed Tom's spiral bound notebook and whistled softly. He looked at his watch. It was ten minutes to ten; that was cutting it close.

He grabbed the phone and started punching numbers.

Across the room, flanked by Secret Service agents, Amy Elwell watched him helplessly, paralyzed with guilt and self-loathing.

This was her fault.

Yes, Heller's timing was tragic, but that wouldn't have made any difference if she had been a better person—or a more skillful bad one. She never should have looked at the journal. It was wrong, it was a violation of Tom's privacy. But ever since the day she had deferred his marriage proposal, Tom had become increasingly remote and military in his demeanor. She knew it had been a mistake to put him off, though Tom's diary concealed his disappointment. That was consistent—it concealed a lot of things. It didn't describe the long silences between them or the many times she had gone to sleep alone. It didn't describe their withering intimacy; her diary could have done that. Though Tom described many conversations with extraordinary accuracy, he hadn't written anything about their most common recent exchange.

It went something like this:

"What's wrong, Tom?"

"Nothing."

"Come on—something's bothering you. What is it?"

"There's just a lot to think about."

"For instance?"

"Amy, please."

"Are you worried?"

"I'm fine."

And then he would write in his journal for an hour. He didn't trust her any more—that was how it seemed. He was closing down, armoring himself. Finally her curiosity about what he was really feeling and thinking had overpowered her good intentions. All she had needed was an opportunity, and Tom had given it to her this morning.

They had left Amos Gramble's apartment early, Amy heading home, Tom beginning the circuitous route that would lead him to the zoo. Amos had made them breakfast and eaten quietly with them. When he was walking them to the door he said, "I have a terrible feeling about this, children. I feel that it's all going to end badly. There's so much bad and so little good in this world. And the bad seems to have so much more vigor."

"The best lack all conviction," Tom quoted. "While the worst are full of passionate intensity."

Amos smiled. "Yes. Yeats understood."

Tom embraced the old man. "Don't lose hope," he said. "Yeats didn't."

Amos hugged Amy and kissed her on the cheek. Then he stepped back, lifted his hand in a half wave, and shut the door.

Amy took Tom's arm and there was a moment of resistance, as if he thought they were being watched. But they weren't. On the subway steps, out of sight from the street, Tom gave her the journal.

"If something happens, if something goes wrong today . . . I don't want anyone to find this on me."

"What could go wrong?"

"I don't know, Amy. Probably nothing will. But 'probably' is a dangerous word. Too many probablies can kill you. So take the book and when you get home put it inside the Atlas. And I'll have one less thing to worry about."

That was typical of his tone, lately—irritable and impatient. She felt like a junior officer instead of a lover or a partner or even a friend.

She was losing him. That was how it felt. That was why she had decided to read the journal. She needed to get in and he'd locked the doors. There was nothing left to do but break a window.

That she was caught in the act was Tom's fault as much as it was hers. He failed to spot the Secret Service team that followed them from Amos Gramble's house. He underestimated Heller's crew, and not for the first time. It was a type of miscalculation that Heller had nurtured meticulously. He cherished Tom's contempt. He knew the priceless tactical advantage of being underestimated.

Amy never saw the two men following her. Tom put her on an express with instructions to get off at 14th Street and walk home from there. He took the next IRT local uptown, planning to catch the shuttle at 42nd Street. He was in his own world, working through various strategies and contingency plans in case something really did go wrong, paying no attention at all to the assorted New Yorkers on the train with him. He could have taken a taxi, but they were too slow and he couldn't afford to be stuck in traffic right now.

If the street gang hadn't pushed into the car, he might never have noticed the Secret Service guys at all. The kids were loud and large and obnoxious, but Tom's urban instincts told him they were essentially harmless . . . just as he knew that the quiet guy with the tattoos at the far end of the car was a bomb waiting to go off. When the man glanced angrily at the boisterous group in their matching leather jackets, Tom was sure for a moment that he was going to pull out a gun and start shooting.

The kids were teasing two girls in jeans and sweaters, with scarves in their hair. The girls studiously ignored them, but a man in a Burberry overcoat sitting a few feet away reached under his lapel in a classic gesture of threat. It was perhaps the most familiar move in the modern choreography of violence—he was reaching for his gun. Tom saw it in a flash-bulb split-second of illumination, and he knew.

He looked up at the ads that ran the length of the car above the windows: answering services, accounting schools, Purdue chicken. He was rewinding the morning in his head, trying to isolate the moment when they picked him up again. He inventoried the empty sidewalk in front of Amos' building. Nothing: if they were there, they must have set up shop in one of the buildings across the street. But for how long? Had they followed him to his meeting with Jim? He had been sure he was alone.

Just like today.

But he had seen them today. They had made a mistake and he had caught it. There were a million possible mistakes, it was hard not to make at least one of them. The body language those guys learned in training was a give away all by itself. He slowed down and thought it out step by step. If he was followed yesterday, Jim was followed from the meeting and Jim was dead now. They would have questioned him about the meeting, and he would have talked. Heller could

be very persuasive, particularly if you had a low pain toler-
ance. And if Jim had talked these Secret Service guys would
be snapping hand-cuffs on him right now, not merely following him uptown.

So—how had they missed him yesterday? One of them
in the bathroom, the other one answering the phone? A
spilled cup of coffee, an argument, a yawn? It didn't matter—he had only been visible on the sidewalk for thirty
seconds or so, from Amos Gramble's front door until he
turned the corner. Thirty seconds out of how many hours?
Hundreds? And a long night of watching an unused front
door. Surveillance was brutal. People got tired, people
made mistakes. Tom grimaced. Including you, buddy, he
said to himself.

Including you.

The kids moved off down the length of the car, pushing and shoving each other. By the time the train pulled
into the 14th Street station, the kids were gone and everything was back to normal—people bunched into themselves, clenched against the noise and the anxiety, reading
newspapers, reading books, avoiding each others' eyes.

Tom didn't waste much time on self-recrimination. He
was concentrating on how to lose the tail. He thought of
just walking up to them and taking them out where they
sat with a pair of flying front snap-kicks. But he rejected
that idea. He didn't want to declare war yet. Besides, he
had no reason to hurt these guys. They weren't bad guys.
They were just doing their job and in fact they were doing
it much better than most of their colleagues. Jake always
said, "Don't fight when you can run." It was good advice.
Few people were as well-equipped for running as Tom was,
especially the kind of broken field running required by
crowded sidewalks.

The train was in the station now.

Time for some subway roulette. The train stopped,

people got off and on. The trick was to dart out of the car just before the doors closed again. Tom waited. A small black kid got on with a massive boom box blasting out a tuneless, abrasive rap song. It was an assault and hearing it on a subway car filled with cowering white people, Tom was finally certain that it was meant to be an assault. It was the aural equivalent of the graffiti on the walls—a way of defacing the world you hated.

Time to go.

Tom jumped up and dodged out the door, which closed just behind him. It would have been perfect, but the doors opened again, for no particular reason. Tom glanced behind him. The Secret Service guys were out and running. One of them was shouting into a cellular phone. That meant reinforcements.

Tom vaulted the turnstiles and sprinted for the stairs. As he came up to street level, he saw two more agents running for the entrance. One of them saw him and pointed.

Tom launched himself into the morning crowds. As he picked up the pace, shifting configurations of people hurtled at him. He leapt sideways between a couple, jumped a baby carriage and did an end-run around a group watching a juggler. He danced across 14th Street against the light, and hit the far sidewalk zig-zagging between nonplussed pedestrians who seemed to be standing still. He heard shouts and car horns behind him. He grinned, distracted for an instant, and tripped over a wire-taut leash. Someone had tied their dog to the pole of a street sign and the big unclipped poodle was straining at the collar. Before Tom knew it he was flying. He hit the sidewalk in a tumbler's roll, knocked over two old guys standing in front of an off-track betting storefront and was on his feet running again.

He crossed Sixth Avenue just ahead of a wall of traffic and then he was tearing east on Fifteenth Street. He risked a quick look behind him: no one. Still he ran for twelve more blocks, north and east. He jogged for 10 more and was walking at a normal pace by the time he reached the Lexington Avenue IRT station at 28th Street.

Behind him, one of the Secret Service men had crashed into an old lady, been mistaken for a purse-snatcher and set upon by a crowd of outraged citizens. Another had gotten clipped by a taxi as he crossed 14th Street against the light. The cabbie got out and started yelling at him. The agent's partner badged the driver with Secret Service ID, but he wasn't impressed. Tom would have been pleased with the cabbie's response:

"Right! Didja get that out of a crackerjack box? If you was the Secret Service the President would be dead by now!"

The last agent was stopped by a simple stitch in the side. Panting and wheezing, leaning forward with his hands on his knees, he knew he had no decent excuse for Heller. The kid had simply outrun him.

Tom was far away, free and clear, still on schedule. He rode the subway to 68th Street, feeling his muscles lightly coated with lactic acid, his blood pleasantly infused with endorphins. They made him unnaturally cheerful and optimistic. It was a beautiful morning. Tom strolled west, past the boutiques and the brownstones, aiming for the park. There were birds in dirty trees. The city was wind-swept and new; it sparkled in the sunshine. The mild air humanized it, somehow. For the first time since he had met the impostor Tom felt confident that things were going to turn out all right. The gentle breeze seemed to ratify his optimism and much to his surprise he found himself whistling as he crossed Park Avenue.

As Tom was ditching the Secret Service, Amy was sitting on the big leather couch in his apartment, drinking a mug of herbal tea and reading his journal. Her primary emotion was relief. There was nothing dark or weird in Tom's notebook. There were things he hadn't said but they were good things, loving things. And the rest of it was just the paperwork of a man with a mission. If the mission was distracting him from the sweet protocols of his love-life, well why shouldn't it? It was just as Jim Gramble had said: they had a job to do now, and that job was much more important than how either of them happened to be feeling.

She had just finished reading about the meeting with Jim and was about to get up and make herself some more tea, when Ira Heller started pounding on the front door.

"Secret Service. Open up."

She recognized that rasping voice through the door and panic emptied her head. She jumped up, knocked over her empty mug, and tripped over one of the legs of the coffee table. The notebook flew out of her hands.

"Open the door or we'll break it down," Heller drawled. Amy scrambled on her hands and knees and grabbed the book just as the first blow hit the door. She lurched to her feet as the second impact resounded through the small apartment. The locks might hold but the wood of the doorjamb was going to splinter any second. She made it to the book-case and she was just jamming the journal into the hollowed-out center of the Atlas when the door flew open and the Secret Service stormed in.

Then, in a moment of almost sublime idiocy that she would remember with rancid self-contempt for the rest of her life, she gave up on the Atlas and let it fall to the carpet while she thrust the notebook behind her back.

Tom had said: "If we act suspiciously they'll get suspicious."

She couldn't have acted more suspiciously if she had rehearsed it. This was a perfect pantomime cliché of guilty behavior. A three-year old could look at her and say "Lady hiding something, Mommy!" Minnie Mouse hid things this way.

If she had been sitting quietly and reading when Heller arrived, if she had set the notebook down casually in plain sight and offered to make them a cup of coffee, Heller might never have even noticed it.

But now she was caught between two big agents, all her new knowledge of small arms useless to her, listening to Heller barking orders into the telephone.

" . . . Take whoever you need, just move it. You've got eight minutes. Yeah? Well, tough luck. I would have called sooner but I hadn't read the kid's confession yet. Look on the bright side—this is a break for us. Unless you screw it up." Heller hung up. "The problem is, that moron could screw up a wet dream. Get her outta here. Let's go."

"Don't you have to read me my rights?" asked.

"No I don't. I'm not a cop. You're not under arrest. You're being taken into custody by the Secret Service under suspicion of high treason. That means you have no rights. So try to stay on my good side. I'm cranky and temperamental and I drank too much coffee this morning. So it aint gonna be easy."

He flicked a hand impatiently at his men and they hustled her out the door.

16

Tom was four minutes late.

He ran towards the sailboat pond from the south, down Pilgrim Hill. He had started running half way across Madison Avenue after a quick glance at his watch. He could feel panic nibbling at him. He didn't like the idea of Jim loitering in the park, alone.

But he wasn't alone. There was a man talking to him on the north side of pond, beside the Hans Christian Andersen statue. Tom forced himself to slow down.

Jim flinched as the man spoke to him. One of the man's hands was in his raincoat pocket—holding a gun, Tom was certain. It was in the way the man's weight shifted to that side. Tom circled behind them, walking. He couldn't afford to draw attention to himself now.

The man said something. Jim answered.

Tom was fifty yards away. He picked up his pace—a typical New Yorker, taking a short cut through the park, in a hurry.

Forty yards.

Jim reached into his coat and pulled out a manila envelope. It was the story. It had to be. The man took it.

Tom leapt into a run, knees pumping to his chin, arms tight at his sides. The ground was clear ahead of him. Twenty yards, fifteen.

Jim saw him. His eyes flicked over the man's shoulder, just for a moment, then back again. But it was enough. The man spun around and saw Tom hurtling towards him Tom got one glimpse of his face—long and dark with a thin pencil mustache—before he turned his back again.

The man fired three shots, dropped his gun and started running himself, smashing through a group of kids, knocking two of them down.

Jim was on the pavement. Blood was soaking through his coat. In an agonized moment of indecision, Tom knew he should chase down the running man. But he couldn't. He couldn't leave Jim to die alone. And Jim was dying, there was no doubt about that.

Tom saw the gun lying a few feet from Jim's head. He dove, grabbed it, rolled to his knees and aimed at the fleeing killer. He squeezed off three shots before he realized that the gun was empty. Jim groaned. He was trying to talk. Tom scrambled back beside the big black man, screaming "Call an ambulance—somebody call an ambulance!" Then he turned back to Jim and spoke quietly. "Its okay, we're gonna get you to the hospital. Just lie still. Don't try to talk. Just breathe. That's it. Nice and easy."

"Tal ..." Jim said.

"Shhh. The ambulance is on the way. But Jim was still struggling. Finally he said it:

"Taliafero." Blood bubbled up at the corners of his mouth. Tom glanced up, but Taliafero was long gone.

When the first cops arrived five minutes later. Tom was kneeling next to Jim Gramble's body, rocking back and forth, making small keening noises, feeling the fabric of his connection to reality tearing along the seams like an old shirt.

He heard Amos Gramble saying "Are you going to help

Jim?" He heard him saying "You're fighting the good fight. Don't lose it. Jim's counting on you. Both of us are."

But Jim was dead and all his father's prophesies had come true. There was the sound of an ambulance from far away, but it was too late.

Too late: if Tom had run ten blocks less, gotten on the subway two stops sooner, run instead of jogged across town to the park—

"On your feet, kid."

"And drop the gun."

Tom looked up sluggishly. Two policemen were standing over him, weapons drawn. He was indeed still holding Taliafero's .38. Still on his knees, he reached up and handed it over. Had Taliafero planned this final touch? It was possible; Tom's prints were all over the gun now.

And Taliafero had been wearing gloves.

"You are under arrest for suspicion of felony assault and murder," the older cop was saying. "You have the right to remain silent. If you choose to speak anything you say can and will be used against you in a court of law. You have the right to legal counsel. If you cannot afford a lawyer, one will be appointed for you by the court."

"Wait a second." Tom stood, His legs were trembling. "I didn't kill him. It was a cop. I'm a witness. A cop did it. His name is Taliafero—tall, thin guy. Pencil mustache. He—"

"Don't make it worse for yourself, kid. Here's a tip for ya—we cops tend to be fraternal. We get pissed off when you accuse other cops of murder. Cuff him, Howie."

Tom stared down at Jim.

This was what Jim had been talking about. This was Hell on Earth—a few shrewd deals, a leveraged buy-out or two, floated by junk bonds (the Devil would have to appreciate junk bonds) and Satan had gotten his Kingdom. Everything was lost or given away—or sold.

And this was what remained: two bulls on Dominic Nosiglia's payroll, accusing Tom of murder.

But the two fat, brutal faces yanked him back to reality: he couldn't save Jim, but he still had a mission and it was Jim's mission, too. These cops thought they could stop him; they had the guns and the handcuffs and they thought that was enough. There were new sirens in the distance—five or six more sets of guns and handcuffs *would* be enough—more than enough.

Tom smiled at the two policemen.

Then he exploded.

He knocked the older one's gun aside and lunged forward with an elbow smash to the throat. Using his hip as a pivot, he kicked the man's legs out from under him and slammed him into his partner. Tom kicked the younger one as they fell, and then he leapt over the bodies and started sprinting for Fifth Avenue. He heard people shouting but there were no gunshots. He still had a minute or two. He angled left beside the pond, back towards Pilgrim Hill and the 72nd Street entrance to the Park. As soon as he was on Fifth Avenue he slowed down to a brisk walk. In ten minutes all exits from the park would be blocked. But two minutes later, Tom was walking east down 71st Street, watching police cars roll by and listening to the convergence of sirens.

He was free for the moment. But he was a fugitive now. Hitting those cops had changed everything. If Heller wanted to stop him he could use the full force of official law enforcement. But would Heller want to stop him? There was no immediate need to panic. If he wasn't recognized at the crime scene, if Taliafero was just a mob goon with no connection to Heller . . . Tom pressed his hands to his eyes.

No—they had to be connected. That was Jim's whole point. Everything was linked together now. Taliafero might even be some kind of liaison: a crooked cop who had dealt with the Secret Service over the years would be a perfect go-between. If Taliafero was working for Heller—

Tom cut himself off. He didn't have time to second guess
Heller now. He didn't have time for anything but a frantic
search of Jim's apartment: he had to find the papers Jim had
hidden there before the cops and the Mafia and the Secret
Service figured out that was where he was going next.

Or maybe they had figured it out already—maybe they
were waiting for him right now, loading their guns and
checking their watches.

There was only one way to find out.

Tom hailed a cab on Park Avenue.

"Ninetieth and West End," he told the driver. He
wanted to walk the last few blocks. A little prudent recon-
naissance might just save his life.

Everything depended on the next hour. Tom sat back,
shut his eyes and concentrated on breathing. He needed
to be calm and focused—he had a puzzle to solve, along
with everything else.

"Don't let the bunny stump you again."

Tom ran Jim's words around in his head, trying to recall the various Easter Sundays he'd spent with Jim and
Eleanor as a child. He was baffled; hopefully the apartment
itself would give him some ideas.

Tom paid off the cabbie and started walking uptown
on West End Avenue. There wasn't a cloud in the sky and
the temperature was in the mid-sixties. There was a light
breeze blowing off the Hudson River.

There were some mornings when late March in New
York made April in Paris look mundane by comparison.
The city opened like a flower in these first days when winter fled. It was picnic-on-the-roof weather, window shopping weather, softball-in-the-Park weather.

And he was going to war. The very air seemed to chastise
him. Tom wondered if the hostile factions in Beirut and Ulster and Sarajevo felt reproved in the same way when spring
finally came to their battered cities and they continued kill-

ing each other in the bright air, their coats off at last, amid the melting snow and the new mud, with that gentle southern wind in their faces. Probably they did, though they went right on killing each other anyway.

Jim's apartment was being watched.

As Tom approached he saw a gray Secret Service Dodge pull up and double park door to door with the blue Secret Service Plymouth that had taken the last shift. Ordinarily Tom would have assumed that it was just a routine changing of the guard. But today he wasn't sure. If Heller knew he was free after a botched meeting with Jim Gramble—and Tom had to assume that was the case—then it would make sense to increase security around the three or four most like places for him to show up.

The anger from the Park welled up in him again. He saw the absolute, impossible stillness of Jim's body, ground his teeth at the obscene, casual ease with which that brave irreplaceable life had been taken. That it was tactically appropriate to eliminate these two surveillance teams was a secondary matter.

He wanted to hurt them.

It was four to one, but he had certain advantages: greater skill and the element of surprise, and his rage, if he could control it. Even the weather was on his side. Hand-to-hand combat was much more difficult, much riskier, in the cold. It was harder to punch with chilled hands, harder to run on icy streets.

A moment before he launched his attack, he smiled to himself. Now he knew a little bit better how the Bosnian freedom fighters had felt when spring came to Sarajevo.

Ed Joseph was leaning against the roof of his car, in the crook of the open door, with his back to the traffic. He was listening as Nate Billings leaned over in the narrow alley between the cars, speaking into the open window to Joel Pressman and Bobby Cross. In the hum and rustle of traffic behind him, Ed didn't even hear the footsteps until his car door was slamming him unconscious against the edge of the roof.

Before Ed could fall to the greasy asphalt, Tom was rolling over the roof, dropping between the two cars. He clamped Nate Billings in a head lock that cut off the blood to his brain and punched in through the open car window, knocking Joel Pressman out with one blow to the temple. As Pressman slumped against his seat belt, Tom pulled the agent's gun from his shoulder holster and jammed it into Bobby Cross' neck. Ed Joseph was unconscious in the crook of Tom's elbow from his blocked carotid artery.

Tom let him crumple to the street before brain damage set in, not that you could necessarily tell the difference with these guys. He hit Cross with the butt of his partner's gun, rolled Ed Joseph and Nate Billings under their car and turned on their emergency blinkers.

Traffic streamed past both ways on West End Avenue. Probably some people had seen him. But no one stopped and he was reasonably sure that no one even called the police on their car phones. No one wanted to deal with the cops.

Tom felt calmed by his outburst of violence. He let himself into Jim's building with his own set of keys, still trying to remember Easters past, keenly aware that as soon as the unconscious Secret Service men were due to check in, the alarms would start to go off. He had ten or fifteen minutes at most.

It was quiet in Jim's building, and stuffy; perhaps ten degrees warmer than the air outside. Tom took the stairs three at a time, As Jake Gritzky invariably did, with his habit of making a punishing exercise regimen out of any routine activity. On the third floor there were the sounds of classical music from one apartment, a television bleating from another and the soft grumbling of the building itself—the mutter of the furnace, the whine of the elevator, not disturbing the quiet but enriching it. There was no guard posted at Jim's door. Tom let himself in and shut it softly behind him.

The apartment had been demolished. The furniture was slashed apart, the floor boards levered up, the appliances smashed. The bookshelves were overturned, the cupboards were gaping open, empty. Tom's first thought was that a bomb had gone off, but this was a meticulous, hand-crafted destruction. The wreckage showed an exhausting attention to detail: things were dismantled rather than destroyed. Experts had been here.

Tom picked his way into the other rooms, past ransacked closets and shredded upholstery, his shoes crunching on broken glass. The place smelled like an open sewer. He cleared a space on what was left of Jim's mattress and sat down.

Given the quality of the search and the number of man-hours it had probably required, it was hard to believe that they hadn't found what they were looking for. Any vestiges of Jim's personal life which might have given Tom a clue were lost in the ruins.

"Don't let the Easter bunny stump you again."

Tom could feel the time passing: his ten or fifteen minutes were down to five or ten.

He stood up, breathing through his mouth. The first thing he had to do was flush that toilet. He eased his way into the bathroom and risked a look under the lid. The stink was raw and acrid. It was like pulling a rope through his sinuses. The lumpy brown mess inside had been there for quite a while. Tom hit the flush lever but nothing happened. He was turning away queasily—as no doubt all the other searchers had turned away—when the memory darted past him, like a quick small shape in his peripheral vision—a squirrel flitting up a tree trunk.

He stood very still, thinking, losing time as a falling man loses space, plummeting through the empty seconds towards the impact of his capture.

He almost had it.

Something about the moment when he lifted the lid and—

That was it. That had to be it. Jim had drained the toilet one year, scrubbed the bowl shiny and then placed Tom's Easter basket inside. Tom had looked everywhere else in the house before he finally gave up, just the way the cops and the Secret Service and the Mafia had given up. Of course, Jim had done a much more elaborate job this time . . . if Tom was right.

He went into the kitchen and found a plastic mop bucket, a bowl and a knife. He returned and, grimacing with disgust, opened the toilet again. He slid the knife gingerly below the surface of the brown water, point first. It went in two inches and then struck something. There was a sharp click of metal against glass.

Tom rocked back on his heels, exhaling a laugh of triumph and respect.

Jim had done it.

He had beaten the professionals at their own game. You didn't need years of training or decades of covert experience to outsmart these guys; all you needed was to be smarter than they were.

Tom went to work, bailing out the shallow mess into the bucket with the bowl, finally using windex and lots of paper towel to wipe off the oval-shaped piece of glass Jim had so carefully caulked around its perimeter. Then he washed his hands.

There was a manila envelope under the glass, just like the one Taliafero had taken from Jim at the seal pond, lying safe and dry on the scrubbed white porcelain. There was a note clipped to it and a key lying on top of the note.

Tom broke the glass, pocketed the key and pulled loose the slip of paper. Jim's sloppy, over-sized handwriting was like a voice from the grave.

"Well done, Tom! I knew you'd be able to find this stuff. Sorry about the camouflage. All my notes and research material are in the bedroom closet of Gary Meredith's apartment—400 East 74th Street, #2010. The building is called The Monarch. I'm leaving a key for you. The material corroborates the article and strengthens the presentation. Use it. That you're reading this means either we haven't been able to meet yet, in which case, you can contact me through my father. Or we have met and I'm dead."

Tom closed his eyes. After a while he opened them again. There was a little more of the note:

"If that has happened, believe me, Tom: I don't blame you. You did your best and we both know how good that is. Thanks. Jim."

Tom was crying. He stood in the pillaged bathroom, in the vandalized apartment, sweating in the steam heat, smelling the septic stench that was the only lingering physical remnant of Jim Gramble's existence, crying for Jim and for his own parents, alone and lonely, overwhelmed by circumstance, missing his father, needing his Mom.

He was finally just a child, orphaned and left to fend for himself, doing his best. But his best hadn't been good enough. It hadn't been anywhere near good enough. Who else was going to die because of him? Amy? Jake? He couldn't—

There was a sound from the other end of the apartment. His self-pitying thoughts fled and Tom pulled in his breath, listening.

People were kicking through the rubble, at least three of them. He crumpled Jim's note and slipped it in his pocket with Gary Meredith's key.

A moment later Tom was facing two automatic assault rifles. Between two Secret Service agents he didn't recognize, unarmed, towering above both of them, six foot five and two hundred and eighty pounds of solid muscle, Duane Claassen smiled at him.

"Take the envelope and get out of here," he said to the others. "Tom and I have a little score to settle."

He turned to Tom, still smiling. "You made a fool out of me, Tom. You got me in trouble. So now you're going to hurt. I'm going to hurt you in the special way that tells you your body is being destroyed. You're going to be crippled and in pain for the rest of your life. Every time you try to take a deep breath or walk upstairs or urinate you're going to remember me, you're going to remember this day. You're going to remember how you begged me on your knees to forgive you."

"I have an idea—why don't we skip a few steps? I'll start begging right now."

Claassen shook his head. The other two agents slipped past them out of the bathroom with the envelope. A few seconds later Tom heard the door to the apartment slam shut.

Claassen stepped towards him, still smiling that maddening, savage, disconnected smile.

They were alone.

Duane filled the doorway: there was no way around him, and Tom knew he had no chance against the giant in the close quarters of Jim's bathroom. He needed room to move, he needed a way out, he needed a weapon. And he had nothing.

"I'm going to rupture your spleen first," Duane said conversationally. "Then I'm going to break your fingers, one at a time. I'm going to bend them backwards until they snap. I may scalp you after that, I don't know. Maybe I'll cut your hamstrings first. Or castrate you. We'll see."

He took a step forward and Tom took a step back. There weren't many steps left to take. His heel bumped into something and there was the sound of sloshing water.

The bucket.

Tom was in action before the plan had even risen to the level of conscious thought. He grabbed the bucket, came up with it, thrusting it out and around in a hard arc. The brown water and feces hit Duane in a projectile spew, blinding him and forcing him back, thrashing at himself in horror and disgust, gasping and howling.

There was just enough space between his legs: Tom hit the slippery tiles of the bathroom floor tucked into a ball and rolled between Duane's knees. He was on his feet before the big man turned around. He tripped over an overturned bookcase and jack-knifed himself onto the bed. Duane was just behind him, bellowing in rage as Tom rolled off the tattered mattress and lunged for the door.

Duane's psychotic tantrum was scary but Tom knew he could use it to his advantage. Angry people didn't think clearly. They made mistakes, and Duane was going to have to make some serious, world-class mistakes if Tom was going to get out of Jim Gramble's apartment alive.

For a second the way was clear through the rubble-strewn living room to the hall and the front door. But just for a second. Before Tom could pick his way through the junk on the floor, Duane had heaved himself forward.

Trapped again.

Duane smiled, wiping the muck off his face with his palm. The guy was huge. Tom forced the fear back and tried to think what Jake Gritzky would do in this situation. Hit one spot over and over again—choose a vulnerable location and just keep hammering it, the way you'd cut down a tree with an ax. The side of the knee, for instance. Tom kicked the giant there as hard as he could. The blow seemed to have no effect. Duane started toward him, pushing the way clear with his feet. Tom kicked him again, and again, backing up all the time. After the fifth kick Duane started to limp slightly. Tom drove a sixth kick into the same spot, then a seventh. The limp increased. Duane wasn't smiling any more. But he wasn't slowing down either.

Tom risked a glance behind his back: in two more steps he would be up against Jim's overturned desk. If one of the legs was loose . . . but they were solid; he grabbed one but couldn't budge it. Then Duane's arms were around him, lifting him off the floor in a merciless bear hug.

He was face to face with the wide-eyed, flat-nosed monster, smelling his sweat and the sweet reek of English Leather cologne, the greasy Chinese food and cigarettes on his breath. Duane's teeth were bared in a snarl of effort as he squeezed Tom's ribs. Tom pushed at the arms, hit them as hard as he could. It was like hitting logs. The pain in his sides was sharp and explosive; soon his ribs would splinter like bread sticks.

But Jake had taught him well. There was only one possible move to make in this situation and he remembered it now. He jammed his thumbs into Duane's eyes, pushing the eyeballs back, smashing them against the optic nerves. It might have seemed like a futile gesture—after all, even a blind Duane Claassen could kill him. But the point wasn't to blind the big man. The optic nerve connected directly to nerve clusters at the base of the neck: enough pressure on the eyeballs can induce unconsciousness.

But when? That was the only question now.

Tom could scarcely breathe. It was like being stabbed, like ice-picks puncturing not just skin and muscle but the bones themselves, metal driving into marrow. If this went on much longer it wouldn't matter if he knocked out Duane Claassen or not. There was no way he could survive the next seventy-two hours with a set of cracked ribs.

He pushed harder.

Duane tightened his grip. It didn't seem possible that Duane's grip could get any tighter, but it did. Tom felt himself blacking out from the pain.

Then, suddenly, Duane's hold relaxed. Tom jumped back against the desk as the giant slumped to the floor.

The apartment was silent. Tom stood very still, feeling his sides, checking for damage, experimenting with a couple of deep breaths, deciding that shallow breaths were a better idea and waiting for the biting pain to relent. He seemed to be intact—sore, badly bruised, but intact. A few more seconds of that bear hug . . . Tom looked down at Duane Claassen, snoring peacefully on the floor, still festooned with the contents of Jim Gramble's toilet.

The agony was backing off a little now. But time was crowding him. Cars could be pulling up at the curb even now and he was in no condition to do any more fighting. He made his way back to Jim's bathroom. He pulled off his soiled shirt and washed himself in the hottest water he could stand—he hated to think what the germs in that bucket had ripened into. There was aspirin in the medicine chest. He took five, swallowing them with water straight from the faucet. Among the slashed jackets and coats in Jim's closet he found a good corduroy shirt. It was couple of sizes too big but it didn't smell like an open latrine.

He changed clothes gingerly, listening for cars at the curb and steps in the hallway outside. When he was ready he stood at the front door for a full minute, listening. He heard nothing. He crossed the empty hall and took the fire stairs to the lobby. He walked out onto the sidewalk into the mild breeze. The street was clear. He turned west and started walking towards Riverside Park. He didn't need to think or plan. His choices had been sheared down to the imperative and the unthinkable—get the material from Gary Meredith's apartment or turn himself in. There was still a decent chance that the Secret Service knew nothing about that drop. He felt the crumpled note in his pocket. No one had seen it but him.

He hailed a cab on Riverside Drive

"74th Street—400 East 74th Street."

The aspirin was starting to kick in, loosening the band of pain at his sides. He needed to go to his bank—his inheritance was waiting for him in a safe-deposit box in the 53rd Street branch of Citibank. But he didn't dare. They'd be waiting for him, and the safe deposit vault was the perfect spot for an ambush.

This was bad. He was being closed off from his territory, from his past and the places that defined it. His apartment and Amy's were off-limits now, too. Amos Gramble's house, his own family's homes on Beekman Place and Nantucket and any place where the Secret Service had logged him spending time—NYU, friends' apartments, restaurants . . . they were all under surveillance.

He was in exile.

They had forced him into motion, driven him away from every sanctuary. His only access to his money was his ATM card, but that was foolish. Heller would certainly have neutralized it the way they did when your card was stolen. He wasn't foolish enough to try it and find out for sure. The only result would be to give away his location to a computer network, accessed by the Secret Service.

He had about fifty dollars in his pocket—that was it.

The driver was listening to the radio. The music stopped and a news bulletin came on. Tom sat forward.

"In a shocking development in the Central Park gunfight that took the life of Pulitzer Prizewinning journalist James Gramble and left two police officers critically injured, Police Chief Warren Dontanville has just released the identity of the primary suspect. The fatal shots were allegedly fired by Thomas Jaglom, the only son of President Edward Bellamy Jaglom. Three separate eye-witnesses placed the troubled college student at the scene of the crime.

"President Jaglom, sequestered in a Des Moines hospi-

tal and still recovering from injuries sustained in the New
Year's crash of Air Force One, could not be reached for comment and the White House offered no statement. In a hastily
convened press conference at City Hall, Chief Dontanville
expressed hope for quick apprehension of the twenty-two-
year-old Thomas Jaglom. "His picture is on the cover of
People Magazine this week," said the chief. "You couldn't
ask for a better 'Wanted' poster."

The driver turned off the radio.

"Can you believe this shit?" he said.

Tom slumped down. He didn't want to give the driver
any reason to identify him later. His thoughts turned morbid. If the papers weren't in Gary Meredith's apartment, if
he had no proof to use against Dominic Nosiglia, then he
would be finished: broke and on the run, a homeless man
full of deranged accusations, one more psychotic street
person.

But famous; the police chief was right about that. His
face was staring out from every newsstand on every corner
in the city. But conjuring such disasters was pointless. The
pain in his ribs had skewed his thinking. Close as he was to
defeat, he was just as close to victory. It would be much
better for him to sit back and close his eyes, to make himself patient and calm, to focus on his own breathing and
try to relax.

After a while, as the cab jolted uptown, the babbling
noise inside him subsided. By the time they pulled up to
400 East 74th Street he was quiet and serene.

And he was ready.

17

"It's a roach hotel," said Ira Heller into the phone. "Remember that ad, Mr. Clark? 'Roaches check in but they don't check out.' That's all you need to know. Leave the details to us. Uh huh. I'm aware of that. But we're not talking about Superboy, here. He's unarmed and I just talked to Duane Claassen ten minutes ago—yeah, he'll be fine. A few headaches, nothing serious, I'll tell him you wanted to know. Anyway—Duane did some damage. The kid is a hurting unit right now, trust me. What?"

Heller shrugged the phone off his shoulder, put down his clip-board and covered the speaker with his palm. He frowned at the agent standing by the door of the cramped, makeshift office across the street from The Monarch apartments.

"I have to be polite with this idiot," he said. "But I'm gonna take it out on you."

He put the phone back to his ear.

"Okay—that's a good question. In fact, we don't know. There's not a whole lot we do know in my end of the business, Mr. Clark. So we play the odds and keep our eyes

open. We're certainly hoping he'll show up, because
frankly we have no idea where else he might go. The
odds are good because there's something he wants here.
If I assume he's gonna stay away I got nothing to do but
pick my nose and watch CNN. Which is not what you pay
me for. I got four teams of six guys each in the building. I
have two command posts set up. He walks in there, he's
mine. Yeah, I will. Yeah. Good. Thanks. I'll get back to
you."

Heller hung up with a disgusted snort.

"All right, now listen up. This is our last clean shot. I
don't wanta be chasing him all over the Eastern seaboard."

"Don't worry, sir."

"Don't say that, Tomlinson. I worry for a living. So pay
attention: nobody peeks around a corner. No improvisa-
tions, no heroes, no photo opportunities. No problems
with the police liaison. Everyone's been briefed and
drilled; nobody should have to give an order. Nobody
should have to say a word."

Tomlinson nodded. "We've rehearsed this set-up a
million times, sir."

"Yeah? Well, this is opening night and there's—"

"—no margin for error?"

"That's right. I say that a lot, huh?"

"Yes, sir."

"O.K. smart-ass. Just remember it."

Tomlinson was at the door when Heller spoke again.
"One more thing—I want the kid alive, if you can manage
it."

"What if we can't?"

Heller stared at him coldly. "Do what you have to do."

"Yes, sir."

Tomlinson saluted and left the office. Downstairs, he
ran across the street and through the front doors of The
Monarch. Heller had walked over to his office window.

He looked out at the big, cheap, undistinguished building across the street as Tomlinson disappeared inside.

The window was open and a mild current of air flowed over the grimy sill, carrying the rumble of buses heading uptown on First Avenue. They always seemed to travel in packs. Seventy-fourth Street was peaceful at this hour—two men in business suits, a lady walking a big Rottweiler. A kid on a skateboard was practicing ollies and kick flips. Heller had reluctantly decided against closing off the street. Tom was a New Yorker—he'd sense that something was wrong and bolt.

Heller sighed. He didn't want a fire-fight, though he knew the soldiers and the cops were keyed up for one. He didn't like the mess and he didn't like the paperwork. He didn't enjoy explaining the exigencies of peacetime combat to Congressional oversight committees.

As he looked down, a cab pulled up to the building and Tom Jaglom climbed out. Tomlinson had gotten inside just in time. Heller walked over to his desk and sat down. There was nothing more he could do now; the morning would be decided by the men he had trained. He sipped tepid coffee, hoping he had trained them well enough.

The lobby of 400 East 74th street was empty. Tom quartered the space with his eyes as he walked toward the elevators. No doorman, no janitor, no one checking their mail, no one sitting in the uncomfortable-looking furniture. It was the middle of the day and middle class people lived here; it made sense. Even the maintenance staff would be taking their lunch. But it made Tom nervous anyway. The place had the eerie, interrupted quality of an evacuated town.

Tom stepped into the elevator and pushed the button for the 20th floor. He was pressed against the side wall, invisible from the corridor, when the doors opened.

The hall was deserted. Tom moved into the corridor as the elevator doors shut behind him. The wall-to-wall carpet crackled softly under his shoes. After about 30 feet, the passageway made a right-angled turn. Tom flattened himself against the wall and peered around: another stretch of gray carpet and blank doorways. Number 2010 was the first door around the corner. Tom pulled out the key and unlocked it gently, cracking it just an inch. With his back to the wall beside the jamb, he nudged it the rest of the way open.

He eased himself into the doorway and the empty living room yawned at him: cheap matching couch and chairs from Sears, scuffed orange carpet, book shelves full of paperbacks, copies of *Billboard* and *Spin* on the glass coffee table. A counter separated the living room from the kitchen. Big windows let in the sun from the North and West. Tom blinked in the dazzle of early afternoon light. You could see most of the East Side from here—the jumble of flat roofs, rising to the looming pre-war buildings on Park Avenue. Water towers dotted the skyline. There was a dense murmur of wind punctuated by distant car horns and the remote wail of a siren, but that was all. No whispers, no one's weight shifting on the rug, no click of a safety going off. The wind gusted. The window rattled in its frame.

Tom moved inside, closing the door softly behind him. He glanced out the window. The apartment below Gary Meredith's featured a small terrace. Apart from a potted Ficus tree and two chairs, it was empty also. Tom moved through a narrow hall, past the bathroom and into the bedroom. That uneasiness was climbing his spine again. Something was wrong—he wasn't alone. But the bedroom was deserted: king-size bed, chain quilt bedspread, upholstered headboard, polished parquet floor. There was a light coat of dust on everything. No one had been here for a while. Tom opened the closet door.

It was empty.

He stared into the blank space, the wood bar with its dangling wire hangers, some still wrapped in dry cleaner's paper, the bare floor.

It was the wrong closet. It was the wrong apartment.

But the key had fit the lock; and there was only one bedroom. This was it, this was the end. Someone knew about this place, after all. Someone had gotten here first, and now everything they had done meant nothing. Jim's ingenuity meant nothing, his death meant nothing. Tom had accomplished nothing and there was nothing more he could do.

There was a sound behind him; the wind again. He leaned against the closet doorjamb and shut his eyes.

He didn't see the movement but he felt it. The rush of air and the creak of the parquet flooring snapped him to attention just in time to feel the gun jabbing into his sore ribs.

"Hands on your head.'

Tom obeyed. He glanced behind him and absorbed another shock. The man said, "Eyes straight ahead." He had memorized that bony face with its pencil mustache and elegantly styled black hair. This was the man who had killed Jim Gramble.

"Taliafero," he whispered.

"Detective Sergeant Armand Taliafero, at your service. My job today is to bring you out of here, preferably alive. But if I have to kill you, no one's gonna complain."

Tom was recalibrating the situation. Taliafero wasn't alone; getting past him would just be the beginning. There would be others, many others. Heller and the cops would have the whole building secured. Tom was hurting and un-armed; if he gave up now he might save a lot of bloodshed.

But even as he considered that choice a final, desperate plan—the logical conclusion of all his other plans—slipped

behind him, cold and dangerous as Taliafero himself, as ugly
and obvious as the ring of metal digging into his left side.

There was, after all, one course of action left open to
him. It was grim and appalling but it was possible. It could
be done; and he was the only one in the world who could
do it.

He sucked air through his clenched teeth. First of all,
he had to escape—and that meant he had to disarm
Taliafero. The man had taken a step back but he was still
within striking range. On any of a thousand TV cop shows
the good guy would lash out and, after a brief struggle for
the gun, with both his hands clamped on the villain's wrists,
either the gun would drop from the bad guy's nerveless
fingers or a single shot would go off and after a moment
of bogus suspense it would become clear that the bad guy
had shot himself. In any of a thousand Martial Arts movies,
Jet Li or Jackie Chan would pull some fancy move and
send the gun flying across the room as the villain howled
and clutched at his shattered wrist.

Tom knew better.

Jake Gritzky had trained these lethal fantasies out of
him a long time ago. In reality, it was almost impossible to
disarm a trained shooter like Taliafero. No matter how fast
you moved, the flick of a wrist and the muzzle velocity of a
bullet were much faster.

"I know what you're thinking, kid," Taliafero said.
"You're figuring the angles. Given your reputation, I'd say
the prudent move for me is to just kill you now and get it
over with. Nothing personal."

Tom turned with his decisions made. He knew his
chances were slender at best. He was likely to be wounded
and if he was wounded even slightly he was finished. But
Taliafero had talked too much and now Tom knew that his
only other option was being gunned down where he stood.

That made any plan look good.

Taliafero smiled at him. "How does it feel to be dead, kid?"

Tom smiled back. "You tell me."

Tom faked to the left and lunged to the right. A right-handed shooter can't move his arm to the right without locking the elbow. It's awkward and clumsy—by the time the gun went off, Tom was outside the line of fire. Inside would have been better, but he didn't have time to quibble. The shot was deafening in the confines of the bedroom. It missed him by no more than an inch. Tom grabbed Taliafero's wrist and thrust it down as he brought his knee up, dislocating the cop's elbow. Taliafero screamed and the gun dropped to the floor.

Just like a Martial Arts movie.

It was a kind of miracle and Tom knew it. Taliafero must have known how the odds favored him—that knowledge had made him over-confident. He'd actually been enjoying himself there for a minute, relishing his tough guy dialogue, when his nerves should have been screaming.

With the flat of his hand on Taliafero's shoulder, still holding the wrist, Tom slammed the cop head first into the wall beside the closet. He scooped up the gun Taliafero had dropped, and looked down at Jim's murderer. He knew he had to kill the man and he heard Amy Elwell's voice in his head, saying "We have these guns and neither of us has ever used one, ever really used one I mean . . ."

Ever killed anyone, she meant.

In the end, though, it wasn't a deliberate choice; it happened too fast for that. Taliafero had a .22 in an ankle holster. Doubling over on the floor to draw the gun, he faced the same odds that had been stacked against Tom; worse odds, really. And he didn't make it.

Tom got off two clean head shots before Taliafero could even aim. The shots were deafening in the small room, re-

bounding off the walls as the recoil snapped up his elbow to
his shoulder. He stepped back, looking down, the gun dangling from his hand. He had done it, proved he could do the
necessary, pull the trigger when there was a living body in
front of the muzzle. He had crossed that final line. But he was
nauseated with himself. He was physically ill. The stink of
blood and gunpowder and his own sweat was lifting his stomach into his throat. He couldn't stop staring at Taliafero, at
the growing pool of blood on the neat parquet floor by the
man's head, the absolute stillness of him, sprawled just the
way Jim Gramble had been sprawled on the asphalt in the
park, turned into nothing, turned into meat the same way.
Death was filling his mouth like wads of mildewed cotton
batting. He tried to swallow and gagged. He knew what he
was, what he had become, how the world would see him, the
way they would describe him in the newspapers.

And they'd be right.

Now he was a cop-killer, too.

He twisted away and lurched for the bathroom, but he
didn't make it. In a moment he was on his knees, vomiting,
giant convulsions that seemed to turn his stomach inside out
and hammered at his injured ribs. He screamed in pain,
scrabbled at the floor. But the spasms kept coming.

After a while he crawled into the hallway and struggled
to his feet. He pressed his fingers to his eyes, squeezing
hard against the bridge of his nose. He focussed on his
breathing, pulling the air in like lengths of rope, forcing
every bit of air out with his diaphragm, letting the pressure bind his ribs.

He eased himself back into the bathroom, splashed
water on his face and rinsed his mouth. He had to master
himself, now.

Remorse was useless. This situation required a murderer. Anyone else would fail. Anyone else would be dead
already.

He jerked himself away from the sink. There were people all around him, heavily armed professionals. They must have heard Taliafero's shot and his own. He had to get out of this apartment before they came to investigate . . . or just launched an all-out assault, assuming Taliafero was already dead.

How much time would they give him? A minute? Less? How much time had passed, how much had he already wasted? He had no idea. Too much—that was all he knew for certain.

As he raced into the living room, the big picture window exploded inward, and three men with assault rifles vaulted inside.

Tom dodged back into the hall for cover, took position and started shooting. All the feeling was gone, emotion replaced by training, scattered the way birds scatter from a gunshot. The sound of gunfire pulled the trigger inside him and he became the machine Jake had trained him to be, the machine he would have to be to survive the next half hour.

Taliafero's gun carried an eight-shot magazine and three rounds were gone already. Tom's first four shots sent two of the men twitching at each other, as Tom dropped to the floor and the third man opened fire. The stream of bullets shredded the sheet rock over his head.

The room stank of cordite, it was all smoke and noise, reverberating hazy light and explosions. Tom had one bullet left. He aimed it at the muzzle flash and pulled the trigger. He heard a body fall and threw the gun down. Another man was hoisting himself through the window. Tom leapt into a spinning back kick. It snapped the man's head around on his neck and blasted him out the window, flailing.

The last member of the assault team dove over the window sill a moment later, just clearing the jagged edges of broken glass. Tom grabbed him in mid-air, dropped him to the floor and pistoned a fist into his throat.

Something banged against the door. It bulged on its hinges. Tom grabbed one of the assault rifles and sprayed bullets at the far wall. There were screams from the hallway outside. In a moment they'd start firing back.

Tom glanced out the window. Three ropes dangled down to the deck 12 feet below, where the man he had kicked lay beside the overturned ficus tree. The men had come from the apartment below. It was probably some kind of field headquarters. If he could knock it out . . .

The men had smoke grenades clipped to their belts. Tom grabbed one, along with the guy's sidearm, jammed the gun into his waistband and plunged out of the window just as the apartment door leapt off its hinges.

The air sizzled with flying metal, splintered glass and sparks from the metal window frame. He grabbed the rope and hit the brick wall hard, his ribs shrieking. He ground his teeth together and pushed off from the side of the building, the hemp cutting into his palms. He managed to shoot out the glass door below him but he had to drop the gun to pull the pin on the grenade. He counted off the seconds, dangling and helpless. Ten, nine, eight . . .

As soon as one of the men from the corridor poked his head out the demolished window and looked down, Tom was finished. He was an easy target at this range. And the trap was closing from both sides: the men in the apartment below him were shooting out the splintered glass door, unsure of the exact situation, fearing a trap. In another few moments they'd be out on the terrace, firing up at him.

Six, five, four . . .

Just a few more seconds. The sight of their slaughtered comrades might slow the men above him enough to—but there was a head at the window, a body leaning out, a mouth yelling. Tom flung the grenade at the gaping face. It rocketed up the five feet between them and struck the man just below the left eye. He staggered back, out of sight, and Tom wrenched himself, stretched to the limit, and caught the grenade as it fell.

Three, two, one . . .

Two men rushed out onto the terrace. Tom dropped on top of them, throwing the grenade at the same time. It detonated inside as he struggled with the two gunmen. Smoke billowed out the door. Shots were coming from above them, now, shattering the clay pot, puncturing the dead man, killing the man on top of Tom.

In the blinding acrid chaos, Tom slithered into the apartment. More shots were going off, people were screaming. The air was thick and white and unbreathable. He reached the front door just as the last two men were getting it open. They stumbled into the corridor, gasping and coughing.

Tom was right behind them.

Across the street, Ira Heller was yelling into a secure line, trying to find out what was going on, when the telephone jumped and went dead. A chip of plastic cut his face as he lurched backwards. There was a soft musical crack as another bullet broke a pane of glass and buried itself harmlessly in the bookshelf on the other side of the room.

That was not the only incidental destruction caused by the fire fight at 400 East 74th Street. Bullets fired in Gary Meredith's apartment and the one directly below it didn't stop. They penetrated walls in three directions, they went through the ceiling and the floor. Thirty percent of the rounds discharged actually traveled into other buildings, including the one across the street where Ira Heller had set up his headquarters.

A woman changing her baby's diaper staggered back in horror as silent bullets ripped into the changing table and her infant's left thigh; a retired high school English teacher was taking a bottle of juice out of the refrigerator when it

burst into shrapnel, shredding his eyes with flying glass. Three
of the men closing a crack deal in the apartment next door
were wounded; the buyer was hit in the temple and killed
instantly. Four televisions, six microwave ovens, a Cuisinart
five computers and a fax machine were destroyed. Many expensive pieces of furniture were wrecked; one shell passed
through every suit in the salesman's closet two doors down. A
child's porcelain doll was smashed; so was an elderly couple's
lamp, whose base was made from the champagne bottle with
which they had toasted their marriage 40 years before. One
man suffered a collapsed lung as he sat on the toilet reading
the New York Post. Another bullet cut upward through the
ceiling of apartment #2010, piercing the box spring, the mattress and the bodies of the man and woman making love in
apartment 2110.

Heller sat on the floor of his office, knowing it was
happening, knowing he would have to answer for every
death and injury, every penny of property damage.

He closed his eyes and waited for it to be over.

In the 19th floor hallway, Tom clubbed the choking
men in front of him unconscious as a bullet splintered the
plaster next to his shoulder. An old man stuck his head
out of an apartment door.

"What the hell is going on out here?" he demanded.

"Get back inside!" Tom screamed at him.

The man vanished behind his door again, assuming
his apartment walls would protect him. The soldier around
the corner of the hall kept shooting. Tom fired back into
the murk. At some point in the deafening barrage the return fire stopped. Tom edged forward cautiously, fearing
a trap. But the man was really dead; half his face was gone.

Tom ran to the elevator and hit the button, listening
to footsteps thundering above him, voices shouting and moan-
ing. When the door opened he was ready, out of sight to the
side.

Two secret service agents plunged out, caution and personal safety forgotten in the supercharged mixture and rage and worry and injured pride that was reaching full combustion inside them. One 22-year-old college kid was not supposed to be able to put up this kind of fight. Tom should never have been able to get out of Gary Meredith's apartment; he was absurdly overmatched—Moving cautiously would be giving a lucky amateur too much credit.

So they tore out of the elevator into the smoky hallway. Tom swung both arms around, catching the first one in the stomach. The impact was so sharp that the agent flipped over Tom's arms but before he hit the carpet the other agent had his gun out, shooting at Tom one-handed and unbraced, from less than four feet away. All three shots missed, which wasn't surprising; Jake had described similar moments—once in 'Nam a Viet Cong guerrilla had emptied a twelve shot magazine at him from point blank range and missed every time, wounding three of his friends and allowing Jake to escape.

Shooting was harder than it looked; so was remembering your training when you started to panic. This particular agent flunked on both counts and as a result he was disarmed and unconscious on the floor three seconds after he fired his last shot.

Tom had the man's gun and two spare magazines and was reloading as the elevator doors closed behind him.

In the lobby, five of Heller's picked troops stood with assault rifles ready, watching the elevator's floor indicator. A gasping report from 19 stories above them had just let them know that Tom was on his way down armed with a Glock 9mm pistol. The orders to "Take him alive if you can" didn't matter any more.

These men wanted blood.

As the elevator sank below the 10th floor, Tom was scrambling through the trap door in the roof. He replaced it care-

fully, crouched between ridges of grimy metal, as he passed
the eighth floor and sank toward the seventh. He had stuck
the gun into his belt and the barrel was digging into his hip
bone. The air was cool and clean in the shaft. He took shallow breaths and tried to think. He knew they were waiting for
him. At the fourth floor he swung onto a stationary cable and
levered open the doors facing the shaft with a pen. It snapped
in half but he was able to force a hand into the crack between
them and push. He released the cable, scrabbled onto the
ledge and used both hands. He squirmed through the gap
and stood up. The corridor was empty. He ran for the fire
stairs.

When he crashed through the door he saw there were
two men on the landing below him. He threw himself down
at them, landed on top of them in a grunting tangle of
arms and legs, banged their heads together and took the
stairs two at a time. He knew his only chance of escaping
the lobby lay in correctly second-guessing the reactions of
the men waiting for him below.

He heard the first shots as he reached the lobby door.

The elevator had arrived and even before the doors
opened the troops had opened fire. Bullets sliced into the
elevator, punching holes in the walls, making the flimsy
box sway on its cables. When the scarred interior was fully
revealed there was a moment of stunned silence as the
echoes of gunfire died out.

The elevator was empty and there was one obvious
conclusion to draw.

Tom crouched by the door, listening. If they figured it
out, he had a chance; if they thought one step further,
they'd be charging the stairs. He was outgunned and out-
numbered. That last jump had battered his ribs and the
pain was making him sluggish and dizzy as he crouched
waiting. He was stiff. His left hand was bleeding under the
nails from scrabbling at the elevator door. His ears were

ringing and his head felt like someone had just hit his temple with a ballpeen hammer. He didn't have many resources left; he could feel it in his stomach, that frenzied adrenaline queasiness. His body was manufacturing drugs to protect him from the pain and shock, but he was about to overdose on them.

One of the men shouted, "He's gotta be on the roof of the car! Cmon! We got him!"

Tom pushed himself upright, his face twisted into a kind of horrible smile by the effort.

It had worked.

Now all he needed was perfect timing, a strong stomach and a body that would obey orders for a few more minutes.

He panted in the shadows, waiting for the first shots.

In the lobby, all five men rushed into the elevator, aimed upward and started shooting. The light bulbs exploded as they perforated the ceiling with bullets in a relentless, particulate geyser of metal. Anything or anyone on the roof of that car would have been ripped to pieces in the massed fire from those five AK-47s. Blood should have been pouring down through the holes. There should have been screams. There should have been the sound of a falling body, the clatter of a dropped weapon.

One of them finally figured that out.

"Hold it!" he shouted, above the chattering, ear-pounding reverberations of the guns. "He ain't up there!"

"What the—"

"He ain't up there! He must have—"

But at that moment Tom appeared in front of them, standing in the Weaver stance, expert and implacable. They were clear targets and he had perhaps as much as five seconds to take them out before they saw him. It was perfect. As elegantly choreographed as a classical ballet, as brutally efficient as a tactical study in a combat manual.

All he had to do was pull the trigger.

That was when it happened. It was like running hard and tripping, like hitting that dog's leash this morning—stopped and flung forward at the same time.

He recognized one of the men in the elevator.

His name was Bob. Bob Anderson, Bob Andrews, something like that. The big nose, five o'clock shadow, going bald on top. The splay-footed way of standing. He had been at the Madequecham compound during the Christmas holiday. Tom's mother had invited him and several other agents in out of the cold and given them hot chocolate and stickey buns and little presents. Bob had gotten a Swiss Army knife with the Presidential seal on it.

He had been flustered. "Gee, Mrs. Jaglom," he had said. "I didn't get you anything."

Tom's mother had smiled.

"Of course you did," she told him. "You're here."

Tom stared at the man now. The Swiss Army knife was probably still in his pocket. His mother had touched his wrist lightly that morning, to make him feel at ease. He had looked down, blushing then glanced up to meet her eyes and said "Well, Thank you. Thank you very much. And merry Christmas, Ma'm."

Tom just stood there, staring. The trance was broken. He wasn't a soldier or a cop killer any more. He was just an orphan with aching ribs, a little boy looking at another human being who had been touched by his mother.

But he had to act, he had to do something. Bob had recognized him, and the others were turning. His time was up.

"Drop your weapons," Tom said. They didn't move. Perhaps they felt the strangeness of the moment, also. "Drop them!," Tom shouted, "Do it now."

They dropped the guns.

"Kick them out of the elevator."

They obeyed and Tom sprinted to the car. He hit the ten button and the close doors button. Even if they managed to stop the car and get out on the second floor, they'd have to run down stairs, and he'd be clear of the building by that time. It had to work—he couldn't have pulled the trigger. His finger was limp; He might as well have severed the nerves with a straight razor.

He dropped the gun and turned around.

The lobby was empty. There was no one between him and the front door. He was in the eye of his own hurricane. The next storm wall would sweep down on him any second—from the floors above, from the service areas, from the street. He sprinted across the lobby, and outside.

The sidewalk was clear: no cops, no Secret Service. They'd all been drawn into the building by the suction of battle. There were no pedestrians either—the only other figure moving in the asphalt landscape was a 12-year-old boy with a walkman kicking his way up the street on a skateboard. The volume was set way too high—that would explain his obliviousness. Tom could hear the music from twenty feet away.

He started for First Avenue. The light had just changed and there was an empty cab crossing 74th Street. It wasn't even off-duty. Too shell-shocked to celebrate, functioning on automatic, he stuck two fingers into his mouth and whistled. The cab stopped. Tom waved as he ran. He could measure his escape in heartbeats now.

Then everything happened at once.

The kid on the skateboard was just a few feet from the corner when a Secret Service Dodge skidded around, taking the right angled turn at 40 miles an hour. The kid was suddenly in front of them, unavoidable as a pot hole. They couldn't stop and they couldn't swerve. Tom saw it happening in his peripheral vision. He made no conscious

decision in that glaring, compressed instant, but he knew he
could save the boy's life and the action was contained in the
perception.

The boy looked up and had one moment of absolute
terror, staring at the onrushing car, before Tom tackled
him, flinging him out of the way, cushioning the fall with
his own body.

Behind them the Dodge ran over the skateboard with
a sickening crack, and hit the brakes.

By the time Tom had time to think about what had
happened, he was lying flat on the pavement, unable to
move, pain binding his ribs like barbed wire, looking up
into the barrels of four guns. The cab was long gone.

Heller was on the fringe of the group. He turned to
his second in command.

"This isn't street Theatre, Crumley. Get him out of
here."

Crumley nodded and the men kicked Tom to his feet.
They pushed him head first into the back seat of the Dodge,
climbed in on either side and handcuffed him as others
slid into the front seat. In a few seconds the car was peel-
ing off east on 74th Street.

The boypolled the earphones off his head, picked up
the pieces of his ruined skateboard and watched, still dazed,
as the car disappeared around a corner. He was alone with
Ira Heller.

Looking tired, rumpled and bored as usual, Heller
strolled up to the boy. He pulled a hundred dollar bill out
of his pocket. He had his own kids; he knew what things
cost. He handed the boy the money.

"Buy yourself another skateboard, courtesy of the U.S.
Government."

The kid took the bill without looking at it. "That man—
he saved my life."

"Yeah. Dumb move on his part."

"He saved me."

"And he just killed at least six people. You balance it out." Heller sighed. "I have a platoon of trained soldiers on the job and it takes a 12-year old kid to nail him. Go figure."

"Is he a bad guy?"

"He's nothing any more, kid."

Heller squeezed the boy's shoulder and walked back into the lobby of The Monarch to sort through the bodies and wait for the ambulances to arrive. There were going to be a lot of questions in the next ten hours, but he had the one answer that mattered. Whatever the body count, the mission had been a success. Tom Jaglom was never going to see the light of day again.

18

Amy Elwell was taken under guard to a Secret Service safe house in the West Eighties, between Amsterdam and Columbus Avenues. The block, a slum area of tenements and welfare hotels 30 years before, had been radically gentrified during the last few decades, every brownstone on the block meticulously renovated, rewired and redecorated, with skylights and hardwood floors, living rooms from Conran's and kitchens from Williams Sonoma.

The Secret Service safe house, near the corner of Columbus Avenue, was one of the more lavish entries. Foreign dignitaries and vice presidents often stayed there when traveling through New York.

Amy was given a cup of tea in the sunny, high-ceilinged kitchen and was asleep, heavily sedated, ten minutes later. When she woke up, the digital clock beside her bed said 12:15. The only illumination in the dark room—apart from the faint glow of the clock itself—came from a bar of light under what she assumed was the bathroom door. Someone must have left a light on. She pulled back the covers and moved cautiously across the room. When she opened the bathroom door she was blinded for a moment, the sudden illumination was so intense. She was blinking in the sunshine; it was noon, not midnight.

She leaned against the doorjamb, disoriented. Back in the bedroom, she found the switch that controlled the metal anti-terrorist shutters that had blocked the big dormer window, and light gushed into the room. It was like filling a tea cup with a fire hose.

Amy sat down on the bed and looked around. It was a pretty room, in shades of blue: blue checked sheets, pale blue waffle-weave blanket, strands of the same blue roped into the hooked rug on the pickled oak floor and the nubby upholstery of the arm chair by the window. The cafe curtains were blue gingham—it was some New York decorator's idea of a farmhouse bedroom.

Amy yawned. She didn't usually enjoy naps, and she was surprised to feel so rested after only a couple of hours' sleep. There was a copy of the *New York Times* on the bedside table. She picked it up and saw the date with a shock: she had missed a day. She must have been sleeping for 26 hours. Her tea must have been doped. She felt a brief tug of anger, then shrugged. At least she was well rested. It was just as Tom had predicted—she was alone now. No one was going to help her. She needed every advantage she could get. There was no reason to begrudge herself a good night's sleep.

Amy picked up the newspaper, and the horror began in earnest. On the top left, with a picture of Jim obviously taken ten years and twenty pounds ago, was the headline "Reporter Killed in Central Park Shooting." She twisted her head away and saw the other story: "Twelve Dead in East Side Gun Battle." She was lucky in a way; Heller had spared her *The Daily News* and the *New York Post.* Their headlines were bigger and considerably more graphic. On the front page of the *Daily News,* 96-point type blared "SLAUGHTER ON FIRST AVENUE."

The *Post*'s front page was taken up with a picture of a cute nine-month-old child and giant letters saying "THEY SHOT MY BABY!"

The New York Times was bad enough:

"A simple arrest turned into a tragic firefight yesterday as tactical police units attempted to apprehend an unarmed suspect in an Upper East Side apartment building.

"Detective Sergeant Armand Taliafero, of the 31st Precinct Homicide Division, along with seven other police officers and two bystanders, were killed and many more were injured in the 15-minute battle which began just after 11 a.m. at 400 East 74th Street.

"Many of the injuries were sustained by those in apartments adjoining the 20th-floor residence where the fighting began. Michael Brownell, an unemployed advertising executive, suffered a punctured lung. Retired Dalton School history teacher Alan McCall was blinded in one eye. Nine-month-old Janice Martin was shot in the right leg. The baby is currently in fair condition at Lenox Hill Hospital.

"The suspect, whose name had been withheld by the police pending further investigation, was killed instantly when—"

Amy knocked the newspaper off her lap.

They had killed Tom.

Everything was over, everything was finished. She felt tears coming, great convulsive dangerous tears, tears that could choke you with the sheer force of sorrow and loss and guilt. Guilt most of all. Guilt—the unbearable devouring knowledge that she had caused this. She had murdered Tom. There was no forgiveness possible, no excuse she could make, no way she could continue to live. She let the tears overwhelm her and she was still sobbing 10 minutes later when she heard the door open. She lifted her head to see who it was.

"Hello," said Ira Heller.

She wanted to leap off the bed and hit him, punch him in the throat as Tom had taught her, shoot him in his fat smirking face as Tom had trained her to do. But she had no gun and no strength. And even through her grief and her rage, through the refracting blur of her tears, she knew it would be a mistake. She was the only one left now. She had to be smart. She couldn't afford any more mistakes.

Heller watched her, saying nothing. He closed the door softly behind him and sat down in the armchair by the window. When the tears had slowed to hitching and gasping she propped herself up on one elbow and started to speak. But Heller raised his hand to silence her. He nodded and shrugged at the same time, giving the gesture a gentle, fatherly quality.

"Since you've looked at the newspaper I should tell you first of all that Tom is alive."

"What?"

"Somewhat the worse for wear, but still among the living, Ms. Elwell."

"But . . . the newspaper said—"

"The newspaper says what we tell it to say."

"You're talking about the *New York Times.*"

"I'm talking about a top-priority National Security threat, Ms. Elwell. They were glad to cooperate. I'm hoping we can have your cooperation, too. That's why we're having this conversation. Tom treated you as an ally, as a full partner. He seems to have a great deal of respect for your abilities—"

"He's in love with me. I'm just a college sophomore from Vermont. I'm not—

"Please. The only thing I hate more than false modesty is the real thing. It's boring and you're not. Don't say anything right now. I'll do the talking for a little while—there's a lot you need to hear. I hope you're ready."

Amy sat up. The fact that Tom was alive was surging through her system like a big breakfast, a double espresso and a long walk in the mountains. All at once she felt lively and strong.

"Try me," she said.

"There are certain facts you have to accept, Ms. Elwell. I know it's difficult. But Tom Jaglom is, in clinical terms, a paranoid schizophrenic, classified axis one, which indicates severe mental illness as opposed to mere personality disorder. Tom's age and high intelligence, along with the history of insanity in his family, make him a prime candidate for this type of psychosis. The particularly well-organized and coherent delusions are typical of his condition. The self-referential structure of the imaginary world can be deceptive . . . even seductive. The subject can appear sane most of the time. I'm quoting Tom's doctor now. Leonard Honig is one of the most respected men in his field, Ms. Elwell. And he asked me to point out to you that as a general rule, humoring schizophrenics does not help them."

Amy flailed for a rebuttal, that feeling of a good breakfast turning sour in her stomach.

"But Jim Gramble," she said. "What about Jim? He said that—"

"Mr. Gramble uncovered a scandal, not a conspiracy. All of this is classified Top Secret but I'm telling you anyway because, quite frankly, I think I'm going to be needing your help soon. Let me run this down for you from the beginning. Edward Bellamy Jaglom and various friends of his were briefly involved with the Mafia in a quite minor way when they were in high school. Mr. Gramble was one of those friends. Another one was appointed Attorney General last year, as you know. Michael Cafferty allowed a man named Alfredo Blasi to be killed by the Nosiglia crime family a week before he was due to testify against them in federal court. This is a very serious matter and it's being handled as such within the

Justice Department. Mr. Cafferty will be asked to resign some time in the next few weeks.

"There were other crime-tainted appointments which Mr. Gramble felt were breeding a systemic corruption from the top down. The President was naive—he had no idea how compromised his people had become. He didn't understand how his life-long acquaintanceship with Dominic Nosiglia, insignificant as it really was, compromised the Oval Office. President Jaglom is a man who lives by the rule of friendship. The tragedy is that he picked the wrong friends."

"But Jim said—"

"Did you talk to Jim?"

"No, but—"

"Did you read Jim's article?"

"No, but—"

"Of course you didn't, or you'd know all this already. You'll have to excuse me, Ms. Elwell. I've developed the irritating lawyer's habit of only asking questions when I already know the answers. It's true that Mr. Gramble exposed alarming ties to organized crime within the Jaglom administration. There's no doubt about that. But it's just as clear that Mr. Gramble's article was the jumping off point for Tom's delusions. The trauma of his mother's death had already accelerated the course of his illness, and now that he was sure his father had been replaced by a double, he needed a coherent framework in which to place that fact. Whether he even heard the bulk of what Mr. Gramble said to him at their meeting is open to question. What we do know for certain is that Mr. Gramble's article did not implicate the President in any way. It did not suggest, by any stretch of the imagination, that the President was personally involved with the Nosiglia crime family. The notion that he instigated some sort of business arrangement with them, putting the health, reputation and stability of this coun-

try at risk is simply . . . insane. I mean, really, Ms. Elwell—
think. Doesn't it all sound just a little bit farfetched to you?"

"But . . . if it isn't true, why did the President's newspaper fire Jim?"

Heller chuckled. "First of all, the Jaglom family does
not own, directly or indirectly, any newspaper or broadcast outlet. You can check that out for yourself. As an accu-
sation, it's absurd. As one section of a complex delusional
system, it is precisely what a clinical psychologist would
have predicted. The good news is that there are drug treatments available that can stabilize Tom's condition. They
don't constitute a cure, but nevertheless—"

"Jim wanted to meet Tom. I heard the message on my
answering machine."

"Yes, I know. I consider that our failure. Mr. Gramble
came to the President asking for protection and the Secret Service was given the job of keeping him alive. We
were negligent. We were remiss. We didn't take the death
threats seriously enough. Mr. Gramble lived as long as he
did by luck and nothing more. When he went underground we spared no expense trying to locate him. We
staked out every location we had ever logged him at during our previous surveillance. That's how we finally appre-
hended Tom, in fact. We're thorough, if nothing else.
Strangely enough, Mr. Gramble had actually been found
by our police liaison Armand Taliafero at the time of the
attack—"

"The attack?"

"Oh. You didn't know. Tom killed Mr. Gramble with
Detective Taliafero's gun. Three witnesses placed him—"

"He couldn't have!"

"I'm sorry. But there isn't much this man couldn't do.
I believe he's capable of almost anything. An hour later
he killed Taliafero. The boy was on a rampage, Ms. Elwell.
But the important thing for you to understand now is that

Mr. Gramble knew Tom needed help. He approached
Tom initially because he needed the assistance of someone he could trust, someone who was capable of protecting
him physically. But that was before he realized the gravity of
Tom's condition, before he realized how his story was exacer-
bating Tom's illness, feeding his delusions. I think he felt
some measure of responsibility. That's why he was willing to
help us. Unfortunately he was scared. He was guarded with
me, partially because he believed he could handle Tom
alone. But mainly because, well . . ."

"He didn't trust you. He thought you were an incompetent and a liar."

"I'm afraid we'd given him little reason to feel otherwise. Taliafero's presence in the park was an extraordinary
coincidence and it should have been a stroke of luck. He
had been trying to track down Mr. Gramble independently
for weeks.

"But things turned out badly. I wish Mr. Gramble had
been more candid with us. His own life and many other
lives could have been saved yesterday. Still, as I say, I blame
myself. If I had acted with greater alacrity when Jim first
came to the President . . . if I had seen his call for help as the
emergency it really was—"

The lies in the room were like moths, fluttering around
Amy's head, confusing her, panicking her. She had to swat
them one at a time. "Wait a minute," she said. "This makes
no sense. Jim wasn't asking the President for help. They
were arguing. We heard them all the way downstairs."

"Well . . . it's true they quarreled. Mr. Gramble wanted
the President to make all of this public. The President preferred to deal with these difficulties more discreetly. These
men are his friends, after all. They have families. But I assure you, none of that had any effect on the President's
desire to secure Mr. Gramble's safety."

Amy pulled her knees up to her chin.

"If only I could see the article. Jim was going to give it to Tom yesterday."

"I have Jim's papers. I think you'll find them very revealing. Taliafero turned them in just 10 minutes before he was killed himself."

He opened his briefcase and pulled out a manila envelope. It was stained with blood. He handed it over and Amy took it gingerly, as if the blood stains were still wet, though they had dried to a dark brown crust. She slid a finger under the envelope flap and pulled out the pages inside.

She didn't have to spend much time reading them. She felt a small stomach-flipping push at her sense of reality; it was like finding daylight in the bathroom beyond her night-dark room when she woke up an hour ago. There was something demented in the moment and the tilt of lunacy came from Heller, not from her or Tom. It was like talking to one of those steely-eyed fanatics who want to convince you that the Holocaust never happened.

Her hands were shaking. She jammed the papers in her lap.

The document she was holding was not Jim Gramble's article. It was the elaborate set of forms required by the State of New York for self-commitment to a mental hospital.

Heller spoke softly: "Ms. Elwell, let me ask you something. Tom told Mr. Gramble about speaking to his mother in the graveyard. He says in the journal that he mentioned this to you."

"Yes, but there's nothing abnormal about—"

"Eventually he stopped visiting the grave. Did he ever tell you why?"

"He said . . . it was getting weird."

"To say the least, Ms. Elwell. To say the least. Did he ever discuss precisely why it was getting 'weird?"

"No, but I mean—"

"He did tell Mr. Gramble. And I think it's something you should know. He stopped talking to his mother for one simple reason. She started talking back. He was still in the denial phase. It's a textbook case. You might not be aware of this, but he was even convinced that I was spying on him—listening to his phone conversations, reading his mail, that sort of thing. I'm sorry. But you have to know the facts."

Amy looked at Heller, smiling paternally at her from across the room, and she knew he was lying. His glib spiel fit the facts, but that didn't make it true. Tom's story was much wilder, but that didn't make it false. Besides, it was all so convenient—there was no hard evidence to prove or disprove Heller's claims. If he wasn't spying on Tom, how could he have known that Tom suspected him? Even the self-commitment forms could be fake. The blood on them wasn't necessarily Jim's blood. What she really needed was a copy of Jim's article—*that* would be tough to fake. Amy knew his style. She was a fan. She was on the verge of demanding a copy, but she stopped herself: that would just be one more blunder.

Amy was in Tom's position now, just the way he had described it in his journal. Her job wasn't to convince Heller that Tom was sane—that would be a meaningless task anyway, since Heller didn't really believe that Tom was crazy. Tom's "psychosis" was the perfect way to neutralize him and take advantage of his intimate family knowledge at the same time.

No: her job now was to convince Heller that she was on his side. Arguing would only land her in the padded cell next to Tom's.

She closed her eyes, trying to concentrate. There was some loophole in their conversation, something false in the logic of Heller's argument. She asked for a cup of coffee and waited for it in silence. When it came she stood and sipped it by the window, ignoring Heller, looking across at the renovated brownstone on the other side of the street. Someone was planting a hugely elaborate roof garden: dozens of flats of zinnias, impatiens, forsythia and others she didn't recognize were being unpacked and set into great troughs of potting soil by a pair of Korean gardeners. She watched them as the coffee worked its way into her system. She realized she was hungry and smiled, thinking of her father saying "I only eat breakfast so I won't have to drink my coffee on an empty stomach."

When she finally figured it out, it seemed embarrassingly obvious. Most good ideas were like that.

She turned to Heller. He'd been watching her calmly. He was patient and it was her move.

"I don't think you fully understand the situation," she said to him.

"Oh?"

"We're basically in agreement."

"We are?"

Amy set her cup down on the window sill. "Did it ever occur to you that I might have been playing Devils Advocate this morning?"

"Why would you do that?"

"To draw you out. To determine your position. To test you. Frankly, I'm surprised you could believe that I was manipulated so easily."

"Well, as a matter of fact—"

"Dr. Honig didn't. You said so yourself. He wanted to caution me against humoring schizophrenics."

"Yes, but—"

"Think about it for a second, Mr. Heller. What evidence do you have that I was working with Tom? What evidence do you have that I believed him?"

"Well, the journal makes it very clear that—"

"The journal."

Heller stared at her, confused. But he was figuring it out

STEVEN AXELROD

fast. She pushed him along. "The catalogue of delusions? The ravings of a lunatic?"

"I understand the point, but—"

"What makes you think that I was the only subject he was lucid about?"

Heller pushed his stubby fingers into his cheeks, sucking air in through his nose. Amy pulled back a smile, watching him. He was caught in his own lie; she had taken it to its logical conclusion. To accuse her now he would have to admit Tom was sane, and he couldn't do that. So he would have to at least pretend to believe her, as she would pretend to trust him, though neither one of them was fooled for a second.

It was an arrangement she could live with.

Finally Heller said, "So . . . you were . . ."

"Trying to help. Just like you."

"So . . . you don't really believe the President has been replaced by an impostor?"

Amy smiled mischievously. "Has he?"

"There are times when he wished he had been, Ms. Elwell—particularly during physical therapy sessions."

Amy sighed. "It's funny . . . he made it seem so real sometimes."

"Of course he did. It was real to him."

"You said you were hoping to get my cooperation?"

"Yes. Tom is currently undergoing a thorough psychiatric evaluation at the Holden Clinic. I suspect he will prove intransigent, given the nature of his delusions. So someone he trusted could be enormously helpful."

Amy couldn't resist. "Helpful in what way? How could a candid conversation about his delusions help you?"

"It's Tom who needs the help. Ms. Elwell. I thought we had agreed on that. Whatever he may have done, however dangerous he may be to himself or others, he is still the only child of the President of The United States, and we are determined that he receive the highest possible level of care."

Amy looked away, chastised. "Of course," she said. "Sorry. Anything I can do."

And inside her the fireworks were going off, the crowds were celebrating, it was the 4th of July, New Year's Eve, Christmas and Valentine's Day, put together. She wasn't alone; there was still hope. Tom was alive. And she was going to see him. The rest would take care of itself.

19

On the morning of his third day at the Holden Psychiatric Institute, Tom was taken to see Dr. Leonard Honig. He'd spent the previous 50 hours sleeping.

When they had first brought him into the building, bruised and hurting, there'd been a cringing animal part of him that was grateful for the silence and the sedatives. He knew he was in the hands of his enemies, that his plans were wrecked and his chances of ever escaping—much less prevailing over Dominic Nosiglia's new world order— were next to zero. But the fact of his defeat meant much less to him than the firm mattress and the soft pillow of his institutional bed. There was a consoling ecstasy, an almost painful physical sweetness, in simply lying down, releasing his weight from his legs, closing his eyes and letting the soft stampede of sleep trample through him.

His slumber was monitored and extended by Dr. Honig, who prescribed a course of demerol injections with dosages decreasing from 10cc to 8cc, 6cc and finally 4cc, which allowed Tom to float upward gradually through the dark fathoms of his drugged oblivion into the pale shallows of consciousness. "Bring him up too quickly and he'll get the bends, just like a skin diver," Honig remarked. The nurse on duty smiled politely, she'd heard this particular observation many times before.

Still, Honig knew his business and Tom awoke feeling a crystalline alertness, with new energy flowing in him like spring water over smooth rocks. His bruises were healing. He felt strong and potent and optimistic. He wasn't dead, after all, despite the best efforts of numerous professional killers.

He stood and stretched, feeling the luxurious tension in his muscles, and looked around his cell: scuffed white linoleum, white walls, white ceiling, indirect fluorescent lighting. Even his cot featured white sheets and a white blanket. There were no decorations, no moldings or baseboards, no chairs, no window. It was an utter blank, a room designed to drive sane people crazy or make crazy people feel at home. There were two other cots. On one of them an enormously fat man was counting and recounting a stash of marbles, clicking them against each other, muttering the numbers to himself. On the other cot a tall, wide-eyed man with a crew cut rocked back and forth, clutching the bed frame in his huge hands, humming tunelessly.

Tom ignored his roommates and did some exercises on the floor, a basic set of push-ups and sit-ups, a hundred of each and then a long slow series of stretches. It was hard work and it helped him empty his mind. Lying in bed he had already begun to manufacture escape plans and that was dangerous. It was easy to get attached to those first thoughts, even if they started out as guesswork. They quickly solidified into a strategy, and you ignored or misread new information.

He stood up and looked around again. A shiny green bubble of snot bulged out of the marble counter's left nostril. Tom looked away. He didn't belong with these pitiful

creatures, anyone could see that. He felt claustrophobia tightening around his head. The clicking and humming, the
sick-room smell that soiled the air, were unbearable. He
breathed quietly through his mouth, focusing on the act of
respiration. The panic relented. The trick was to make his
mind as blank as this little room, to make no decisions or
plans, to wait and watch and listen. Something would occur
to him—something always did.

The walk to Honig's office half an hour later started to
fill in the details. It was an old building, solidly built, with
thick walls and high ceilings. The only apparent conces-
sions to high technology were the surveillance cameras
mounted high on the corridor walls and the magnetized
cards that unlatched the knob-less doors. It wasn't Attica,
but it was daunting enough.

Walter Honig was a short, slim man with curly gray hair,
wire-rim glasses and an attitude of gentle condescension
that made Tom want to pound him senseless. Somehow,
though, Tom knew that even as Honig was being stomped
into jelly, he'd manage to say something like "Now, what
issues are we actually expressing with this anger? I think it
represents a much deeper problem, a systemic dysfunc-
tion we won't begin to understand until we uncover the
sources of your rage . . ."

The first thing he actually said, as Tom sat down in an
armchair facing his, was "Do you know why you're here,
Tom?"

It was clear immediately—this guy was going to use
his first name a lot, to create a sense of intimacy. It was a
salesman's trick. The only question was, what was this guy
selling?

"You didn't ask if you could use my first name," Tom
said.

"May I?"

"No."

"What shall I call you, then?"

"You don't have to call me anything. There's no one else here."

"But suppose I needed to get your attention in the cafeteria?"

"You do that a lot? Bother people while they're eating?"

Honig took a deep breath, resettled himself on his seat, resettled his glasses on his nose. He smiled encouragingly. "I think we got off on the wrong foot. So let's start again. Do you know why you're here?"

"Where am I?"

Another smile. "Fair question. You're on the sixth floor of the Holden Psychiatric Institute on Eighty-first Street, between Second and Third Avenues on the upper East Side of Manhattan. Now, why do you think you were brought here?"

"Because I got caught."

"And do you know why people were chasing you?"

"Overdue library books?"

"Don't feel you have to amuse me, Tom."

"I don't feel it's possible to amuse you, Dr. Honig."

Honig nodded, "That's very insightful. Now turn that insight on yourself. You're a very frightened young man. Do you have any idea what it might be that frightens you so much?"

"You, Dr. Honig. You scare the shit out of me."

"Oh my. That's most unfortunate. I want to help you. I want you to trust me."

"Then let me out of here. We'll schedule regular sessions at your office."

"Well, of course I can't do that. It's out of the question. You're a criminal. You've committed murder, Tom. You've killed members of the Secret Service and the local police. These are very grave matters. It was only by convincing the authorities that you were criminally insane that I got you brought here instead of prison."

Tom stared at him. "Send me to prison."

"What?"

"If I go to prison there'll have to be a trial. I'll be given a hearing. That's how our criminal justice system works, Dr. Honig. I get to hire a lawyer and tell my side. But you can't afford that, can you?"

Honig nodded. "Now we approach our area of interest. Tell me your side, Tom. That's why we're here."

"You've read my journal. You know my side."

"Yes but I want to hear it from you."

"Put me in jail. Arraign me. Set a trial date. I'll tell my side on Court TV. I'm sure a lot of people in America would be interested to hear it."

"Tom—"

"You're doing it again."

"I have to call you something!"

"Don't lose your temper, Doctor. It's not only unprofessional, it reflects certain dysfunctional syndromes we should explore. Did your father have a bad temper?"

"I want to talk about your father."

"And that's why we're really here."

"Young man, let me explain something to you. I know you want to get out of this institution. But there is only one way to do that. I have to sign a paper that says you're fit to rejoin the world as a stable member of society. And believe me, without your co-operation, that will never happen."

"All right. I'll tell you something about my father. He taught me to take no crap from bullies. He used to say 'Standing up to a coward is the safest way in the world to look like a hero.'"

"So?"

"So don't bully me, Doctor. It won't work."

"You speak of your father in the past tense,"

"That's right. Because he's dead."

"On the contrary. He's being released from the hospital in two weeks. There are going to be great festivities in Washington and all over the country. It will be a great day for everyone else. For him it will be darkened by the death of his wife and the descent of his only child into destructive mental illness."

"So—I'm crazy?"

"You suffer from a severe personality disorder. That doesn't make you a bad person, although you have done many bad things as a result. We are beginning to learn a number of solutions to your problem, chemical ways of dealing with the chemical imbalances in your brain. But I firmly believe that old-fashioned therapy sessions like this one are equally important. Schizophrenics keep secrets, Tom. They are spies. They are secret agents in the pay of their own . . . imaginations, if you will. Their distorted world view. My job is to break into that clandestine world, to . . . blow your cover, as it were. To bring you out. The drugs will help, rather in the way that a computer spreadsheet program helps a businessman organize his financial affairs; The drugs, like the computers, are our servants. They are useful but mindless. The real work is up to us. We have to explore the territory of your mind together. You have to be my guide. I need to understand the world as you see it." He sat forward. "For instance . . . you're certain that your father has been 'replaced' by an impostor. I need to know how you know that, Tom. I need to know what you see in the President that no one else does."

Tom laughed. "I bet you do."

"Excuse me?"

"I don't get it. Why not just interrogate me? Put me under with some drug, hypnotize me, whatever. You could get all the information you'd ever want. Stuff like . . . this guy doesn't get the jokes. He doesn't have my Dad's sense of humor. He's like some white guy at a jazz club clapping along with the music on two and four. He's off the beat, and my Dad was always right on it."

"I'm not exactly sure what you mean. Tell me how it felt to be with him. Tell me about the hospital. The details are so important. We have to train ourselves to remember the details."

"I remember the details just fine."

Honig sat back, elbows on the arms of his chair, fingers steepled in front of his chin, his lips pursed faintly, one eyebrow raised with prim skepticism. He was so smug, so intensely irritating, Tom found himself wanting to answer. To convince him? To prove something? To stand up for himself? To defend his memory and his sanity? Or was it just to dazzle Honig, to talk rings around him, to wipe that mild dismissive smile off his pudgy face?

Tom didn't know. But he was talking:

"You want details? Here's a perfect one. We were in the solarium of the hospital—they had him up and walking around for a few minutes at a time. They even let him have a cup of coffee. He fixed it himself off a food service trolley—milk, no sugar, just the way he likes it. Except he put in too much milk."

"I'm not sure-"

"Dad just tipped in the smallest amount he could. To 'take the curse off' he used to say. The color barely lightened at all. This guy's coffee was pale beige. Does that seem trivial?"

"No detail is trivial to me."

"Good, because it's the whole point, right there. That's what I'm saying. I know my Dad ten levels down from the level where they've briefed this guy. He knows to add milk, but he doesn't know how much. Anyway, he said something that morning about the country running pretty well without him and I said 'Maybe you should just quit.' And he says, 'I never know when you're joking, Tom.' Big mistake, Doctor. My Dad always knew when I was joking."

"What did you say to him?"

"The conversation must have been taped. Check the transcript."

Honig smiled that professional smile again, the one he used for talking suicides off high ledges and taking loaded guns away from the hopelessly deranged. "Now, now," he replied. "I think we both know that nobody was taping your conversation. But if you can't remember . . ."

Tom cut him off. "I remember. I said, 'I'll wink next time if you think it will help,' and he said something about 'not liking my tone of voice', which was totally out of character. It was like he was trying to sound 'Presidential' even with his own son. But that was the last thing my Dad ever cared about. Then he asked me about law school and it was as if we'd never had the conversation before. Which was actually true, though that couldn't be the impression he wanted to give. You know, it's funny in a way—a couple of years ago we were going around and around on this same subject and I remember thinking to myself, we're going to be fighting about this stuff forever. I'll be in my fifties and he'll be saying 'If you had only gone to law school . . . .' On his death bed, he'll still be trying to talk me into it. Then I thought, at least when he dies we'll finally stop having this stupid argument. It was a bad thought. Now I feel like I'm being punished for it. I mean he's dead but I have to keep having the same argument anyway, only with some stranger." Tom shrugged. "Well . . . at least that part is over now."

Honig was grinning. His eyes were bright. "This was most productive," he said. "An excellent session, after a rather rocky start. Of course, we only scratched the surface. But I feel we're developing a real rapport. We've opened the floodgates now, Tom. I'm sure our next session will be a revelation for both of us."

Maybe it was the repetition of his first name; maybe it was the look of victorious greed on Honig's face. But Tom knew with a sickly twinge in his stomach that he had made a terrible mistake. Somehow, Honig had tricked him into talking. He knew Tom needed to talk, that was part of it. Honig had taken advantage of his vulnerability with surgical skill. Of course: exploiting emotional weakness was his specialty. Despite his fuzzy academic demeanor he was expert at his job and he was dangerous. The false intimacy of Honig's clinical 'concern' had to be broken. He couldn't let his own need for human contact rule his reactions any more.

But the fact remained, stubborn as the winter chill of an underheated room, the cold linoleum underfoot: he was lonely. His blunder had forced him to face that fact, if nothing else. He had never felt so alone in his life. There was Honig, and the shovel-faced orderlies, and the gibbering lunatics around him—he might as well be in solitary confinement. In fact, solitary confinement would be an improvement. At least he'd be alone.

As he was escorted to the cafeteria for lunch, feeling the orderly's hand clutching his upper arm, thinking about how easy it would be to break his grip (and his wrist), thinking about how useless and impossible it would be to attempt an actual conversation with the guy, the simple childish thought occurred to him: "I need a friend."

It was a perfectly timed wish: fifteen minutes later he met Charlie Flegg.

20

It happened the same way at every meal. Two big patients, both named Larry, both with choppy crew cuts and infected tattoos, would shamble over to the frail, fifty-year-old man's table and steal some essential part of his meal. At breakfast they took his bacon or his sausage; at lunch and dinner they stole his dessert. They were massively built—they bulged out of their institutional t-shirts in slabs of pink muscle. You couldn't fight with them and their frowning, slack-jawed faces made it clear you couldn't argue with them, either.

The little man never did.

The two Larrys had arrived at the Holden Psychiatric Institute a little less than a year before, and this sad and anemic-looking man, hadn't eaten a complete meal since. He was used to it by now. He knew the orderlies didn't like him and he never expected them to help. He had mastered the art of low expectations and it had served him well at Holden.

At some point in the thirty-odd years of his incarceration he had given up on people and retreated into himself. In

the old days he had been annoyingly garrulous, declaiming
his hare-brained political theories to anyone who'd listen
and quite a few who wouldn't. Now he hardly spoke at all.
They let him have books and he read only the fat ones: everything from John Jakes' Civil War trilogy to *War & Peace*; from
Atlas Shrugged to *Gravity's Rainbow*. *The Lord of The Rings, Ha-
waii, Buddenbrooks, The Stand*—quality and subject matter made
no difference. All he cared about was length. The longer the
book, the farther it could take him away from the tension and
discomfort of human contact. The last thing he wanted from
anyone now was a gesture of human kindness. He wasn't
even sure he'd know how to react.

But as it turned out, he hadn't lost the knack entirely.

This particular lunchtime, Tom Jaglom, eating his first
meal in the Institute's cafeteria, watched the whole drama
unfold. When one of the Larrys snatched the little man's
key lime pie, Tom stood up to help. One of the orderlies
on duty saw him and extended his arm out straight with
the palm vertical, like a traffic cop. Tom sat down again,
but when the Larrys had gone back to their table to argue
over who got the crust, Tom picked up his own slice of pie
and walked over to the little man's table.

He sat down next to the man and pushed his pie over.
"Here. Take mine."

The man looked down. "No, thanks."

"I saw what they did."

"Yeah? Well, they do it every day."

"No one ever stops them?"

"I'm not exactly a favorite around here."

"They play favorites?"

The little man looked up with a bitter smile. "They
play many interesting games. As you'll soon find out."

"Come on," Tom said. "Take the pie."

In the strange seconds of silence that followed, Tom
saw unshed tears glittering in the man's eyes.

"Don't be nice to me, okay? Please. I can't handle that right now."

"You don't have to handle anything. Just eat. I don't like dessert anyway."

It happened again at breakfast. The two Larrys stole the man's bacon. Tom offered his own. Bacon evidently meant more to him than key lime pie: he took it, but glanced suspiciously at Tom as he ate.

"Why are you doing this," he said when he was finished.

"Why shouldn't I? You deserve a break."

"How do you know?"

"Hey—everybody deserves a break."

He pointed across the room at the two Larrys. "Even them?"

"They get all the breaks they want by scaring people."

"They don't scare you, though."

Tom shrugged.

"Which I find a little strange, I don't mind admitting. I mean . . . all those muscles . . ."

"It's good to fight muscle-bound guys. It's easier than it looks. They're slow and tight. They don't move well. And they're cocky."

"You sound pretty cocky yourself."

"I don't mean to. Fighting is just something I've learned how to do. And guys like those two need to be physically intimidated. In the interest of justice, you know what I mean?"

"Better than you do."

"They need to be—"

"Scared. Hurt. Humiliated."

Tom laughed. "Something like that."

"Teach them a lesson."

"Well, no—they'd never really learn anything. But I'd feel much better."

"Me, too. I'd buy tickets for that one, kid."

They ate in silence for a while. When the little man set

his plate aside, he said "Thanks for the pie—and the bacon. You took me by surprise there. But I appreciate it. Those guys haven't let me eat a strip of bacon in 10 months." He stuck out his hand. "Charlie Flegg. Good to meet you."

"Tom Jaglom."

They shook hands. Flegg had a firm grip.

"Jaglom, huh? Any relation?"

"Not any more."

"What happened?"

"It's a long story."

"Yeah? Well, I've got lots of time and a good attention span for a psycho." He grinned, showing his gums.

"Some other time."

"You drink coffee?"

"What?"

"I'm gonna get myself some coffee. You want some?"

"Sure, thanks. Milk no sugar."

When Flegg returned he set down Tom's mug and said, "What are you in for?"

"You make it sound like jail."

"I wish. Jail you can get out of. There's a parole board. You have a sentence. You can reduce it with good behavior. We're in this place for life. Now me, I was with the Weather Underground. In the '60s. I blew stuff up. Buildings that held draft records, plants that made napalm. They caught me but I wouldn't rat on my friends. That was my big crime. That's why I'm here. They say I'm crazy, but I'll tell you something: I made a difference in this world."

"So . . . how, long have you been here?"

"Jeez, let me think. Since '71, I guess. Before you were born, But I ain't cured yet! Never will be. Which reminds me. Have they started with the pills yet?"

Tom shook his head.

"Well, they will,. Probably today. The pills turn you into a zombie, kid. You gotta cheek em."

"Cheek them?"

"Learn the language. We mental cases have our own jargon just like everyone else: It means hold the pill under your tongue until the orderly splits. You pretend to swallow it but you really don't. That's cheeking. You gotta do what you can. It's tough to keep your brain intact around here."

The pills began that night, as Flegg had predicted. Tom used the system, but he didn't know he was taking Haldol and he didn't know the precise effect the drug was supposed to have. His imitation of a zombie was apparently inadequate. Two days later, the orderly, whose name was Henry, stayed in the room after administering the dosage.

It was an unusual thing to do. Tom noted that he had the undivided attention of his roommates for the first time.

"Don't you have some place to go?" Tom asked.

"Nope."

"Come on—get out of here."

"Can't."

"They told you to stay?"

"Huh?"

"You're quite a conversationalist."

"What?"

"Nothing."

Silence settled in. After fifteen minutes a pink foam started bubbling out from between Tom's lips. The plastic capsule was dissolving in his mouth.

"Swallow," Henry said.

Tom spat out the remains of the pill. Henry was unperturbed. He handed Tom another pill.

"Take it."

Tom shook his head.

"I can make you.."

"Not by yourself."

They stared at each other. Tom felt the threat of violence

between them like a cool wind on a summer evening. It re-freshed his spirit, braced his sluggish nerves. It was a child-ish moment, a school-yard confrontation. And Henry's re-sponse was appropriately adolescent.

"I'm telling Dr. Honig," he said.

Tom had a session with Honig that afternoon and the doctor came right to the point.

"Henry tells me you've been refusing your medica-tion."

"Henry doesn't miss much."

"He says you threatened him."

"Actually he. threatened me. I merely pointed out that the threat was unrealistic."

Honig sighed. "I don't know what to do with you, Tom. I'm at my wits' end. We're trying to help you, but you're fighting us every inch of the way. You're determined to see me as your enemy."

"If you're not my enemy, let me go."

"I can't do that. As I've already explained-"

"You could help. Those papers you were talking about—"

"Please. This is futile. We must move away from this constant discussion of your release. The chances are that you will never be released. Our efforts have to be directed toward making your time here productive. Toward mak-ing you whole again. Anything else is just destructive fan-tasy."

"My specialty."

"I think we should start by talking about your hostility. You seem to distrust the therapy process."

"No I don't."

"Perhaps not consciously."

"Let me ask you something, doctor. If you know my unconscious mind so much better than I do, why do I need to be here at all?"

"Good point. Very shrewd. Let's make a deal, shall we? I won't try to bulldoze you with psychiatric mumbo jumbo— but you have to give me some straight answers. For instance . . . what precisely did your mother say to you in the graveyard?"

"I don't know what you're talking about."

"You're agitated."

"So are you."

"But this denial response has to be—"

Tom wagged a finger. "Mumbo jumbo, Doctor."

Honig took a breath. "You told Jim Gramble you heard your mother talking to you."

"I did not."

"Why would he lie?"

"He wouldn't. But you would."

"That's absurd."

"O.K. Listen to me. Here's what I'm going to do:

I'm a prisoner of war and I'm going to act that way. A soldier would give you nothing but his name, rank and serial number. I don't have a rank or a serial number and you've already got my name. But that's all you're going to get."

They stared at each other. Neither one of them moved. Neither one of them looked away. Finally Honig picked up the telephone.

"Claudia? I want Tom Jaglom scheduled for a course of electro-shock therapy. Yes. As soon as possible. Thank you."

Tom never remembered much about his first electroshock session, just the long walk down the blank corridors, flanked by two burly orderlies (Henry conspicuously absent); the gray room with its monitors and steel cabinets and the big table, all polished metal and leather like some benign high-tech exercise machine. He remembered his decision not to fight, his show of docility, walking slowly between his guards like a trained animal in a cheap circus, spiritless and eager to please.

A nurse had an IV of Brevital, an anesthetic, waiting for him. Honig waved her away. He didn't want this to be painless. He did slip in an IV of succinylcholine, "To relax your muscles and prevent broken bones," he explained mildly as they strapped Tom down. They struck a rubber block into his mouth and an oxygen mask over his mouth and nose. "We don't want you to bite off your tongue, or suffocate," Honig explained. "During the seizure."

Then they vaselined his temples and attached the electrodes. Tom tensed himself waiting, trying to anticipate the pain.

But there was way he could prepare himself for the chrome-glare twanging pulse of agony that seemed to shake everything loose inside him, a seismic tremor in the blood that threatened to jar his organs from their cavities, his nerves from his muscles and his muscles from his bones. When the second jolt took him, he could feel his thoughts shaking loose from his brain, his identity fracturing as if ragged chunks of who he had been would tumble to the floor if he dared to move.

He knew that something irrevocable, something unfixable, would happen if they threw the switch again. He was like a rickety little house in an earthquake, where survival was measured in the smallest increments of time. Another few seconds and he would collapse from the inside. They wanted to turn him into rubble and they had the power to do it.

He was immobile and helpless.

He closed his eyes and waited for something much worse than death to snake through him.

But it didn't come.

They unstrapped him and helped him to stand. It was a good thing they did. His legs and arms were numb, his knees

were jelly—cartilage floating in aspic. There were tears in
his eyes. He was crying from gratitude, the craven animal joy
of survival.

But he couldn't survive another session.

Anger had replaced fear, and hate was traveling along
the secret reaches of his spine. Honig didn't know it yet,
but he had just created the most dangerous creature on
earth: a 22-year-old fanatic, expert in every art of warfare,
with a cause to die for and nothing to lose.

All Tom had left was his mind and they wanted to take
that, too. He smiled, just a flicker of cold amusement. Let
them try. Next time he would fight, next time those two
orderlies would get a surprise.

Next time there would be blood on the linoleum.

They could turn him into a vegetable—a smiling puppet face who would embrace his father's look-alike on national TV. But it was going to cost them. They were going
to pay as bullies always paid when they miscalculated their
victims, as America had paid in Viet Nam.

Tom was about to start his own Tet offensive.

It couldn't last long; but it was going to be a fine time
while it lasted.

21

Tom was ready to take his stand at the next electro-shock session, but he got his chance sooner than that, when Henry and two other orderlies arrived the following morning with his medication. Though Tom's room-mates took their meds without a struggle, Tom's defiance had sparked their interest. They may be crazy, Tom thought—but they're not stupid. They know something's up. He had to smile—this was probably the only live entertainment they'd had in years.

Henry smiled at him.

"You said I couldn't make you swallow your pill alone," he said. "I'm not alone today."

Tom smiled back, rising to his feet. "I'm not sure you can do it, even with your back-up."

The grotesque exchange of smiles continued. "Let's find out."

Henry extended the Haldol tablet on the palm of his hand. Tom shook his head.

Henry addressed the other orderlies. "Hold him."

One of them grabbed Tom's arm, expecting resistance; Tom let himself be pulled and the man stumbled backward, off balance. Tom followed him, driving a side-thrust kick into his stomach, then spun around as the other orderly jumped at him It was a clumsy attack and Tom didn't even bother to block or side-step it. He just snapped a punch into the lunging solar plexus. The big man doubled over with an explosion of breath, and Tom brought a knee up into his face. The impact broke the orderly's nose and snapped him upright again, dazed and bleeding. Tom batted him aside and then he was face to face with Henry again.

"Your turn," he smiled.

By now his roommates were bouncing up and down on their beds. The giant who rocked back and forth all day had actually released his grip on the frame and was applauding, with his hands directly in front of his face. The men on the floor groaned softly as the weird ovation continued.

"Okay," Henry said. "You asked for it." He pulled a little black box from his pocket and pushed a button. A red light went on and Tom could hear an alarm ringing somewhere down the corridor outside. "One last chance," Henry said. "Take the pill."

"No way."

Henry shook his head. "This way," he replied.

Then the door burst open and six more orderlies charged into the room. Tom took out the first two with a pair of flying front snap kicks and flipped the third one over his back. The other three were armed with rubber clubs. Tom was a blur of motion, ducking under a swinging bat, blocking a punch, shattering a knee cap, hammering a fist into a lunging face. He twisted away from the arc of a club; then another connected with his bruised ribs.

The pain was unbearable.

It chopped him apart like an ax splitting a frozen log. He was brittle, cracking along the grain, blacking out. He crumpled to his knees and saw Henry looming in front of him, grinning now, relishing the moment. Then the fist detonated on the side of his head and another club knocked him flat.

He never even felt the needle.

He woke up in a strait-jacket, his arms crossed and lashed to his sides, in an empty room with upholstered walls. A padded cell. So there really were such things as padded cells. Amazing. The floor was soft, too. It was comfortable. He tucked his legs under him and fell asleep again.

The next time he awoke there was a man in the room with him

"Congratulations," the man said. "You have permitted us quite an extraordinary breakthrough. Indirectly of course. Unless you are the proponent of some revolutionary new therapy which uses vicarious violence to re-connect violent psychotic patients with the real world."

Tom just stared at him blankly.

"No, I thought not."

The man had a rich, modulated Hispanic accent, like a Brazilian diplomat with a Harvard education, his baritone voice smoothed and softened into an instrument of gracious charm by a thousand state dinners. Or perhaps this was just the way he spoke to the criminally insane. If the guy was trying to set him at ease, it was working. Tom leaned back against the cushioned wall, and stretched his legs.

"I'm not really sure what you're talking about," he said. His mouth was dry and his voice felt alien and obstructed, as if he was talking through half-chewed shredded wheat. If they had given him pain killers after the beating they were wearing off. Every single part of his body hurt him. His right ankle felt like it had been struck on the point of the bone with a baseball bat.

The man was still talking.

Tom squinted up at him and made an effort to concentrate.

"Claude Demming, your roommate, ended his disassociative period yesterday," the man was saying. "During your confrontation with the orderlies. You probably didn't have time to notice, but he was clapping. Even more remarkably, he wanted to talk about the incident afterward, with anyone who was willing to listen. Not that he was particularly coherent. Have you ever heard an excited five year old describing a complicated TV show? There's far more enthusiasm than precision. That isn't important, though. The key thing is that you somehow *roused his interest.* You were actually more compelling to him than his own interior world. Quite an accomplishment."

"Do I get a reward?"

"Well . . . I can take that jacket off you."

"Aren't you afraid I'll go berserk?"

The man shrugged. "Your spirit may wish to . . . 'go berserk' as you put it. But I doubt the flesh is willing. You resemble nothing so much as the raw strip of pounded veal I prepared for my dinner last night."

Tom smiled; it hurt. "That reminds me of something my Dad used to say. Which is just the kind of thing you people want me to tell you."

The man started to speak—some knee-jerk contradiction, no doubt. Tom squinted to silence him. "We'd be making a soufflé or something and the cook-book would say, 'fold in the beaten whites'. He'd always say, 'That means us, kid.' "

"Well, today I would have to agree with him," the man said as he untied the lacings and pulled the jacket off. The man took Tom's hand. The pressure made him wince. "My name is Miguel Osona. I'll be working with you from now on. Dr. Honig's approach was determined to be unproductive."

"And dangerous."

"Yes. The attrition rate among the orderlies was reaching alarming proportions. The union lodged a complaint. Apparently dealing with patients who fight back was not included in their last contract negotiations."

"Okay—I get it. This is like good cop, bad cop, right? Good shrink, bad shrink. Aren't you supposed to offer me cigarettes or something?"

"Yes. I'm familiar with that method of interrogation. The victim is broken down by the constant violation of his expectations. I have no interest in 'breaking you down'. Nevertheless . . . the term is curiously appropriate in this context. So far as I'm concerned, Dr. Honig is a very bad shrink indeed. One of the worst I've ever encountered."

"And you're the good shrink."

"I try to be."

"Well . . . you're doing all right so far."

"Better than you think. For one thing, I've arranged that you be given a private room. On the sixth floor, with a view of the street, a writing table, a comfortable chair with a reading lamp . . . I even procured some Winslow Homer watercolor prints for the walls. Just as if you were someone important, Oh say . . . the President's son, for instance. I've been given full responsibility for your medication and I'm taking you off the Haldol and the Stelazine. At least for the moment."

"And then what?"

"Then we talk."

"What if I don't want to talk?"

"Then you're back with Honig. And he wants to start you on Clozopine."

"Clozopine?"

"It's a relatively new drug, one the most potent anti-psychotics currently available. It's contra-indicated unless every other approach has failed because the side effects are so extreme."

"Like what?"

"Like . . . agraulocytosis. I won't go into a lot of detail but it's a condition where the shape of your white blood cells changes."

"And what happens then?"

"You die."

"But you're cured!" Tom laughed and it stabbed his ribs like an awl. He realized he'd been breathing shallowly since he woke up to lessen the pain in his sides. Good thing he didn't have to sneeze.

Osona nodded. "Yes, that's the good part. Yet for some reason patients don't find it particularly consoling. I suspect that talking to me will prove to be a more practical alternative. You might even enjoy yourself."

Tom readjusted his back against the wall. "You know, my living room when I was growing up had walls like this. The fabric was a lot nicer, though."

Osona glanced around. "I'm sure a good interior designer could do wonders with this room. Whether the average resident would care is another question."

"But that's exactly the point, Doctor. I'm not the average resident. You can sense it. That's why you're talking this way."

"Now wait a moment. Perhaps you—"

"Listen to me. I'll take as many sessions with you as you want, marathon sessions, we can go at it all day long. I don't care. But you have to understand what I'm doing it for. And it has to be on my terms."

"No, no, you can't possibly—"

"They're easy terms, Doctor. Just hear me out. Then you can decide. Let me tell you what I want and how I'm thinking. That's your job anyway, isn't it? Listening to this shit? So listen to me. Please. I'm not trying to get well. I'm not trying to resolve any interior conflicts or stabilize my personality disorder. I don't even have any 'issues' to deal with. All I want to do is . . . I have to convince you I'm not crazy. Somehow. By taking my time and explaining everything clearly, laying it all out for you. I know I can do that, if you'll let me. If you'll really listen. I'm in a crazy situation, but I acknowledge that fact— which actually proves I'm sane, doesn't it? A crazy person wouldn't notice this stuff. Or it would seem normal. I'm sane, Doctor. That's what I have to make you understand. Nothing else matters to me."

"And so, your 'terms' are . . .?"

"That you give me a chance. That you have an open mind. Most of all . . . that you listen to me as a *person*, not as mental patient."

Osona sat down on the other side of the cell, exhaling a long, tired breath. He pressed his index fingers between the corners of his eyes and the bridge of his nose. It was a refined gesture, expressing an aristocratic fatigue, as if it was the shabby world around him, not any ordinary lack of sleep, that had drained his energy.

"First of all," he said. "It is untenable and destructive to allow a patient in your situation to set the terms of his therapy. The arrogance of the request could be seen as signifying a whole other delusional system at work."

"Maybe. Or maybe I'm just a spoiled snotty rich kid."

They sat in silence for a few moments, listening to the hiss of the air filtration system. Then Osona stood up.

"There's a story I heard several years ago, about a reporter who went 'under cover' to investigate claims of malpractice and abuse at a state mental hospital. He actually got himself admitted to the place. He was supposed to be psychotic but he had no training, he wasn't an actor, he wasn't versed in the behavioral details of his pathology. He was sure he'd be found out immediately. He didn't even know how he could keep his notebook up-dated without arousing suspicion. But he had nothing to worry about. The doctors watched him scribbling away, documenting their crimes and misdemeanors. And they did nothing. One of their reports says, 'The patent exhibits note-taking behavior.' Doctor Honig is a bit like that."

"But not you."

"Any psychiatrist is a bit like that, especially in a place like this. Still . . . I dislike easy assumptions."

"So you'll accept my terms?"

Osona laughed. "Let me get this straight—it's being pampered and spoiled by wealthy parents that makes you this arrogant?"

"No, I was pretty much born this way."

"You amuse me. I have to be careful about that. It can be dangerous."

"But fun."

"Fun is not the point of therapeutic intervention–"

"My point exactly."

"All right my poor little rich boy, prove you're sane if you can. But don't think it will be easy."

Tom stared at him. "Until this morning, Doctor, I thought it would be impossible."

Alone in the padded cell after the doctor left, Tom found himself feeling a wary optimism. He picked up the strait-jacket; it was a surprisingly flimsy garment when it wasn't on your body, festooned with dangling laces.

Tom knew Osona's attitude could be a trap, but he didn't quite believe it. Honig wasn't insightful enough for such shrewd match-making. The only question was how best to use Osona's sympathy, how to build an escape plan on the delicate foundation of a psychiatrist's sense of humor, on the unflinching intelligence in a stranger's eyes.

How to do it: he smiled, thinking of Jake Gritzky's all purpose (and purposely cryptic) advice:

Very carefully.

Amy Elwell was asleep when the phone rang.

She had started sleeping at odd times, staying up most

of the night, dozing in front of sleazy cable movies and infomercials on television; she actually watched some of the long-form talk-show style advertisements for car waxes and self-improvement. She day-dreamed about improving herself. She listened to pledge-drives on public radio. She envied the people taking calls, the banks of anonymous volunteers—at least they were doing something.

She no longer cooked, she just ate frozen food out of her microwave oven. Mess was accumulating in her house. She let it happen, watching it like an advancing tide. Dirty dishes and clothes already out-numbered the clean ones. Soon there would be nothing to wear, nothing to eat off, no patch of floor visible under the clutter.

Ira Heller had told her to resume her normal life, but she couldn't remember what that had been. Her one brush with the outside world had been Jim Gramble's funeral.

There had been more than a thousand people at Grace Church for the service and she couldn't help thinking that each of them had at least ten wonderful Jim Gramble anecdotes; so there were ten thousand stories on the street with her that day.

She was shunned at the cemetery.

As Amos Gramble pointed out to her, most of those people believed that her boyfriend had murdered Jim in cold blood. Of course they were angry. But Amos knew better. He hugged her in front of all of them and said, "Make his death mean something."

She promised that she would.

But the words were hollow. Her life now consisted of waiting for the phone call that would give her permission to visit Tom.

"I'll get you in there as soon as possible," Heller had said.

His men had debriefed her, long sessions every day, in

which she'd told them everything about Tom she could remember, even describing intimate moments and the later
coldness, the military demeanor that had prompted her to
read the journal in the first place. There was nothing to lose—
everything was lost already. And she wanted to gain their
confidence. She had no idea if the strategy was working, but
Heller hadn't called. Her mother and father called; friends
from school called. Every time the phone rang she feel her
nerves curling and snapping back like a whip. When she
came home she saw nothing in the house but the blinking
red light on her answering machine. But it was never the
message she wanted.

Until this afternoon.

The phone woke her from an absurd, terrifying dream
of being chased by vicious but impeccably groomed little
poodles. Heller's voice swept the images out of her mind
brusquely—straight-arming them like dishes off a table,
clearing a space and setting his proposition down in front
of her.

"You get to see him, you convince him to cooperate
with his doctors, you tell me everything he says."

"What if I can't remember everything he says?"

"You won't have to. You'll be wearing a wire."

"No way." She slammed the answer back without even
thinking about it.

"It's all been arranged, Ms. Elwell. You'll be in no danger and I personally assure you—"

"Forget it. I'm not wearing a wire."

"You don't want to feel like a spy? You don't want to
feel like you're betraying his trust? Is that it?" Amy said
nothing. He pushed on. "Well I find that somewhat ingenu-
ous. You are going to be a spy, whether you like it or not.
You are going to betraying him, whether you use our technology or your own faulty memory. The only question is how
effective a spy you're going to be."

"Effective? He's going to hold me, we're going to touch, he'll feel it and—"

Heller raised a hand, smiling indulgently. "I'm afraid you've been watching too much television, Ms. Elwell."

For some reason, Amy thought of those endless infomercials—would those clear-eyed, shovel faced self-help salesmen have some good advice for her now? Somehow she doubted it.

Heller went on: "The applied science of surveillance has progressed far beyond what you see on the average cop show. Trust me. There's no way Tom could discover the wire—unless he was in a situation of . . . much greater intimacy than will be possible at the Holden clinic. So. I have three primary concerns. First of all I worry that Tom is plotting some escape plan with like minded and gullible individuals inside the institute. Patients are free to mingle and I'm sure he'll be able to find a ready audience among them for his delusions. Any information you give me about such plans could avert a catastrophe down the line. Second . . . "

Heller paused as if he wasn't sure he wanted to proceed.

"What?"

"All right. This is tricky, Ms. Elwell. The President wants to meet with Tom. The first thing he wants to do after being discharged from the hospital is to put flowers on his wife's grave. And the next thing is to visit Tom. I think it's safe to say that the whole nation wants that, too. There are wounds that we have to heal together, collectively. For that reason, it may be the biggest single human interest story since the death of JFK jr. That's why I have to know how Tom feels about the meeting. It's critical for the Administration that the reunion goes off smoothly. America wants to see the First Family pulling together. Wild accusations, acrimony of any kind—it could be disastrous. And not just to

America, but to the rest of the world, which looks to America
for leadership. I'm sure you can understand that."

Amy nodded.

"There is another aspect of the situation which I have
to clarify for you. I find this embarrassing, but . . . well, I
suppose it's unavoidable. Rumors have surfaced which . . .
well, they're similar in tone, at least, to some of what Tom has
been saying. Where they come from, I'm not sure. I know
Tom talked to at least one reporter before he was captured.
But this stuff could have started on its own. At first it didn't
matter—stories in the tabloids about the President being
abducted by aliens and replaced with an extra-terrestrial.
According to the *National Inquirer*. According to the *Star*, he's
an evil twin recruited by Saddam Hussein. That sort of thing.
It started to get serious when one of the Network
newsmagazines ran a story on the rumors. Perhaps you saw it.
They showed before and after videos—the President in news
conferences, bootleg videos of him walking in the hospital
corridors versus him walking to Air Force One last year. And
I have to admit that he looks different—so would you if you
had been through what this man has been through. Anyway,
it's pointless for us to deny it. Denials are basically self-in-
crimination. They won't contain this lunacy. It's all over the
internet. There are at least thirty web-sites devoted to 'fake-
President' conspiracy theories. And you can't believe the
hits they're getting—thousands, every day." He paused and
took a breath. "No. The only way to stop this is to prove beyond the shadow of a doubt that the stories are false. That's
why we've invited a camera crew from *60 Minutes* to join the
President when he visits Tom. They're going to broadcast
live from the Holden Clinic. We expect the biggest television audience in history. The love between Tom and his Father, the family connection there . . . it will be obvious for
everyone to see. And these destructive rumors will be put to
rest forever."

Amy nodded. "Sounds like a plan."

"So you'll . . . sound him out for us?"

Amy nodded again.

"My final concern is for Tom himself. To aid his recovery, to speed the work of his doctors. To get him out of there so that the two of you can resume some sort of normal life together . . . within the obvious limits of Tom's illness. Having access to thoughts he would only share with someone he trusted could be invaluable to the therapeutic process. How can you argue with that?"

"I can't. But I won't wear a wire."

"Then I can't trust you. And we have no deal."

"No! Then you'll have to trust me. Which is what our deal is all about, anyway."

"But you yourself said you might no be able to—"

"I'll remember. Just be sure to debrief me right away. I waited on tables for two years, and I never got an order wrong. My memory's fine."

There was a long silence at the other end of the line. Finally Heller said, "All right. we'll try it your way. Just don't let me down."

"I won't."

"Tomorrow morning at ten A.M. I'll have a car pick you up. Be downstairs waiting."

Heller hung up without saying good-bye. Amy pushed the disconnect button and set the phone down, smiling. She had won this round. It would be easy to feel cocky now—quicker and smarter than Heller. Still, slow as he seemed, Heller had managed to catch Tom. It was worth remembering that. And Tom was much better at this stuff than she was.

Amy got out of bed, dressed and put on a pot of coffee. She burned her tongue on the first sip and then sat there silently in the sunny kitchen, waiting for the cup to cool.

They met on the fourth floor terrace of the Holden Clinic. It looked out over the courtyards and gardens between Ninety-first and Ninety-second streets. Amy waited alone, pacing the weathered brickwork, sitting briefly on each of the uncomfortable wrought iron benches. It was early April but she felt no hint of spring in the morning air. It was cold and cloudy, dark as late afternoon under the heavy clouds. Amy buttoned the top button of her coat, wishing she'd worn a hat. The sounds the of city lifted up to her faintly on the steady East wind—the rustle of traffic, broken by car horns, shouts, the slap of a basketball on asphalt. Five minutes became ten; then fifteen. She was going back inside to get warm when she saw Tom on the other side of the big glass doors.

He looked terrible—the way people look on the news when they've just been rescued from prisoner-of-war camps or religious cults: thin and stiff and tentative. He smiled when he saw her and the life came back into his face. There was a moment of awkward comedy as he pulled at the door, which had to be pushed from his side; and Amy pushed when she should have been pulling. She smiled morosely: a fine example of the well-oiled team work that was going to save America from the clutches of organized crime. But it was just a moment; then they both figured out what was going on.

Amy stepped back and Tom was through the door, grabbing for her, pulling her to him. They stood in the damp wind, just hugging for a long time before he kissed her and it was the same kiss as ever, another drink from the stream that was always running between them, as unmistakable as the sweat-sharp musty smell of him, as the sound of his voice when he said,

"You came."

She stroked his hair. "You knew I would."

"I knew you'd try. But Heller—"

"I convinced—" She started talking but thought better

of it. She whispered in his ear, instead. "I convinced Heller I was on his side."

"Come on." He walked her to the railing at the far end of the deck.

They just stood there for a while, listening to the city, feeling the wind on their faces, struck dumb by simple proximity, amazed and grateful to be together again.

Amy put her arm around his waist and leaned against him, loving the hardness of his body, his height, the physical fact of him. He put his arm around her shoulder, tilted his head down to rest on hers. And it was enough. Maybe I'm the crazy one, she thought—this is all I want. She was happy and she knew it was absurd to be happy now; it was dangerous. But she needed to feel this way if she was going to have the strength and the stamina to do the things Tom needed her to do. So she shut her eyes and let the feeling take her.

"What did you tell him?" Tom asked finally.

"I tricked him. Well—actually, he tricked himself. Your journal was the only evidence he has against me, and he has to deny it's true. Since his whole point is that you're crazy."

"Amy, wait. I don't get this. How did Heller get his hands on my journal? I gave it to you to keep it safe. You were supposed to—"

But Amy was crying.

At first Tom thought she was just shivering with the cold, but she was shuddering. She turned and pressed her face into his shoulder, clutching his arms and sobbing. They were big, chest tearing sobs and Tom held her tight and them roll out of her. He stroked her hair and repeated "It's okay, it's okay," over and over although he was just starting to see just how far from okay things really were.

Finally she was just sniffling and gasping, her breath coming in little hitches. He waited while she pulled herself together. She pulled away a little and looked up at him.

"I read it, Tom. I had to. I was scared. I didn't understand what was happening to you. You were so cold and distant and strange. You seemed so far away and I didn't know how else to . . . I don't know—to break through that wall. So I read it and Heller caught me and I tried to hide it but I didn't do—I . . . if I had just acted normal like you told me to, he probably would have—"

She was crying again.

"You must hate me now," she said, when the surge of self-loathing misery had subsided.

"Amy, please . . ."

"I ruined everything."

"No you didn't."

"It's over."

"It's not. It's not over until we give up."

"But, I just—can't you at least get angry at me? You're supposed to get angry at me. You would have, before, when you were—"

"What?"

"Before they put you in here."

He stepped away from her, leaned against the parapet. "Maybe you're right. But I am in here and we can't afford temper tantrums now. Remind me in a couple of years—if we both live through this. I'll get angry then, all right?"

"Will you scream and throw things?" She was smiling a little.

"Absolutely. I'll even walk out on you and slam the door and hang up on you when you call me. As long as we can have really good make-up sex afterward."

She took his hand. "It's a deal."

"Just don't give up, Amy. That's the most important thing. Because this is good. It's good you told me. I'm starting to see what really happened. How they caught me and why they brought me here and—the whole thing. Jake always says— the most critical things for any military operation are lines of supply and information. Intelligence—knowing what he enemy is thinking. If—"

"Tom—"

"I have to—"

"It doesn't matter. Don't you see? You're stuck in here and there's nothing you can do, anyway. They'll never let you out and I can't—It's . . . there's no way I can help. I'm just one person, I'm not qualified, I'm not a spy or a secret agent, I couldn't even hide your notebook, and I—"

"Amy, wait."

"No, it's true, I—"

"Just wait a second. Please. It's not over yet and there's a lot you can do. You can find Jake, for one thing. He'll be able to help. Tell him the whole story. And you can track down some of the key players in this thing—Doctor Jerome, for instance. The plastic surgeon who worked on my Dad. Maybe he's had a change of heart. Maybe he never knew the whole story. Maybe you could poke his conscience, if he has one. I don't know. But it's worth a try. You can keep me informed when you visit and I can—"

"But that's the point. I don't know if they'll even let me visit you again. I'm supposed to be getting Heller information. I'm supposed to tell him something when we're finished, but I have no idea what I can say. He wanted me to wear a wire, but I refused."

"Did he brief you?"

Amy took a breath and looked out over the line of courtyards. A golden retriever was sniffing the bushes in the nearest one; next door, a couple dressed in heavy sweaters were braving the chill to drink their morning coffee at a round green metal table on the flagstones. The other yards were deserted. There was a screech of brakes from First Avenue, then horns blaring. Faint rap music stuttered from a distant boom box. Amy felt like the whole city was closing in around her. She didn't know where to begin.

"The President is going to be visiting you," she said. "The meeting is going to be on television—there's going to be a crew from *60 Minutes* there." She turned to face him. "Actually, this is good news—There are rumors that the President is a phony. People must have sensed that something's wrong. That's a break for us, don't you think? It's a start, anyway. So Heller thinks that a big reunion will fix everything. The First Family smiling and hugging for Morley Safer. Or whoever. And he wants me to find out what you think . . . what you're going to do. But I don't—"

"It's okay."

"You don't—"

"Listen, it's okay. It's going to be all right. I have an idea."

He took her arm and started walking her to the far side of the terrace. But he stopped after a few steps—it didn't matter any more. Of course they were watching. It didn't matter whether Amy was wired or not. They had directional mikes that could pick up his heartbeat from a hundred yards away. The business of the wire had to have been something else, some kind of psychological warfare, a way to break Amy down, force her to feel she had changed sides. Tom loved her for refusing. She would never change sides, never even consent to the appearance of it.

And all of Heller's technology was irrelevant, that was what he had just realized. The idea was coming together in hard precise sections. It was like assembling a sniper rifle: the clean solid ratcheting sound as each section snapped into the rest—sight into stock, stock into barrel. You started with bits and wound up with something both elegant and lethal.

He took both of Amy's hands.

"Think about this," he said. "We've lost the element of surprise. They know all my secrets. They beat us. But now we can turn that defeat around. Because we have nothing to hide any more."

"I don't understand."

"In the hospital I couldn't ask the impostor the kind of tough questions he couldn't answer because I didn't want to blow my own cover. But now I can say anything I want—my cover is already blown. I have nothing to lose. They have every-thing to lose—with network news cameras and half the country watching. I can show this guy up in front of the whole world."

All he needed was an ally inside the Holden clinic; and he thought he might just have found one. But he kept that to himself. Even the most sophisticated surveillance system couldn't read his mind.

Amy was wide-eyed. "Could you really do that?"

"You can watch me do it, on *60 Minutes*."

"But . . . they'll kill you."

"They won't be able to. They're trapped, Amy. Their whole plan depends on secrecy, that's why they're freak-ing out right now. Once this is out in the open, it's over. So you can tell Heller what I'm planning to do—that should earn you a few more visits. They have to suspect it anyway. So confirm their suspicions. No, really. I'm serious. I like the idea of making them squirm. They've built this trap for themselves and now they're caught in it. I just wish I could see the look on Heller's face when he figures out what's happened."

"No, Tom—they'll do something, they'll think of some-thing. They'll drug you."

"It would show. The President's reunion with his son doesn't mean much if the son is a Haldol zombie."

"They could threaten you physically."

"Let them."

"They could threaten me physically. With me as a hos-tage you'd do whatever they wanted."

"That's another reason for you to get in touch with Jake. He'll protect you. Make that your first priority, Amy. I have to know you're safe."

Amy pulled her hands away and crossed her arms over her chest. She stared out at the buildings that blocked her view of the East River. All the windows with all the lives transpiring inside them. All the little urgencies. She wondered what they thought about the couple on the terrace of the Holden Clinic, if anyone even noticed them. Some sad crazy boy having a lover's quarrel. She could just see some cynical New Yorker having a chuckle over that—not even crazy people get a truce in the war between the sexes.

She turned away from the windows. Imagining other people just made her lonelier. She felt bad, suddenly. She felt hollow inside. There was something terribly wrong with Tom's plan, but she couldn't explain it—even to herself. It was too easy. The forces arrayed against them had too much riding on the outcome to allow Tom's little scheme to work. Maybe they even had an impostor for Tom himself, ready to step in and play the role of the loving son if Tom failed to cooperate. Anything was possible. The situation as constituted proved that. To dismiss a possibility because it seemed too absurd or extreme was just foolish. Their world had gone insane—to try and deal with it logically now would be suicidally stupid.

"You can't let them know in advance, Tom. You can't. You've thought you had them out-smarted before. That's why you're here right now. I'm sorry, but it's true. If they know what you're going to do, they'll stop you somehow. Even if you manage to embarrass the impostor in front of the television cameras, they'll edit it out, they'll cancel the show, they'll . . . I don't know. They could even take a digital impression of you from the video tape and construct a computer generated image that would say whatever they wanted."

"Amy—"

"They can do that. They were putting John Wayne into potato chip commercials ten years ago. God knows what they can do now."

He slumped a little. "Maybe you're right. But whatever happens, a crew of top journalists will see it. They'll see it's the scoop of the century, the first great political scandal of the new millennium, and they'll run with it. They'd never drop a story like this."

"But that's why you have to keep it secret. I'll tell them you're confused. You're afraid you made a terrible mistake. That you miss your Dad and love him and the shock of seeing him so battered and flimsy and strange sent you over the deep end and now you don't know what you think. I'll say you said, 'I just want to be with my Dad.' You're lonely and scared . . . I don't know, maybe I can make them think that a good performance by this guy could turn you around. I mean . . . with all the drugs they've been giving you . . . "

"Forget it."

"What—?"

"They're listening to us now. They have to be. Or at least . . . we have to assume they are. They certainly have the technology. The time for hiding is over, Amy. I'm going to do what I have to do. And they're going to do what they have to do. No more bluffing—all the cards are face up. So just be honest with them. Your only value is the subjective impressions you've made of me—whether you think I'm capable of pulling this off, or too far gone to be a real threat. You can tell them what you saw in my eyes. That's the one thing their cameras can't show. You know me. They don't. So tell them the truth. Then I'll get to see you again and we'll still have a chance."

"But—"

"You have to be on their side right now. So do it right. And pray. And kiss me good-bye."

"There's only one part of that I feel any confidence about at all," she said. So she kissed him and it was a long deep urgent kiss and when it was finished and she was walking away back to the glass doors and the debriefing by Ira Heller,

both of them were thinking the same thing—that the fate of
the world might just depend on whether she could perform
her other tasks with the same skill and passion. She had
been raised with strong values but no religion at all, in a
family of agnostics who valued loyalty above everything else.

Betrayal and prayer.

She couldn't help wondering . . . which one would be
more difficult?

As it turned out, betrayal was easy.

She corroborated Heller's surveillance transcripts (It
was easy to imagine the complete text of her conversation
with Tom stored on some Secret Service Zip drive somewhere); she gave her personal opinion of Tom's state of
mind ("Too unstable to be much of a threat to anyone");
she even offered to wear a wire at the next meeting. Heller
met her ironic smile with a chilly one of his own.

"That won't be necessary," he said, and as usual they
understood each other.

22

Amy Elwell loved the telephone. At moments of heart-break and stress, at moments of victory and jubilation, she always found herself on the phone. There were times when the sound of a sympathetic voice late at night had kept her spirit alive. She understood the concept of suicide hotlines, and had volunteered for one at NYU.

That was the worst part of this situation somehow—the telephone was off-limits. There was no one she could fully trust, no privacy, no secure line to use . . . even if she could find someone to listen.

There was Jake, but she knew somehow that she had to see him in person and look him in the eyes when they spoke. She needed the comfort of his physical presence—Jake was, among other things, a professional body-guard, and had pro-tected dignitaries as diverse as Desmond Tutu and Tony Blair when they visited America. Surely he could protect her from the Secret Service. Of course that was another irony—that she now felt the presence of Heller's people as a potential threat. But it was true—they could snatch her off the street any time they wanted, to coerce Tom's cooperation. Her disappearance would be hard to explain, perhaps; but there wouldn't be any need to bother. It wasn't the *Public* Service, after all—or the *Gossip* Service or the *Full Disclosure* Service.

It was the Secret Service.

And Heller knew how to keep a secret.

That was why she walked the half a block to First Avenue without looking back, hailed a cab, climbed in, and said, "LaGuardia Airport, please."

She was going to Nantucket.

Amy timed it perfectly—she walked right onto a direct flight. The air was clear and the trip was smooth. She was walking across the tarmac an hour later, spirits buoyed by her own efficiency. She was like an arrow, released by Tom with a hard twang of the bow, slicing straight for the target.

But the target was elusive.

Jake prided himself on being hard to find.

Amy walked inside and waited until the girl behind the Nantucket Airlines counter was free. It took a while. They were having a busy morning.

"Excuse me," she said finally. "I'm looking for Jake Gritzky?"

The girl focused on Amy for a moment; then shrugged. "He hasn't been in for the last couple of days."

"Do you have his phone number? It isn't listed."

The girl laughed. "I guess not. Jake doesn't have a phone."

"Oh . . . I see. Well, it doesn't matter. I really just need to see him anyway. Can you give me his address?"

"No, sorry."

"Is that company policy? Because—"

"Our company isn't big enough for a whole lot of *policies.*"

She made the whole idea sound bizarre—as if Amy had

asked about purification rituals or particle accelerators. Or
Potpourri. Amy bit down on a laugh; she was getting punchy.

"Did I say something funny?" the girl asked, annoyed.

"No, not really. You were saying—about Jake?"

"It doesn't matter—nobody really knows where he
lives. Out in the woods somewhere, I think. He's kind of a
hermit."

"But . . . his address must be on file with his W2 forms."

"It's a PO box."

This was getting nowhere—an arrow stuck in the dirt.
She took a breath and gave it one last try. "Well—the next
time he comes in, will you tell him to call Amy Elwell? Tell
him it's about Tom. And it's urgent."

The girl actually wrote down the message.

"I'll let him know," she said. And then she was on to
the next customer.

Flying back to New York, Amy was reminded of a recurring dream she'd been having for years. It was a fairly
common, stress-related nightmare: she was in school,
about to take a major test in a class she had been cutting
all semester. She hadn't gotten in trouble so far because
the teacher didn't even know she was supposed to be there.
But now they had found out and she was being dragged
down the hallway by the assistant principal who was saying
"You're not going to be able to talk your way out of this
one," as he led her towards the classroom.

The nightmare was coming true. She noticed the date
on another passenger's newspaper and realized with a
sickly drop of her stomach that midterms began in two
days. She had accepted a lot since New Year's Eve, changed
in many ways—she was willing to break the law, to lie and
steal and even kill if she had to. She was willing to lose
Tom, to go to jail fighting for his cause, even to die.

But she was not going to flunk her Twentieth Century
American Literature survey course at NYU.

That was where she drew the line.

Looking down as they banked across Manhattan toward Newark Airport, Amy felt the curious comfort of a normal moment. This was stress she could handle. This was the kind of problem someone like her was supposed to be having. She smiled almost happily as she leaned her head against the nose tickling vibration of the Plexiglas window.

She had a lot of studying to do.

Tom had been talking for six hours. Doctor Osona had canceled his other appointments; apart from that one short instruction to his secretary, he hadn't spoken at all. He just let Tom talk, and Tom had a lot to say. This was the third day of the grueling marathon Tom had promised. He had begun at the beginning, methodically recapitulating everything that had happened since Christmas. It was an impressive story. The deaths, in any case, couldn't be ignored: Blasi, Polidakis, Helen Jaglom, Buster, Douglas Baird . . . and Jim Gramble himself.

Tom finished with the story of his own capture, then sat back against the cushions of Osona's couch. It was a comfortable piece of furniture. It was so comfortable, Tom sank so deep into the pillows, he sometimes felt it was ingesting him. He was content to be swallowed by the soft fabric today. He stared at Osona, waiting for the man's response. A lot depended on it.

"Well," Osona said, rising. He paced their office during their sessions. He had a difficult time thinking when he was seated. This, he had explained once with a self-deprecating smile, had made medical school unusually challenging for him. "First of all, I have to say that constructing a personally coherent explanation from disconnected facts is part of the textbook definition of paranoid schizophrenia."

Tom levered himself away from the maw of pillows, but

before he could speak, Osona raised a hand; the man's gentle smile stopped Tom more than the gesture. He leaned back again.

"The problem," Osona went on, "Is that it is also part of the textbook definition of good detective work. And I am faced with the uncomfortable fact that you seem to be one of the most rational, practical and well-grounded people I've met in years. Of course," he smiled, "I spend much of my time with mental health professionals."

He walked to the window

"Your story is bizarre, obviously. The lack of corroborating evidence troubles me. I'm sure you realize that there is nothing at all to substantiate your extraordinary claims. Mr. Gramble's story has disappeared . . . since we are assuming at least for the moment, that it even existed in the first place. The files he mentioned were gone when you arrived at 401 East 74th Street and haven't turned up since. Mr. Gramble himself, who could be the key to this whole matter, is of course . . ." Osona shivered slightly. He rubbed his palm over his mouth and then down his throat. He rubbed his neck to loosen the knot of muscle there. "Naturally, many people familiar with your case assume that you killed Mr. Gramble for precisely that reason."

Again Tom started to speak. Again the lifted hand.

"Certainly it seems unduly coincidental that the one man who could definitively refute your charges was murdered before he could talk to anyone except this detective Armand Taliafero . . . whom you admit to killing less than an hour later. It's a tidy case, Tom."

"But turn it inside out, Doctor. Jim was also the only person who could clear me, who could help me prove that what I'm saying is true. I'd have to be nuts to want to—"

Tom was pulled up short of the amusement in Osona's eyes.

"What?"

"Well that is the point, isn't, my spoiled little rich boy?
You'd have to be . . . 'nuts' as you put it. It's not clinical terminology, but it serves the purpose well enough."

"It was a figure of speech, Doctor. The kind sane
people use all the time."

Osona moved to his desk. "There is another anecdote
I wanted to share with you. It's been on my mind for several days. A kind of footnote to the Watergate affair. It happened long before you were born of course, and if you
are not a student of Presidential scandal and the abuse of
power you could easily have missed it. It's not the sort of
thing they teach in school. Watergate burglar Bernard
Barker's son went to the police, claiming that his father
and Gordon Liddy were involved in covert domestic intelligence operations inside the CIA. What happened next
bears a chilling relevance to your own situation. His father arranged to have him placed in a mental hospital,
where he was detained for more than two years. If what
you claim is true it would not be . . . unprecedented."

Tom felt a physical relief; it was like the moment when
you could begin to feel the aspirin unraveling your headache. He took a moment before he spoke.

"It's good to hear you say that," he said softly.

Osona shrugged. "I operate according to a private rule
. . . a policy, if you like. I trust my senses. I believe what I see
and hear. I believe in first hand experience. I trust eye-witness testimony. It may be flawed and inconsistent but it's
generally superior to the alternatives—hearsay and speculation. So, here I am . . . I've been told various things about you,
I read your case history, and I come to certain temporary
conclusions. I listen to Honig—but I like to see things for
myself. I can be quite stubborn about that. It annoys people.
I don't take people's word for things. Especially people like
Leonard Honig."

Tom smiled. "This is working."

"Yes. Are you familiar with the great Victorian poet, Matthew Arnold?"

"I know the name."

"I have always admired his definition of integrity. Actually, he was speaking of 'piety', but it comes to the same thing. He said it was simply . . . 'Acting what one knows'. My father was a psychiatrist. He fell in love with one of his patients. It was a disaster. My mother left him, he lost his license."

"What did he do?"

"He married his patient and they opened a book store. In Princeton, New Jersey. Twenty years later, it's still doing quite well. And they're still happily married. They're like sixty-year-old teenagers. I asked him one day, 'Do you think people should do what you did? Should people break the rules?' And he said, 'Other people's rules don't matter. Follow your own rules.'"

"So he was an anarchist."

"But a law-abiding one. People make up lots of rules, Tom. The 'Golden Rule' for instance. Whatever our religious persuasion, most of agree that Jesus was onto something there. It applies to every aspect of life. For instance . . . I wouldn't want to be treated as you've been treated here."

"So you'll break the rules to help me."

Osona looked back at him steadily.

"Their rules. Not mine."

He sat down against the edge of his desk and looked at his watch. "They'll be serving dinner in a few minutes. You should get a move on, or you'll be late. When breaking the big rules, you should strictly uphold the small ones. Best to be punctual."

Tom stood and shook his hand. "Thank you, Doctor."

Osona smiled. "You know, you really are extraordinarily well-mannered—for a spoiled snotty rich kid."

"We get a bum rap. I think it's the deprived polite poor kids. Those little shits are always bad-mouthing us."

Osona laughed, pushing him towards the door. "Go on, get out of here. We'll continue this tomorrow."

Tom walked down the long corridor towards the dining hall, past Henry and two other orderlies, careful to keep the excitement off his face.

In this place there was nothing more suspicious than happiness, and the last thing he could afford to do now was raise anyone's suspicions.

23

The TV weathermen and *the New York Times* had made it official: Spring was in full retreat. After a deceptive start, this was going to go down in the record books as the coldest April in fifty years. Amy Elwell sat on the train from New York to New London Connecticut staring out the window through the freezing rain at the gray miles of industrial suburbs, glad to be in the overheated compartment, still bundled in her coat and reluctant to take it off. The damp chill had gotten inside her this morning. She was reading the *Times*, hoping for some distraction, but the front page carried a stories about the President's approval rate shooting to 87% and in the very next column, the news that more racketeering charges against Dominic Nosiglia being dropped by the Justice Department. It was too depressing. She set the newspaper aside, shivering. If she had been thinking she would have brought a thermos of hot chocolate. But she had been on auto-pilot this morning. She was starched with exhaustion, with a screeching headache behind her eyes that felt like someone was playing the violin, scraping a horsehair bow over her retinal strings.

She thought of the crumbling frost belt infra-structure,

the rusting factories sliding past her window, the track she was riding on and the bridges they crossed. She had read somewhere it was all about to fall apart from age and negligence and metal fatigue. She smiled as she started to unbutton her coat. For some reason the concept of metal fatigue comforted her this morning. It was nice to think that even metal got tired eventually.

With a sustained burst of effort unlike anything she had ever contemplated—much less actually accomplished—before, Amy had studied for three mid-term exams over the previous weekend: the American literature course; "Social Engineering in Post War America", whose first semester had focused on the planning and construction of the Levittown housing development; and a Biology exam. The Biology class was like a curse, the last hated remnant of her long discarded plan to study pre med at NYU. She had to fulfill her science requirement, anyway, she knew that—but there were lots of easier ways to do it than with Nobel laureate Professor Theodore Halpern's "Advanced Molecular Biology." Still, she was half way to the finish line and next year would be easier.

If she was going to have a next year.

Amy turned away from the gloom, inside and outside her head—the fatalism of her situation, the dreary landscapes chugging by as the train approached the Connecticut border, and the dreary men from the Secret Service watching her from the other end of the car.

In school at least, she was safe. She knew that many people took exams and came out of them with no idea how they had done. That baffled her. She could always predict her grades exactly, and in this case she knew she had scored two Bs and a C. It wasn't great, she wouldn't make the Dean's List, but at this moment that was the least of her problems. She had done what she had set out to do, that was what counted.

She was on her way to see Dr. Clifford Jerome, the plastic surgeon who had worked on the impostor. Getting the address had been an education in the kind of thinking her new lot in life required. It was a puzzle she had to solve, one whose solution was hidden in its own interior logic.

She had started by looking up Jerome in the newspaper files at the Public Library. The momentum of study and research had helped her as she scrolled through six months worth of the New York Times.

She had been in the library most of the day before she came upon the story about Clifford giving up his practice and moving back to his old home town of Waterford, Connecticut. He was virtually retiring from a high profile, wildly successful career at the age of thirty nine, with no explanation beyond the standard one of "Wanting to spend more time" with his "family"—an estranged wife whose affairs with his glamorous patients had made her a staple of the tabloids for years; a college-aged daughter whose tell-all autobiography had been rejected by every publisher in New York; and two cats (Who probably didn't like him much either).

It was the kind of transparently phony explanation politicians gave when one too many scandals had forced them out of office. But Amy had a very good idea of what Jerome's real reasons might be.

He was guilty.

He hated what he'd done.

Maybe he would seize the chance to make up for it, somehow. Maybe Tom was right, If she said the right things, laid the situation out properly, he might change sides. If he did, his testimony would do more than even Jim Gramble's article could have done to destroy the Nosiglia crime family's hold on the White House.

In another part of the library she had found a Waterford telephone book and looked up the name Jerome. There

were plenty of them, the family had been there for genera-
tions. She started calling, and that was when she hit the wall.
No one would talk to her, no one would give her any information. Some of them were quite insulting. After two hours—
and almost fifty dollars in long distance charges—she was no
further than when she began.

She thought of just going to Waterford and ringing door-
bells, checking the address labels on peoples' mail. The
article said Jerome had a view of the Niantic River—that
should narrow it down a little. Then the image of herself tip-
toeing from house to house with two blank-faced Secret Service guys trudging along behind her made her laugh out
loud.

And that was the answer: the Secret Service.

All she had to do to get the address was to *ask Heller for
it*. As the surveillance slapstick she had just imagined
proved, there was no way she was going to find Jerome
without the Secret Service knowing about it . . . and they already knew she was planning the visit anyway, didn't they?
Tom certainly thought so. Actually, requesting the information from Heller would be a good way to find out. If he
didn't know her plans, if in fact he hadn't been eavesdropping with high-tech equipment on Friday, then he would
have no reason to doubt her cover story—that she wanted
to shake Jerome's hand and thank him personally, "As an
emissary from all the ordinary people who owed him so
much". It was corny, but Amy was a twenty two year old
from Vermont. She wasn't supposed to be sophisticated.
He would give her the information. If he refused or even
stalled, then she had to assume Tom was right.

Much to her surprise, he had chuckled, said, "You know
that's a very sweet idea, Ms. Elwell." Then he had given her
the phone number and the address. It was that easy. "Be sure
to send him my regards," Heller had said, just before they
hung up. The only moment of disagreement had come when

Heller asked to send a news crew with her—to make the
most of the encounter "from a public relations point of view."

She had refused. He had been gracious about it.

And that was that.

She had called Jerome last night, told him she wanted
to come and speak to him in person—that it was urgent, and
that she believed he understood the nature of the urgency.

"Yes, come," he had said. "This is overdue. Do you have
my address?"

"Twenty-nine Oswegatchie Road. Heller gave it to me.
Along with your phone number."

"Did he really? How helpful of him. I'll expect you
around lunch time."

She glanced back at the two agents and smiled at them.
The trick would be to get inside Jerome's house quickly,
and lock them out. She only needed five minutes alone
with the plastic surgeon. Then this would be over.

The cab dropped her off in a neighborhood of small
houses dwarfed by big trees and charged with the sense of
water nearby. She could see the flicker of blue through
the branches of the trees, dense with budding leaves. The
other cab that had been following her since the railroad
station parked a couple of houses down the street. They
were making no visible effort to intercept or join her.
Good sign or bad sign? It was too complicated to figure
out. She just walked up the driveway and rang the doorbell.

The woman who opened the door had obviously been
beautiful once, she held herself with the untouchable calm
dignity Amy had always associated with rich beautiful
women of a certain age. It was a kind of ease that came
from the knowledge, derived from decades of experience,
that you would be sought after, deferred to, obeyed. She
was dressed casually, against type—jeans and a Smith Col-

lege Centennial sweatshirt that said "Celebrating a hundred years of women on top" across the chest.

Looking at her, Amy could tell something was very wrong. The woman's face bore all the marks of insomnia—the circles under the eyes, the sallow complexion—but she was ravaged by something far worse than a sleepless night.

"You've come to see Clifford, haven't you?" the woman said in an uninflected voice. Someone else's voice—a mail-order voice to use until she got her own back. "You're the girl who called yesterday."

"I—"

"You're too late. He committed suicide last night."

She felt the words like a blow, like something had struck her whole body all at once, like walking into a tree.

"I'm so sorry—"

"You know what this is about, don't you? You do. You know why he did it."

"I don't—I can't—"

"He didn't leave a note. I think that's the worst part. He always despised people who walked out on arguments. People who hung up on you. But this is so much worse. He left me with nothing. Can you understand that?"

Amy was thinking clearly enough to shake her head. She couldn't understand and she hoped she never would. She studied the granite paving block she was standing on. She sensed that the Secret Service men were hovering but she didn't turn around to look at them.

"Tell me why," the woman said. "Something about your phone call was . . . unbearable. Something you said forced him to this. What was it? Look at me!"

Amy looked up into the harrowed, merciless face.

For a moment she considered telling Mrs. Jerome the truth. But the story was so implausible, so grotesque, it would only seem insulting. There was no way she would believe it. And if even if she did, it would just put her own life in danger.

STEVEN AXELROD

It was pointless. Amy was turning away.

But then the thought jabbed at her: this woman might be able to help. It was possible. Jerome might have talked to her. He might have left notes, or diaries. There could be evidence in this house right now. If she found it and used it that could mean that Clifford Jerome hadn't died for nothing.

And beyond that, Mrs. Jerome deserved to hear the story. Even if she didn't believe it. Because she would have to believe it eventually, if they won, if they beat Dominic Nosiglia somehow.

The woman was still staring but her face had softened.

"Please," she said. "I need to hear it."

Amy nodded and walked inside.

They shut the door on the Secret Service men. They walked into the living room. It was elegantly and meticulously furnished, but it was obviously one of those rooms that were never used in the ordinary course of life. It was for "entertaining". And for dealing with the aftermath of your husband's suicide. Amy sat down on the uncomfortable brocade couch and told the shortest version of the story she could: Edward Bellamy Jaglom's lifelong acquaintanceship with Dominic Nosiglia; the thrown election; the deal that clinched his Presidency. The change of heart that sealed his fate. The extraordinary contingency plan that was now being acted out at 1600 Pennsylvania Avenue. And of course, Tom—how he knew, how he had convinced her, how she had come to be here.

It took half an hour.

It had seemed that Mrs. Jerome was about to speak at several moments, but she had controlled herself. Now she just stared.

"How dare you," she whispered at last. "How dare you."

"Mrs. Jerome—"

"You come into my house after what you've done and

spin this demented fairy story—and I mean literally *demented*, the boy you're talking about is in a *mental hospital* right now! All to cover up your own . . . Ugghh." She shuddered. "Why do it? That's what I don't understand. Why come here at all? If you wanted to rub my nose in it, if you wanted to torture me . . . I could almost understand that. But this makes no sense."

"Please, I don't know what you're trying to—"

"Are you pregnant? Is that it? Is that what pushed him over the edge? Is that what you were threatening him with? Or was there something else? Do you have some disease? That was his greatest fear when I cheated on him. He made me get tested every six weeks. He was terrified about it. Paranoid about it. Yes, I cheated on him, is that why you're staring at me? All right, fine. I had affairs. The tabloids were right about that. They often are. Does that make you feel better? No one's any better than you. We're all in the dirt together. So tell me the truth. I deserve to hear it."

Amy spoke slowly. "I'm sorry, Mrs. Jerome. I'm sorry for your loss. And I'm sorry about . . . your suspicions. I never even knew your husband except for a couple of meetings in the hospital. I doubt he even noticed me. He had more important things on his mind. But what I told you is the truth. You say the tabloids are often right. Read what they're saying about President. Watch *60 Minutes* next week. They're going to do a live broadcast of Tom's meeting with . . . this man. It may change your mind. If it does, and if your husband left any notes or journals, if he said anything to you that seems significant in retrospect, please call me . . . I'll write down the number for you."

Mrs. Jerome sat very still as Amy scribbled the number on a piece of paper from her purse. She handed it over and watched as the woman tore it up into much smaller pieces than was necessary.

"Get out of my house, you little whore. If you ever come back I'll make sure they put you in jail."

Amy just stared at her.

"Get out!"

Amy left quickly. The Secret Service agents were just outside the front door when she stepped out into the chilly drizzle.

"Everything okay?" one of them asked.

It was the perfect conclusion to the morning, to her absurd mission, to the last four months. She wanted to laugh but it caught in her throat and came out sounding like something between a cough and a sob.

"No," she said. "Everything isn't okay. As a matter of fact, nothing is okay. Everything sucks. And it's getting worse all the time. But thanks, anyway."

She turned and walked back towards the waiting cab with their wide-eyed, uncomprehending faces gaping after her. Their dullness, their blindness stoked her anger again. Mrs. Jerome was just as blind, the whole country was blind. She thought of the newspaper she had been reading on the train to New London. It had just made everything seem more futile and sad, but now she realized it was a call to action. There was one more effort she could make, one last person to confront.

It would probably make no difference, she was probably crazy to even consider it—but she was alone. Her gut feelings were all she had left to go on.

She sat back in the cab with her eyes closed, ignoring the bleak spread of strip malls beside I-95. She would be at the station soon, and back to New York. Then she was going to Little Italy, to Il Cortile, the favorite restaurant of a certain Sicilian gentleman. She thought of Don Quixote riding his horse, attacking a windmill; this was more like attacking a nuclear power plant on a tricycle.

The image made her smile. It was her first smile all day.

And she felt strangely at ease with this new certainty: She had been tangled in the web long enough.

It was time to meet the spider.

24

No one in the group therapy session except Charlie Flegg had been able to follow Tom's story. They said nothing, they hardly moved; it was like hanging out in a wax museum. Dr. Osonoa was presiding, of course, but he liked to remain as unobtrusive as possible. These patients were used to hearing about simple delusional systems—people who got radio transmissions from space aliens from the fillings in their teeth; people who believed their families were trying to kill them. They weren't used to dealing with the political ramifications and macro-economics of taxing the Mafia.

But Flegg loved it.

"Listen, man," he said. "If I came in here and said I believed the President was financing a bunch of Nazi wannabees in South America by selling weapons to terrorists, they'd lock me away forever. But it happened, all right? The people running this country are the psychos. You gotta be crazy to want the job in the first place. It's the minimum fucking requirement, man. I don't know. All I can tell you is—this shit makes perfect sense to me. I'm just surprised nobody thought of it before."

After the session Flegg came up to him and said, "We have to talk. Meet me in the exercise room Monday morning. If it's still relevant. On the exercise bikes in the corner. If we're pedaling hard enough and we whisper they won't be able to hear us."

"What's going on?"

Flegg held up both hands close to his chest in a self-mockingly puny fending-off gesture. "Monday," he said. Then he trotted off down the hall and around the corner out of sight.

Tom began his two O'clock session with Osona with a blunt question.

"Is this office bugged?"

"No."

"How can you be sure?"

"It was the subject of my first major conflict with Dr. Honig. He carelessly dropped a comment that indicated he was privy to one of my sessions. I knew the patient wouldn't have spoken to him. I told him he had violated doctor-patient confidentiality and that if the situation was not corrected instantly I would not only quit, I would go to the press and to AMA and make sure this place was closed down and that he lost his license. I promised to discredit him so thoroughly that he wouldn't be able to get a job writing an advice column in a local newspaper."

"And he backed down?"

"He had no choice. Except to kill me, an idea that may well have been bruited about by his superiors. This is, after all, a Government-run clinic. And the United States government has been known, at various moments in its history, to treat human life with some measure of strategic disregard. Fortunately I come from a wealthy and influential family. My death would have caused more problems than it solved. Not that I wish to suggest that as a reason for my continued good health. I'm not paranoid." He smiled.

"Of course not," Tom smiled back. "But it was a factor."

"Perhaps. In any case, the upshot was that the office was thoroughly screened by an outside security organization, one I found myself through a random search of the Yellow Pages."

"Did they find anything?"

"Oh, yes. They found many things. All sorts of listening devices—in the telephone, in the desk blotter, in the plants, in the framed diplomas, in the wiring of the lights, in the ceiling radiant heating, in the books. The levels of systems redundancy would have made NASA proud. To keep Dr. Honig honest I have a crew—different ones each time—come in at random intervals to be sure the place is still clean. At my own expense, I might add."

"When was the last time?"

Osona grinned. "They were actually here this morning—while we were in the group therapy session. So—what secrets do you wish to share with me today? What confession requires such stringent security precautions?"

Tom sat forward. "I'm going to end this charade on Sunday night. I'm going to ask the impostor all the questions I couldn't ask him in the hospital. The private stuff they could never have briefed him on. And then the whole country is going to watch him flunk the only test that matters. But I need your help. I need you in that room, fully committed to helping me get through it any way you can. And I want to go over the questions I want to ask. I want to fine tune them. I want to rehearse. Your specialty is dealing with people. I'm not much good at it. You don't know my family, you can give me some perspective on the kinds of questions I should ask. I don't want to waste time with stuff that's too weird or obscure. I need maximum impact because no matter what we do they won't let it go on for very long."

Tom stopped talking. He caught his breath and they assessed each other across the quiet, book-lined office.

"So," Tom said finally. "Will you help me?"

Osona walked over to him solemnly. Tom stood and he shook Tom's hand with both of his own. Their eyes met.

"Absolutely," he said.

Tom continued shaking his hand, stupidly, unwilling to break the physical connection. "Thank you," he said. "Thank you so much. I—"

Osona patted his shoulder. "There's a lot of work to do before Sunday. We should get started."

"Sure, you're right, but I just—I need a few seconds here. I have to sort of . . . absorb this."

"I understand. But our time is limited today."

"You're right. Sorry. I'm ready now."

"Shall we begin?"

Tom nodded; and they began.

Despite the fact that he had almost been killed there twice, Dominic Nosiglia continued to eat most of his meals at an Italian restaurant in little Italy called Il Cortile. In a violation of perhaps the only appealing Mafia cliché, his mother had been a terrible cook. And his wife was worse. These women couldn't even boil water. Literally—he remembered the first (and last) time Margaret had attempted to make him spaghetti: standing over a pot of water on the stove, yelling at her, "No, no! Wait until it bubbles!"

" But steam is coming off it," she had bawled. "It's steaming, Dom." She hated it when he yelled at her.

"*Some* of the water is boiling," he had answered slowly. "You have to wait until *all* the water is boiling. You can tell that because it *starts to bubble*."

Pathetic.

He wasn't a bad cook, himself. But he had never enjoyed it. It was more of a public relations problem than anything else—how was a gangster supposed to be lovable if he didn't stir a pot of marinara sauce from time to time?

He bought rounds for everyone at the bar and he tipped

big, but he knew it wasn't the same. He had more or less given up which was just as well this afternoon because this lunch was strictly business. His five Capos were here, and his Consiglieri, and he was pissed off at all of them. Two of them were stealing from him; one of them was sleeping with his underage daughter. The rest were just incompetent. He couldn't decide whether to send them to a management training seminar or just shoot them.

He was about to begin when he saw the girl.

She caught his eye and walked up to the table. Everyone stopped eating and everyone stopped talking as the two of them stared each other down. The girl was good looking but her face was hard.

"So this is Dominic Nosiglia,"said Amy Elwell. "The man himself. In person." She spoke softly but they had no trouble hearing over the clatter of the restaurant. "You're the scary gangster I've been reading about all my life? Sorry, I just don't get it."

Nosiglia smiled at her. "Gentlemen—this is Amy Elwell. The President's son is her boyfriend. He recently went insane, which may explain her appalling lack of manners. And by the way, Amy? Can I call you Amy? We don't like being referred to as 'gangsters'. We feel it stigmatizes us as criminals. We prefer 'illegal activity engineers.' "

"What are you talking about? You're criminals, all right! You're just—"

"Amy, Amy, Amy. Please. It was a joke. Don't lose your sense of humor! You can call me anything you like. Mobster. Thug. Hoodlum. Though I must tell you my personal favorite is 'Crime Lord.' "

Amy went along with the joke—she wasn't going to let some sleazy killer accuse her of having no sense of humor. "How about 'Kingpin?" she asked.

"Kingpin! I like it. Now what can I do for you?"

"You can listen to me very carefully. It's over."

"What is? Lunch? Because I plan to have some Cannelloni for dessert. And several espressos. You're welcome to join us."

He smiled up at her again; she waited it out. When his face was serious again, she said. "I spoke with Cynthia Jerome. She gave me the journals that her husband kept last winter. The daily notes he made over the course of the surgeries he performed in Des Moines. It's a complete record. It's conclusive. Like the Nixon tapes. So your arrangement is over, Mr. Nosiglia. That's what's over. And no thank you, I won't be joining you for dessert."

"Ah. This sounds sinister. This sounds mysterious. I'm intrigued. You are clearly in possession of something powerful, something earth-shaking! We could be witnessing history in the making! So what is it that you would have me do, young lady?"

"Call it off. Have the President resign . . . for health reasons. That's one of your favorite explanations, isn't it?"

"There are many ways to secure one's health, Amy."

"Are you threatening me?"

"Do you really think I need to?"

"Call it off—Dominic? Can I call you Dominic?"

"Young people today. So disrespectful. Or perhaps it's just young Americans. We Sicilians teach our children manners." He took a bite, chewed and swallowed. He took a sip of wine and set his glass down. "Let me ask you something, Amy. If indeed you did possess some fantastical document of the kind you describe . . . why not just publish it in the newspapers? There's no need to disturb my lunch unless you're trying to bluff me. Or am I missing something?"

"Two things. First of all, as long as the documents stay private, I'm safe. I've arranged that they be published automatically, if anything happens to me."

"Just like in the movies! A good plan—and very dramatic."

"Secondly . . . I don't want publicity any more than you do. I happen to care about Edward Bellamy Jaglom's reputation and his place in history. There doesn't have to be a scandal."

"Well put. Now . . . if only I had some idea what in the world you were talking about."

"You know exactly what I'm talking about."

"I wish I did—it sounds so interesting."

"Why would you have listened to me otherwise?"

"Two reasons. I always enjoy listening to a pretty girl. And I love stories."

"You have one week."

She turned and walked out of the restaurant, her neck tingling with the expectation of a bullet. But that was presumptuous. They wouldn't bother to kill her—they didn't take her seriously enough for that. Nosiglia could call her bluff with phone call. Mrs. Jerome would—truthfully— deny giving any papers to Amy. On the other hand she would lie if she *had* given Amy the papers, so perhaps her word didn't mean much. Nosiglia would have other ways of finding out.

Other ways . . . Amy felt a sudden lurch of nausea. She had just put Mrs. Jerome at risk. She hadn't considered that. What else had she neglected? One thing she knew for sure—she would never be able to think of everything. The situation was too complex. The longer she stayed on her own, the more mistakes she was going to make and the more people she was going to endanger.

She stepped out of the restaurant onto the crowded sidewalk, feeling an irrational physical relief when the door swung shut behind her. She tried to be optimistic in the bright, rain washed sunlight, walking along, jostled by busy people. She took a deep breath. It wasn't a bad plan. Bluffing worked in poker—it was how the really good gamblers made the really big money. And she had shown Nosiglia a good poker face, right up to the end.

She had given him a deadline. That was the most important thing. By this time next week she would know if her plan
had worked.

By noon on Sunday, April 13th, the Holden Clinic was
no longer a psychiatric hospital. It was a broadcast studio,
a political rally, and a street carnival. Inside, there was no
way to get any work done. The patients who were coherent enough to watch television in the lounge (and most of
them were), the orderlies, even the nurses and doctors
were caught up in the excitement of the live broadcast.
Everyone was hoping for a glimpse of The President . . . or at
least Leslie Stahl. They were like teenage girls at a Backstreet
Boys concert. Leonard Honig was annoyed and bemused by
the spectacle. He had met Presidents before. And female
newsreaders were interchangeable as far as he was concerned.
This was clearly not a common sentiment, however. One
glance outside his office window proved that. A noisy swarm
of supposedly jaded New Yorkers had crowded the street,
completely blocking the sidewalk. Local news trucks were
backing the traffic up half way to Central Park.

There were cops, and dozens of Secret Service people
along with the reporters and the ordinary citizens. Barri-
cades were being erected. Someone was shouting through
a megaphone in an attempt to assert his authority. That
was a good way to get trampled to death, in Honig's opinion. He had always hated crowds; they turned into mobs
so easily and mobs had an unsettling tendency to lynch
people with very little provocation. He turned away from
the window and lowered the blinds.

It was going to be a long day.

In the fifth floor solarium, two producers and an assistant director spent most of the afternoon setting up the
lights with stand-ins for the President and his son, doing
sound checks and coping with curious doctors and staff. They
wanted three camera set-ups so that they could cut freely

between all participants in the discussion. Crews had been installing the temporary broadcasting equipment since the night before. The wiring in the old building and proved too unreliable and everything had to be run through a fuse box in the basement.

By five in the afternoon, they were ready.

Tom submitted to the attentions of a make-up person and a wardrobe person. The idea was to make him look "natural". The irony of marshaling such heroic artificiality to this cause eluded them—so did the greater irony of the "stand in" for the President in the next room. Tom forced himself to relax, waiting for the real stand in to arrive. At a little after six the sound of sirens and the increasing noise from the street told him that the Presidential motorcade was arriving. That was another little tug of irony: in the old days he had resented this relentless media attention. It smothered any sense of privacy or fun or festivity for his family. But now he embraced it. It was his last hope. The bigger and more smothering the audience for this 'private' moment the better.

The minutes crawled by. Osona came into the room to wish him good luck. "Go slow," he advised. "Keep your cool. You have a lot of people to impress this evening."

Finally one of the Assistant Directors led him to the Solarium door, explaining that they wanted the first moment father and son actually saw each other to be captured on tape.

He listened as Leslie Stahl began her introduction.

"We are inside the top security Holden Clinic on the upper East Side of Manhattan to witness a reunion that must be bittersweet for a President who has lost so much this year. The personal tragedy he awoke to last month is not unique. Schizophrenia strikes thousands of families in the country every year—often taking the brightest and most highly motivated kids . . . just as they are taking their first tentative steps into adulthood. This disease can ravage any family—even the First Family. That's the message that Edward Bellamy Jaglom wants the world to hear this evening. No amount of success, money or fame can grant you an exemption."

'Jaglom' spoke up: "It's a humbling experience, Leslie."

"Many people wonder what survives in a family torn apart by mental illness. I think we're here today to prove that . . . well, that love survives."

"Exactly. They say 'love conquers all.' Well . . . I guess we all know that's not true. Love isn't much of a conqueror. But it's one hell of a guerrilla fighter. Kind of like the Viet Cong: it can move through the jungle, it's got the whole population on its side, and networks of tunnels to hide in. You can invade and occupy. But you can't win. Love hangs in there, Leslie. It's tough."

Leslie Stahl laughed a little nervously. "Spoken like a true veteran, Mr. President. Would you like to see your son now?"

He nodded "Very much."

Amy, sitting in front of her television in her West Village apartment, realized she was squeezing the arms of her chair so hard her palms ached. She shook her hands out, then laced them together between her legs. She knew something was wrong. She felt like she was standing on one of those rickety railroad bridges she had ridden over last week, in the moments before it collapsed in a haze of rust. There was nowhere to run and nothing to do but watch the television and wait for disaster.

At the 'President's' words, The AD prodded Tom. He walked into the glare, taking in the two people seated in front of him and the small army clustered at the other side of the lights. This was live television; the moment was his, a deadly weapon if he could use it properly.

He hugged the impostor, smiled and sat down. He let a little silence pool between them before he spoke.

"It's good to see you," he began. "You know, I've been thinking a lot while I've been in here, about when I was a kid." He turned to Leslie Stahl. "There was a game we used to play. Dad would say to me, 'I'm looking for a little boy named Tommy Jaglom. Have you seen him anywhere?' And I'd say, 'I'm him!' He'd squint at me and frown a little and say, "Well . . . you do *look* a lot like him, but I can't be sure until I ask you a few questions.' This was the part I always loved because the questions were so specific and personal. Like, he'd say, 'The Tommy Jaglom I know has a stuffed tiger that scares him somehow. Now, if you knew that tiger's name or why he was so spooky, then maybe—' And I'd shout, 'His name is Wally! His eyes glow in the dark!'." Tom turned to the impostor. "Remember that, Dad?"

"Of course I do."

"But Dad would never let it go at that. He'd shake his head—very serious—and say, 'I don't know. You might have heard someone talking about it. Stuffed animal gossip is a big problem in this neighborhood . . . ' So he'd ask more questions, until I finally proved I was me beyond the slightest shadow of a doubt, and then he'd say "Tommy! It's so good to see you!' and we'd hug as if we'd been separated for a year instead of just an afternoon."

"That's lovely," Leslie said, "But I'm not sure exactly what you—"

"I was just thinking, that game was always such a comfort to me. It sort of . . . reaffirmed how connected we were? So maybe if we played a round or two now, it might do the same thing for the American public. It might . . . reassure them that everything's okay, the way it reassured me when I was a kid. What do you say, Dad? I'll do it with you, this time— all right? Want to give it a try?"

He expected some nervousness, some hesitation. But the impostor was calm. He smiled and nodded.

"I think that's a great idea. And you know Leslie . . . it

might give a personal glimpse into our family life that people would enjoy. Go ahead, son."

"All right. You look like my Dad, but I can't be sure until I ask you a few questions. I liked telling stories so much when I was a kid, describing the last TV show I'd seen or the last movie, or the last Hardy Boys novel I'd read . . . that my Dad made a rule at the dinner table. What was it?"

"Three sentences. You could tell any story if you did it in three sentences. It was hilarious, when you got older, watching you brood all through a meal, trying to break down *Moby Dick* or *Gone With The Wind.*"

Tom felt the first chill of uncertainty. How could the impostor have known that? Did his Dad describe it in some article somewhere, some personality profile for some newspaper during one of the campaigns? It was possible, but it didn't matter. There was more where that one came from. Tom frowned, playing the game by the rules. "You could have read that somewhere," he said. "But my Dad has had a recurring dream for years. And no one else knows what it is."

"I'm on a plane and it's trying to land on a city street. But the street is too narrow and I can tell it's going to break off the wings. It's strange you should mention that dream, Tom. I haven't had it even once since . . . the real plane crash."

The man smiled at him and he smiled back. There was no way he could have known about the dream. He had to keep talking until he could understand what was going on. Osona was frowning at him from across the room.

"Uh . . . that's good . . . but it's a common nightmare. You could have made a lucky guess. Do you know how I know about the dream?"

"Sure—I told you about it to comfort you. When you had that recurring nightmare about being drowned by the bullies at school playing water polo."

For the first time since his initial meeting with this man in that Des Moines hospital room, Tom felt like he really was going crazy. His breath was caught in his throat. These things were private. The recurring dreams would never have been discussed in an interview or anywhere else. His father never even went to a shrink.

"Do you believe me yet?" the impostor was asking impishly, still sticking to the game.

"I don't know," Tom managed. "My real Dad would know what the phrase "green towel" meant in our family."

"That's easy! It was one of the longest running fights I ever had with your Mom. We bought green towels for the bathroom but eventually they faded to a kind of dull yellow. I started referring to them as yellow towels but they were always 'the green towels' to your mother—no matter what. When we moved out of the big house into Beekman Place, she called that apartment 'the house' for years. It drove me crazy. I'd turn to you and say—'Green towel.' and you knew exactly what I meant. It was our private little joke on her."

This was impossible. He stared past the impostor at the video crew, at the smiling anchorwoman, at Osona's averted head.

Osona.

That had to be it. The realization was like the weight of the bully's knees on his shoulders, forcing him underwater in his childhood nightmare. It was drowning him and there was no way to wake up. Osona's office was bugged. It had to be. That was the only explanation that made any sense. Despite what Osona said or believed, they had outsmarted him. Their listening devices were more sophisticated than his detection devices. It made sense—no private security company was going to be able to keep up with state of the art government technology. Tom felt a hot surge of shame. He was a fool. He should have seen this coming. He had wanted to feel safe and so he had let his guard down. He had trusted Osona because he had to trust somebody. And because of that his plan was wrecked.

It all made sense, he thought bitterly—No wonder everything had been so uneventful in the days leading up to the broadcast. Of course, Amy hadn't been kidnapped. Of course he hadn't been drugged up. Of course, no precautions of any kind had been taken. It didn't matter. They knew everything he was going to say in advance—he had set his own trap for himself.

All they had to do was sit back as the cameras rolled, and watch him walk into it.

But he wasn't helpless. There were still moves he could make. He hadn't talked about everything with Osona— there was still plenty of stuff that no one knew about. All he had to do was chose some little detail from his father's life, one last stone for his sling-shot. But it was like trying to find your car keys on the floor of an unlit hallway, in a burning building, at night. He was groping and fumbling when speed was crucial. It didn't even matter what he thought of, any detail would do, as long as he thought of it before they—

"Tom?"

Leslie Stahl was staring at him. So was everyone else. Including something like half a billion people around the world, if the audience estimates had had heard were correct. The silence was nerve-wracking. That old fashioned stopwatch, the symbol of the show, was ticking away the last seconds of his last chance to set things right.

"One more question," he said, speaking the words as an incantation, hoping they would summon forth the frail demon of a final thought.

"Yes?"

Then he had it. "If you were really my Dad, you'd know the pet name you used for my Mom." It wasn't great, but it was good enough.

The man smiled—why was he smiling? He should have been feeling panic at this moment, fear should have been twisting that smile into a grimace.

"Minky," he said.

"What?"

"Minky. I called her Minky."

"No you didn't."

This was it, the impostor was busted.

But he was chuckling. He sat forward so that he could reach across and pat Tom's knee. "Now, now, son—I think I should know a little better than you what I called my wife in the privacy of our own bedroom. Even if you did listen at the door from time to time."

"I never—"

"Well, then. There you are."

That was it, he had lost, it was too late. It was just his word against the impostor's now, and he'd already given the man all the credibility he could ever need. Tom had done the exact job they had intended him to do, from the beginning. This was why they had kept him alive and evidently it all been worthwhile. All Tom could do now was make things worse, make himself look crazier. Wild thoughts cascaded through his mind: jump the guy and snap his neck. Take out a Secret Service agent, grab a hostage and escape. But there were too many Secret Service guys, too many contingencies, too many things that could go wrong.

He couldn't afford to wind up in a strait-jacket again.

No—best to give them what they wanted. Take this defeat in style, and hope for another opportunity.

He jumped up. He saw at least six hands diving into jackets, but before the guns could come out he said.

"Daddy! It's so good to see you."

He played the game out to the end: he hugged the impostor for the second time that morning, and everyone ap-

plauded and Leslie was grinning and all Tom could think
about was that first hug in the hospital room last month.
What had he accomplished since then? A lot of good
people were dead, he was a prisoner, Amy was alone and
the conspiracy he had tried so hard to stop was—thanks to
his performance today—more successful than ever. If he
had done nothing at all, everyone would be better off now.
At least he'd be free. Jim Gramble would be alive, Amy would
be safe. But no, he had to be the hero, he had to save the
world—and he had just ruined the only chance they would
ever have to convince the world of what had happened.
He had failed. He had bungled everything. He felt tears
coming. Everyone would assume they were tears of joy—
the perfect end to the First Family's long awaited reunion.

Then they went to commercial.

"That was wonderful, Mr. President—Tom, that was
extraordinary. This is going to mean so much to the American people." Leslie was wiping away a tear. In fact, there
wasn't a dry eye in the house. Even the hardened Secret
Service agents had been touched by that final embrace.
This was going to be one of *TV Guide*'s great moments in
television, right up there with Neil Armstrong's moon walk
and the last episode of *M*A*S*H*.

And the Kennedy assassination, Tom thought grimly.
But no one knows it.

The next segment went by in a blur—reminiscing about
his mother with a stranger who had never met her; discuss-
ing his homecoming though he knew full well it was never
going to happen. He was expendable now. Some generic
'relapse' would be leaked to the press and Tom Jaglom would
disappear forever.

Osona confirmed this prediction the next day in his
office.

"They're transferring you to Bethesda Naval Hospital in
Washington next week," he said. "The top floor."

"The psycho ward."

"I'm afraid so."

"Then it's all over. I'm finished. They'll never let me out of there."

"Tom—"

"You have to stop them."

"There's nothing I can do."

Osona walked to his window and looked out.

"You believe them now," Tom said.

"I don't know what to believe."

"Your office is bugged."

"No, I already told you—"

"It doesn't matter. Your office is bugged. It had to be. There's no other way he could have known the answers."

"Unless he really is your father."

"I asked him a question we didn't rehearse. You heard it yourself. My Dad never called my Mom 'Minky'. Minky! It's absurd."

"It's human. It humanized him."

"It's a lie."

"I would have to take your word for that, Tom. And even if I did, it would only discredit me. It wouldn't help you."

"If we could prove they bugged your office, it would."

"But they didn't bug my office."

"They beat you, Doctor. Their technology beat your technology. Can't you at least admit that's a possibility?"

"I suppose. But think a moment—if it's true, then they're listening to us right now."

"So what? There's nothing more they can do to me."

"Not to you, no. Your fate is sealed."

Osona stared at him and Tom felt a faint tremor of hope rock his nerves. The Doctor had put himself in danger. The game he was playing was intricate; the rules were changing all the time. His co-operation with Tom had been shielded before, since it was being used without his knowledge to orchestrate the *60 Minutes* performance. Now he had to put some distance between himself and his patient. Some clear-eyed skepticism might save his career—or his life.

"Amy won't be visiting any more, will she?" Tom asked after a while.

"I don't think so, Tom. And even I won't be able to visit you at Bethesda."

"Can I at least call her—before I go? It may be the last time I ever talk to her."

"I think I can arrange that. But the call will be monitored, Tom. I can't guarantee you any privacy."

"I could have figured that one out for myself, Doc."

"Yes, I suppose you could have."

"Sorry—that was the spoiled rich kid talking. Actually . . . I want to thank you. You really tried to help."

"I did what I could. I wish I could have done more."

"You may get your chance."

"I hope so. But I doubt it. I think all our chances are used up, Tom."

"We'll see."

Osona could give up if he wanted to. Tom had been trained differently. While he was still alive he would keep on fighting. He wasn't quitting until they killed him. And they knew that—that's why they were transferring him to the most secure mental hospital in the country. The top floor of Bethesda was a high-tech fortress, and he had a week before the transfer. One week to come up with another plan when his most solid strategy had just fallen apart in his hands like a rotten pumpkin. His one ally inside the clinic was backing away from him; his allies in the real world were out of touch or helpless or dead. He thought of his old room-mates, rocking and muttering and chanting, becalmed in their own private oceans, as eerily content as dogs or Zen masters. He envied them right now.

They were free.

He desperately wanted to call Amy. He needed to hear her voice. But he refused the temptation. It was an empty gesture, a last nod of deference to the concept of hope. Despite his despair he couldn't bring himself throw away that last phone call, that last moment of contact with the outside.

Somehow, some way, he might still need it.

At that very moment, Amy Elwell was waiting by the telephone, watching the news with the sound turned down low. Her own hopes reminded her of the cigarettes in her father's ash tray at home—burned, used up; crumpled into foul smelling little piles. In the interests of decency and cleanliness the only proper thing to do was dump them in the trash.

But she couldn't quite do it.

The phone could ring at any moment.

On the television The President was arriving back in Washington D.C. The ecstatic crowds were waving to him. He was waving back. The band was playing *Hail to the Chief.*

Everyone was hailing the chief.

The utter defeat and futility invading her body were like an infection—she had it all: the fevers, the chills, the headache, the loss of energy.

She had been crying and dozing, pacing and shivering, screaming into her pillow and jamming her eyes shut until the red swarms flooded the darkness behind her eyelids, since watching Tom's humiliation on *60 Minutes.*

Except of course it wouldn't be seen as a humiliation by anyone else. It was America's newest Kodak moment. It was closure—everyone wanted closure. And now they had it. They had watched the President and his son hug and make up. Now they could go on about the business of disposing of all the new disposable income President Jaglom had given them. And just how exactly he had managed that didn't need to be examined too closely. Prosperity was good, and America hadn't been this prosperous since the end of the Second World War. She was feeling it herself. Maybe she should just relax and try to enjoy it, like the rest of the country.

She watched the television, waiting for President Jaglom's news conference, the one where he would announce he was stepping down for "health reasons."

She watched the phone, willing it to ring.

But the President called no news conference; and the phone stayed stubbornly silent.

Amy had a private theory about luck. She believed that you got an amount of it at birth, your personal ration of propinquity and good timing—some people used it up quickly, some people spaced it out throughout their uneventful lives. No lottery wins, but no genital herpes, either. She had been lucky all her life. Blessed with health and great parents, born into the upper middle class and well educated, she was in the top one tenth of a percent not only of people on the planet now, but of all the people who had ever lived on the planet. Even being born in this era, with everything from indoor plumbing to the internet, was a cosmic jackpot. She could very well be living on the cusp between man's conquering of the environment and his ultimate self-destruction. Talk about timing. So perhaps that was it. She had been given more than her share of good fortune. It made sense that her luck was turning bad at last.

Right now, she was too weak and exhausted to care. Giving up felt good. It was like turning off the alarm instead of going out for a run on a winter morning. No one could blame her for curling up under the covers and going back to sleep.

But in fact there was one person who would blame her.

And he was downstairs at that exact moment, painlessly

taking out the Secret Service team assigned to guard her. A little pressure on the carotid artery, cutting off the flow of blood to the brain, and they would be napping for hours. He dragged them into the alley next to the building, set them up against garbage cans, poured a little Thunderbird wine over them, and put a pint bottle in each of their hands. They'd have an interesting time explaining this one when they woke up.

Jake Gritzky laughed, slipped the doorman a twenty and put a finger to his lips as he walked inside.

Amy's luck was about to change.

25

Charlie Flegg was waiting for him.

The little man was already working up a sweat on one of the two excr-cycles in the far corner of the physical therapy room when Tom walked in on Monday morning.

Tom smiled at him and climbed onto the other bike.

"You had yourself quite a night last night," Flegg said.

"Yeah."

"Sorry about that, kid. Seems to me like someone had an ear at the keyhole. So to speak."

"Really?"

"Cheat a cheater—get cheated. That's what my Daddy used to say. You can'[t go up against those big boys. They'll get you, every time."

"I don't know, Charlie–for once I knew that–" "There you go. Will Rogers said it best. It's not what people *don't know* that gets 'em in trouble. It's what they *know* that just *aint so.*"

"Yeah, I guess he had a point there."

They rode in silence for a while. The weight machines at the other side of the room rattled and clicked; two patients were splashing in the small swimming pool under the alert direction of a PT instructor.

"You know," Flegg said finally, "I was a plumbing and heating contractor before I got political. Family business. The big shots here let me do some of the work when they renovated the place. That was back in '85. I do good work—and you can't beat the prices! Anyway . . . these old buildings—they're funny, you know. They have quirks, just like people. For instance . . . there's this one heating duct that runs all the way from the basement to the roof. You can access it from the staff lounge. But that's always been a major problem for me since I'm kind of a small person and the staff around here looks like the Miami Dolphins defense. Too bad, because once you were on the roof, it would be easy to climb down—all the bars on the windows would make great handholds and footholds."

Tom stopped pedaling. "What are you talking about, Charlie?"

Flegg grinned back at him. "Escape."

Amy had turned off the television with the remote and was sitting staring at the blank screen, when she heard the knock on the door. She didn't answer it and the knocking came again. It was louder this time, more insistent. She had the idea that if she didn't move, whoever it was would go away. But they didn't go away—they just knocked again.

Then she heard the voice.

"Amy? Are you in there? Amy! Open up!"

It was Jake.

She jumped up awkwardly and banged her shins on the edge of the coffee table. She let out a gasp of pain and hobbled over to the front door. Jake! She was overwhelmed, it was too much. It was like entering her building, coming in from a frozen, windy night into the dense dry heat of the lobby, your skin crackling like Bennington pottery. The human mind and body weren't designed to manage such drastic changes.

She was fumbling with the locks, it took forever, then the door was open and he was standing there, unshaven, in his black jeans, his denim jacket and his old blue corduroy shirt. She took him in from his scuffed work boots to his wide, squinting face. His hair was longer than she remembered. He looked wild—some crazy fugitive from a logging camp, wanted in six states for hacking up his co-workers.

But that was good. She needed Jake to be a little bit crazy today. Who but a crazy person would believe the story she had to tell him?

"Amy?" he said. "You all right?"

She threw herself into his arms, his chest was as solid as a brick wall. His voice was rough as bricks too, but she could hear the concern and the simple affection in it, and that was what made her cry.

"Oh Jake—Jake—"

She was sobbing in his arms, with the door open, in full view of anyone who happened to pass by in the hallway. But she couldn't stop. She was shaking. Jake held onto her, thinking about racing with the cops in his old Chevy Nova with the bad alignment, bouncing over a rutted dirt road at fifty miles an hour. He had been sure that old car was going to shake itself apart. This girl wasn't in much better shape.

He eased her into the apartment and pushed the door shut with his foot.

"It's okay," he said. "It's gonna be all right."

He maneuvered her over to the couch, disentangled himself and got her a glass of water and three aspirin. Jake never took less than three aspirin. There was no point to it. He sat down next to Amy and helped her take the pills.

"I'm sorry," she said. "The place is such a mess . . ."

Then he set the glass down and said, "It's not so bad. Tell me what's going on."

"I don't know where to start."

"The beginning is usually a good bet. Or you could start at the end and work backward."

She smiled and drank the rest of her water. "It may take a while."

He patted her knee. "I'm not going anywhere."

So she told him the whole story. They started out on the couch, but Amy got up eventually and cooked dinner. They were half way through a second pot of coffee and the Sara Lee cheesecake she'd pulled out of the freezer, when she finished describing the *60 Minutes* interview. Jake didn't own a television and hadn't seen it.

He pushed his plate aside and poured himself some more coffee. The story seemed to keep moving, filling the silence with the momentum of its implications.

"You should have come to me before," he said.

"Contacting you would have made Heller suspicious. Until . . . well, until Mr. Gramble died, it seemed like we'd made the right decision. Everything was going so well. And then, Mr. Gramble was killed and Tom was caught . . . and— I don't know. Everything just fell apart. Then I couldn't find you, and I thought—I just, I guess I just kind of gave up on you. But here you are." She smiled gamely. "You want to help me finish off this cheesecake? There's just one more slice left for each of us."

"Sure, pass it over."

They ate in silence. They cleared the table and it was not until they were doing the dishes (Jake washing, Amy drying, as casually efficient as an old married couple), that Amy spoke up again.

"Is there anything we can do?"

"Well, I've been thinking about that. Right now it don't look good. You can bet that Clinic is set up like a medium security prison. Guards with side-arms, electronic surveillance. I could round up a tactical unit—maybe ten guys I trust. We could get in, we could probably get Tom, but getting out again would be tough. A lot of people would die, that's a guarantee. Guards and orderlies, my friends . . . maybe me. Maybe Tom. You know how in the movies you always see these amazing gun battles between the good gang and the bad gang, and no cops anywhere?"

She nodded; she knew where this was going.

"Maybe that was just pre-Guilliani. But I don't think so. The reality is that the police would be on top of that scene like a fitted sheet on a mattress. They'd seal off a five block area, complete with SWAT teams and helicopters. And that's not even mentioning the Secret Service and the FBI. The only hope would be some jurisdictional squabbling. That might buy us some time. But basically you're looking at a bloodbath. And every second we were caught there, our chances would be getting worse. I don't like it."

"So what should we do?"

"First of all, you have to call him. You have to talk to him. We need to know more about the set-up inside. And he has to know I'm here."

"They won't let me see him."

"I'm just talking about one five minute phone call. They'll allow him that—they should be happy with him, he did exactly what they wanted."

"Would you have? I mean . . . did he do the right thing? He could have killed the impostor right then and there."

"Not necessarily. You don't know how many guns were on him. The cameras didn't show that. Sometimes you're better off not fighting. Most of the time, in fact. That's one of the first things I ever taught Tom. So listen. Bright and early tomorrow, get Heller on the phone. For tonight, just relax. I got a feeling this is all gonna work out fine."

They finished putting the dishes away and went back into the living room.

"How are you doing, Jake? You look a little . . . I don't know—"

"Like I just came from some militia compound in Montana?"

She looked down. "Something like that."

"Bigfoot—captured at last."

She laughed. "So you're okay?"

"Oh, yeah—I've been a good boy. No drinking, no brawling. Car registered, taxes paid. The boss asked me why the other day. I said 'Doncha get time off for good behavior?' And he said, 'Time off for what? This aint prison, it's life.' I wrote that one down, so I wouldn't forget it."

"You don't sound that okay to me."

"Maybe I wasn't. But I'm feeling better tonight."

"Me, too."

"Listen . . . I know this has been hard for you and Tom, but I gotta tell you—I'm grateful to you both. I want to thank you. And I want to thank him."

"I'm not sure I understand."

"You two have given me something I thought I'd never have again."

"What's that, Jake?"

He stared at her for a long moment before he answered. "A war," he said, finally. Then he patted her knee. "You go on and get some sleep, now. You're gonna need it."

As it turned out, Tom called the next morning.

The phone rang at nine thirty, waking Amy out of a confused dream where she was trying to explain some emergency, trying to make herself understood in some squalid foreign shantytown where no one spoke English.

"Amy?"

"Tom? Is that you?"

"It's me—at least until the next electro-shock session."

Despite the grim joke his voice sounded lively.

"What's going on? Are you all right?"

"I'm fine, but I don't have much time to talk. They're moving me to Bethesda Naval Hospital sometime in the next few days. Once I'm there you won't be hearing from me again."

"Tom—"

"It's okay. The most important thing is that you study for your final exams."

"Finals? It's only mid-April, Tom. I just finished with my mid-terms and—"

"Still, it's never too early to start studying for your final exams."

The code! He was using their code. She caught her breath—what did this particular phrase mean? She thought frantically. Then she remembered: she was supposed to meet him at the Alice in Wonderland statue in Central Park.

He was going to escape.

"Jake is here," she said.

"Good. He can help you study. I have to go, Amy. I love you."

"Still?"

"More. Hug Jake for me."

Then she was listening to a dial tone.

Jake was at the kitchen counter when Amy came in. He had a pot of coffee going. There was a pan on the stove, with chopped scallions sautéing in olive oil. He was slicing a green pepper. A bowl of beaten eggs sat on the counter.

"Good morning," he said. "Want to split an omelet?"

The smell was savory and welcoming.

"I'd love to."

"Coffee's on the stove. And there are bagels warming in the oven. One thing about Nantucket—they still don't know how to make a New York bagel."

"That was Tom on the phone," she said, pulling out the bagels. "Butter?"

"Cream cheese."

She got it out of the fridge. "He says they're moving him to Washington D.C. in a few days. To a mental hospital there."

"Makes sense. Bury him—but don't kill him. You never know when he might come in handy."

"He's planning an escape."

Jake looked up.

"I told him you were here."

"Good."

He tipped the chopping board of green peppers into the pan. They sizzled invitingly as he pushed them around with a teflon spatula.

"He used a phrase we agreed on," Amy continued. "It means I'm supposed to be at certain place at a certain time for the next three days."

"The Alice in Wonderland statue."

"That's right. How did you—?"

He smiled. "Tom and I go back a ways."

"So what do we do?"

"We meet him there."

"But, I mean . . . I want to do more than that. I want to help him."

"You can't—not now. Leave that to me. I don't want to have to worry about protecting you in a battle zone. That kind of distraction could get us all killed. No offense. I know you're tough. But this is going to be a strict military operation and there are professional soldiers I'd think twice about using."

He poured the eggs into the pan. "Do you have another spatula?"

"Left hand drawer."

He pushed the firming eggs to the middle of the pan

and tilted it so the liquid flowed into the dry spot. Then he moved away a little. "Gotta wait now," he said. "Can't rush an omelet." After a few moments he performed the same motions again; now he had a nice ridge of egg down the middle of the pan.

It sounded like he was talking to himself when he spoke next: "If they're moving him they'll have to take him down to the street first. That's where they'll breach security. The fifteen, twenty seconds it takes to get him from the building to the vehicle. That's the window. I'll be staking the place out, starting tonight. I just need someone to spot me. Maybe Alphonse Dryer."

"Who's he?"

The way Jake looked up, he was startled just a little, confirmed Amy's thought—he had been talking to himself.

"Al? He's the guy who taught me how to shoot. A very dangerous person. He can take down a police helicopter from a hundred feet—with handgun."

"Did he teach you that?"

"He taught me a lot. But there are some things you can't teach. They're just . . . who you are. Al is part gun. Human armament. Which he'd take as a compliment. That's the kind of sick fuck he is. But don't get me wrong. I love the guy. Gimme a second here. I have to concentrate."

Jake wedged both spatulas under the omelet, and with an apparently casual flick of his wrists, flipped it. The result was browned and fluffy—it looked like a picture in a magazine. Amy was impressed.

"Just about one more minute. Grab us some plates, will ya?"

For the next fifteen minutes, they concentrated on breakfast.

Buttering her second bagel, Amy said, "It seems like all I've done since you got here was eat and sleep."

"Good. I need you rested and well-fed."

She gave him a little mock salute. "Thanks, Sarge."

"Any time. Now clean your plate."

She dutifully swept up the last of her egg with her bagel.

"What if something goes wrong?" she asked a little later.

"Then we improvise."

"I don't like the sound of that."

"No? Well, it's one of the things I do best."

"But I meant . . . you know . . . what if it's a total disaster? That could happen."

"Worst case scenario—go to ground and hide out."

"Where?"

"For me—Nantucket. You should think about that for yourself. Always go to ground where you know the territory. Keep your enemy on unfamiliar ground. Then you have the advantage—that's how the Viet Cong beat us in 'Nam. It was their world and we didn't know shit."

Amy sipped her coffee, wondering what place she would choose. Her neighborhood? The NYU campus? She realized that she had never given either place much strategic thought. She didn't even know the West Village or the University that well, aside from a few well-worn paths to and from her specific classes. She thought of Tom always studying the exits and access points wherever they went, always sitting with his back to the wall and a good view of the restaurant when they ate out, always careful to walk in the middle of the sidewalk, where it was that little bit safer, whether the attack came from a shadowed doorway or from between two parked cars. He had taught her some soldier's tricks—hand to hand combat and shooting. But he hadn't taught her to think like a soldier and that was what she needed to do the most.

She had thought the world was a relatively safe place until she met Tom.

And the fact was—until she met Tom, it had been.

Jake was still talking. " . . . for the moment, just act normally. Stick to your routines. Go to classes, study at the library—whatever. But check your messages a few times a day. When it goes down I'll let you know. As soon as you hear my voice on the machine, find your way to the park."

"And what happens then? When we're all together?"

"I'll tell you. When I was a kid I worked the rodeo circuit for about a year. That was '66—the year before I was drafted. Where we are now is like the few seconds when you're on the horse in chute, before the gate opens. When it does, you know that horse is going to just fucking *explode* into the ring, all right? You're not in charge—he's in charge. All you can do is hold tight—and stay on him. So that's what we're going to do, Amy: hold tight and stay on. Think you can manage that?"

She smiled at him and said "Jake, I have absolutely no idea."

"Me neither, honey. But what the hell. It's gonna be a great ride while 'till it's over."

They left it at that. There was nothing more to say. A few minutes later, with a last quick hug and a kiss on the cheek, Jake was gone.

Amy had one more cup of coffee, raked the living room with an unforgiving glance, and then pulled out her bucket of cleaning products, her mop and her vacuum.

It was time for some house cleaning.

26

Flegg's plan was simple; that was what convinced Tom it could work. It had started with the building itself—not just the heating system, but the floor-plan. In particular: there was a relatively short straight corridor leading from the patients' dining hall to the main staff lounge which accessed the vertical heating vent Flegg had described to Tom. There were three doors between the two ends of the hall, and they opened inward, towards the dining area. If you could get enough people—hopefully, staff members responding to an emergency—charging through them in one direction, it might be possible for a quick and agile person to take advantage of the chaos and slip through going the other way. The staff lounge would be empty and the path would be clear. It was all a matter of timing. Tom had run dozens of variations on the sequence in his head over and over again—at best, a good diversion would give him five minutes to get through the corridor and into the vent. It wasn't much time, but with a little luck it could be done.

"If the plan involves emptying the staff lounge instead of fighting your way through it, how come you never tried this before?" Tom had asked Flegg at the end of their cycle session.

"It takes two people," Flegg had replied. "You have to trust somebody."

"And you never did?"

"Are you kiddin? Look around you! There's a bunch a psychos in this joint."

They set the plan in motion the next night at dinner. The two Larry's approached Flegg just as he was about to start his dessert, as they did every night. The two orderlies on duty looked on, amused by this ritual, lulled by the predictable choreography of it.

But tonight was going to be different.

"Give it," one of the Larrys said.

Flegg just sat there.

"C'mon—give," the other one said.

"You wanta get hurt?" The first one added.

Flegg glanced at Tom. Tom nodded.

"Get away from me!," Flegg shouted. "I've had it, ya stinkin' piece of shit." They were both staring at him in slack-jawed amazement. Flegg slammed his chair backward into one of the giants and brought his whole tray up, cracking the other one in the temple. He staggered backward amid flying crockery and coffee, half the key lime pie smeared across his face. Flegg jumped to his feet, grabbed his chair and swung it feebly at Larry's ribs. Larry grabbed the legs ripped the chair out of Flegg's hands, hurled it aside and lunged for the little man. But Tom was in motion by then. There was just enough open space between the tables for a perfectly executed *yoko tobi geri*—a flying side snap kick that rammed into the back of Larry's head and snapped him forward, unconscious. The bulk of his falling body knocked over the first of the orderlies sprinting into the fray. Tom tripped the second one, grabbed a tray and drove it like an ax blade into the neck of the other Larry. Both bullies were unconscious on the floor.

"Justice?" Tom asked.

Flegg grinned at him. "Better than that, kid—poetic justice." He kicked the sprawling orderly in the head. "Now get going."

The flying chair had struck another patient, who lashed out at the man next to him. A table was over-turned, more glasses smashed and then the whole dining room was erupting into a furious brawl, pent up misery and frustration bursting out in kicks and punches and howls of rage. Men were screaming, alarms were ringing. It was turning into a full-scale riot. Tom dropped to his hands and knees and crawled between thrashing legs toward the exit. A plate whizzed past his ear. A stamping foot just missed his hand.

Finally he stood. He was still ten feet from the door. He side-stepped one attack and flung his arm out, palm up into the face of another charging psychotic. The man flinched his face backward and his legs ran out from under him. Tom jumped the tumbling figure, punched another man through the doorway, and followed the staggering body into the hall.

Dr. Osona heard the alarms, and he knew what was happening. What had Tom said to him? Something about still being able to help. He had demurred and Tom had said "We'll see," with that strange knowing look on his face. Could he have been planning an escape even then? Perhaps; in any case, this was it. It was happening now, and there really was something he could do to help. He ran to the stairwell and stared up towards the third floor surveillance control room.

Tom made it through the first door, against the tide of scrambling guards and orderlies. At the second door, a guard leveled a gun at him. But the man's line of sight was blocked for a second and Tom slid at him like a ballplayer stealing second base, hooked a foot behind his calf and drove his other foot into the guard's knee, shattering it and sending him pin-wheeling backward, his gun discharging into the ceiling.

There were two orderlies coming through the last door. Tom threw himself at them in a cross-body block and they hit the linoleum in a flailing tangle of arms and legs. Tom jack-knifed himself forward, with his full weight and momentum behind two punches. Two heads banged into the floor and he scrambled to his feet, away from the inert orderlies. He lurched into the staff lounge. It was empty. For the moment he was alone. The noise of combat and pursuit were diminishing behind him. He looked around the room—four tables, with plastic chairs, a couch at one end, a line of vending machines at the other. The vent grating was screwed into the ceiling above the ping pong table. Tom looked around for a tool. Time was running out.

Two floors above him, Dr. Osona stepped into the surveillance room. Three guards were watching the melee on the video screens as if it was an episode of *Cops*. A new show, perhaps—*Psychos*. That would be a sure ratings winner. Another screen showed the staff lounge. Tom was taking a knife off the coffee trolley, and jumping onto the Ping-Pong table. If any of the men shifted their attention six inches to the right, they'd see him. Tom started working on the first of the screws.

"What the hell are you doing here?" Osona shouted. The guards swiveled in their chairs.

"Doctor Osona," one of them started "We—"

"This isn't a TV show—it's real! There's a riot going on down there! It's out of control, can't you see that? People are getting hurt! They need you! Grab your weapons and get moving!"

The guards jumped up awkwardly and three-stooged their way out of room bumping into each other. They'd been sitting here, on mind-numbing TV patrol, eight hours a day for years. Quick action wasn't their strong point. Two of them jammed into the doorway at once, puffing and cursing. Osona almost expected them to tweak each other's noses, poke each other's eyes and slap each other silly. Finally they tottered into the hallway and were gone. He had to smile as he turned back to the screen.

Osona's gein froze on his face. Leonard Honig was standing in the staff lounge doorway. He had a gun. Tom spun around with the grating in his hand. Osona stared at the monitors helplessly.

"Set the grating down and climb off the table," Honig was saying. "Move slowly. Keep your hands in sight at all times."

Tom did as he was told. Honig was too far away to attack. And he was smart—he kept his distance. Tom felt the adrenaline turning rancid in his blood. His last chance was being sucked away from him, like smoke out a car window. He was staked to the dying moment by the barrel of Honig's gun. His mind whirled uselessly—he was out of options. But he didn't have to be nice about it.

"You look like a real New Jersey thug with that gun in your hand, Doctor Honig," he said. "It suits you. I think you missed your true calling."

"Shut up. I don't have to—"

And then he was pitching forward and Flegg was looming behind him, holding a scavenged gun by the barrel, grinning crazily.

"I nailed him! I nailed the bastard! Did I nail him or what?"

"Charlie—"

"Get outta here! Go on!"

Tom hoisted himself into the vent and started climbing. It was easier than he had anticipated—there were metal hand-holds welded into the pipe.

Dr. Osona watched until Tom's legs wiggled out of sight.

Then he walked out of the surveillance room and headed for the elevators. Perhaps he could be of some use downstairs. He was exhilarated and impressed—but warily. He found it hard to believe that Tom could actually escape from the Holden clinic—or if he did, that he could stay free on the outside for very long. And he didn't like to think about what would happen to Tom when he was finally recaptured.

In turning away so quickly, Osona missed a last turn in the drama taking place downstairs. Flegg knew he ought to screw the vent back in place; it would buy Tom a little more time. But as he stood in the empty staff lounge with Leonard Honig gradually regaining consciousness at his feet, he recognized the moment at last.

It was his moment.

He would never have another chance to escape. And once his part in Tom's plan was discovered (he knew he was being recorded on video tape even now) his life at Holden would become a living hell. He only had a few seconds to decide and in those seconds his old reckless spirit flared up. The door was open but it was shutting fast.

It was time to bid adios to the Holden clinic.

It was time to show some guts and join the only friend he'd found in the last twenty years.

It was time to be free.

He threw the gun down, kicked Honig once more in the ribs for good measure, climbed onto the Ping-Pong table and with a mad cackle struggled up into the vent and disappeared.

Tom reached the top of the duct and kicked the grating out. It took five solid blows, but it clattered onto the tar surface and Tom rolled out after it. He could still hear the alarms going off, muted, from inside the building. No sirens yet. That was a good sign. Tom sprinted to the edge of the roof, and leaned over the low retaining wall. His feet could reach the first of the bars easily, and there was a decorative pattern

of raised bricks for the first treacherous handholds as he
dangled into the void trying to feel the metal cage with his
toes. It was a long way down and he hated heights. Well,
technically, no—what he hated was falling.

So don't fall.

Good advice—exactly the kind of tough, amusing and
unsympathetic advice Jake Gritzky would have given him
at this moment. He could sense Jake's presence in the
street below. He hoped he was right.

Once he started down it was easy. In three minutes he
was dropping the last ten feet and standing in the alley
beside the Holden Clinic. An ambulance was pulling in to
the emergency entrance. Things were finally going
right—he could take out the driver, steal the ambulance
and—

That was when he heard the shout.

It was thin and terrified. And it was coming from directly above him.

"Tom! Help me! I can't get down!"

Flegg was clutching one of the barred windows, three
stories up, too frightened to move.

"Charlie! What the hell are you—you weren't supposed
to—"

There were sirens in the distance now.

The alley would be full of guards and orderlies any
second.

Tom said "Shit!" and leapt back onto the wall, climbing it like a spider. He had never moved this fast in his life
before. From the entrance to the alley, Jake Gritzky
watched him in utter amazement.

Inside the clinic, the guards had found the staff lounge
vent opening. Honig was awake. Someone was giving him a
glass of water.

"They're on the roof. Get up there," he croaked. "Post

guards in the alleys and the court yards. They've got nowhere to go but down."

"Are you all right, sir?" the orderly who had given him the water asked. "Do you need to go to the infirmary?"

Honig spoke slowly and softly. "I need you to catch that kid, Kimmelman. That's what I need. And that's all I need. So do it!"

"Yes, sir."

Kimmelman and the others took off. Honig felt nauseous, his head throbbed. He eased himself over to a chair and sat down. The staff at the Holden clinic were well-trained. They had been through dozens of escape drills and escape dry-runs and escape tactical response exercises.

The only thing they hadn't been through was an actual escape. And this was not an ideal first experience. He would have preferred some old loon wandering out of the ER wearing a stolen surgical mask and hospital flip-flops.

Instead, he was stuck with a one-man army.

At that moment, the army in question was hanging from a barred window, helping Charlie Flegg clamber onto his back.

"Hold on around my neck, Charlie," he said. "No, no that tight—you're—arrghghhhh . . . ."

Flegg loosened his grip.

"Sorry."

"Hold on and shut your eyes. We'll be down in a minute."

Tom took a couple of seconds to catch his breath then started the descent. He knew instantly that this was going to be much harder than the first one; in fact in might not be possible at all. He was hanging from one set of bars with Flegg's weight on his back, searching for the next set with his toes, feeling the rusty metal bite into his palms. His foot finally touched metal. Lowering himself to the lowest point on the window cage was relatively easy, but grabbing the raised bricks he had used for intermediary handholds strained his hands to the breaking point this time. It was like his fingers were being pulled out of their sockets, tendons torn from the bones.

On the roof above them, guards were crashing out the roof access door, checking the open vent and then charging the parapet. Leaning over, they could see Tom with Flegg on his back. It was dark and the range was problematical, but they started shooting anyway.

Flegg flinched at the first sounds of gun fire and Tom lost his grip. He leaned out too far from the building and gravity took them both. There was a moment of free fall that seemed to bring his whole stomach up into his throat. But he caught the next set of bars. The impact jolted him all the way to his shoulders and his sore ribs started screaming again. There were sparks as a bullet whined off the metal just above his head. It was too far to go. They weren't going to make it.

Then Flegg howled in pain. "They shot me, Tom! They shot me in the ass! O Jesus, they shot me!"

Tom swung down to the next floor recklessly, pain and doubt canceled by the sheer need to move. With a sickly chill he realized that Flegg was a layer of body armor. He was wearing Flegg like a shield. In another few seconds another bullet—even a stray bullet—would connect. They were ten feet from the ground. He released his hold and dropped to the rough asphalt. Somehow he kept Flegg above him so the impact was cushioned for the little man.

In the alley, a metal fire door banged open and a group of guards piled out of the building, just as Tom was easing Flegg off his back.

"Freeze!," one of them shouted.

He had obviously wanted to say that since he was a kid watching TV. But Tom didn't believe he could back it up with action.

"Run!," he told Flegg, pushing the little man. "Get into the ambulance."

Flegg started hobbling away and a shot dug up the asphalt an inch from where Tom was standing.

"I said *freeze!*," the guard shouted. Tom started after Flegg. There were more shots. A piece of brick caught him on the cheek. "All right," the voice shouted. "Take them out! Fire at will!"

But the next muzzle flashes came from the front of the alley. Five shots; and five of the guards spun and staggered, or crumpled to the ground, shot in the shoulder or the knee—precision shooting meant to disarm and disable but not kill.

Jake was here! Tom grinned and thought "I knew it," though he had only hoped it. But perhaps hope that intense was a form of knowledge; it certainly felt that way right now—as if he had materialized Jake by sheer desperate force of will. He raised a fist in acknowledgment, then dove for the filthy asphalt just ahead of another volley of shots. Flegg stayed standing for a moment. Then it was as if someone had kicked him. He sprawled face first on the filthy asphalt, with a grunt of surprise.

Tom belly-crawled back to him. The whole back of Flegg's shirt was stained with blood. Two cop cars had pulled up to the front of the hospital, and Tom could hear more sirens coming. In a few minutes the whole block would be closed off.

And Charlie Flegg was dying.

Honig limped out into the alley shouting "Hold your fire! Hold your fire!"

He was beside them when Flegg managed to speak.

"Make a difference kid. Scare the shit outta those fascist fucks." He turned to Honig. "That means you, asshole," he said to the doctor. And then he was dead.

In an instant Tom realized that Honig thought he was

injured too. He didn't know Jake was in the alley; there was still a chance. He squeezed Flegg's limp hand once, mouthed the word "Good-bye", and then yanked Honig's legs out from under him.

Tom rose as Honig fell and ran the last few steps to the ambulance. The driver was cowering flat on the front seat. Tom pulled him out, slammed the door and gunned the engine. The cop cars were blocking the alley. He had to crash through between them. He stamped on the gas. If he could gather enough speed, he could break through the road-block. If not he'd be jammed between the bumpers of the two police cruisers, a perfect target in the raised cab of the ambulance. There was no time for anything but total commitment. More shots rang out uselessly behind him. A cop jumped out of his way as he braced his arms against the wheel and smashed into the wall of metal. The ambulance bucked hard, almost stalled out. Tom let up on the gas and then jammed the pedal to the floor. The top-heavy truck surged free, spinning one of the cop cars across the street. He yanked the wheel into a teetering right turn and roared West on 91st Street.

Jake watched the cops diving for their cars. Another one was skidding around the corner from York Avenue. The flashing red and blue lights were turning the dark street into a garish amusement park midway. The sirens bounced against each other and off the walls on either side. The air stank of gunfire and burning rubber. The cops were right behind Tom. They were faster and more maneuverable. They'd have him boxed in before he could go one block.

Jake had no back-up tonight, but that wasn't going to be a problem. He slipped a new magazine into his Colt, jacked the first round into the chamber and shot out the rear tires of all three cruisers. They fishtailed into each other and the cars parked on either side of the street, amid the sound of tearing metal and blaring car horns. The pile up would effectively block Tom's rear—no one else was going to be driving up 91st Street for a while. The kid had a chance now.

It was time to go.

Jake walked slowly east and started downtown on York Avenue. Three more cop cars screamed past him. He stopped walking to gawk at them, like the other pedestrians. Then, like them, he shrugged and walked on, just another jaded New Yorker, drawing his boundaries against other people's catastrophes, the next neighborhood's nightmare, the chaos around the corner.

Tom ditched the ambulance on 89th Street and Lexington, double parked it in front of the Dalton School and jogged towards Central Park, looking for someone roughly his size and shape. He needed a change of clothes quickly—his hospital pajamas were conspicuous—and far too flimsy for the chilly night air.

As he was crossing Madison Avenue he found the man he was looking for. Tom was especially pleased about the new Reeboks and the leather jacket. When Arnold Lohman woke up half an hour later, the police were arresting him for indecent exposure and stuffing him into a squad car. He was wearing nothing but his underwear and his socks; hypothermia was setting in. He couldn't explain what had happened, because he didn't know. Tom had loomed up behind him, knocked him out with a single blow, dragged him into a service courtyard between two pre-war high rise apartment buildings, stripped him and changed into his clothes, all in less than five minutes.

When he was finished, Tom had checked Lohman's Cartier watch. It was ten after eight. A little more than an hour ago, he had been sitting down to dinner in the Holden clinic.

He thought of Flegg, mourning the old man's recklessness, his unrepentant radicalism and his guts. He'd be alive now if he'd had sense enough to say behind. Or if Tom had been smart and quick enough to save him. Or if Tom had never been caught in the first place, if none of this had ever happened. If he still had a father, if his father had never met Dominic Nosiglia . . . if, if, if.

If I had ham, I'd have ham and eggs.

If I had eggs.

As his grandfather used to say.

Tom shook his head. He didn't have time for this. He had a busy night ahead of him.

He walked to the courtyard entrance.

He zipped up his new jacket, looked both ways and disappeared like a frog off a leaf, into the dark pond of the anonymous city.

27

Amy watched it all on television. The escape dominated the local news at ten O'clock, but there had been bulletins all through the evening. Honig was interviewed; Osona was interviewed. Apparently an inmate of the clinic who had worked on the building and was familiar with its infrastructure had instigated the escape. He had been killed in the ensuing firefight. A convicted member of the Weather Underground, he had been incarcerated for almost thirty years, and would not be missed. "Charles Norman Flegg was a terrorist at a time when a certain kind of politically correct terrorism was fashionable. Those times are long gone and his reign of terror has ended forever." Honig said, speaking from hastily prepared notes.

"The President's son is also free at this hour," the news reporter continued. "An all points bulletin has been posted for his arrest. He is considered armed and extremely dangerous." They showed a picture of Tom; the cover of *People* again. It was going to be a regular collector's item.

Osona described the progress he had made with Tom, recalled the historic reunion of the previous Sunday night,

and expressed his hope that Tom's relapse, however potentially dangerous, was a only temporary one. Questioned about
the security procedures at the Holden clinic, Osona pointed
out that there had never been an escape before, in the whole
eighty years of the institution's existence.

Guards and orderlies were questioned briefly. None
of them seemed to have a clear idea of what happened
during the critical period from the time Tom landed in
the alley until he took off in the ambulance. But the con-
sensus was he had to have had some help from the outside.

"I don't know who it was," one of the wounded orderlies said with real awe in his voice. "But that guy could
shoot."

Amy turned off the television. She had seen all she
needed to. Tom was safe; no one had even identified Jake.
The good news was confirmed a few minutes later when
Jake called from a pay phone. All he said was "See you
tomorrow," but it was enough. If he and Tom could stay
out of sight until the rendezvous, they would all be together
again in . . . she checked the clock, did the math: something
less than sixteen hours.

Two O'clock, at the Alice in Wonderland statue.

She paced the silent apartment, listening to distant sirens, wondering who they were chasing. She checked the
refrigerator—a bleak reminder that she needed to do
some marketing. She and Jake had eaten her supplies
down to the canned beans and grape nuts. There was a
half-gallon of milk but it was expired. That seemed appropriate, somehow. She tried to cheer herself up with a pep-
talk. Tom was free, he would be holding her soon; Jake
was on their side, now. And they had finally won a small
victory. There was a lot to feel good about.

She knew that; but all she could feel was dread.

She woke up in the morning, knowing she needed a

plan. There were two Secret Service agents posted in front of her building. That was the team she knew about. It was more than enough coverage under normal circumstances. But she was their best link to Tom, now. She would lead them to him, or they would be ready to pounce when he found her. Either way, they couldn't afford to be short-handed. That meant there was going be at least one other team, maybe two or three other teams, involved with her surveillance today.

She had to find a way to lose them.

But that was Tom's department, not hers. She walked over to the living room window and looked down at the street. They were there. She considered the short list of alternatives. She couldn't out-run them, that was for sure. She couldn't fight her way past them. Even threatening them with a gun would be foolish—they would surely know how to disarm a nervous twenty-two year old girl. No, she had to out-think them somehow.

Something Jake said came back to her—that business about going to ground on your home turf. Someplace you were comfortable and they weren't, where you knew the lay of the land and they didn't. At the time she hadn't been able to think of any such location . . . except perhaps her home town in Vermont—especially her old high school. Now, if she could just lure the Secret Service up to Bennington! She knew all the ins and out of that old building better than anyone. She had sneaked around to make out and smoke cigarettes in hidden store rooms and abandoned stairways for years.

But there was no building on the NYU campus she knew that well.

It was kind of sad and weird to realize this, but she'd probably spent more time in Bloomingdales, between shopping and working there part time, than she had in any of the NYU buildings where she'd been getting her education. Of course, Bloomingdale's was a kind of education itself: a virtual symposium in the reality of capitalist economics, human relations and stress management. Not to mention critical things like which designers got the biggest mark-ups. Her lips were sealed on that one—but she was sticking with Donna Karan.

She wondered if Bonnie Traynor was still the third floor manager (She had been hoping for a promotion); if her gay friend Raoul was still giving our perfume samples in cosmetics on the main floor.

She had quit just before Christmas and she knew Bonnie had felt abandoned. She had felt a little lost herself. The place had become a kind of second home to her over the last couple of years and—

But that was it.

Bloomingdale's.

If any place in the city was home turf, it had to be Bloomingdale's. It was perfect: all she had to do was lose some guys in a Department store. Men were sure to be clueless there, anyway. They sort of went into zombie-mode, waiting for their wives to do whatever it was that women did in such places, instantly exhausted and miserable. Her Dad even had a word for it—"Department Store Foot." It was real. His feet would start aching after as little as fifteen minutes. All men suffered from it—that's why there were chairs and couches near the changing rooms. She smiled to herself—if you thought American soldiers seemed lost in the Vietnamese jungle, wait until you saw the Secret Service stumbling through the Bloomingdale's lingerie department!

She felt a rush of new energy.

This might even be fun.

She showered and dressed, had a dry handful of grape nuts and a glass of water. Then she went downstairs to greet the Secret Service. She saw them from the lobby—One at the curb, leaning down to talk to the other, behind the wheel of a Chevy Nova parked in front of a fire hydrant. She shrugged—they didn't really need to be inconspicuous any more.

She stepped outside into the cool bright sunshine, crossed the pavement and tapped the agent on the shoulder.

"Hi," she said. "How are you? Beautiful day, isn't it? Listen . . . I have some shopping to do, and I'm heading uptown. I thought, you know—since you were going to be following me anyway? Maybe you could just give me a lift. Would that be okay?"

He stared at her and she gave him her most flirtatious smile.

"It would save me a cab fare. And we could get to know each other a little."

"Uh, sure, I guess so. Let me just call it in."

On the ride uptown she found out that his name was Tim Evarts. The driver was named Mike Dalnegro. Mike was new on the job; Tim was breaking him in, "Showing him the ropes," as Tim put it.

Amy squinted at him. "I've never understood that phrase," she said. "What are these ropes, exactly? And why does he have to be shown? Can't he see them for himself? Is there something special about them? Are they like . . . trick ropes, or something?"

Tim was non-plussed. "Uh . . . I'm not sure, Ma'am."

"Call me Amy. I'm younger than you are."

"Okay . . . Amy."

"But I'm serious—I mean . . . how much rope do you actually use in the course of a given day?"

"Uhh . . .none."

"That's what I'm saying. It's bizarre. We use these phrases all the time and we have no idea what we're saying."

"I guess you're right."

"Like—dog eat dog. What is that about? Have you ever

seen a dog eating another dog? My dog wouldn't even eat kibble."

"I know what you mean. 'A tough road to hoe' I never got that one."

She laughed. "But that one's easy—it's a tough *row*— like in a garden, when you're planting seeds. A hoe is a tool—you sort of chop the ground with it. If the soil is rocky that would be a tough row to hoe." She patted his knee. "Guess you haven't spent much time in the country, Tim."

"No, Ma'am."

She gave up after that. Whatever else they had been trained for, these guys had never learned how to keep up their end of a conversation. Which was actually just as well—she needed a little silence now, to think about her tactics.

They parked in front of another hydrant.

"Can you do that any time you want?" Amy asked. "Because it would be worth joining the Secret Service just for that."

"This is official government business, Ma'am."

"Right."

It was hopeless; but she wouldn't be saddled with these stiffs much longer. As soon as she walked into the mirrored ground floor of Bloomingdale's, with its perfumed air, muted clatter and dinging elevators, she began to feel good. This was possible. Raoul was at his old post, dispensing puffs of Obsession. Amy broke free from her escort to give the tall, impeccably dressed queer a hug. He liked the word queer; he said it described him perfectly. And he was odd, there was no doubt about it, one of those intensely affected homosexuals who seemed to be pickled in their own lisping precision. Then there were the body piercings and the tattoos, but Amy didn't need to dwell on that stuff right now. She threw her arms around him and said quickly, into his ear, "Raoul, you may have to help me lose the two suits behind me."

"Good to see you, too, sweetie."

"Sorry, how are you?"

"Same as ever. Dispensing Obsession—isn't that perfect? I'm the poster boy."

"Speaking of Obsession—how's Claude?"

"He got a restraining order last week." Raoul sighed dramatically. "I just don't know what to make of that."

"Well, my guess is . . . the first flush of romance is over."

"Don't be so negative—I think he's playing hard to get."

"Yeah—but you think pepper spray is a form of flirtation."

Raoul laughed and held her shoulders to study her affectionately at arm's length. "Oh, Amy, " he said. "You always call me on my bullshit. Why couldn't you be a man? Oh, well—with my luck, you'd be straight."

She stepped back, took his hands and squeezed them.

"Maybe I'll see you later," she said.

"Be sure to stop in and see that cute little Tommy in shipping. Remember him? The one you wouldn't kiss under the mistletoe at the Christmas party? You said it was 'used up' and he believed you. I just *loved* that. Stupidity is so cute."

She squeezed his hands once more and then she was moving past him towards the lingerie department.

"I'm buying some bras," she said to Tim when he had jogged into place beside her. "You should get something nice for your wife—or girlfriend, whatever."

"Uh, I don't think—"

"I'll have them put it on my charge, no problem. Shelley can help you."

She had a bad moment, thinking Shelley wasn't working, but then she saw the tall blond walking away from one of the fitting rooms. There was no one in the world better qualified to distract, stall and befuddle two strait-laced civil servants.

'Strait-laced,' she thought—that's another one. What the hell does 'strait-laced' mean? What are they lacing up? And what kind of person does it crooked? Her kind of person, she was willing to bet.

She caught Shelley's eye and broke away from the two Secret Service agents.

"Amy," she said.

"Shelley, hi."

"Look at you! You are *such* a celebrity. Complete with Secret Service hunks. Just like it said in *People* Magazine. "Not that I read *People* Magazine—but . . . you know. When there's someone you know, not that I even recognized you, you looked so weird in those pictures. Didn't you have any control over that?"

"Not really, no. Listen, Shelley, I need to get rid of those Secret Service . . . hunks. Show them some lingerie. Distract them."

"You're not in trouble are you?"

"Not yet."

"Amy, I don't know—"

"Please. It's for a good cause. And I'll owe you one."

"You already owe me, like—twelve or something."

"Please."

Amy grabbed some bras and started for the changing rooms. The Secret Service guys were actually kind of hunky. Especially Tim. That might be enough for Shelley.

And it was. She turned to them and said, "Amy tells me you're picking out bras for that special someone in your life. And you look like you could use some help."

"Well," Tim began.

"Are we talking about a wife or a girlfriend?"

"Uh, she's my wife, but I—"

"What size is she? Would you say roughly . . . my size?"

She arched her back; Tom looked down but she had
Mike's full attention. She handed each of them a filmy
undergarment, smiling as they blushed. "Doesn't that feel
nice. Soft but sort of . . . electric."

"It's—I—"

"So . . . is your wife a little smaller than me? I'm actually a
little smaller, too. But I'm wearing the wonder bra. Do you
know about the wonder bra?" She eased them behind a corner display of slips and nightgowns. "It sort of lifts and defines,
but not in any obvious way . . . it's more like . . . I don't know. I
can't describe it. Let me show you. I'm wearing one now."

By the time she had the third button undone, Amy was
long gone, sprinting for the street.

For one lovely moment she thought it was over; But, it
was just as she had suspected—there was another team
waiting for her on Lexington Avenue.

She spun around in front of the revolving door and
dashed back towards the escalators. She didn't look back
but she could hear them behind her, grunting and excus-
ing themselves past shoppers and clerks. She looked
around for Raoul, but she had come out on the opposite
side of the cosmetics department. She reached the escala-
tor and took the moving stairs two at a time until she was
stopped by a clot of people. She edged past them as the
Secret Service guys started up behind her.

"What's your rush?"

"Kids today!"

"In a hurry—going nowhere."

She left the disapproving chorus behind. The next
flight was clear. She needed to reach the dressing rooms
near the DKNY section before the agents caught up with
her. She grabbed a dress at random and slipped into the
changing area just as they came in sight, bobbing their heads
above the racks of clothes like dogs in high grass.

Amy caught her breath. The chase had winded her.

She hung the dress—it really was awful, it had tassels—on a hook in one of the cubicles. She was okay, they wouldn't follow her in here. And this changing area was special: around the corner of the short, L-shaped corridor there was an employee-only security door. It led to the workers' lounge and the freight elevators. It was supposed to be locked but most of the time it wasn't.

She jiggled the handle for a few seconds, but it didn't budge. Just her luck—today of all days someone decided to follow the rules.

She was trapped here. Unless . . .

She walked back out onto the floor and asked the salesgirl to help her. The Secret Service guys were there. One of them was talking into a cell phone.

Who was he talking to? How many more of them were there?

She got the girl into the dressing room hallway.

"The door back there leads to the lounge. You have a key. Open it."

"Excuse me?"

"I need to get into the staff lounge and the door is locked."

"Customers aren't permitted in that area. That's an employee only area."

"I know that. I worked here for two years." She grabbed the girl by the bicep and squeezed hard. "Just open it."

"I'm sorry—I'd have to talk to my supervisor—"

"I have a gun. Don't make me use it."

The girl's eyes widened. Amy stared her down thinking it would probably be a good idea to actually have a gun at a moment like this. But the girl believed her. She unlocked the door. Before Amy let her go she said. "Don't say a word to anyone. Or I'll come back for you."

The girl was on the verge of tears.

"I hate New York," she blurted. "Everyone says 'I love New York.' Well, I hate it! People pretend stuff like this doesn't happen but it does."

Amy felt bad. "Sorry. I just needed the door unlocked. I don't really have a gun, if that makes you feel any better."

"It makes me feel worse! I believe any crazy girl who says she has a gun! How am I supposed to survive here? I'm going back to Mahwah."

Amy had lived in the city long enough to have developed a native contempt for New Jersey, with its smelly refineries, monotonous tract subdivisions and its blighted suburban mall mentality. But for the moment she kept her opinions to herself.

She gave the distraught girl a quick hug. "Maybe you should do that," she said gently, then slipped through the door and away.

She ran down the corridor toward the freight elevators, but she could see that neither one was on this floor. She didn't have time to wait. She burst through the door to the fire stairs and leapt down them. She got to street level, tore down a couple of right angled halls and ran out onto the loading docks.

She saw the pair of Secret Service guys—of course they would be covering all the exits—and Tommy the shipping clerk at the same moment. Tommy . . . what was his last name? Raoul would know. Hardesty, that was it.

"Well, Tom Hardesty." she said, walking up to him.

"Uh—wow! Amy! I—uh—hi, how are you?"

"I'm a little rushed right now."

"Too bad you missed the Christmas party this year—I got some *real fresh* mistletoe. Hardly used at all—the florist swore up and down on it."

"I hope it worked."

He gave her a thumbs up. Oh, well . . . if he was really

bright he'd probably have been doing something else by now. She moved a little closer to him and spoke softly.

"See those two guys coming toward us?"

"Uh—what? Yeah . . . I guess . . . but—"

"If you help me get away from them, you won't need that mistletoe."

"Really? You mean it? Cool."

"Thanks, Tom."

"You go. I'll handle them."

She turned back inside, but paused to watch. The Secret Service guys were climbing onto the loading dock.

"Here fellas—gimme a hand."

Tommy grabbed a big box and heaved it at one of the agents; before he could respond, Tommy had slung another box at his partner. They were heavy boxes. Tommy was strong. The impact knocked them off balance.

"Hey! Sorry!" Tommy called out. He ran between them and seemed to lose his own balance. He tripped them up and as they fell his own arms flailed for a second; then his fists connected and they sagged to the pavement.

"Whoops! I think I knocked them out."

Amy had come back outside. She was right behind him.

"Thanks, Tommy," she said, and when he turned around she went on her tiptoes to kiss him on the lips. She lingered for a moment, and moved back down a step, smiling up at him. "I've owed you that one for a long time."

He stood there stunned with delight, but before he could think of an answer, she was gone.

Amy slipped back through another door near the pay telephones and moved at normal browsing speed through the store. For the moment she was in the clear. The trick was not to call attention to herself by rushing or pushing past people. This wasn't a sale day at Filene's—it was an ordinary shopping day at Bloomingdale's. No one was in a hurry.

She was just one woman among hundreds—it was perfect camouflage if she could control her need to run.

She was a few yards from Raoul's position, almost at the doors, when he saw her and waved and called out "Amy!" to get her attention. That was all Tim Evarts and Mike Dalnegro needed. They had been quartering the store desperately—they had grabbed three different women who looked like Amy and then released them with gruff apologies.

Team #2 was checking the third floor dressing rooms.

Team #3 had gone off the air. A team never went off the air, it made no sense. Tim knew he should check with team #2 and get them downstairs for back-up, but there was no time, Amy was on the move, almost at the street and anyway he could handle the situation alone. She had tricked them once but it hadn't done her any good and it wasn't going to happen again.

Amy slammed into Raoul so hard she almost knocked him over.

"Remember why they almost fired you last year?" she asked him.

"Well, of course I do. It was a moment of pure spontaneity. I have no regrets."

"Well, have another moment, Raoul—I have to stop these guys."

"I'll be fired for sure this time."

"Good. You were talking about quitting this job a year ago. Take some time, get your modeling portfolio together. This is fate." She knew he liked the idea of fate. The thought of life as a chain of meaningless coincidences demoralized him.

Mike and Tim were almost upon them. They had pushed some guy who pushed back. They had to badge him before they could move on. Raoul followed her eyes, saw the two big men shouldering their way through the last of the crowd. In a few seconds they'd be on open floor.

"You run along, sweetheart," Raoul said. "I'll take care of it."

"Thanks."

She squeezed his arm once and then dashed for the front doors.

Raoul blocked the path of the two Secret Service agents.

"Care to try Calvin Klein's Obsession?" he asked sweetly.

Then he sprayed the perfume in their faces.

As he had learned the year before, it didn't work as well as pepper spray and it didn't work as well as mace.

But it worked well enough for him.

The men were on their knees, screaming and clawing at their eyes. Raoul bent down in a flurry of apologies. Another pair of agents who had been upstairs were bounding off the escalators toward the front doors. They veered towards their injured comrades as Amy pushed into the street.

Raoul felt a thrill of victory as he watched her vanish into the crowds on Lexington Avenue. He didn't know exactly who these men were, but they looked like government men, with the short hair and gray suits and military demeanor that he had always hated. When America finally decided to round up all the fags, he was sure it would be one of these guys, formal and polite—but with a gun in his hand—who would come to his door.

Good luck, sweetheart, he thought as they hustled him away. You run like hell.

And thank God you wore flats.

28

Amy arrived at the Alice in Wonderland statue fifteen minutes early. She had been wandering through the Metropolitan Museum for hours, strolling aimlessly through the American Wing, glancing at the Colonial furniture and paintings, the muskets and military uniforms on display, letting her mind drift back hundreds of years. Supposedly things were simpler then, but she doubted it. More uncomfortable and inconvenient, that was for sure. Dirtier; but just as complicated. Emotions didn't change. She thought of Thomas Jefferson falling in love with one of his slaves, transfiguring her most intimate moments, making them a part of her country's history. If she and Tom succeeded they would be part of history, too. So would Dominic Nosiglia. His name would be right up there with Benedict Arnold in the high school textbooks. If they succeeded.

Now she was sitting on one of the benches on the raised pavilion next to the sailboat pond, watching the kids scramble over the bronze statue. It was a dull brown, except for the places kids used as handholds. Those gleamed

gold in the sun. A little boy fell and his Jamaican nanny ran to
him as he started crying under the giant mushroom. It was
mostly nannies out in the park today. And you could see
there was a class system among them. The English nannies
lorded it over the Irish Nannies, who lorded it over the German nannies, who lorded it over the Jamaicans. The kids had
their own pecking order, too; all the busy worlds within worlds.

She looked at her watch: five minutes after two. She had
been here twenty minutes, but that didn't mean that Tom
and Jake were twenty minutes late. They were five minutes
late. There was nothing to worry about. If she started worrying she'd feel like a fool when they finally showed up. It was
a waste of energy. But what if something had happened to
one of them? Or both of them? She hadn't heard a news
report since this morning. They could both be under arrest
by now; or dead.

She looked at her watch again. Seven minutes after
two.

She resolved not to start worrying until two fifteen.
Someone sat down next to her, uncomfortably close.

"You keep checking your watch, someone's gonna
notice. They're gonna say 'Who's she waiting for? Why is
she so nervous? She looks familiar. Oh yeah—the crazy
kid's girlfriend. Maybe they do their civic duty and call the
cops. All because you looked at your watch once too often—and forgot to wear sunglasses."

It was Jake.

Something fell away sweetly inside her, like those tunnels she used to dig at the beach—when she'd finally stand
on the frail bridges and make them collapse and she'd
drop into the sandy trench feeling like the queen of the
giants.

Jake was here.

She twisted sideways on the bench to hug him.

"Any sign of Tom?" she asked to his cheek.

"Not yet. But he'll be here. You holding up okay?"

"I'm fine."

"Looks like you lost the Secret Service."

She smiled and tried to look casual. "No problem."

Tom arrived a few minutes later. He was wearing Dockers khaki trousers a size too big, a green wool turtle neck and a bulky leather jacket. At least his running shoes fit. His hair was tangled, his hands and face were dirty—he looked like an Ivy League frat boy still reeling from an all-night drunk.

Amy jumped up and held him hard. "We made it," she said.

He stroked her hair. "Not quite yet," he said.

He hadn't shaved. His face was rough. But as usual she felt absurdly safe and comforted with his arms around her. It was especially absurd right now—being with him was the most dangerous place in the world for her to be, unless she wanted to seek out some Third World Civil War. But it was like having cash in your pocket when your bank account was overdrawn—you still felt prosperous, somehow. The image was particularly apt, since Jake was broke, both of their banks were under surveillance . . . and Tom had a wad of cash, almost fifteen hundred dollars, in his hand.

Amy was baffled.

"Remember the money I told you about? The money my Dad and I buried in the park? Most of it was still there. After all this time. That's got to be a sign, don't you think?"

"I don't know," Amy said, "But I think your Dad would be happy to know he helped."

Tom kissed her and they were really together. Tom embraced Jake and then the three of them started back up the path to the Museum.

"Let me lay it out for you guys," Jake said. "I've been thinking about this. The way I see it, we can't expose this guy—the impostor. We needed Jim Gramble for that. He's

gone and his story is in the shredder. No one's gonna believe
you. So you have just one way to go."

Tom nodded. He had thought of this a long time ago.
"Assassination."

The word jolted Amy. "No, wait," she said, "there has
to be some other way, something else we can do . . . "

Jake's voice was cold. "Do you have a plan?"

Amy looked down. "No. But I don't get it, I don't understand how we got to this place where we, I don't know . . .
its like we used up all our choices. We chose and chose and
now we can't choose any more. Everything's decided. We have
to either let evil win or . . ."

"Or assassinate the President."

"It sounds so insane when you say it out loud."

"He's not the President, Amy," Jake said quietly. "Someone already assassinated the President. That's why we have
to do this."

"I know."

They walked along.

"Daffodil Day is coming up," Tom said. "It's a fake
Chamber of Commerce holiday on Nantucket. Everyone
parks their antique cars on Main Street and then they all
drive out to the east end of the island for tail-gate picnics.
Dad always rode out in the Jensen-Healy. They'll have to
stick with that tradition."

Jake was nodding. "There are trees on both sides of
the road—good tall thick ones on the North side around
the Tom Nevers turn-off. Clear lines of fire. If you could
get into position early enough . . . "

"All I need is a weapon and some ammo . . . and a place
to stay or a few days."

"You can use my Winchester 70—it's a 300 magnum with
a Weatherly scope. I use it for hunting. I'll head back to
Nantucket now—set everything up. You guys . . . get off the

street for a while. Tom's a wanted man and everybody knows your faces."

"Thanks, Jake."

Jake just grinned. "Any time," he said.

He jogged off downtown, towards the statue. They turned and watched him go. Two women ran past in designer sweats with matching headbands, pushing strollers ahead of them.

"Now what?" Amy asked.

"Now we hole up for a while. And I know the perfect place . . . if a certain new friend of mine is in the phone book."

Miguel Osona didn't strike Tom as the kind of guy who'd have an unlisted number. And as it happened, he didn't.

The number was 989—7644; he lived at 2 Charlton Street in the West Village. Tom didn't want to risk a phone call. It was better just to show up. And it would be pointless to show up until after work.

They walked across town to the multiplex Theatre on Third Avenue and 86th Street, and Amy described her confrontation with Dominic Nosiglia and her Bloomingdale's escapade as they treated themselves to another lunch of Papaya King hot dogs.

Then they hid out in the dark theaters, watching movies into the evening, strolling into the lobby between films to replenish their giant sodas and their twizzler supplies. Amy insisted that they only see teen comedies—no horror pictures, no thrillers.

She remembered a comment from his journal—she hadn't quite understood it at the time.

"I know what you mean about suspense," she said ruefully, taking his hand. "I used to like it, just the way you did. Before I knew what it was."

Like most New Yorkers, Miguel Osona had dozens of

take-out menus in his kitchen drawers. For a man who hated restaurants but rarely had the time or the energy to cook, they were the perfect solution. Tonight it was Szchuan chicken from a place on Houston Street. And a couple of Coronas.

It had been a grueling day. The police had interviewed him, so had the Secret Service. Tom had described Ira Heller so he had a pretty good idea of what to expect; and Heller had lived up to his worst expectations, bored and bullying, cynical and snide. He wanted to know what Osona had been doing in the surveillance room—why he had ordered the guards down to the cafeteria. Their negligence had bought Tom the few extra minutes he needed. Osona's story was plausible—he had been trying to help.

"So what did you think of Tom? Did you like him?"

"I try to like all my patients."

"He was trying to convince you he was sane."

"Most of my patients try to convince me of that."

"Was it working?"

"That's confidential."

"This is a National Security matter."

"Then arrest me."

The two men had stared at each other. Heller had rubbed his jaw and smiled.

"I just want to know what you felt about the kid."

"He's a good kid."

"But crazy?"

"Probably. I didn't have much time with him. We had just gotten started, Mr. Heller."

"Because if you did get sucked into his fantasies, if it turns out you actually helped him escape . . . and if he manages to kill the President of the United States as we strongly suspect he is planning to do right now, then you will be considered an accessory to the crime and you will be executed for treason. That means the gas chamber in this state. And if you wind up strapped into that chair in that little room . . .

I'm gonna bring a picnic to Sing Sing and open the champagne while you hold your breath and drink a toast when you
have to suck in that first lungful of gas. Because I hate traitors, Dr. Osona."

"So do I, Mr. Heller. Just as much as you do."

This time the stare went on much longer, and Heller
didn't break it with a smile. He just turned and walked out
of the interrogation room, turning Osona over to the police. He told his story ten more times and was finally released around three in the afternoon. No charges were
brought against him.

There was a meeting with Honig and the other members of the oversight committee. Honig made it very clear
that Osona's therapeutic approach had failed miserably.
Despite their adversarial relationship, Honig had calmed
Tom down and gotten him to open up emotionally on several occasions. Under Osona's more compassionate regime, Tom had escaped.

"Not much more needs to be said," Honig had concluded. "But I'll be taking this matter up with the board of
Directors next week. I'll be demanding a thorough inquiry
and full disciplinary action."

Osona opened his second beer. No one could prove
he helped Tom escape from the Holden clinic; but he
knew it was true. No one could accuse him of believing
Tom was sane; but he did. Or at least he had started to.
These diagnoses were difficult and confusing at the best
of times. Five competent psychiatrists could come to five
completely different conclusions about the same patient.
He could sometimes come to five different conclusions
about the same patient all by himself. But if Honig and
Heller were right and he was wrong . . . Well—then he would
deserve the death penalty. He thought back. Would he have
done anything different? Would he turn Tom in if he had
the chance now?

Such questions are usually abstract—like the absurd speculations in those 'test your ethics' party games. He had actually broken up with a girlfriend over one of them, years ago, when he admitted he would save Michelangelo's Pieta . . . even if it meant letting a kitten die. "Fortunately, it's not the kind of choice that comes up very often," he had joked to lighten the mood. It hadn't worked, though. The girl had stalked out of the apartment.

"Cat killer!," were her last words to him as she slammed the door.

He had tried to avoid such games after that, but the choice of whether or not to turn Tom Jaglom in to the authorities was no idle diversion.

And it was about to come up again.

In fact, it was coming up quite literally at this very moment, in the elevator of his building.

Tom and Amy had slipped into the lobby with a group of teen-agers, and were watching the floor markers, crushed into the back of the car by large, noisy crowd of sixteen year olds. At the seventh floor they pushed their way out into the quiet corridor. As the door closed behind them, Amy said,

"High school kids. They make me feel old."

Tom shrugged. "They made me feel old when I was in high school."

"You *were* old in high school."

"So—what does that make me now? Ancient and wise?"

She looked him up and down appraisingly. "Geriatric and cranky."

"Thanks alot."

She kissed his cheek. "Just kidding. At least about the geriatric part."

They were at Osona's door. They glanced at each other nervously before ringing the bell. It was one thing to know he was going to help them; it was quite another to actually find out.

Osona was watching Tom on the news when he heard the doorbell. The largest manhunt in decades was happening "at this hour," as the self-important local news people liked to say. Even in New York, there was rarely a breaking national news story of this magnitude for them to cover and already the network teams were closing in, trying to take it away from them.

Osona's answering machine had logged forty-one messages during the day, all from press people wanting interviews about the *People* magazine cover-boy. There had been no reporters in front of the building but the superintendent, a burly Swede named Horst Lindvall, explained that he had chased them away with a baseball bat. No one was seriously hurt but two cameras were smashed and one aggressive reporter "Is going to have bad tummy ache tomorrow," Lindvall had grinned.

Osona had given him a fifty dollar bill.

"No, no," he had protested, "I do for free!"

"I know." Osona had replied. "That's why I'm tipping you."

The doorbell rang again.

"Hold on a second," he called out. The story about Tom was almost finished. The police and the FBI were covering all the bus and train stations, the airports, the harbor—even the toll-booths on the major arteries leaving the city. The streets were full of informants—everyone who had ever worked for the police was on the look-out tonight and the general public was urged to examine everyone passing them on the street. Jaglom could be anywhere. There was a hundred thousand dollar reward for any information leading to his arrest

"That's how it stands, Kathy," the reporter in the street was saying. "Despite the best efforts of national and local authorities, a young madman with devastating combat skills, an intimate knowledge of the First Family and a lethal grudge against the president is still out there . . . somewhere. This is Todd Robbins, Newscenter Five."

Osona turned off the TV with the remote and went to the door.

Somewhere: he looked through the peep-hole and a jumble of emotions pushed through him, like a crowd squeezing out of subway car. First there was shock, to see Tom standing in front of him. Then relief, that the boy was safe. And vindication—something in the way he stood, with his arm around Amy's shoulders . . . it was the body language of sanity, the posture of someone at home in his skin and on the planet. The surge of resolution was next—he would help any way he could; and fear, right behind it, even as he was unlocking the door. Anyone could come out of another apartment at any moment and recognize Tom. There was even a flicker of resentment as he fumbled with the dead-bolts—he was being drawn into the center of this terrifying situation and he hated that. Osona had always liked the periphery of things. He liked to watch from a distance and make notes.

But no detachment was possible now. He was about to commit a whole raft of crimes. He didn't even know them all: aiding and abetting a fugitive, conspiracy, accessory to God knew what . . . but there was a privileged satisfaction in the fact that Tom had chosen to come here, of all places, for safe harbor.

"Tom!" he said, embracing the boy. "And you must be Amy. Please come in—quickly, before someone sees you."

He pulled them inside and shut the door.

"So you really are one of the good shrinks," Tom said when they were safely inside.

"Absolutely," Osona said. "Possibly the best shrink."

He took them into the living room, ordered more Chinese food and listened as they described their last twenty four hours and outlined their plans. He was struck, as they had been, by the awful logic of what Jake Gritzky had proposed. Murder was a crime and murder was a sin; to even consider it was appalling.

But they didn't have the luxury of virtue. No one was going to do their dirty work, as the army did for pacifists or the police did for anarchists—making it safe to sneer at warfare or the rule of law.

They would do what had to be done—and they would take the consequences—because there was no one to do it for them. That was exhilarating, as well as frightening. They were the only people left in the country with the power to change things, to make restitution. And it wasn't often that one had a chance to really make a difference in the world . . . or so Amy and Osona decided as they cleaned up the dishes after dinner. Tom was on the couch in the living room, listening to some classical music on WQXR. He had gotten almost no sleep the night before, and Osona had insisted that he rest.

"Thanks, Doctor. We both appreciate this so much."

Amy would always remember that moment—her hands in warm soapy water, holding a dinner plate while Osona dried a glass with a dish towel—that last innocent mundane moment before everything changed. It would scarcely seem real in retrospect—like trying to recall what you and your sister were arguing about in the seconds before the car crash. Ordinary stuff, of course. In this case, Osona was offering the use of his queen-sized bed, assuming that could get Tom off the couch.

That was when Amy heard him talking.

She held up a hand to Osona.

"Tom?" she called out.

But Tom kept on talking. She called his name a little louder, again with no effect. She walked to the kitchen door, so that she could listen to him and Osona followed, instantly stealthy, as if a burglar had broken into the apartment—which wasn't all that far from the truth. Someone was in the living room now that neither of them knew.

Tom was talking back to the radio.

"I know that," he was saying. "But I can do it, Mom. I'm going to do it. I'm going to purge it in blood! Fire and blood. They're going to *drown* in blood. That's why I was able to escape, Mom—this is meant to happen. I am *instructed.* I know . . . I know . . . and I *will.* I can *do* it. He's going to *see* the fire, he's going to *choke* on the blood. Yes, yes—but not just for me. For you. For all of us. I'm going to slaughter him. He's going to die die die—"

Tom must have felt Amy and Osona listening. He turned towards the kitchen. They flinched back as the door swung open. His face was raw and harrowed, stretched into some leering demon mask.

"Tom," Amy said. "What's going on—what are you—?"

"I have to go."

"No wait—I don't understand—"

"Tom I need to talk to you, just for a few moments. Before you leave." Osona's voice was softer and deeper, modulated to soothe unstable people. He took a step toward the doorway. Tom flowed into a combat stance, like a hound on point

"Stay away from me."

"Tom, listen. You're exhausted. You need to rest. I was just saying to Amy—"

He reached out a hand and Tom exploded. He knocked the proffered arm aside and dropped Osona with a single punch. Blood streamed from the Doctor's broken nose. Tom turned to Amy. He didn't seem to recognize her.

And he was unrecognizable.

"You can't stop me," he said. "Don't try."

He jumped Osona's body, grabbed his jacket off the back of a chair and darted out the front door. He left it open and they heard the door to the fire stairs open and shut. The

classical music played on. Something by Mozart. That relentless teutonic frivolity. It was hideous, chilling—like the smile
on a clown.

"Oh my God," Osona gasped from the floor. "He really is crazy. And he's going to assassinate the President."

Amy was staring at the open doorway. She still didn't
understand. "We don't know that," she began. "We can't
be sure that–"

Osona held up a hand to stop her. He pulled himself
to a sitting position and touched his bleeding nose. "I'm
sure. Aural hallucinations are the primary symptom of
Tom's condition. It's all . . .Everything fits. He must have
been hearing his mother's voice at the cemetery, just as
Jim Gramble said. That may have been where this new
cycle began."

"Wait a second. I don't understand this. He didn't seem
crazy to me. His journal wasn't crazy."

"But it was. Don't you understand? It presented the
complete structure of a fully realized delusional system.
Of course it made sense. Everything proceeded logically
from the premise. Everything made perfect sense to *him*."

Osona pressed his hands to his face "Oh God," he said.
"Oh shit. Oh no."

Amy knelt beside him. "Dr. Osona—?"

It was a while before he spoke. But when he looked
up his eyes were clear.

"My career is over. I believed him, Amy. I'm a trained
clinical psychiatrist and I believed him. And now . . .Do
you happen to know what happened to the doctor who set
John Wilkes Booth's broken leg after he assassinated President Lincoln? He was hanged, Amy. And he didn't even
know who the man was. A stranger came to his door with a
compound fracture, that was all. I knew Tom. God help
me, I actually participated in his escape from the Holden
clinic. I harbored him as a fugitive."

"But wait—Tom talked to the impostor, he tricked him. The man didn't know about the money Tom buried in the park with his Dad. He described the whole thing . . . he told me . . ."

Osona just shook his head.

"Amy, you are going to have to accept the fact that this conversation never took place, except in Tom's mind. I know Tom seemed rational to you. He seemed that way to me as well. Schizophrenics in the early stages go through prolonged periods of lucidity and denial. But if you look back I'm sure you will be able to see incidents, moments that should have been warning signals. Or perhaps I should say . . . moments that should have been warning signals to a trained observer."

He added quietly, with a bitterness that was more convincing than his words, "Such as myself."

Amy thought back. There were things that troubled her. The way Tom had made such a point of escaping from Heller's team in Central Park after they had just saved his life—and his fixation with their constant surveillance; his violence in the Chicken Box; his obsession with his mother's grave and then his fear of the place; his increasing distance and coldness. That was why she read the journal in the first place. She knew something was wrong. His words had reassured her. But that was the point. Reading the journal had put her into his world, into the self-referential upside down dreamscape of his psychosis, in which an old friend like Jim Gramble, who had met with Tom in a last ditch attempt to convince him to commit himself to a state mental hospital, became something else entirely—the man with the last pieces of the conspiracy jig-saw puzzle. But there was no conspiracy, no puzzle to solve. Except the purely medical one, the enigma of a young man's brain chemistry slipping helplessly awry.

Which meant that Heller was right.

STEVEN AXELROD

Which meant that Heller one of the good guys.

It was too much to think about. It was too horrible. It punched everything she'd said and done and thought for months inside out. If Tom actually succeeded, she would be an accessory before the fact. She wasn't fighting some shadowy nefarious plot, trying to expose and destroy it.

She *was* it.

She was a criminal. And she was a fool.

She was blinded by love, but she was guilty of high treason. She had plotted with a lunatic to assassinate the President. That was the truth.

Heller was right.

And everything else was wrong.

PART THREE:
ASSASSINS

29

New York City was too big and diverse to be seriously affected by the doings of its inhabitants. It absorbed events and catastrophes effortlessly, the way the sea absorbs shipwrecks. A burning high-rise on the upper west side was nothing but a faint sound of sirens in the distance to an advertising executive on Madison Avenue; even the World Trade Center bombing had been just one more unexplained detonation, uptown. If you didn't watch television and stayed off the Internet, it was possible to live as isolated from the world as a hermit in a mountain cabin.

That was what Tyler Mackenzie had chosen to do. But as a native New Yorker he appreciated the fact that although the world scarcely reached him, he had all the access he wanted to the world . . . or at least to street music, salt bagels and Sabrett hot dogs. Not to mention cheap electronic parts and marine paint supplies.

Those supplies, especially the three hundred grit sandpaper and the spar varnish, were going to be especially useful today, since he was finally doing some bright work on his forty-two foot Grand Banks trawler. He had been a 'live aboard' in the 79th Street marina for more than two years, ever since the extraordinary month of June when he had sent his last child off to college, divorced his wife and quit his job at one of the city's largest brokerage houses . . . all in the space of less than two weeks. Of course the legal aspect of the divorce had dragged on for months, and Caroline had wound up with everything she had ever wanted from him—and more than even her horrible, relentless lawyers had dared to ask for: the house in the Hamptons, the Sutton Place apartment, the XJ6 (Purchased out of the Nieman Marcus catalogue and presented as a Christmas gift during a happier year), the art (including some Jim Dine hearts and some Hockney photo-collages) the books (including his Jim Thompson, David Goodis and Charles Willeford first editions), the silver, the furniture, the audio equipment . . . everything but the boat.

Caroline had always hated the boat.

Which was fine with him; it was all he wanted. He had even given up custody of their black lab, Sam. He was tired of dogs. He just couldn't have these undiscriminating, brainless yet vaguely sentient creatures around him anymore. He needed smart, funny, surprising creatures around him. Like say, for instance, *human beings*. Like his girlfriend Polly, for example, who was going to be spending the weekend with him on board the *Arcadia*. He had to admit it, he was a snob. People were better than dogs. People were good. Dogs sucked. When he came back to the car with a grocery bag and saw Sam sitting expectantly in the driver's seat he was never tempted, even for one second, to let the dog drive. He understood that dogs wanted to drive, they longed to drive, they even got cocky sometimes and thought, "Hey, how hard can it be? The bipeds do it." But it didn't matter. When they could clean the house and keep up their end of a simple conversation . . . then he'd talk about driver's ed. Until then, forget about it.

He didn't miss Sam at all. But he did miss Polly. She was the opposite of dogs, come to think of it—the anti-dog, the antidote to dogs. He loved the supremely discriminating affection in her eyes. He glanced at his watch. She was half an hour late. He looked up past the big Sag Harbor sport fishing boats with their tuna towers and the Chris Craft cabin cruisers, but the dock was empty. He went back to sanding the mahogany. Wooden boats were a lot more trouble but they had soul. They were beautiful, they were flexible and they handled better in rough seas. Of course he couldn't keep up with some of the yachts moored out here—his twin Lehman 135s had a top speed of maybe twelve knots. But he wasn't in a rush any more; these days, he enjoyed taking his time. And it really was *his time*, now, in a way it hadn't been since college. He owned it, every minute of it—and he could spend it any way he wanted.

On the telephone, Polly had said she might be caught in traffic—some new calamity (she knew better than to go into the details) was clogging the streets. The only evidence of a crisis Tyler had seen was a couple of extra cops prowling the piers, stopping people and talking to them. But even the cops were gone now. The marina was deserted.

Tyler didn't know it but the police—as well as two other unlucky boat owners—were unconscious and tied up in the basement of the chandlery store at far side of the marina. He wasn't expecting trouble and he wasn't aware that anything was wrong until he felt the barrel of the flare gun against his temple. He felt his wallet being slipped out of his pocket. For a moment he thought he was going to be robbed. But the intruder just checked the name on the license and put the leather billfold back.

"I'm borrowing your boat, Mr. MacKenzie" Tom Jaglom said softly "We're going to take a little river cruise together."

"Listen, buddy—take it easy . . . put the gun down."

"I need you to take me as far north as Lyndhurst. Then you can let me off and head back." Tom removed the gun from Tyler's head. "I'm not going to hurt you unless you make it absolutely necessary."

"Hey—I'm cooperative. Ask my ex-wife. You on the run or something?"

Tom had to smile. "You could say that."

"Tyler!"

Both men looked back toward the city. A lovely, dark haired girl at least ten years younger than Mackenzie was jogging up the pier. She was wearing jeans and a rust colored turtle neck. A dark blue pea jacket billowed out behind her in the freshening west wind.

"That's my girlfriend Polly. This was supposed to be our weekend together."

"It will be. This is just a three hour detour. Then I'll be gone."

Polly had stopped short—it was as if she'd come to the edge of a cliff.

"Oh my God," she said. "It's him."

"It's who? Who *is* this guy?"

"Jesus, Tyler! I know you pride yourself on being out of it . . . but I mean—Jesus. He's President's Jaglom's son. He's a psycho. He's a killer. He just escaped from a mental hospital! They think he's going to try and assassinate the President. Every cop in the city is looking for him . . . and you're just standing here *chatting* with him? I don't believe this. This is so fucked." She turned on Tom. "So what are you going to do? Are you going to kill us? The TV says you're armed and dangerous."

"I wouldn't believe everything you see on TV, Polly. Besides, three quarters of the people in this city are armed and dangerous. It's not much of a distinction. If I were unarmed and polite—that would be news."

Polly caught herself smiling and tightened her face.

The three of them stood there tensely. Tom felt the seconds passing. He wanted to get on the water. But he couldn't pilot the big boat alone.

"You're sure you're not going to kill us?"

"I won't even hurt you, if you help me get out of the city."

She turned to Tyler. "I'm scared, Ty."

"Me too."

"But you're supposed to know what to do."

"She doesn't trust you," Tyler said to Tom.

Tom could feel time like a current, pulling him towards a waterfall. Soon he would be launched helpless into the roaring mist, smashed on the rocks below. It could come in any of a dozen ways. They could be seen by other boat owners, the river traffic, police helicopters. More cops could show up. This girl could just start screaming.

"You're both safe–I told you that."

"She doesn't believe you."

"I don't–"

"Put the flare gun down. Trust us and we'll trust you."

Tom shrugged. "Okay."

"Make him give it to you," Polly blurted out. "He's some kind of karate guy. I saw it on the news."

Tyler nodded. "Give me the gun Tom."

"That's not trust."

"Are you one of the good guys?"

"As a matter of fact . . . yes I am. That's the whole point."

"Then prove it. Good guys don't take hostages."

They stared at each other. Tom heard a siren in the distance. He glanced at Polly. Her face was hard. He handed Tyler the gun but he didn't let it go for a moment.

"If you turn me in it will be a national disaster, Mr. Mackenzie. You'll be doing more harm than you can possibly imagine."

He released the gun.

STEVEN AXELROD

"Call me Tyler," MacKenzie said. He stuffed the flare gun into the waist-band of his pants.

Polly gaped at him. "You're really going to do this?"

"A deal is a deal."

"But—"

"Hey," he said, taking her hand. "I told you this would be an adventure."

They worked together, untying the dock lines, unscrewing the shore phone cable and warming up the engines. Tyler had locked away the flare gun and was just putting on the UHF and the Global Positioning Satellite receivers as Tom swung down into the center salon.

"Top of the line," he nodded. "You really need GPS?"

"Maybe once in ten years, if it's night and it's snowing and I'm lost. Infantry guys in Desert Storm had miniature receivers—about the size of two packs of cigarettes? It could be dust blowing and pitch black, they always knew exactly where they were." He shrugged. "I like knowing where I am."

"Me, too."

"Boys and their toys," said Polly, coming in from the deck. "I don't think you should be acting so friendly with this man, Tyler. I mean, *technically* we're still his hostages."

"Yeah, well—this hostage is planing to make the best of it. Who wants lunch?"

He served sandwiches and beer as they churned up the Hudson towards the George Washington Bridge. Even from the river you could see a massive bumper-to-bumper traffic jam on both levels, turning the West Side Highway into a parking lot. Tom had a pretty good idea what was causing the problem.

An hour later with the city behind them, Tom began to feel safe. They ate and chatted about Wall Street and Washington D.C. Mackenzie's father had run a powerful arbitrage house; he was a legend on Wall street, so Tyler knew what it was like to grow up in a great man's shadow. Tom had shrugged. "My Dad made it easy," he said.

Tyler just swigged his beer. But Polly noticed the past tense.

"You make it sound like he died," she said.

Tom just blew out a breath. "That's a long story," he said.

"Tell us."

For a moment he actually considered it. "No," he said finally. "But by next week, if I get some luck, if things go the way I hope they will . . . you'll know everything. Let's just leave it at that."

Tom and Tyler started clearing the table. Polly moved to get up, but Tyler touched her shoulder gently to keep her seated. She took his hand and kissed it. Tom turned his attention to the sink, waiting for the water to run hot.

"I'm sorry about your mother, Tom," Polly said. "I guess everybody is."

"She was an amazing person."

"I read your eulogy in the *Times,*" Tyler added, handing him the plates. "That thing you said, about . . . you know— about appreciating the people in your life, treating them as if they could be dead tomorrow . . . I don't know. It got to me. I called my Mom that night."

"I think everyone in America called their Mom that night, Ty," Polly said. "I would have, but . . ."

"Her Mom died a few years ago."

Tom turned to her. "I'm sorry."

"It's okay, don't—I'm dealing with it. You just deal with it. Because you have to."

"Yeah."

"It was horrible at first. I felt so alone. You're never really alone when you know you can E-mail your Mom. She loved E-mail. After the funeral I just felt totally—I don't know. Isolated? Just cut off from the world. I felt *grown up* for the first time in my life and I thought, this sucks. I want to go back to being a kid."

"That would be nice," Tom nodded.

"I'm happy to say I have no idea what you guys are talking about. My parents are beyond healthy. They're . . . dangerously robust. And they've assured me that they're planning to live forever. Which means I'm never going to have to grow up—which is quite a relief, believe me."

"Ty."

"What?"

"Ty, that's just ridiculous. You're a Dad."

"Yeah, well—kids make you feel like you *need* to grow up. And fast. But that's different."

Polly turned to Tom. "Don't listen to him. He's the most thoroughly *adult* man I've ever met. He can fix a carburetor and tie a bow tie. He can wear a tuxedo. He can talk to people—he can argue a traffic cop out of a speeding ticket in a one street town and impress a wine steward in a four star restaurant. He can use power tools. We go to the *opera*, Tom. He translates for me. He runs every morning. He actually has discipline. He doesn't brag—I never knew he'd been this incredibly famous college football quarterback until his father told me. What else? I don't know. There's tons of things. He never loses his car keys or the TV remote. He's organized—he has *files*. He can listen to a five year old describe a Jackie Chan movie without interrupting and he can listen to a woman's troubles without trying to solve them. He does his own taxes, for God's sake. And he can re-fold a road map."

Tom laughed. "That's the ultimate test."

She stood and stretched. "It's stuffy in here. I'm going to go up on deck for some air. Ty?"

"I'll be there in a second. I want to help Tom finish up the dishes."

"Okay."

She left and they worked in silence for a while.

"There's something I didn't tell you about this little cruise this weekend," Tyler said as he stowed the last of the glasses above the sink.

"What?"

He dug into his pocket and pulled a small brown felt box with tiny gold hinges. He opened it to show a dazzling diamond wedding ring. "I was planning to propose."

"Then do it. You have to. I don't want to blow that for you. Just—pretend I'm not here."

"No, it's not that. I mean . . . that's part of it. But she obviously thinks I'm crazy to be going along with this."

"It's not like I gave you any choice. I'm a dangerous lunatic, remember? What were you supposed to do—fight me? You could have gotten yourself killed."

"I guess. She just seems a little cold, that's all. But who wouldn't be? This is a pretty strange situation."

"You're wrong, though. I mean it—she's ready. Didn't you hear that little speech she just gave? She's nuts about you. It's obvious. Take it from a total stranger. The way she was looking at you just now . . . you ever read any Ring Lardner?" Tyler shrugged. "He has a line somewhere, he describes that look exactly. He says, it was the kind of look 'you could pour over a waffle'."

Tyler laughed. "You really think so?"

"Listen—I know you're the world's number one adult and everything . . . but you sound pretty much like a high school kid getting ready to ask the head cheerleader to the prom."

"Aint it the truth."

"Go on out there and ask her. She's waiting for you to do it."

"You think so?"

"I'm positive."

"Then you ask her."

Tom smiled and shoved him toward the hatch.

"Go."

Ten minutes later, Tyler called Tom from the deck and he climbed up into the cool air and the river smell, the wind tugging at his clothes. Polly was right—it was stuffy down below. She and Tyler were standing at the starboard rail, holding each other, laughing.

"Look what he gave me, Tom," Polly said.

Tom crossed the deck to them and she held out her hand, cocked upward at the wrist, to display the ring. It was lodged just before her second knuckle.

"It's beautiful," Tom nodded.

She was struggling with it. She twisted it and pushed simultaneously and it finally cut into the base of her finger. She immediately saw that her last effort had been a mistake.

"Ty . . . it's so tight. I may never be able to get it off."

"It's okay—I can have it sized for you. It's a service they offer right when you buy the ring."

"That's nice . . . but we have to get it off first, and I don't think I'm going to be able to—"

She lost the rest of the sentence in the struggle. She was really fighting with the ring now. It was sitting directly on her second knuckle, jammed there.

"Here," Ty said. "Let me—"

Tom stepped forward. "Polly," he began.

"There!"

That was when it happened. It all happened at once, with an eerily perfect timing that Tyler and Polly would always attribute to a once in a lifetime miracle of coincidence.

But Tom knew better. He knew it was a sign, proof that he was doing the right thing.

He knew it was the hand of God.

The ring dislodged from Polly's knuckle but the force she had used propelled it off her finger like a stone from a sling shot. The ring hit the rail and ricocheted up in a glittering arc over the water. For Tyler and Polly, paralyzed with shock, it seemed to happen in slow motion. But even as they stood there gaping, Tom was hurling himself over the side of the boat.

He had the ring in sight, but it hit the water a second before he did. For a moment, in the turbulence of his own dive and the murk of the river, he couldn't see it. Then there was a gleam of gold and he plunged his hand down towards it. The ring bounced off the side of his hand and he had to take a stroke and pull himself deeper before he could twist around and make a last grab for it.

Up above, Tyler killed the engines, and ran back to the rail as the boat slowed. There was no sign of Tom.

He was quartering the surface, frantically methodical, when he saw the River police cutter approaching. Had they seen Tom? He calculated the angles and realized that the three of them had been standing with the bridge and its brightly striped Bimini cover between them and the cutter. That was why none of them had noticed it. But they hadn't been seen either.

For the moment, Tom was safe; but his head could bob up in front the patrol boat at any time.

"Ahoy, there!," came the amplified voice of the captain. "Request permission to come aboard."

Tyler waved toward himself in a 'come on' gesture and in a moment three river Cops were climbing onto the deck.

A hundred and fifty feet away, Tom came to the surface with the ring in his hand. The two boats were bobbing together in the wake of a third and getting from one to the other was tricky. No one noticed his head in the water fifteen yards south. Tom took a few deep breaths, ducked under again and started swimming for the *Arcadia*.

"I'm sorry to inconvenience you, sir—Ma'am. We're checking all the river traffic heading away from the city."

As he spoke, three of his men climbed down into the salon to check the interior of the boat. Tyler thought about the glasses and plates—the lunch for three that had been sitting on the galley table half an hour before . . . all cleaned up now and out of sight. Polly often teased him about being a 'neat freak'. But it had certainly come in handy today.

"No problem," Tyler said, forcing himself to look away from the water. "What makes you think he'd try the river?"

The officer smiled. "Thinking isn't really our job, sir. We're just running down every possibility. Car rental places have the kid's picture. So do cab companies and limousine services. Even car dealerships—somebody figured he might just steal a car off a lot during a 'test drive'. Anything's possible with this kid. There's teams covering the heliports, the PATH stations in Manhattan and Jersey. Traffic's backed up at both tunnels, the bridges . . . even the Staten Island ferry. Though what good the ferry would do him I have no idea. The Verrazano Narrows Bridge is pretty much closed off right now. So we're checking out the river. And the Coast Guard is dealing with small craft traffic up and down the coast. Lots of angry fishermen! But no one wants to be the idiot that let this guy get away."

"I can understand that."

"Have you seen anything suspicious today? Any trouble at the marina?"

Tyler shrugged. "Nothing."

"No strange people? No one sneaking around?"

"Well . . . I have to say I was a little distracted. I just proposed to my girlfriend."

One of the other cops popped his head out of the hatch. "All clear down here, sir."

"All right, we'll get out of your hair. Thanks for your cooperation . . . and congratulations."

"Thanks. And good luck to you."

Hanging onto the ladder on the starboard side, Tom heard the engine note of the cutter deepen and then fade as it headed south. Polly watched the ship pull away.

"Why did we just do that?" she asked Tyler.

He put his arm around her waist and pulled her to him. "Because we like the guy," he said.

"This would be a good question on the Newlywed Game," Polly laughed. "Would your husband turn over a wanted fugitive who had just rescued your engagement ring from a polluted river?"

"Marriages founder on questions like that."

"Not this one."

He kissed her and in a few minutes Tom climbed back aboard and gave them the ring. An hour later he was shaking Tyler's hand, hugging Polly, wishing them good luck and sprinting off down the Lyndhurst public landing. They watched until he had vanished in the crowd.

"Do you think we did the right thing?" Polly asked as they pulled away from the dock.

"We'll find out soon," Tyler said.

They couldn't believe he was insane. But then, neither could Amy, or Jake Gritzky, or Miguel Osona, who was a highly qualified mental health professional.

None of that surprised Leonard Honig—as he explained to Ted Koppel on *Nightline* and Katie Couric on the *Today* show and Geraldo Rivera on MSNBC . . . and anybody else who'd point a camera at him and listen to him talk.

"A convincing and seductive killer is on the loose," he said, again and again. "And the President's life is in mortal danger. Anyone who listens to this boy and lets themselves get pulled into the world of his fantasies will be pushing us toward a national tragedy. No potential assassin has ever had the intimacy with his potential victim, or the inside knowledge that this one possesses. And fewer still have had his deadly skills. I urge anyone who sees Tom Jaglom to turn him in immediately. Do not engage him in conversation. Don't question him. Just call the police."

It was sound advice but Tyler and Polly didn't hear it. They were happily incommunicado, drifting north past West Point towards Albany, drinking champagne and making love.

Tom, meanwhile, had stolen a car, gotten on to 287 and was now heading up 95 north to Hyannis and Nantucket. The Daffodil Day parade there would be starting up Milestone Road in less than forty-eight hours.

And if Tom had his way, it was going to be the most memorable one ever.

30

"What the hell happened here?" demanded Ira Heller.

Osona's apartment was full of cops and crime scene techs and Secret Service agents. EMTs had bundled Osona onto a stretcher and taken him to the hospital. The Emergency Room doctors would take care of his nose.

Heller and Amy were standing in a corner by the window. Amy stared Heller down. This was familiar combat.

"Tom took us hostage," she was saying. "He beat up Osona and left."

"Just like that."

"Pretty much."

"So he knew about Osona."

"Knew what?"

"Come on, Ms. Elwell. He thought the doctor's office was bugged. He confronted Osona after the *60 Minutes* interview. Osona denied it, of course."

"What are you saying? Was the office bugged?"

"It didn't have to be. Osona was thoroughly debriefed after his sessions with Tom."

"What about doctor-patient confidentiality?"

"What about it?"

"Osona could lose his license."

"On the contrary. He had information pertaining to attempted murder, conspiracy and high treason. He was legally obligated to tell us anything we wanted to know. He understood that. So . . . if Tom figured that out . . . it might explain his little tantrum."

"It might."

"Did he say anything?"

"No, he just went nuts and flipped out. He was talking back to the radio. He heard his mother talking to him. He's really going to do it, Mr. Heller—on Daffodil Day, during the parade. He worked out the plan with Jake Gritzky. Jake has the rifle, a Winchester with some kind of special sight. Listen to me—You have to do something. You have to stop him."

"We'll do our best, Ms. Elwell. That's our job and we're actually quite good at it. We only get publicity when we fail. We don't generally advertise our successes."

"Can I help somehow? I know him, and I—"

"Ms. Elwell, please. You've already been a tremendous help. More than you know. There's nothing left but the field work now. Leave the warfare to the soldiers."

"But—"

"I'm afraid I must insist. Still, there is one thing you might help me with."

"What? Anything."

"Well, I'm not exactly sure how you wound up with Tom in the first place. You lost several teams of my people yesterday morning—that was nice work, by the way. We couldn't figure out why you went to all that trouble. And then when you surface again, you're with him. What's going on, Ms. Elwell?"

Amy looked out the window. This was the question she

had been waiting for; and dreading. "I had agreed to meet him if he escaped. I thought I could convince him to turn himself in. I knew the Secret Service would scare him off— or there'd be a struggle or a gun fight, or . . . and I knew you wouldn't give me permission if I asked for it. So I just went under and did it on my own. One of Tom's first rules is that you should never ask permission. People will always say no, if they get the chance. It feels good. It makes them feel powerful. You're much better off going ahead and doing the thing and then saying 'Gee, I had no idea that would be a problem' when they catch you."

"That's a dangerous, anti-social attitude, Ms. Elwell."

"But it works. I got to meet Tom instead of being put under house arrest or used as bait."

"So, despite everything you told me, all your very convincing assurances, you still believed Tom was sane."

In the street a line of cars was being blocked by a delivery truck. Horns blared. Amy stared down into the angry stasis, hoping Heller would just go away. In fact he took a step closer.

"Isn't that right, Ms. Elwell?"

She turned to face him. "I hoped he was. And there was evidence that he was. He had fifteen hundred dollars he'd taken from places around the park where he'd hidden it with his Dad."

"Did you actually see the cash?"

"I don't know, I didn't really notice."

"It would have to have been all old currency, Ms.Elwell, from before the change-over. And it wasn't."

"How could you know that?"

"Because I interviewed the thirty or so people Tom mugged in the park last night. Their total losses came to just about one thousand, five hundred dollars. Quite a coincidence. Mostly new bills, of course. But you conveniently failed to check that detail. It's a pity because it might have changed your mind about Tom a little sooner. And you might have been able to help us."

"I was trying to help you. I tried to talk him out of it, and I learned about his plan. Just for the record—I just gave you the only hard information you have about Tom right now. But there was nothing I could do, Mr. Heller. Dr. Osona tried to interfere and Tom . . . well, you saw."

"Yet Tom didn't hurt you at all."

"And that's suspicious?"

"It's odd. Given what you know, it would have been far smarter to kill you."

"He loves me, Mr. Heller."

"And love makes people stupid. Which may be the only good thing about it."

By the middle of the next morning Heller was certain Tom had slipped through the net. He didn't berate himself—Manhattan was a big place, and he had asked a hastily assembled army of law enforcement people to set their normal duties aside and concentrate on tracking down one lone fugitive. It was like trying to find a cockroach in a housing Project. Heller didn't know anything about needles and haystacks—he was a city guy.

Morale had been low, there was a lot of disorganization at the beginning of the operation, a lot of chain-of-command foul-ups. It wasn't hard to believe that Tom had managed to get away. Besides, Heller firmly believed in the luck of the Devil. If Tom had been an American spy in World War II, trying to reach Berlin and assassinate Hitler, someone would have caught him, even if it was only by accident. Good guys with true hearts on noble missions generally got squashed like bugs. That was Heller's experience. Whereas the bad guys did just fine.

All he could do now was strengthen the security on Nantucket, which meant—as the head of the Board of Selectmen had just finished telling him at the top of his whiny voice—there were going to be a lot of unhappy tourists. Heller was the wrong person to plead with on that score. He liked unhappy tourists. And he liked making fat spoiled petulant self righteous small town big shots go red in the face. There weren't many perks in his job. Heller took them wherever he could find them.

The airport was sealed and every person on every incoming flight, public or private, was checked. Heller even had an agent at the Nantucket Cottage Hospital making sure Tom didn't hitch a ride from Boston on the MedEvac helicopter.

The Steamship dock was just as tight. Every car, every walk-on passenger, was stopped and identified. The ferries were backed up more than five hours. And the little old ladies who liked to sniff that "It used to be nice on Nantucket" really had something to complain about for once.

Heller had the Coast Guard out patrolling Nantucket Sound, but they didn't notice the lone wind-surfer who tacked across the thirty miles from Hyannis to the island in the darkest part of a moonless night.

Simple plans worked best, that was what Jake Gritzky always said. So when Tom had arrived in Hyannis, he ditched the car, and went looking for another one. He found a Chevy Suburban in the Cape Cod Mall parking lot with a wet suit and other equipment inside and a windsurfer lashed to the roof rack. It was another little favor from God; one more proof that he was doing the right thing. He stole the car and waited until nightfall. The wetsuit was baggy on him but there were booties and a hood, which were essential—the Atlantic was bone-piercingly cold at this time of year.

Tom actually passed as close a couple of yards from one of the Coast Guard cutters, getting air as he crossed the big boat's wake. It seemed like no one saw him, but it made him nervous. He knew the Coast Guard had radar. He scuttled the sail and paddled the last five miles, flat to the water and invisible.

It was a good thing he did, because the first cutter doubled back to check the area where he had been sailing and another boat arrived soon afterward. Tom angled to the west, off his original course, paddling hard. Another boat almost ran him down.

Still, by five in the morning, he was beaching the sailboard at Eel Point. He would have expected to be exhausted but the sleepless night and the long paddle had exhilarated him. He peeled off the Billabong wet suit (sending out a little prayer of thanks to the man who invented velcro), took his dry clothes and a towel out of the big plastic garbage bag he had worn strapped across his shoulders, and got dressed.

He stood on the beach in his warm clothes, staring out at the dark placid water, touched with the first light of dawn. The wind had died down to a breath; he would have had to paddle anyway if he had started out much later. It had been a long dangerous trip, but it was over now. In thirty six hours his mission would be accomplished, the impostor killed, his father avenged, his mother resting easy in her grave.

She started to talk to him now, whispering out of the dune grass, shaping the pale night breeze into words of encouragement and praise. He walked up the beach, past sleeping houses towards Eel Point Road, speaking softly, answering her questions, making his plans.

The night before the Daffodil Day festival, Amy Elwell was watching television at a friend's house. Actually, Julie Ananthan was more of an acquaintance than a friend. But by some fluke they had wound up taking every class together. The first week of the semester had been a series of small surprises that became alarming and then finally comical. That girl again!, they both thought at each new encounter. What's going on? Is she stalking me? When they realized it was nothing more than a preposterous coincidence of interests and requirements, they relaxed and got to know each other. Julie soon showed evidence of numerous annoying beliefs—she was passionate about both astrology and Scientology; she was sure that fate had led them together and certain they had known each other in a previous life. Amy was agnostic about most things, including fate and reincarnation, and largely ignorant on the subject of Scientology.

But astrology really annoyed her.

She refused to disclose her sign or her birthday, and watched with great amusement as Julie guessed wrong over and over again. Finally she told the plump red-head that she was a Libra, which she wasn't. Then the second act of the comedy began: she learned in passionate detail that she was a "typical " Libra in every way. Amy even produced a time of birth on request—a total guess, she had no idea what time of day she was born. Julie made her quite a beautiful chart, full of planets in other planet's houses and things in retrograde. It was sweet and thoughtful; intricately stupid and impossibly dull.

Julie had redeemed herself in various ways, though. When it became clear that Amy was dating the President's son, she had been one of the few people whose behavior didn't change. She didn't want anything and she wasn't impressed. She wasn't much interested in politics anyway and had never voted. Though that itself was kind of annoying, it had helped turn her little apartment on Bleecker Street into a haven for Amy. They had spent many evenings studying there (Julie was startlingly smart for someone with so many woolly-headed beliefs), eating John's Pizza or KFC, then watching videos. Julie was a connoisseur of junk food, and Amy had started to gain weight. After that it was strictly bring your own hummus. But she remembered those nights fondly.

Julie's apartment was the perfect place to wind up after a day that had included another grating interview with Heller and a tense lunch with Miguel Osona at his favorite health food restaurant in the West Village. Her emotions towards the doctor were too scrambled to deal with. It was like the salad she had ordered at lunch with him. It had arrived at the table with big cucumbers and wheels of tomato and spikes of celery ticking out among the flower-cut radishes and mescal greens and endive, the arugula, the basil and the raddichio. The four colors of julienned peppers; the shaved Brussels sprouts. The asparagus and the artichoke hearts. It was like some evil carnival turned into vegetables by a mad wizard. She was weary and sad and didn't even know where to begin eating it. She wound up sending it back and all she could say to the waiter was "Sorry, it's just too . . . complicated for me tonight."

She wanted to push Osona away, too. She was furious at him for betraying Tom, and glad he had done it since Tom actually was crazy, and disappointed in him for not realizing that sooner. She was grateful that he had helped Tom escape, and afraid of the things he knew that could still hurt Tom if Heller debriefed him. She knew Tom needed to be caught but hated Osona for helping to catch him. She felt guilty for his injuries—if she had seen the truth of Tom's illness she never would have agreed to visit the doctor, she would have done something, turned Tom in or, called the police, or . . . what? There was really nothing she could have done and she knew it. But the guilt persisted. She was worried about Osona, too, and it was good to see that he was able to joke about his new nose making him more dashing and attractive. He said he was sorry, and Amy didn't even know what he was apologizing for. Maybe for everything: that the world sucked and there was nothing he could do to fix it.

So Julie Anathan's apartment was the perfect place to end the day. They were eating Chinese food with the TV on and the sound off, talking about Julie's parents (They were getting divorced after thirty years of marriage), when Amy saw Barbara Walters in the rose garden of the White House, interviewing the President.

"So it's like my whole life has been a lie," Julie was saying.

Amy grabbed the remote.

"Hold it," she said. "I have to see this."

"What—?"

"—Frankly, Barbara, I'm hoping I can use this most recent tragedy in my life to come to some good purpose. If I can take the 'bully pulpit' of the Presidency to alert other Americans about the dangers of Schizophrenia . . . if even one parent gets their child the help he or she needs before it's too late . . . then I'll feel that all of this sorrow hasn't been in vain."

He was on his knees, weeding the area around the rose beds. He picked up his pruning shears. Barbara stepped closer.

"I have to ask this next question, Mr. President. I think so many Americans are wondering how do you keep yourself going? You've lost so much."

"Well, this little patch of ground means a lot to me."

"It's lovely."

"But also . . . working with my hands. Doing simple things. That's what keeps me going. That and Mozart. I guess you might say . . . I whistle while I work."

"You're not just whistling Mozart's fortieth," Amy said softly.

"Amy . . .?"

"Shhhhh."

"Could we eavesdrop? It would be an honor to share a private moment with such a public man."

"Well . . . all right, I suppose. Though it's nothing special."

Amy sat forward. The President started working, whistling the violin part from the first movement of the Symphonia Concertante. It stung her for a moment; how much her life had changed. She hadn't touched her violin in months.

Then she started really listening.

Later on Julie Anathan would use one word to describe what happened next: terrifying. It was like watching a seizure. A friend of Julie's had died on the beach in Florida two years ago at least partly because Julie didn't know CPR. All she could do was watch. It was the same way now and though she had learned CPR since that horrible day, it didn't do her any good on this occasion. She didn't even understand what was happening.

Amy sat up sharply, staring at the screen wild-eyed.

"Oh my God," she said. "I have to help him."

She was already jack-knifing out of her chair, running, half-stumbling toward the hall closet, when Julie managed to speak. The helplessness closed her throat.

"Amy—what are you talking about?" she finally gasped. "You—he . . . you can't help him! He has the *Secret Service* to help him! He has the . . . the police and the army to help him, and . . . You don't—Amy!"

But Amy was already gone, and the door was slamming behind her.

31

Jake Gritzky lived in an underground bunker. He had built it himself, deep in the scrub pine forest between Tom Nevers and the old 'Sconset dump. He dug it out over three nights, fortified the walls with plywood stolen from job sites, paved it with granite flagstones that held the heat from his small wood stove in the winter and stayed cool in the summer. He had enlarged it over the years. It was three small rooms now, all with hand-made teak-wood fold away beds. He had an electric generator and a sky-light that he could conceal from inside with a roll away carpet of turf and weeds and twigs. The only visible sign that the place existed was a chimney that broke the surface among a tangle of roots, twenty feet away. Jake had fuel and food stores for a month, weapons and ammunition for a siege. He was ready—some said he was even eager—for any national catastrophe, and he hadn't been able to conceal his disappointment when the Y2K breakdown had fizzled on him.

But even in peaceful, ordinary conditions, it was a good snug eccentric and most of all free place to live on an island with the highest real estate values per square foot on the Eastern seaboard. Set into the earth, the bunker was naturally insulated and out of the wind. He often thought of the snobs with their thirty-five hundred dollar mortgages and thousand dollar heating bills in their gale-battered houses wobbling on the eroding beaches, and smiled. Jake liked beating the system . . . especially this system, the toxic capitalism which was over-developing and ruining one of the few places on earth that he still loved.

Only two other people had ever seen the inside of his little fortress. One was a woman. That was a long time ago.

The other was Tom Jaglom.

Tom had only been there once and Jake was starting to worry that he wasn't going to be able to find it again. He was already an hour late. There was nothing Jake could do. He was helpless and he often felt that way with Tom, whether the kid was confronting his Dad, going out on a date or taking his SATs.

Jake had learned the quiet art of stepping aside, of withholding advice that wouldn't be taken. That detachment served him well this morning: he had trained Tom rigorously, but he knew that getting here was going to take more than training and skill. Inspiration was required; and that couldn't be taught.

Jake was meditating half an hour later, when he heard Tom open the trap door. He rose smoothly to his feet on a long exhale, with his legs still crossed at the ankle. He checked the clock and shrugged. It was all right—he built delays into all his plans. They could still make it. They'd just have to move a little faster.

"You're late," he said, giving the boy a bear hug as he stepped into the main room of the bunker.

"Ninety three minutes. Things got complicated."

"They always do. You scared?"

"What do you think?"

Jake grinned. "Hey—there's always plan B."

"I know," Tom said. "That's what scares me."

Amy just missed the last direct flight out of Newark for Nantucket, and she got into Logan ten minutes too late for the last trip from Boston. It was infuriating—it wasn't even nine o'clock. She thought of renting a car and driving to Hyannis, but the airport there would be closed down already and the first ferry in the morning didn't reach Nantucket until ten thirty—which might very well be too late.

She booked herself onto the first flight in the morning and checked into the airport Hilton, hoping she could use the time and get a good night's sleep. But it was hopeless. She was wide awake through *Tonight* and *Late Night* and *Later.* She would have gladly watched *Way Too Late* and *For God's Sake Go to Sleep You Insomniac Freak* if they had been available, if anyone cared to push another set of cocky hosts, ironic side-kicks and self-involved guests that much further towards dawn.

Finally, though, she had to simply lie in the dark and think.

Her plan was nuts, she knew that. She wasn't up to it. She was scared. She had no confidence, much less the arrogance she needed. She felt futile and puny. But she had two facts to hold onto: she was doing the right thing . . . and there was no one in the world who could do it but her. There was a kind of strength in that fatalism: she would do these extraordinary things because she had no choice.

Because she knew now that Tom was right.

She had the proof. Yes he was insane, she had seen the proof of that also and it had been one of the worst moments of her life, like the floorboards giving way under her, and everything she believed in collapsing under her own weight, gravity yanking her down into the dark. But she had survived the fall.

Because Tom was right.

He was crazy, but maybe it took someone crazy to see the truth and get the job done. She thought of something he had told her once—it was a quote from Henry Kissinger. Someone asked the Secretary of State why he trusted Nixon's judgment of people—since the President was so obviously paranoid. And Kissinger had replied, "Even paranoids have real enemies."

She should have remembered that when Heller was questioning her. But she had been rattled and confused; she'd been trying to help. She had told him everything she knew, including the location of the secret passageway from the boat house to the main residence on the Madequecham compound. She had thought Tom might use it to penetrate the estate's security. She couldn't have imagined at the time that she was going to be using it herself. There would be guards posted there now. But once again, it didn't change anything. She still had to try it because there was nothing else she could try, no other way she could break into the Presidential mansion.

She rolled over and doubled the flimsy pillow under her head. It was three in the morning. She had to sleep somehow. She thought back to the night before, to the Barbara Walters interview. She played it in her head. Was she absolutely sure? Everything depended on a few seconds from a television program she had only watched by accident.

She pulled the covers up to her chin.

It was true. The President was a fake. And that meant everything else was true also, everything was real—Jim Gramble's article, Dominick Nosiglia's conspiracy, Heller's betrayal . . . all of it. Tom's mission was real and it was her mission too.

She thought of that line from an old James Taylor song her Dad loved so much: "All I've got to do is the best I can. If I can."

Well, she could. And she was going to. And that was all
the resolution she needed, at least for tonight.

She was asleep a few moments later.

It was a standing joke on Nantucket that Daffodil Day—
which was meant to celebrate the coming of Spring—was
inevitably cold and rainy. It amused old timers that the tourists the bogus holiday lured to the island got to stand
around in the icy drizzle looking at the same set of antique cars every year and eating damp sandwiches. This
year was better than most—at least it wasn't raining. But it
was chilly: somewhere between forty and forty five degrees,
with a scalpel-edged wind slicing off the Atlantic. And it
was more crowded than ever, with everyone hoping for a
glimpse of the President.

Every car on every ferry had been thoroughly searched,
except one. Ira Heller was on duty at the Steamship wharf
when the black Cadillac stretch limousine rolled off the
Eagle. One of his people, an officious little turd named
Ingalls, was hassling the driver when Heller walked up to
them.

"One more time," Ingalls was saying. "I need everyone out of the car now. I want to see picture IDs and I want
that trunk popped pronto."

"Listen—" the driver began.

"No. You listen. You're holding up the line, obstruct-
ing the Secret Service and interfering with Presidential
security. So just—"

"Ingalls."

The little agent turned and found himself looking up
at Ira Heller.

"Yes, sir?"

"Leave this car alone."

"But—"

"Do you have any idea who's in there?"

"No, sir—"

"Good. Now apologize to the driver and get back to work."

Ingalls stared at his boss in disbelief. Heller lifted his eyebrows and inclined his head slightly, as if to say "I'm waiting." Ingalls was furious. He had joined the police and later the Secret Service to intimidate people not suck up to them. On the other hand, he was expert at sucking up to Heller. He bowed his head.

"Yes, sir." He leaned down to the car window. "Sorry to bother you sir. You're free to go."

The driver gave him a sarcastic salute and pulled away.

The limo almost ran over Amy Elwell a few seconds later. She was coming out of The Upper Deck with a shopping bag in her hands, so focused on the job on hand that she was paying no attention to her immediate surroundings. The screech of brakes woke her up. She jumped back just as the big car surged forward again. She stared after the massive limo. There was a kind of malignancy about it, something smooth and predatory, like a shark in shallow water. She watched until it turned onto South Water Street.

She almost ran after it. But that was a ludicrous idea. She hated movies where guys chased cars on foot. And even if she caught up with it, what was she going to do? She forced herself to concentrate. She had an actual task to carry out.

She had purchased a full wet suit with hood and booties along with a skateboard deck. A few questions about the south shore cross rip had put the last piece of her plan together. All she had to do was swim out a hundred feet or so, somewhere around Tom Nevers and then let the current carry her east towards Madequecham. The skateboard deck was the best she could manage for a weapon on short notice. She was not going to raid that beach unarmed. She hefted the oblong of hardwood, shrugged. Swung hard enough, it could do some damage.

All she had to do now was get a cab out to the old naval base at Tom Nevers. She shivered. She didn't know whether it was the damp, wintry air (She wasn't dressed for it), or the thought of the frigid Atlantic. Most likely it was the even colder thought of what she was going to do when she finally climbed out of the water. The truth made her shudder again. Her teeth were actually chattering. She opened her mouth a little and let them vibrate in silence. She thought of that limousine. It was an omen. It was a vision of death. She was going to kill today, or be killed herself.

Or both.

Five miles away, Tom was sitting on a branch twenty feet up a tree, in a dense stand of old growth pine beside the Milestone Road. He was wearing Jake Gritzky's camouflage fatigues, virtually invisible from below as long as he made no sudden movements. He loaded a last round into the Winchester and checked the sight again. He recalibrated it a degree or two, pleased with his position and the angle of fire down into the road. He checked his watch. The parade would be starting in a few minutes. The trick was to concentrate on breathing, to not imagine the coming scene, to not anticipate. It was like playing music, the way Amy described playing the violin. First you trained your fingers; then you let them do the work. You couldn't think about the up-coming b-minor arpeggio; the part of your brain you used for thinking was useless. Those notes were lodged in the muscle memory of your hands or they were nowhere. It was the same with a jazz solo—you didn't devise the melody, you just let it happen.

Like this killing: it would be bungled . . . or it would be too swift for thought.

So he forced himself to stop thinking. He emptied his lungs, forced the last milligrams of oxygen out. Then breathed in slowly, for a count of five, pulling hard at the end to fill his lungs totally. Then out again; then in.

He was perfectly calm when he heard the first motors approaching.

Heller was in the President Jensen Healy with three agents, including Duane Claassen, who seemed fully recovered from his last encounter with Tom—there was just a little residual bruising under the eyes. There were two police cruisers ahead of them, a pair of motorcycle cops flanking them, and the whole parade lined up behind them, cars painted yellow and festooned with daffodils, matching the flower beds by the side of the road. Claassen was silently checking the thin, wind-scraped forest on either side of the street. Heller was shouting into a cellphone.

"I want you in the air at all times! I want the compound air space sealed! Goddamn right, both Apaches! They're not lawn ornaments, Hansen! I don't care what the Coast Guard has! Some shit box Sikorsky. You can fly rings around them in an Apache. No! Absolutely not. I don't care. These orders come directly from the President. You want to talk to him? He's sitting right next to me. Good. That's what I like to hear. Now get moving."

He slapped the phone closed.

"Fucking idiot. Pardon my language. I deal with fucking idiots all day long. I swear to God it's making me stupid, now. This shit is contagious. Am I right, Duane?"

Duane never took his eyes from the trees. "Yes, sir," he said.

They drove on in silence. Behind them people honking their horns, shouting to each other. The last of the clouds had blown away and the day was brilliant with glacial sunlight. Heller pulled on his North Face parka, happy he'd brought along a thermos of coffee. But he'd been through Daffodil day before—by now he knew what to expect.

The two police cars passed Tom's position and he settled the rifle against a branch, aiming down into the road, waiting for his shot.

He got it thirty seconds later.

The impostor's head was caught perfectly in the cross-hairs: the shot would take him in the left temple and blow his head apart. Like hitting a pomegranate with a sledge-hammer. Tom tracked the car, finger resting on the trigger and starting to squeeze.

The sun caught the swiveling rifle barrel and Duane Claassen saw the glint of light, high in the trees. He threw himself at the President at the exact moment Tom pulled the trigger. The shot slammed into and through the passenger side door, whining against the asphalt.

A second later, Claassen was up, shouting and pointing. "He's in the trees! Right there! Move it! Flank him!"

Heller was hustling the President out of the car, getting him down safe on the other side of the Jensen Healy. Behind them the parade had turned into chaos. Cars were slewed across the road, people were screaming, pouring into the street, running back towards town, or into the trees for protection. Heller didn't have the time—or the man-power—for crowd control. They didn't matter. Nothing mattered but catching Tom.

One of the agents had already run into the trees. Tom had half-climbed, half fallen from the big tree. He was on his feet when the agent crashed through the brush at him. Tom swung the rifle up like a golf club. The crack was so loud Tom thought he'd broken the Winchester's stock—then the agent was sprawled senseless in the pine needles. Tom jumped his body, angling towards the car. Claassen was clambering out when he saw a blur of motion—the butt of the rifle. It crashed into his head and Claassen crumpled into the back seat, unconscious.

Tom jumped into the driver's seat and gunned the engine. He had learned how to drive in this car—he knew how to make it fly. He revved it high and then let out the clutch in second gear. The big car actually leapt forward as two shots shattered the windshield. A third one nicked his ear. One of the motorcycle cops was right behind him, firing wild. The other one was right beside him, shouting. Tom swerved into him. The big Harley skidded off the road and Tom slammed on the brakes. The other cycle rear-ended the Jensen and the cop was catapulted over the car and onto the hood. For a second he looked like the absurd center piece of the flower arrangement. He was too stunned to hold on and as he fell to the road, Tom floored the gas pedal.

He thought he was in the clear; then Claassen woke up.

The big agent was groggy but still strong enough to grab Tom around the neck. Tom braked again and the Jensen swerved into a road swallowing skid. It only broke Claassen's grip for a second, but that was all Tom needed. He dove out of the side door and hit the street in a tight roll. In a second he was on his feet and sprinting for the trees. There was a cacophony of sirens and car engines, screams and gun shots. He didn't look back. Bullets chipped the trees around him as he plunged into the forest on the south side of Milestone Road. He was less than a mile from Jake's bunker. He just had to keep a straight line and leave as little evidence of his passage as he could. Blundering through the overgrowth would lead searchers to Jake. So he moved carefully, assessing his injuries. They were slight—bruises around the neck, and from the dive to the pavement. Scrapes and scratches from the tree. His ear had stopped bleeding, but there was glass in his forehead and his cheek—bits of the shattered windshield. The sounds of the road were diminishing behind him. He slowed to a walk. Even jogging through this tangle of undergrowth could result in a mishap and something as ordinary as a turned ankle or a sprained wrist could ruin his last hope for success. It was a bizarre and terrifying thought: one careless step could change forever the fate of his country.

Everything depended on him, now. He had to take care of himself.

"Give me some good news," growled Ira Heller. He was standing with the Nantucket police chief, Dave Holdgate, who looked awkward and ill-at-ease. He was used to dealing with stolen cookies from the Bake Shop, the occasional drunk driver or drunken brawl at the Chicken Box. This was way out of his league and he knew it.

"It's an island, right?" Heller was going on. "There's nowhere he can go."

"Well . . . that's a tough call, sir. That kid knows the island pretty well. Once he's in the scrub forest around the old dump, he going to be almost impossible to find."

Heller was losing it. "He's running in the goddamn bushes! What's the problem? We don't have to track him. We have two Air Force Apache helicopters up there."

"Yeah, well . . . it's like a jungle, sir. You can't see into that stuff from above. Especially now, with the leaves coming out."

"So we've lost him?"

"No, no . . . but we're going to have to start beating the bushes. Some of my men know the island even better than Tom does. But all the helicopters in the world aint gonna do squat."

"Then what are you waiting for? Get them out there! He's already got a fifteen minute head-start."

"Yes, sir. Right away sir."

Heller turned away in disgust, "Idiots," he said under his breath. "I guess stupidity isn't contagious after all. If it was I'd be doing finger paintings with my food by now."

At seven in the evening, Jake decided it was time to awaken his protégé. Tom had arrived at the bunker just before noon, cut and dirty with twigs and pine needles in his hair, looking wild eyed and physically strung out and almost as crazy as the radio and the newspapers said he was. He told Jake what had happened. He was clear and lucid, despite his appearance. The plan had gotten fucked up, but the kid had handled himself well. Plans generally got fucked up; how you handled it was what counted.

Jake gave Tom a bowl of the beef stew had had going on the wood stove, a cup of herb tea and a handful of pain-killers. He made Tom get into bed and the kid literally fell asleep in the middle of a sentence. It exactly what he needed. If he went without sleep for too much longer he'd be useless, to himself and everyone else. He had been running on sheer adrenaline for more than forty-eight hours.

So Jake sat in the next room all afternoon, while Tom slept, drinking the occasional cup of coffee and reading *The Book of Dignity*, a brilliant treatise on martial art by an obscure tactician named Karasuma Kantaro. He read one last paragraph before he closed the little book:

Most modern factory issue weapons are serviceable. It is a matter of technique as to whether the weapon is adequate to the solution of a given problem; that is to say, a matter of the ability of the technician to select the appropriate tool and utilize it effectively. This is true of the whole range of logistical apparatus. If the fire arm tends to heat up rapidly, fire it more slowly; do the job with fewer rounds. If the sight is not calibrated for five hundred yards, get closer. If the slide is not cycling, clean it. If the tool cannot be used effectively despite its proven capability, it is the technician, and not the tool, that needs work. This is true of every sort of weapon, from the modern electric gattling gun to the jawbone of an ass.

To the point, and on the money—as usual.

Jake set the paperback aside, thinking back to Viet Nam; all the ludicrous equipment failures that paralyzed missions and set intricate strategies awry. Almost no one was able to think beyond the immediate situation, to conjure an alternative even as the first plan was falling apart. They wanted to take it up with a committee. But the committee was back at Alpha base in Da'Nang, forty klicks away.

They wanted to run it by the lieutenant. But the lieutenant was dead. So they died too.

Was that why he had survived? Jake wondered. Because he was smart enough to make things up as he went along and tough enough to follow through? Or was it because he backed off at crucial moments, kept moving ahead when he should have gone back, or taken another pass a hundred feet lower, despite the anti-aircraft fire?

He didn't have to ask the questions. He knew the answers—he should have done more.

And if he had died? Then he would have died with his friends, *for* his friends, instead of living with this soul-shriveling disgrace. That was the real post-traumatic stress syndrome: the humiliation of living on because you weren't enough of a soldier; knowing that you failed, that you couldn't embrace death in those few vital split-seconds of decision when you needed to most.

Those were the seconds you lived with forever, the flashes of truth that made all the medals and ribbons into a mockery and a joke.

He had gotten rid of all his military awards—sold them to collectors. They were like cheap costume jewelry to him.

The only medal he wanted was a posthumous one.

And there wasn't much chance of that.

He walked to the set sink and poured out the last of his last cup of coffee. He glanced around the bunker. You could easily mistake it for a prison cell. That was what the VA shrink had told him—that he had had constructed his own jail. But he was content with that. He was content to do his time. And especially so today. Despite the stress and tension all around him (twice teams of searchers had tramped over his head, calling out to each other; the island had imposed a curfew and was virtually in a state of war), Jake felt good. This little cave he had built for himself was like an oasis of calm today in the military chaos of Nantucket. To sit reading while the boy who was the closest thing to the son he would never have slumbered in the next room was an education for him. He had always assumed happiness required romance and money and travel, success and vindication. All the bells and whistles. He had never imagined that it could be so simple, or so plain.

He ducked into the smaller adjoining chamber and shook Tom's shoulder gently.

"Time to go," he said. "It's getting late."

Across the island, Amy was wading into the icy Atlantic. The currents were strong but the surf was small, and she was grateful for that. She didn't want to fight heavy breakers. She needed to conserve her strength. Being in the ocean at night scared her anyway, and the last light was just smoldering above the trees inland. She shrugged; a night approach to the beach at Madequecham had always been intrinsic to her plan—she needed every edge she could get against the guards who would be posted at the boathouse. It was overcast, clouds had been rolling in since late afternoon. That was a lucky break—a black wet suit against a dark beach on a starless night would be hard to see.

She was in up to her chest now. It was strange to feel the weight of the water against her, but not the coldness of it. Then a small wave broke in front of her. White water churned over her bare face, knocking her backward. She was underwater for only a few seconds but she was gasping when she freed herself from the dense foam. The sudden touch of frigid water on her cheeks and forehead seemed to collapse her chest. She was paralyzed for a second or two. She thought her heart had stopped. Then she started swimming and soon she was beyond the breakers. But she felt like she had fallen face-first into a snowbank. The owner of the Upper Deck had warned her about "ice cream headaches". Now she knew what he meant.

She found that her skateboard deck, her humble weapon, also served as a flotation device. She held onto it lightly, braced herself as icy salt water flooded through her suit and then warmed against her skin. All she had to do now was keep her eyes on the coast and hope she could recognize the lights of the Presidential compound. The main house was one of the biggest on the island, with a cupola on the peak that would serve as a beacon. She studied the other mansions drifting by, and let the current carry her west.

32

They were almost at the road when the cop car passed by, shining its search-light into the trees. They pressed themselves against a pair of big pines. They were motionless, dressed in black with charcoal-smeared faces. They didn't even breathe. The cop slowed down, then stopped.

Jake glanced across at Tom, gave him a flat palm gesture that meant prepare to attack. Tom had two Army Ranger-issue combat knives, one in each hand. Jake had his Officer's edition Colt 45 ACP with the best sound suppresser his extensive military connections could procure. He also had fifty feet of heavy gauge rope coiled around his shoulder and across his chest, slowing him down.

The cop was getting out of the car.

But he turned the other way. There was a pair of guards at the airport perimeter fence, obviously locals also. They were just talking. Wait—they were handing something off. Cups of coffee. Tom let out a long slow breath and relaxed. Jake's gun was by his side again. But still the glare of light stabbed into the forest, directly at them.

Finally the car moved away.

That made the timing perfect. No one would be check-ing in with these guards again for a while. Tom put the knives away. He wouldn't be needing them; with the pa-trol car gone, this was a routine attack.

They came out of the trees crouched low, from oppo-site sides, closing a circle. Tom took his man out from the front, just as he was taking a sip of his coffee—a single strike to the head. The other cop started to cry out, but Jake rose behind him. There was a dull thud and he slumped to the ground.

Tom picked up the paper cups and dragged the two bodies out of sight while Jake cut through the chain-link fence.

The big Coast Guard Sikorsky was only fifty feet away but the pilot had heard nothing over the mutter of the wind. Jake studied him for a moment. He was smoking a cigarette, bored and restless, in the state of oblivion that Karasuma Katana referred to as 'Condition White.' He was surrounded by rings of guards and patrols, far removed from the action which had in any case come to an appar-ent halt. The Secret Service and the FBI treated the Coast Guard with dismissive contempt. No one expected him to do anything tonight but put in his time.

So it seemed safe to relax; a dangerous illusion. Jake thought of a quotation from the first Shogun of Japan, Tokegawa Ieyasu, cited somewhere in *The Book of Dignity*. "After a victory, tighten the cords of your helmet."

The pilot, one David Cranepool, learned that lesson the hard way a few seconds later. He was crushing his ciga-rette against the side of the helicopter when he felt Tom Jaglom's knife at his throat. Tom whispered in his ear:

"Don't move. Don't say a word."

"Get him into the chopper," Jake said.

"Are we going to kill him?"

"Hell no—we need him." Jake turned to the pilot. "Take it easy son. No one is going to kill anyone and nobody has to get hurt. Just punch in your security code and get me on freak—now."

They climbed into the chopper and Cranepool did what he was told. It took him two tries because his hand was shaking.

"Calm down," Jake said. "Slow and easy."

Jake started the engines as the pilot typed in the security code and tuned to radio to the proper military frequency.

"Thanks, kid. You did good," Jake said with a warm, friendly smile. Then he clipped the boy with his elbow. They eased him out of the seat and lay him down on the grass. Tom was staring down at the prostrate figure. Jake read the anxiety on his face. "Don't worry. He'll be out for ten minutes anyway. And that's all the time we need."

Tom nodded and they swung back into the cockpit. As they lifted off, Jake picked up the microphone.

"Request permission for Coast Guard recon. patrol. Over."

"We got two Apaches up there friend. Just stay out of compound air space. Over."

"Yes sir. Over and out."

They were banking out over the dark ocean now. Jake's face was unreadable in the dim light from the instrument panel.

"Those Apaches are serious shit," Tom said. "They have simultaneous target attack, infra-red night sight, full shrouding . . . you name it. They come after us it'll be like trying to outrun a Porsche in a go-cart. We can't fight them."

"We're not trying to. The best we can do is fool 'em. And hope we fool 'em long enough."

"Are you sure about this?"

"Are you kidding? I've been waiting for this since 1968. Now get that rope ready."

Tom secured it to one of the support bars. They were heading inland again, dropping lower and curving east. "Tell me about how well this plan worked," he said.

Jake grinned. "It was a night raid on Hanoi. We had to fly low to stay under the radar so a standard jump was out. A ground attack was pointless, same as here. The brass were stumped. So they went all the way down the line to the crazy-ass, gung-ho, shit-kicking grunts—see if they had any ideas. And we did—ten dumb-ass ideas and one good one. The brass picked right for once. Plan went off smooth as a field dress parade. And the kids dangling from those ropes had a hell of a lot less training than you do."

The radio crackled to life before Tom could answer.

"Coast Guard 206 Bravo, you are approaching compound airspace. This is restricted airspace. Over."

"We'll be heading out to sea momentarily. Everything all right down there?"

"So far so good. Hell of a day though."

"Yeah. We're headed out now. Over."

Jake turned off the radio. "I don't think we're gonna want to hear what they have to say next. Get ready, kid." Tom pulled on Jake's leather gloves.

The compound was coming into view. So was one of the Apaches. Jake dropped down to fifty feet above the ground "Now," he barked.

Tom plunged from the cockpit into the battering wind and the whipping noise of the rotors. There were a few seconds of stomach-lifting free fall and then the rope brought him up short. Swinging wildly under the big chopper, he almost lost his grip. The house was rocketing towards him.

Jake dropped even lower—too low. Tom was going to slam into the roof. He screamed but his voice was lost in the howl of machinery. The Apache was less than fifty yards away, vectoring in from the east. Tom braced to hit the building.

Jake pulled up, the roof blurred under him and Tom let go of the rope. He was over the widow's walk; he dropped ten feet and hit the deck dead center, but rolling out of the fall, his shoulder hit the railing and splintered two of the wooden spindles. He looked up. Jake was already turning hard, out to sea and away from the compound.

Tom straightened himself out, dazed and winded. There were splinters in his hands. His arm was bleeding. Before he could move the flood light from the Apache hit him. It was as bright as day in that little circle. He shielded his eyes.

The amplified voice rocked him backward: "PUT YOUR HANDS ON YOUR HEAD AND THROW DOWN YOUR WEAPONS."

The Apache's co-pilot was watching the cumbersome Sikorsky's attempts at evasive action as it pushed to escape. Nice try, fella. But you're finished. He picked up the radio and got the other Apache on the box. It was hardly necessary though. They had done this drill a thousand times. It was like hunting deer with an Uzi.

"He's headed northwest. Intercept at will. We'll take care of the intruder."

The big sleek helicopter was hovering twenty feet over the roof. Tom was struggling to get the trap door open. There was a warning salvo from the helicopter. Big bullets ripped through the decking and splintered a section of the rail. He jumped to his feet, hands up. They had the fire power to shred him—and the house itself—if they wanted to.

'THROW DOWN YOUR WEAPONS! YOU HAVE TEN SECONDS TO COMPLY. TEN—NINE—EIGHT . . ."

Jake saw the other chopper cutting off his escape. There was no way to slip past them; no way to out-run them. He would be obliterated in a fire-fight.

It was over. Jake smiled.

His moment had come at last.

"Okay, kid," he said quietly. "Let's finish it."

He cranked the Sikorsky around, back towards the house.

"SEVEN—SIX—FIVE—"

The pilot saw Jake approaching in the mirror. For a moment he just froze.

"Mike—look—What the hell is he—? Oh my God, look at that—Jesus Christ—!"

The co-pilot turned. The Sikorsky was almost on top of them. He flinched backward, screaming, covering his face, as if that would help. He had no time to use any of the big machine's sophisticated security systems, no time to save himself, no time even to pray.

The last thing he ever saw was the joyous grin of victory on Jake Gritzky's face.

Then the two helicopters collided in a deafening fireball. Every window on that side of the house shattered as the tangle of burning twisted metal pin-wheeled to the ground. Tom was flat on the deck. The shock wave stomped him like a giant foot and he could feel his shirt and his hair catch fire. He rolled over, squirmed frantically and managed put out his flaming jacket. He pulled it over his head, using it to snuff out his blazing hair.

He stood for a second in the stink of scorched metal and smoking diesel fuel, and raised a fist in salute to Jake Gritzky. Tom was in tears, shaking from the blast and the fire but most of all from Jake's sacrifice, from the beautiful, appalling gesture his friend had just made.

It was selfish, too, Tom knew that—Jake had wanted this, needed this for years. He had finally done it. He had changed his own destiny, and everyone else's, too. He had saved them all. And he had cleared the way for Tom, passed the torch to his student. As Jim Gramble had, by digging out the truth and trying to tell it—as his father had, too, by repudiating Dominick Nosiglia and his own crazy ambitions, by changing sides, by finally standing up for what was right, even if it killed him.

And it had—the truth had killed all of them. Only Tom was left.

He grappled the trap door open and plunged down into the house. It was up to him, now.

It was time to end it.

A hundred yards away, Amy Elwell was wading out of the Atlantic. The two guards posted in the dune grass beside the boat house were transfixed by the ghoulish fireworks of the crashing helicopters. The distraction was only going to last for a few more seconds.

She fixed her grip on the skateboard deck and ran up behind the first of the guards, arms over head in a back swing. She brought it down hard once, then again. As the first guard fell, the second one turned to her. She swung up hard from below and caught him full in the face. He folded into a heap like a silk jacket tipped off its hanger. She grabbed his gun, dropped the skateboard and ran for the boathouse door.

If she had been more experienced, she would have known that one off-balance blow to the head delivered by a hundred and sixteen pound girl was not going to knock out a well-trained two hundred pound man. But her whole exposure to violence had been the movies, in which it was commonplace to see–for instance—a fifteen year old gymnast drop kick a velociraptor out a second story window.

So she didn't give the prostrate Secret Service agent another thought.

The agent, his name was Rick Antonowsky, watched her disappear into the little shack, grabbed his partner's gun, got to his feet and followed her.

When the helicopters crashed into the raked shell driveway they sent a small avalanche of burning debris at the cars parked there. A Jeep was crushed by the impact, and two other vehicles were set ablaze. The debris swept into and under several other cars including the black limousine that Amy had seen earlier in the day. It was badly scratched, and one window was blown out. But the significant damage was invisible. A bouncing sliver of the Sikorsky's rotor punctured its gas tank. The fires burned all around the big Cadillac; but none of them were close enough to ignite the growing puddle on the ground below it.

Inside, Tom was flying down the widow's walk stairs. There were three guards in the hall. He threw himself off the stairs, throwing both knives at once. One went wild, but the other buried itself to the hilt in a guard's throat. Tom torpedoed at the other two, knocking a gun aside, bringing the point of his elbow down behind the man's ear and felt him go limp, finger still on the trigger. The other guard was about to shoot. There was no time to grab the gun. Tom swiveled the limp arm, around and yanked the nerveless finger. The Glock must have been adapted for automatic fire: eight shots sent the guard reeling and twitching backward before Tom could release the weapon.

He stood up to see a bulky man in a dark suit coming out of his father's office. The man's face was pock-marked with old acne-scars. He smiled, sinister and charming. Time seemed to stop. They were alone in the corridor, though more guards were approaching from below.

"Tom Jaglom," he said. "You look just like your old man. It's all in the genes."He had a gun in his hand, a snub nosed .38.

"The sins of the fathers shall be visited on their sons. That's what it says in the Bible, Tom. You ever read the Bible?"

Tom couldn't speak. He had finally realized who he was looking at.

"No? Too bad. Most people like a little religion at a time like this."

But just as he pulled the trigger another man barged out of the office, bumping into him, saying "I got the stuff—let's go!"

The shot missed. It was echoing in the narrow hallway as Tom lunged forward.

But someone grabbed him from behind. There were more guards charging into the hall from downstairs. Tom kicked backward viciously. Someone screamed and fell. The big man and his accomplice were gone. The office door was open. Tom twisted behind him, grabbed a gun from the man who had tackled him and lurched into the office.

He took in the scene with one shutter-click flash of perception: two Secret Service guys, Heller and the impostor. The goons behind the desk, both armed; the impostor sitting down. A gun on the blotter. Heller in the corner. Everyone going for their weapons. Tom shot one of the Secret Service guys. Three more shots from the automatic Glock (Tom had time to think, no wonder these things are illegal)—and the guy was catapulted into the billowing curtains and through the blast shattered window.

"Drop it."

Tom spun around.

Heller had a big Heckler & Koch leveled at him. Tom swung the Glock around at the impostor.

"No way," he said.

"Listen to me, kid. The plan is working. Can't you see that? Things are good. Things are better than they've ever been. Your Dad was a genius. He just didn't have the guts to finish what he started. You blow the lid off this now . . . think about your father. His reputation. His place in history. He'll be disgraced. Do you want that?"

The door started to open. Tom kicked it shut and locked it, his gun still aimed at the man behind the desk, who looked so much like his father.

It was all he could do not to pull the trigger.

Downstairs, two bulky figures dashed from the house into the gruesome chiaroscuro of the fire-lit driveway. They climbed into the battered limousine and gunned the engine. There were guards in front of the house now, but no one tried to stop them from leaving.

Edward Bellamy Jaglom's office was strangely silent in the pandemonium of the Presidential compound, the shouts and sirens and the roar of the fires. Tom thought— this is what it must be like in the eye of a hurricane. The weird glassy stillness among the ruins, waiting for the next storm wall to take down whatever was still standing.

"No one comes in until we're finished," he said. "Talk to me, Ira. Bullshit time is over."

"I'm not sure what—?"

"How did they do it?"

"What exactly do you—?"

"The mob, Ira. How did they pull it off? How did you sabotage Air Force One? It's the best guarded plane in the Western Hemisphere. How do you replace the President of the United States with an impostor? How did they *do* it?"

Someone was trying to force the lock.

"A bullet from this gun will go right through the door, Ira. And I don't care who it hits. I'm crazy, remember? So back them off."

"We're all right," Heller shouted. "Stand away."

Tom stared at him. "Now talk."

"All right . . . there are three redundant hydraulic systems on the 747. We placed charges on all the lines."

"Who did? You're not even allowed on that plane without an Air Force escort. No one is."

"Jack Swithen placed the charges. He's Chief Mechanical Engineer and he runs the ground crew. They . . . they got to him somehow. Like they got to Clifford Jerome. They can get to anyone. Nosiglia says that people are the key to any security system. People are the weak link."

"How did they get to you?"

"Tom—"

"What did it take to buy you, Ira? Were you a bargain? Or did you get a good price?"

"You little bastard. You know nothing. Nothing. So listen to me. One of my daughters was kidnapped when we were visiting Disney World three years ago. She was only gone for a few hours. She said the men were nice to her. They brought her a Mulan doll. But they gave her a shot. It was HIV, Tom. They injected my daughter with . . ."

He stopped, too distraught to continue. It took him a few breaths to regain his composure.

"They gave her AIDS. And they told me to be glad I had one daughter left. One daughter who wasn't going to die slowly in front of my eyes. Sound like a good enough price to you?"

"I'm sorry, Ira. I—"

"We put Jennifer on that fucking 'cocktail' you read about in the papers. Twenty pills a day. I guess they help some people. They didn't help her. She died six months ago, Tom. Just before her eleventh birthday."

"Ira—"

"Shut up. I'm not finished. You want to hear the story or not?"

"I want to hear it."

"Then listen. Your Dad was supposed to die in the crash. That was the plan. But he didn't, and that actually turned out better for us. We had the real President to show to the staff at the hospital and the press. We didn't have to do the total security number. So nobody got suspicious. We did the switch much later. It took twenty minutes at three in the morning and nobody had any idea . . . well—no one but you, that is."

"What happened to him? What did you do to my father?"

Heller looked down. Tom almost pitied him.

"I've been with the Secret Service for twenty three years, Tom. Don't make me say this."

In the silence, Tom could hear fire engines approaching from town, the two-note drone getting louder as they approached.

Tom's voice was iron. "Say it."

"I failed. All right? The President was in a coma and I knew they were going to kill him. There were three of these Mafia capos in the room with me and one of them pulled a gun. I knew what I had to do, I knew my duty. But I couldn't do it. I couldn't move. And just before the gun went off I realized that it didn't matter, anyway. What if I had put myself between the President and that bullet? It wouldn't have saved him. He was dead already and I was part of the plan. I had put him there. Performing some fucking charade now, some Secret Service dance step, that wasn't going to do anything but show just how far down I'd come and what I'd turned into. I almost took the bullet anyway. But I still have a family, Tom. So I just . . . I let it happen. I'd been letting it happen for months. Yeah, I guess you could say I assassinated the President. Is that what you wanted to hear? But I didn't do it alone."

Tom said nothing. Heller looked away. "We gave your father a John Doe cremation. The ashes are in the oval office safe. And that's it. I hope it's enough for you, because it's all you're gonna get."

Heller ran his left hand up his forehead and through his thinning hair. He blew out a tired breath. The confession had diminished him. He was sagging a little. He looked his age. It was just for a few seconds, though; then he pulled himself together with a visible effort, standing up straight, working a kink out of his neck. When he spoke again his voice was calm and businesslike.

"I'm calling in the troops now," he said. "I want you to put down that gun and go quietly. You're surrounded, you're all alone. There's nothing you can do—"

At that moment the bookshelves swung open.

Amy was standing there—in the Weaver stance. The gun was pointed at Heller.

"Put down your weapon," she said, slowly and clearly.

"What are you talking about? He's insane and he's about to kill the President!"

"I don't think so." She turned to the impostor. "You made one mistake, 'Mister President'," she said. "You whistled off-key."

That was when she felt the tiny circle of metal pressing into the back of her neck.

"Please lower your weapon, Miss," said agent Antonowsky politely.

"What the hell happened to you, Antonowsky?" Heller barked.

"I—uh—I think I broke my nose, sir."

"And how exactly did that happen?"

Antonowsky was spared the embarrassment of having to answer: Tom spun around and shot him.

Heller shot Tom.

The impostor went for the gun on the blotter. Amy's shot took him in the chest and knocked him backwards out of his chair. The last Secret Service agent was coming around the front of the desk, lunging across the room at her. She fired but the gun was empty. Tom was prostrate in front of the agent, but he managed to grab the man's ankle. Momentum took him head first into the wooden arm of a chair in the corner. He was out.

It had all taken less than six seconds.

Tom was on the floor dying. The impostor was dead.

Heller still had his gun. Amy dropped hers.

All she had now were her wits. She understood the logic of the situation. She just had to find some way to use it.

"The world is waiting out there, Ira," she said. "You tell them or I will."

"Not if I kill you."

"It doesn't matter. You can't cover this up. The autopsy will prove he's not Jaglom. You know that. Killing me won't help you. Tell the truth. You'll get immunity. You'll be put into a witness protection program that really works because it's not going to be operated by Dominic Nosiglia any more. You'll get a book deal. This is the story of the century and you're the only one who can tell it. With your evidence you can put these gangsters away forever, pay them back for what they did to your family. You can be one of the good guys. Ira. You can make this right. Tell the truth. See how it feels. You might even like it."

Heller didn't shoot her. That was a good sign. He just looked at her; finally he shrugged and picked up the phone.

"I want a chopper on the pad five minutes ago. We have a kid here who needs to get to the hospital."

Amy kneeled by Tom, stroked his head.

When he spoke, his voice was a cracked whisper.

"So . . . the crazy guy did okay, after all."

She just nodded. "I love you," she said finally.

He smiled. "Still?"

"More."

"So, we can get married and live . . . not happily . . ."

Amy squinted down at him. She didn't understand and he was fading fast. "Tom—"

"Interestingly. Curiously. Passionately."

She smiled, remembering.

"Ever after?"

Tom shut his eyes. "Ever after," he said.

And then he was gone.

33

Amy was walking alone on the Madequecham Road. She had held Tom as long as she could, cradling his head in her arms with her head on his chest. She had sobbed as the room filled with people—paramedics, Secret Service agents, staff and local police. Finally they had pulled her off him. She was offered a ride to the hospital, or to town to a hotel. But she wanted to walk. She wanted to get away from all the people, from the noise and the scurrying officials and the looks of concern on strangers' faces.

There were press trucks in the driveway, reporters in the yard. The last of her privacy was about to be torn away. She was part of a public tragedy and she knew that. She just couldn't deal with it tonight. She grabbed one of Helen Jaglom's bulky coats from the peg rack in the mud room and slipped out the back of the house, across the rear lawn and through the stand of birch trees that separated the estate from the road.

A chill drizzle had begun. She pulled the coat tighter. She had circled beyond the yellow police lines, unseen. The road was comfortingly dark. It felt good to walk. She felt like she could walk all night.

She had almost reached the Milestone road when she saw the limousine. A few more steps and she knew it was the same black Cadillac she had seen that morning. She stopped, suddenly afraid.

But of what? She wasn't superstitious, but the first half of her premonition had come true already. She had killed the impostor, pulled the trigger, felt the jerk of recoil and watched his body flip over backward in a spray of blood. It hadn't been premeditated, he was going for his gun.

But now she was going to have to live the rest of her life with the memory of what she had done. She didn't even know the man's name, or how he had come to be there. Did he have a family? He had a mother somewhere, she was sure of that much. And now her son was dead. For years Amy would dream of the gun jumping, death squirming like a live thing in her hands.

She stared at the limousine.

There was still half of her premonition left to go.

She wanted to run the other way, but there was nothing in that direction but the swarming compound. She braced herself and walked forward. She didn't believe in premonitions, anyway.

When she was ten feet away from the big car, someone climbed out, a heavy man in a dark coat. He recognized her instantly. And why not? Never forgetting a potentially dangerous face had to be part of his job description.

"Good evening, Ms. Elwell," said Dominick Nosiglia. "We seem to have run out of gas. I sent Carlo into town to replenish our supplies. The cell phone was damaged in the blast."

"You were there."

"Of course I was. I'm what you might call a hands-on manager."

"'Hands-on'—would that be the throat or the testicles?"

"Such crude language. And from such a lovely girl. I had

to reprimand you for your manners the last time we met, also. But to answer your question . . . generally all it takes is a squeeze of the shoulder, or a friendly slap on the cheek."

"And a man with a gun standing behind you."

"I have my own gun, Ms. Elwell."

He pulled his hand out of his pocket and pointed the gun at her.

"Well, I hope you enjoyed managing the government. Because that's over now."

"What is?"

"Your plan. Your coup-d'Etat. You obviously left the party early. So let me fill you in. Your ringer is dead. Heller is going public. The story's going to be in every newspaper in the country tomorrow. Cops who've been sitting on their hands for a year and a half are going to be going wild. The good news is you get to be in the history books. You get to be the worst traitor in American History. The name people use to curse each other out. The new synonym for evil. 'That guy turned out to be a real Nosiglia, didn't he?' Stuff like that. You're going to be the bogeyman that scares kids into eating their vegetables. The face on the dart board. I hope you get a piece of that action, Dominick. Because you're not going to be getting anything else, from now on."

"Heller wouldn't betray me."

"It's already happened. They're moving his family right now. You'll never find them. He's going to write a book about all this. It should outsell the new Harry Potter ten to one."

Nosiglia shook his head.

"Two kids," he said. "How did two kids manage to ruin everything?"

"It wasn't just us. It was Jim Gramble, and the people who talked to him. And it was President Jaglom. You know that. He finally just said 'no'—that was what ruined you. That

. . . and the fact that his son loved him enough to tell the difference."

"Isn't that touching. The triumph of family values. Well, there's one consolation for me anyway."

"What's that?"

"The admittedly minor satisfaction of killing you. A small thing perhaps. But the memory of watching you die will comfort my twilight years."

He cocked the gun.

Amy looked around frantically. She was standing in the middle of the road. There was no cover, nowhere she could run, no chance of reaching him before he pulled the trigger.

"Wait," she said. "Please . . . ."

"Are you going to beg? I'd enjoy that. Offer yourself as a sex slave—that might sway me. I haven't had a girl as young as you in a long time."

"Go to hell."

Amy shut her eyes, every muscle bunched, every nerve scraped raw, waiting for the unimaginable shock wave of pain.

She heard the gun go off.

The flat crack echoed off the trees.

But nothing happened. Had he missed? It didn't seem possible.

She opened her eyes. Nosiglia was lying on the ground on his back. There was a neat hole just above the bridge of his nose.

Heller stepped out of the trees.

"I was following you," he said. "Good thing, too." He grinned. "Now I have the last chapter for my book."

"You're such a nice guy, Ira."

"Come on, let's find you a hotel room. You need a good night's sleep. You have a big day tomorrow."

"Let me ask you something," she said as they walked away from the car and the remains of Dominick Nosiglia.

"Feel free."

"The money Tom had in the park . . . that really was the money he buried with his father, wasn't it?"

Heller nodded.

"All old bills."

Heller nodded again.

"So no one was mugged that night."

"Not by Tom."

"You gambled that I hadn't noticed."

"Not much of a gamble. Most people don't notice shit."

"Ira Heller, you are a cynical and devious person."

"You make those words sound like terms of endearment."

"Good."

They walked along.

"Hey, listen," Heller said after a while. "I've been thinking about what you said in Jaglom's office—about the witness protection program. It sounds okay to me. I think I might enjoy being somebody else for a while."

She smiled at him and offered her arm. He took it with a certain formal gallantry and they walked off together towards the Milestone Road.

The aftermath of that night dominated the news for weeks. The break-up of the Nosiglia crime family, the transition of power in the White House as vice-president Lamar Crane was sworn in, the President's funeral (Tom was buried beside him), the posthumous award of the Medal of Valor, the highest civilian honor, to both Tom and Jake Gritzky . . . those were the highlights. In between, everyone was grabbing their moment in the media spotlight. Talk shows and news programs saw everyone from Duane Claassen to Roy Fisk and Leonard Honig giving their versions of the events. Heller signed his book deal. Tina Brown was going to publish a big chunk of it in *Talk* magazine.

The only person who refused to deal with the press was Amy Elwell. No one understood it—she could have made a fortune. Oprah Winfrey called her personally and was stunned to be turned down. "Though it was really great talking to you," Amy had hastened to add. She wasn't as polite to the reporters who caught up with her at the Jaglom grave in Arlington cemetery.

"Were you lovers?" the man from *Hard Copy* asked. "Did Tom die a virgin?"

She didn't answer. She slapped him. Hard.

"Shame on you," she said, and walked away.

She didn't come back to the grave for a long time.

But the story continued to get ratings and sell newspapers. Every detail of Tom's historic struggle was picked apart and deconstructed. His journal was published. So was Jim's story—Fisk had kept a copy, after all. There was only one mystery that remained stubbornly unsolved. No one could quite figure out how Tom had escaped from Manhattan during the biggest manhunt in the city's history.

It was the subject of a Dateline segment in September. Tyler and Polly MacKenzie were just back from their honeymoon—they had gone to Paris and were still a little jet-lagged. Polly was clicking through the channels when she saw the report. They were under the covers, she was in the crook of his arm, where she liked to be best.

"How do you like that?" he said. "It looks like we saved the world."

"Well—we *helped*," she admonished him gently.

"I knew he was a good kid."

"Shhhh."

Stone Phillips was wrapping up the rather disappointing investigation, saying: "How did Tom Jaglom escape from the city on that fateful day? We may never know."

"Shall we tell them?" she asked. "We'd be famous. We'd get to meet Stone Phillips."

STEVEN AXELROD

"There's a thrill."

"We'd get to go down in history."

"I like that idea."

"Or we could just keep it our secret. I think that's what Tom would have wanted."

He kissed her head. "Marriages founder on questions like that."

She smiled. "But not this one."

"No."

Stone Philips was saying. "If you have any information that could help us clear up the mystery of Tom Jaglom's escape from New York, please write or E-mail us here at NBC. We're prepared to offer a substantial reward to anyone who can help us put the last piece of this historic puzzle together."

Polly clicked off the television.

"I like a man who can keep a secret," she said.

Then she kissed him, and he turned out the light.

And everything else was private.